Beyond Her Manner

EMILY BANTING

Sapphfic Publishing

**Beyond Her Manner
Copyright © 2025 Emily Banting
Published by Sapphfic Publishing
ISBN: 978-1-915157-16-4
First edition: January 2025**

This is a work of fiction. Names, characters, business, events and incidents are the products of the author's imagination. Any resemblance to actual persons, living or dead, actual events, or fictional characters is purely coincidental.

All rights reserved. This book, or parts thereof, may not be reproduced in any form without permission of the author.

Although Artemisia Gentileschi is a real historical figure, some references or suggestions regarding her work and its context in this book are purely fictional and created for the enjoyment of the story. They should not be interpreted as factual representations of her life, career, or artistic legacy.

Sapphfic
Publishing

*CREDITS:
Editor: Hatch Editorial*

1 2 4 5 6 7 8 9 10

ABOUT THE AUTHOR

Emily Banting is an award-winning and bestselling author of contemporary sapphic romance featuring LGBTQ+ characters and plenty of British humour. History obsessed, she throws her sapphic leading ladies into historic buildings and environments at every opportunity and strongly believes in representing women over forty in literature.

www.emilybanting.co.uk

FIND ME HERE

I love to hear from my readers. If you would like to get in touch you can find me here…

www.emilybanting.co.uk

Or follow me here…

facebook.com/emilybantingauthor
instagram.com/emilybanting
x.com/emily_banting
bookbub.com/authors/emily-banting
goodreads.com/emily_banting
amazon.com/author/emilybanting
bsky.app/profile/emilybanting.co.uk
tiktok.com/emilybantingauthor
threads.net/@emilybanting

ACKNOWLEDGMENTS

Finally, I bring you the last book in the South Downs Romance Series. It's out later than I'd hoped, but life threw some curveballs in 2024. Giving up work and becoming a full-time author has at least allowed me to focus on writing, and get some much-needed downtime. I also lost Maddie, the black lab who inspired Rodin in *Reality In Check*, which hit hard.

As always, books aren't birthed into the world by an author alone. So, thanks go to Conny, who never stops believing in me, never stops encouraging me, and never lets me stop believing in myself. I couldn't have done this without you and epic amounts of handholding. I'm sorry if I ever squeezed too hard.

Also, to my early readers, Lou, Chloe, Laure, and Rachel for your thoughts and helpful comments, as well as to my ARC team, who are always eager to get their eyes on anything I write.

To friends and family who are always patient with my random questions — particularly, Catherine, for your kitchen appliance expertise, Dad for your helicopter knowledge, and Natalie for her horsey advice. Not forgetting Dudley for the rides he has given me over the years — the gentle giant is real!

Thank you, Jess, for editing and to Dad for always being the last eyes on it. Any mistakes are his!

Lastly, I want to thank everyone who has read and supported the South Downs Series. Whether you've been here from the very beginning or just discovered these stories, your enthusiasm and encouragement have been vital in bringing this series to its conclusion.

Writing can often feel like a solitary journey, but knowing that these characters and their lives have resonated with you makes all the difference. To those who've reached out with kind words, shared these books with friends, or simply enjoyed them alone — thank you for being a part of this journey and for spending time in the South Downs world.

For Maddie (Rodin)
There at the beginning, gone before the end.
RIP

CHAPTER 1

Gillian Carmichael wiped her eyes with a tissue, knowing it would remain dry. No tears had been shed, and none would be shed, not even as she watched the pallbearers lower the coffin of her late husband, Jonathon, into the frozen January earth.

It wasn't that she hadn't loved him; it just wasn't in the way a wife should. Their relationship had grown into a companionship rather than a traditional marriage, devoid of deep emotional attachment or affection.

She'd known what she was getting into when she agreed to marry him. They had both gone into it knowing it was transactional, and they had fulfilled their roles precisely. Jonathon would get a beautiful woman on his arm to show off to his wealthy friends, and Gillian would have all the money she could want. In recent years, though, the money had dried up almost as much as she had.

The arm of her best friend, Bridget, slipped around her own and squeezed, no doubt bringing comfort to the stout, unassuming woman. She was the type of person who was always there for others — not that Gillian was ever in need of anyone else. On this occasion, she would let Bridget feel useful, even though she didn't require the comfort herself. It would do her no harm to look like a grieving widow in need of some support from a friend.

As Bridget's body began to vibrate, Gillian stepped forward. She didn't need to be standing beside someone crying real tears. She threw an orange lily into the grave and finally felt she'd broken free from her shackles. This was her chance to redefine herself. Turning away from the grave, the weight of the past lifted slightly from her shoulders, leaving her uncertain yet quietly hopeful about what the future might hold.

A ringtone sounded, cutting through the heavy silence. A rustling rippled through the crowd of mourners as they checked their phones. Realising the sound was coming from inside her handbag, Gillian dived in to retrieve it. As she silenced the phone, she noticed several glares aimed her way, which she ignored. Life continued, relentless as ever. It always had, and it always would.

She watched as the large, solemn, black-coated crowd began to disperse, noting that it was mainly comprised of local villagers with nothing better to do. Taking the crowd's dispersion as her own cue to leave, Gillian turned to a tall, grey-haired man, resplendent in a white alb.

"Thank you, Reverend. A *satisfactory* service as always," she said dryly.

He opened his mouth to reply, then, seemingly thinking better of it, closed it again, giving her a slight inclination of his head in acknowledgement. It reminded her to have words with him about his recent sermons. They were too depressing for a Sunday morning, and far too long.

Signalling to Bridget that it was time for them to leave, they took the public footpath through the Kingsford Estate, following an avenue lined with beech trees that connected the manor house to the church. Once a path between two places, it now felt like a corridor leading her to a new chapter of her life. An Elizabethan house came into view with wisteria wound around its Ardingly Sandstone façade and mullioned, leaded glass windows. A trio of steeply pitched slate roofs with gable ends topped it off.

Despite every attempt to keep a smile from her face, she couldn't fight it. The manor was all hers now. She was finally free to take charge, make decisions, and, most importantly, implement changes. No longer would she voice her opinions only to have them shut down as too expensive, untenable, or ridiculous, which had always been Jonathon's three go-to responses whenever she proffered an idea to improve the estate.

She inhaled the earthy scent of the beech trees as she surveyed the view over the Kingsford Estate, her home for the last thirty-five years. It comprised fifty acres of land, a Tudor manor house, a Georgian lodge, and three old farm cottages in the village, which were, regrettably, in a poor state of repair.

She'd encouraged Jonathon for years to invest in the properties, only to be told they were not a priority. She could never quite determine his exact priorities, but it was clear they centred on collecting anything he believed held hidden value or might appreciate over time. Despite his abundance of self-belief, Jonathon did not have an eye for antiques; everything he had sunk money into turned out to be worthless.

He had sold off most of the tenable land over the years to neighbouring farms, claiming it was a pain to manage. A lot of the remaining land was less suitable for farming and of little use for anything other than recreational purposes. Having acres of land to run wild with Dudley, her Friesian horse, suited Gillian perfectly. She was looking forward to taking on some new horses for herself as well as extending the stables and livery. There was so much potential in the estate that Jonathon hadn't had the foresight or business acumen to exploit.

Continuing along the path, she and Bridget passed a bench on the brow of the hill. It was Gillian's favourite place to sit and admire the estate. The low winter sun caught a gold memorial plaque screwed into the backrest, another reminder of how precious and short life could be. She made a mental note to ask one of the gardeners to give the old oak bench a sand and a fresh coat of oil to ready it for the spring.

Although tempted to sit and prolong returning to the manor, which would be full of people with words of condolence she could do without, she refrained. Bridget was in the throes of updating her on a rather heated meeting of the Women's Institute she had missed last night, and she didn't want to ruin the serenity. Bridget was inclined to go on a bit when left to it, and this appeared to be one of those moments.

Gillian couldn't help feeling that if she'd been at the

meeting, there would have been no opportunity for disagreements. Attending such a gathering the night before her husband's funeral, however, wouldn't have given the right impression.

Once they reached the manor, they slipped into the back hall, a cosy space with a servant staircase leading from it and doors to the cellar, kitchen, great hall, and a small cloakroom. Gillian needed a moment to compose herself before facing the crowd of mourners. She suspected most, if not all, of them had only come for a free feed and to socialise. They were like a rent-a-crowd. With the average age of the villagers being over sixty-five, it felt like there was a funeral every few weeks. It was the only time some of the villagers left their houses.

Passing her black woollen coat and black hat to Bridget, Gillian shook out her shoulder-length, blonde, wavy hair in the mirror beside her. She poked and prodded at it until the shiny locks relented, reaching the shape she desired.

"Right, let's get this over with. A large glass of wine or two is in order, don't you think?"

"Most certainly," Bridget replied, heading for the door to the great hall.

Catching another glimpse of herself in the mirror as she passed it, Gillian backed up and took in her appearance again. Stretching out the muscles in her face, she slapped on a more appropriate sullen look and followed Bridget.

She stepped into the wood panelled great hall, where a fire flickered and glowed in the original Hamstone fireplace. A smile spread across her lips as she took in the grandeur of what was now entirely hers. The stone floor and high-vaulted, elm-beamed ceiling echoed her guests' voices and the chinking of crystal and silverware. Chandeliers hung from the crossbeams, casting a warmth across the tapestries which hung between the tall windows.

The room was mainly used for dining when they entertained and was a particular favourite as a venue for all the local events, which Gillian organised. She considered it to be her forte. Having spent the best part of thirty-five years as hostess at Kingsford Manor, she could manage any event necessary.

Her stomach rumbled as she passed an array of culinary delights exquisitely laid out on the old banqueting table. Mrs Johnson, her cook, had prepared everything to Gillian's exacting standards. Waiters weaved their way through the throng of people, offering up trays of hors d'oeuvres and wafting a symphony of aromas around the hall. Her stomach rumbled again, begging to be satisfied. It would have to wait; etiquette prevented her from mingling with a mouthful of food.

Noticing Bridget had already abandoned her in favour of the buffet table, Gillian approached the nearest group of people.

"Ah, Mrs Hawkins, so glad you could make it! I hope you didn't have to close the shop."

"No, got my daughter to run it, didn't I?" she replied.

Gillian suppressed a wince at the grating twang of the woman's accent; it never got easier to listen to. When she'd moved to the village, Gillian had been tempted to offer the woman elocution lessons until she realised it would involve spending a considerable amount of time with her.

She flashed a smile, hoping it would be an end to the conversation, only to find Mrs Hawkins opening her mouth again.

"Anyway, I wouldn't miss this. End of the Carmichaels, innit?"

"*I* am very much alive, Mrs. Hawkins," Gillian countered through gritted teeth, her jaw tightening as she tried to maintain her forced, polite smile.

"I mean the proper Carmichaels. You're married in, aren't ya?"

"Please excuse me. I must mingle," Gillian said, biting back a response. Any other time she would have given the woman a stern talking-to, but spotting her hairdresser from the village standing alone, she needed to seize an opportunity.

Walter, the family solicitor, stepped into her path.

"Gillian, I must speak with you."

"Not now, Walter. Can't you see I'm entertaining?"

Stepping around him, she approached a small-framed young woman.

"Hannah, it's good of you to come." Lowering her voice, she added, "Book me in for a cut and colour a week tomorrow. Usual time."

"I'll have to check I don't have anyone else booked in."

"You do that. I'll see you then," Gillian replied, giving the girl a tap on the arm. She felt it was important to support the locals in their endeavours. "Do help yourself to something to eat, won't you?"

As she moved away, an arm slipped around her waist in a vice-like grip, and a booming voice resounded in her ear.

"Gillian, my dear. You've outdone yourself yet again."

The arm belonged to Major Hargreaves, a short, rotund man in his seventies who looked like he'd sneezed a large slug onto his top lip. Gillian always found him to be a rather odious, pompous sort of man, but at least he was of the right breeding.

"Thank you, Major. Now I must mingle."

She pulled away, slipping from his tight grasp as unwelcome memories flooded her. Jonathon always had a way of making her feel trapped too. What had initially felt like attentiveness turned out to be control; his touch was more about possession than affection. At parties, he paraded her about like a trophy, keeping her within reach to ward off any other man who might dare approach. She was his, and he made sure everyone knew it. The thought still turned her stomach.

It took a year or two of marriage for her to realise what she had fallen in love with was Kingsford Manor, not Jonathon. By then it was too late. All other aspects of her life were perfect, so she convinced herself she could be content in the marriage. Living on the estate was worth any hardship she had to endure, particularly in the bedroom.

She was still young — well, fifty-five, but she wasn't dead yet — not that she would be looking to remarry again. There would be the required mourning time to go through. How long was that? A week or two? A month? Hearing the major laughing heartily at what was undoubtedly his own joke and still feeling the grip of his fingers on her waist, she vowed to stay off men entirely.

Relieving a passing waitress of a glass of Cabernet

Sauvignon, she gulped at it and checked her watch, desperate for the charade to be over so she could get on with things. There was much to do and many changes to make. Taking another sip, she regretted not serving champagne. Bridget had pointed out that offering it at such a time might come across as inappropriate, and at the time, it had seemed like sound advice. Now, in desperate need of something light and bubbly, not doing so felt like the wrong choice.

The octogenarians from Kingsford House, the second-largest property in the village, approached with their arms linked. Childhood friends and both unmarried, they had moved in together after one inherited the house from her aunt. Despite their age, they were always eager to lend a hand at the Women's Institute and other village events. They were amongst the few people in the village Gillian could tolerate.

"Oh, Gillian, you must be in pieces. We're sorry for your loss," Elouise said, squeezing her arm. Her companion, Louisa, nodded her agreement.

"Thank you, ladies; I will bear it as best I can. Stiff upper lip and all that."

The two women smiled and nodded.

"You must excuse me, it's time for me to make a speech."

Taking a spoon from the buffet table, she took a couple of steps up the grand wooden split staircase on one side of the hall to elevate herself. A high-pitched sound silenced the crowd as she tapped the spoon against the crystal glass.

Walter appeared in front of her again, his face pale and

his eyes wide. "Gillian, please," he implored, his voice strained.

Gillian lifted a finger in his direction in response, hoping he would get the message. His shoulders slumped in defeat, and he stepped back.

"Thank you everyone for joining me on this sad occasion. Jonathon will be sorely missed by everyone who knew him. Death is never the end but a chance for a new beginning, and we now enter a new era at Kingsford Manor. With me at the helm, it will be transformed. I have big plans for the estate, starting with increasing the livery offering. If anyone is in the market, do let me know. Over the years, Kingsford has been synonymous with openness, generosity, and, above all, courage. I aim to continue this ethos." She raised her glass. "To Kingsford Manor," she said, before adding quickly, "And Jonathon."

Voices echoed in agreement around the hall, and the crowd dispersed into smaller groups. She hoped her speech would mark the end of the proceedings, but the villagers did like to linger.

"I must insist we speak, Gillian," Walter's voice hissed from behind.

"Can't it wait until another day, Walter?" Gillian asked, swapping her empty wine glass for a full one as a waitress passed.

Walter's face twitched. "It's urgent!" He took a glass of wine and handed it to her. "You're going to need more than one."

Gillian's stomach tightened at his firm tone, and she relented, gesturing for him to head to a door off the large hall. Following behind Walter, she issued a few smiles to guests as they moved through the hall.

"What's this about, Walter?" Gillian asked as she closed the door to the drawing room behind them.

"I've finished assessing all the finances for you," Walter replied as he sat on the brown leather Chesterfield next to Agatha, a small black cat.

Placing her wine glasses on the coffee table, Gillian took a box of matches from the mantelpiece and lit the ready-made fire in the hearth.

"It can't have escaped your notice that funds have been a little tighter in the last few years," he continued.

Lifting one of the wine glasses as she sat opposite Walter, she noticed a chip in the rim. Turning it around, she took a large gulp and placed the glass back on the table.

"Jonathon spoke about redirecting funds into some investments," she confirmed. "Tightening our belts a little now to enable us to live more comfortably in our final years, he'd said. I'd always thought there was no better investment than the manor." Noticing Walter shifting uncomfortably and scratching at his balding head, she asked, "Why? Have the investments gone bad?"

"Not exactly."

"Oh, good," Gillian added, exhaling noisily with relief.

Walter winced as he said, "I'm afraid they were never good."

Gillian's body tensed as if each muscle was under an invisible grip. "How much is left?"

"Very little, I'm afraid."

"But I have the estate; I have the manor." Gillian's

breath caught in her throat. "Please, tell me I have them at least."

"Well, yes. If you can pay for them."

"Pay for them!" Gillian screeched. "Jonathon owned them… I own them!"

"Not according to the mortgage taken out four years ago, you don't."

A cold sweat ran through her. She wiped her hands on her knee-length, black dress. "Mortgage?" Gillian chuckled. "Is this some kind of joke?"

Walter remained silent, his lips pressed together as he met her gaze, the sadness in his eyes speaking more than words could.

"What about my plans? I can make the estate pay; I just need the chance!"

"I'm afraid you won't have the chance." Walter extracted some paperwork from his briefcase and placed it on the table between them. "From what I can establish, he re-mortgaged to cover some bad debts and has been rerouting money from other loans to cover the payments ever since."

Gillian ran her hand around the back of her neck and rubbed it to relieve the tension which was building as Walter continued.

"As you can see, the monthly payments are here." Walter pointed halfway down the page.

Gillian's hand shot to her chest, feeling the wind knocked out of her. "No wonder the bastard had a heart attack. I think I'm about to have one."

"The bank has decided to foreclose. I'm sorry, Gillian, but you will have to sell the estate. It's not simply the mortgage; it's the other loans as well." Walter proceeded to extract more papers from his briefcase.

Gillian's mind raced as another cold sweat made her shiver. This couldn't be it; there must be something she could do.

"Walter, the Carmichaels have owned this house for over four hundred years. We've lived through civil wars, world wars, famines, plagues, and even the decimation of our local railway network. Are you telling me there is nothing I can do to save it?"

"I'm afraid so. I've made some calculations and have some suggestions that won't leave you completely destitute. You'll have a small income, but you will need to tighten your belt — considerably. I'll fetch you another glass of wine before we talk details."

Gillian looked at the two empty glasses in front of her, not even recalling having drained them. Her hand reached out to Walter as he passed, grasping at his arm in desperation, wanting him to take it all back.

"It's finally mine. All mine. I can't give it up! I can't."

He patted her hand and sighed. "I'm sorry, Gillian, but you don't have a choice."

"I made *that* speech. Why didn't you warn me?"

His gaze fell to the floor. "I did try."

Gillian's arm dropped as Walter walked away, and she slumped back into the sofa. Would she have to sell her beloved Chesterfields? They had been a wedding present from Jonathon's mother. They may be a little tatty now, but it was part of their charm and character. They were part of Kingsford Manor, like everything else. Like her.

"Is everything okay, Gillian?" Bridget said, poking her

head around the door. "I saw Walter leaving looking rather concerned."

"Come in," Gillian said, dejected.

Bridget took in the room as she entered. "What a lot of sympathy cards."

"Yes. I find they cheer the place up a bit."

"Oh, Gillian," Bridget chided her with a smile.

"What? You know there was no love lost between me and Jonathon." Bridget was the only one who knew their marriage wasn't all it had appeared to be. "I despise him even more now he's left me destitute."

"Destitute? Surely not."

Gillian nodded, her jaw clenched as she fought to keep her anger and tears in check. Her hands began to tremble so wildly she sat on them. Even in front of Bridget, emotions weren't something she displayed too often.

"I'd strangle the bastard if he wasn't already dead!"

"Is there nothing you can do?" Bridget asked, sitting beside her.

"Apparently not," Gillian replied, letting out an exasperated sigh.

Bridget gave her a soft smile as she tucked strands of her light brown long bob behind her ear. "You'll sort it out. I've never known you not to solve a problem."

Bridget wasn't wrong. This time, however, she wasn't so sure, and her friend's blind belief in her did nothing to improve her mood.

"Why don't you eat something? It always makes me feel better," Bridget said with an encouraging smile.

"I'm afraid I've rather lost my appetite."

CHAPTER 2

*G*illian heard a tapping sound against the drawing room window. Looking up from the framed photograph of her younger self winning the point-to-point steeple chase, she noticed Bridget's face squashed against the glass and her hand gesticulating towards the front door. Gillian placed the frame into the cardboard box beside her and got up.

"Sorry, Bridget," she said as she opened the front door. "I heard the bell but forgot I'd dismissed the staff. It's going to take a bit of getting used to."

"Have you ever answered the door yourself?" Bridget asked with a grin as she stepped into the small, covered porch.

Gillian sniffed. "Of course I have. There was the time when Bramingham caught flu in 1998. We were without a butler for a whole week."

Bridget laughed as she removed her coat and hung it on one of the pegs.

"I'd put it back on if I were you; all the heating is off now. Mind the boxes as you come through."

"We missed you at the Women's Institute meeting last night," Bridget said, putting her coat back on as she negotiated the boxes blocking her way into the great hall. "I thought you said you would consider coming."

"I did consider it. Then I decided against it."

"Why? You missed a fascinating talk on the history of knitting."

"In which case I definitely made the right decision."

Apart from the fact her hair still desperately needed a cut and colour after she'd cancelled her last appointment — she couldn't risk her card bouncing — Gillian had felt no desire to see anyone other than Bridget. She'd cut off all contact with the village following the wake six weeks ago and had no wish to show her face.

"You still haven't told me why you decided against it," Bridget said, following Gillian into the drawing room and seating herself beside a sleeping Agatha.

"Haven't I?" Gillian was hoping to avoid answering the question. She couldn't bear to face the village, not after her speech declaring how she would be taking the helm and all the changes she would be making. The humiliation was too much. She'd been lady of the manor all her adult life, and now she was lady of nothing. The villagers looked to Kingsford Manor and herself as a constant in the community. She exhaled slowly, her breath heavy with the weight of everything pressing on her. "Oh, how am I going to show my face in the village again?"

"People understand it isn't your fault," Bridget urged as she stroked Agatha's head.

"It doesn't change the fact it's happened. The last thing I need is pity!"

"You'll have to come out of hiding at some point. We have the summer flower show to organise."

"I am not hiding," Gillian bit back as she began pacing the room, knowing it was exactly what she was doing. "Where are we to hold the flower show now? Where are we to hold any event? This building was more than my home; it was the very heart of the village."

"We'll have to use the village hall."

Gillian's top lip curled.

"Oh, it's not so bad," Bridget replied with an optimistic grin.

"It's not so good either. It's not Kingsford Manor for a start."

"We'll manage. Who knows, the new owner might be as amenable to hosting village events as the Carmichaels are — were."

"No one is as amenable as the Carmichaels," Gillian replied, pushing aside the thought of having to attend, let alone organise, all the village events in what would be her former home. "We've prided ourselves on opening our home to the community, providing them with jobs for over four hundred years, and now we are reduced to this? Simply being one of them?"

Bridget grinned and rolled her eyes.

"We don't even know much about them," Gillian added, her voice beginning to crack. "They could be some ghastly city type who will erect a six-foot steel fence around the entire estate."

"They couldn't do that even if they tried, not with a public footpath going through it."

A new thought caused a chill to run through Gillian. "The only reason the footpath is there is because we never disputed it." She leaned forward in her seat, hand clutching her stomach. "What if the new owner reroutes it around the outside of the estate?"

Knowing she could legally access the grounds and no one could stop her from returning to the land she'd called home had kept Gillian going. Over the years, it had become her escape — a place to be alone, ride Dudley, and find peace.

"Take a breath. If it happens, then we'll deal with it," Bridget insisted. "The whole village will. Together."

Gillian inhaled slowly, trying to push the fear away.

"What time do you have to be out by?" Bridget asked.

"Three o'clock."

Bridget looked at her watch. "Shouldn't the removal men be here by now?"

"We are the removal men, Bridget — or women. The staff moved the few items of furniture I was keeping and everything from the kitchen before they left. There are only what's left of my personal effects boxed in the hall and in here; everything else has already gone into storage."

"What about all the tapestries and paintings? All the furniture? You can't leave it all."

"They are an integral part of the building. You can't remove them; they've been here for centuries. Anyway, where would I put them? I can only store a few personal possessions. It would cost a fortune to store hundred-year-old four-poster beds and thirty-foot banqueting tables. Walter said the new owner was more than happy for them to be left and that they would include them in any future sale. I need them here for when I return."

Bridget's eyebrows shot up. "Return?"

"Yes. I have every intention of getting my home back one day."

"How?"

"I don't know yet, but I won't rest easy until I'm back where I rightfully belong." Gillian reached for a button beside the mantelpiece. "I'll have some tea brought through." As she pushed the button, she realised her mistake and let out a sigh. Having no staff was going to take some getting used to. "I will make us some tea," she corrected herself.

"Can you remember how?" Bridget teased.

Gillian narrowed her eyes at her friend as she left the room. Since moving into Kingsford Manor, she'd barely lifted a finger to prepare food or drink. It all arrived at the touch of a button and was served to her liking. When she returned with the tea tray, it was to find Bridget beckoning a sleepy Agatha onto her lap, where she curled up into a ball.

"Why does she never do that for me?" Gillian grumbled, setting the tea tray down on the table.

"Have you tried asking her?"

"No. I pick her up, put her there, and then she walks off."

Bridget snickered as Gillian passed her a cup and saucer.

"We only got her to save money on pest control."

"A cat isn't a commodity, Gillian. Try treating her like a member of the family rather than a member of staff." Taking a sip from her cup, she asked, "Have you changed tea?" Leaning forward, she lifted the lid on the teapot. A single teabag bobbed about in the murky water.

Gillian's face flushed, and she set her cup and saucer on the table. "Tightening my belt is going to be a challenge."

"What are you doing about Dudley?"

"The new owner has agreed he can stay where he is until I make new arrangements. I can't bear moving him; we've never been apart. I was hoping they might allow him to stay, depending on their situation with their own horses, of course."

"They might not have any."

"Don't be silly, Bridget; all the right country folk come with horses."

"I don't."

Gillian lifted an eyebrow at her. "You can't ride." Checking her watch, she drained her teacup, winced at the taste, and stood. "I'll clear up."

"Is there anything I can do?" Bridget asked, as she quickly finished her tea.

"Would you mind checking the top floors? To make sure I haven't forgotten anything."

"Of course," Bridget replied with a smile as she followed Gillian into the great hall and then made her way upstairs.

Gillian headed into the kitchen to wash up. As she packed the clean china into a box, she took in the kitchen.

It was the first thing she'd changed when she moved in. Jonathon was a socialite and enjoyed drinking and partying to excess, and Gillian knew the space wouldn't be able to keep up with the kind of future they had planned for the manor.

She designed the kitchen with the practicality of a commercial setup in mind, fitting it with stainless steel surfaces and appliances from top to bottom. A small area near the kitchen table, which held a stunning view over the estate's southern expanse, was left more homely for family use, featuring a handful of cupboards, a marble worktop, and a traditional butler sink.

Whilst the kitchen remodel may not have aligned with the house's Tudor character, it had been well received by the staff, earning her their admiration. It went on to cater countless parties over the decades. Even though it had become a little tired in recent years, it was still perfectly serviceable.

She opened the door leading off the kitchen, stepping into a space that starkly contrasted with the sleek stainless steel. The dining room, in particular, was one she would miss spending time in. An elegantly carved table was positioned at the centre of the room, in front of a large window. Being south-facing, the sun provided an abundance of light for meals throughout the day. A warmth radiated from the dark wooden floors, wood panelling, and historic fireplace, particularly in the winter months. French windows on the west side of the room led into a well-manicured garden and allowed a welcome breeze to flow in during the hot summer months.

Returning to the kitchen, Gillian collected the box she'd

left there and, taking one last look around the room, suppressed the urge to be sick.

She found Bridget coming down the grand wooden staircase as she returned to the hall.

"All clear up there?"

"Yes, except for what looked like some old paintings in the attic. Should I bring them down?"

"No, leave them. They can be someone else's problem."

"Aren't they worth anything?"

"No, just another money-wasting hobby of Jonathon's. He went through a phase of picking up old paintings, thinking they would be worth something. The problem was he knew nothing about art. Thinking back, I don't think he knew much about anything."

"Shall we get these boxes loaded then?" Bridget suggested.

"I'll make a start. Would you mind rounding up Agatha?" Gillian asked, picking up a cat box. "I get the feeling she might be more cooperative with you."

Bridget took the box with a chuckle and disappeared into the drawing room. By the time she reappeared, Gillian was emerging from the porch, tying a scarf around her neck.

"That was more difficult than I expected," Bridget said, her face flushed.

"Did you try *asking* her?" Gillian smirked, picking up the last box from inside the great hall.

"I did, but I don't think she wants to leave."

A wave of nausea hit Gillian again. "That makes two of us."

Her eyes swept the hall one last time, a flicker of sadness crossing her face as she took in the familiar space. Swallowing her emotions, she walked to the front door, stepping outside with Bridget following silently at her heels. She closed the large, wooden door behind them, turned the key in the lock, and took a step back.

Looking above the door at the coat of arms chiselled into the stone, she wiped a tear from her eye. It might not have been her ancestral home, but she'd lived and breathed as a Carmichael for most of her life. The ties to this place coursed through her blood probably more deeply than they ever did through Jonathon's. He had taken it for granted; it was natural when you grew up with it, and few knew the real pain of poverty.

Her stomach knotted as memories surfaced of a time before Kingsford. She couldn't return to that life; she wouldn't. She'd come too far. The knot tightened as her thoughts shifted to the future. Without land or wealth, who was she?

Bridget's hand lightly gripped her shoulder, pulling her from her thoughts.

Grateful for the support, Gillian gave it a tap. "I won't breathe easy until I get it back, Bridget."

"Don't rest everything on that hope. Try and see this as a fresh start."

"It's not a hope."

"Look to the future, not the past, eh?" Bridget encouraged.

"What if the future *is* the past?"

"The future is never the past."

"Hmm." Gillian turned on her heel, in disagreement with her friend. The past was always in the future; it followed you everywhere, serving as a constant reminder of everything you would rather forget.

They headed for her trusty old beaten-up Land Rover Defender. It didn't quite carry the look of Jonathon's new Range Rover, which had been repossessed. Discovering it wasn't even hers and had been bought through a hire purchase agreement was another little surprise she'd been gifted by Jonathon from beyond the grave.

Thankfully the old Defender carried the same sense of class, if not more. It didn't have all the modern conveniences, but in a way, she preferred it. This one was a symbol of old money while the other represented new wealth — and there was nothing ghastlier than that.

Bridget climbed into the passenger seat beside her, lifting the cat box with little grace onto her lap. An angry meow came from within.

"Sorry, Agatha."

Gillian watched Kingsford Manor become smaller in the rearview mirror as she drove away, and she brought the vehicle to a stop just before the estate gates. Putting on the handbrake, she turned off the engine and stepped down from the Land Rover, taking in the small, one-bedroomed Georgian lodge.

"I must say, it was an awfully good idea of Walter's for you to move in here," Bridget remarked, joining her outside the vehicle, still clutching the cat box.

"It didn't sit easy to begin with, I can tell you. Separating the estate wasn't ideal. If I couldn't afford to keep it all, though, I could at least avoid selling everything."

Looking back down the drive to Kingsford Manor, she smiled. This lodge would do for now. She would be able to keep an eye on the new owner and do what she needed to keep it safe until she could work out a way to get it back.

CHAPTER 3

TWO MONTHS LATER

"This is simply ridiculous!" Gillian griped as she entered the small entrance hall of Kingsford Lodge.

"He says you don't have a say because you aren't on the church committee anymore," Bridget replied, closing the front door behind her.

"Because he removed me! How dare he!" Gillian snapped, her fingers trembling as she tore off her gloves and threw them down on the hall table. "I've always been on the committee! I *created* it, for Christ's sake — literally! When the church was on its knees and begging for a new roof. I bet he's forgotten that!" Her chest heaved as she struggled to compose herself.

"You were never on it in an official capacity," Bridget

rejoined, "not like me as parish clerk, only as owner of the manor. And since you're no longer — "

"Yes, thank you," Gillian glared at Bridget, passing her coat to her to hang up on the stand next to her. "I don't believe I need the technicalities pointed out to me. If I'd been able to predict the Carmichaels' future removal from the manor thirty odd years ago, I would have ensured our continued position on the committee regardless of it. I wouldn't have left it as an honorary position so it could be snatched from me, but unfortunately, I did not. And this nonsense about moving the church service from ten to eleven, it's the thin end of the wedge I tell you! A ten o'clock service gives me enough time to ride Dudley before lunch at one. It's always been that way."

"On the plus side, it gives you time to make your lunch now you have to do it yourself," Bridget pointed out.

Gillian glared at her friend and shook her head. "That does not bring the comfort you think it does, Bridget. Did you notice the quality of the toilet paper in the chapter house has gone downhill too?" Gillian made her way into the small sitting room, scarcely drawing breath before she continued. "I'll feel less guilty about stopping my donation to the church now. The reverend has never been my biggest fan. Men like him don't appreciate women guiding them as to the right way of things. If he insists on remaining unmarried, then how will he ever know the right way of things? Reverends come and go, but we Carmi — "

Gillian stopped, realising she really was the end of the Carmichaels. Pushing the thought away, she took a brief breath before beginning again. "After everything I have done for that man. And having the gall to ask me to move back a pew at the service yesterday! We have sat at the front for over four hundred years. No doubt we paid for the blasted thing. It's not a Kingsford Manor pew; it's a Carmichael pew. I won't be moving, that's for certain. The new owner hasn't even deigned to visit their house; I can't see them visiting *their* pew anytime soon."

"Still no sign of movement then?" Bridget asked, joining Gillian by the window.

"No. Why buy it only to leave the place empty for two months? Houses need to be lived in, especially that one. I bet they won't even live in it full-time; it will become a weekend pad." Gillian picked up a pair of binoculars and directed them at the manor. "I could do with getting my post."

"Your post? Did you not redirect it?"

"It's an expense I can ill afford." Although that was true, the real reason was to make an introduction to the new owner when they arrived. The estate agent insisted she left the estate for any viewings, so she had never met them. The one time there had been any report of activity at the manor was a few days after it sold. Because it coincided with a day out for Bridget's birthday, Gillian had annoyingly missed them again. "Why should I pay when they walk past my house to get to the manor? I'm effectively saving them money, or at least the weight of carrying my post the extra distance."

"Could you not tell the postman?"

"Oh, I did. He said it was more than his job was worth to be misdirecting post from how it's addressed."

Directing the binoculars to the drawing room window,

she could see the curtain closed as she had left it. It was a room she should be in right now, sipping from a cup of loose-leaf Earl Grey. With her budget not extending to her favourite tea, she was losing her taste for it. Every cup of inferior bagged tea from the local supermarket served as a reminder of how far she'd fallen. A surge of anger bubbled up inside her and lodged itself in her throat, where it tightened and pulsed with a burning intensity.

"I'm afraid I won't be much company today, Bridget," she said. "I need some air. I'll take Dudley for a ride. The benefit of the place being empty is there is no one to tell me where I can and cannot ride."

"Small mercies." Bridget chuckled. "I'll see myself out."

Gillian followed her into the hall, taking herself up the small staircase that wound around it. Even after two months of living in the lodge, she was still struggling to adjust to the scale of it. She'd never considered herself to be claustrophobic before, but then again, decades had passed since she'd lived in such a small house. Shuddering at the memory, she wondered if she would ever adjust. Reminding herself of her plan to return to the manor one day, she told herself it didn't matter if she didn't adjust; this was a temporary situation after all. She would need to keep reminding herself of that.

Having strapped herself into her black riding jacket, beige jodhpurs, and black boots, she headed out to the stables. Located on the eastern side of the estate, the stable block had been added at the same time as the lodge and was situated directly between it and the manor.

Comprising four stables, a coach house, a small

groom's flat, and four garages, all set around a cobbled courtyard, it was too convenient to lose. If she were able to retain accommodation for Dudley, it would likely cost her, but hopefully it would be for a fraction of the price that others were asking — that was, if there was space. Losing it would mean travelling twice a day to check on him. The time she had; the money she did not.

Dudley trotted over to see her as soon as Gillian came into sight of the small plot of land partitioned off behind the stable. She rubbed the bridge of his nose, careful not to catch herself on the electric fence as she did so.

"What are we going to do with you, eh?" she murmured to the horse.

The black horse stamped the ground with his hoof, sending a brief cloud of dust into the air.

"Don't you worry. I won't see you go hungry. I'll make sure you get your rations first. Let's get you tacked up, and then we'll stretch your legs."

The feel of the breeze against her face ten minutes later, as she cantered across the parkland, was like nothing else. Pulling Dudley to a stop on the hill opposite Kingsford Manor brought a tightness to her chest, though. To see the building empty was the harshest punishment Jonathon could have exacted on her. Being poor was unbearable; seeing Kingsford alone and abandoned ate away at her core. Tearing her moistening eyes away, she pulled the reins and directed Dudley back across the field towards the stables.

Maybe she should have made a clean break, left the area entirely, and started fresh somewhere new — somewhere she could be herself. She wasn't even sure who she was anymore, and what was she without the manor anyway?

A low hum filled the air. Looking around, she spotted a helicopter coming in their direction. She expected it to veer off in another direction, but it only came closer. The hum became a thrumming that began vibrating the air. The wind whipped the loose hair cascading from under her riding hat as the helicopter passed above her head.

Dudley reared up at the sound. Feeling herself losing control, she instinctively slipped her feet from the stirrups and whipped her leg around, allowing herself to slide off the side of him and onto her feet. Running around to the front of him, she retook the reins.

"Whoa! There's a good boy."

As she tightened her grip and regained control of the animal, her mind leapt to what could have happened if her instincts hadn't taken over. How lucky she was, and how some were not. Freezing at that point could have cost her everything. With the fresh reminder of life's harsh unpredictability, her legs weakened, and a numbing chill filled her veins. Her pounding heart felt like it was pumping ice through her, tensing her muscles and making her body feel as if gravity were intensifying.

In the distance she could make out the helicopter, its echoes quieter now, telling her it was about to land on the lawn. Removing her black leather glove, she stroked Dudley's neck. His soft hair soothed her as she closed her eyes and drew in some deep breaths. Dudley nuzzled at her as if to apologise.

"It's okay, boy. It wasn't your fault. Let's get you safely

in your stable, and then I'll give that inconsiderate pilot a piece of my mind."

∼

Having completed her shutdown checks, Viola Berkley opened the helicopter door and jumped down onto the expansive grassy lawn clutching a small box. Giving a nod of gratitude to Douglas, her concierge pilot who would be returning the helicopter for her, she grabbed a Louis Vuitton Keepall and shut the door.

Stepping away from the landing site, she covered a yawn with her hand. Despite the short flight from London, the intense concentration required to pilot the helicopter always left her drained.

As she walked across the lawn toward the house, she noted the need for proper lighting to make nighttime landings possible. Her thoughts were interrupted by a woman striding toward her with determined speed. As she drew closer, her stiff posture, clenched fists and contorted expression made Viola's steps falter. The woman stopped abruptly a few metres away.

"I demand to speak to the pilot of this ghastly contraption!" The woman's voice, seething with anger, easily projected over the sound of the idling helicopter blades. She glared at Douglas, who was manoeuvring himself into the pilot's seat.

"That would be me," Viola replied, raising an eyebrow.

"You!" The woman sniffed. "You can't be the pilot."

Viola tucked a strand of her long, wind-blown auburn hair behind her ear. "And yet I am."

The woman glared, blue eyes piercing into her. "But… but you're a woman."

"Well observed," Viola replied, her voice laced with sarcasm. "Amazingly, it doesn't stop me from flying a helicopter. My ovaries are cleverly concealed, and even the helicopter is fooled."

The woman's gaze lingered on Viola. Her stern expression wavered, almost softening, as she studied her.

"I see being a woman doesn't prevent you from being misogynistic," Viola continued.

"Don't be ridiculous," the woman snapped back, her face hardening again.

"I'm not the one who is being ridiculous."

"You threw my horse. I could have been seriously injured or worse. This is the countryside, not Monaco. You can't land here!"

"Why can't I?" Viola demanded.

"I own the place," the woman retorted, lifting her chin.

Viola arched a brow and folded her arms across her chest. "That makes two of us."

The woman pulled back in surprise, fiddling with her riding gloves. "Oh! You're the new… owner."

"Viola Berkley. You must be the old one."

The woman's twitching upper lip told her she may have chosen the wrong word, using 'old'; her reply confirmed it.

"*Previous*… owner, yes," she replied through gritted teeth. "Gillian Carmichael."

"I hope your horse is all right," Viola said gently, feeling she should at least try to diffuse some of the tension.

"Yes. He's in the stable."

"Ah, yes, that would be my stable too."

"Yes. I'm grateful to you for allowing me to stay on whilst I seek alternative suitable arrangements."

Viola shrugged. "I don't ride, so feel free to continue."

She was torn about giving such an offer, but she'd always believed in killing people with kindness, and right now, it was clearly having that effect on Gillian. She could have been petty and told the woman to fuck off, yet the look on her face was far too satisfying.

Gillian finally responded, her smile stiff and reluctant. "Thank you."

And that was the icing on the cake. Viola sensed those words were rarely uttered by the woman. Gillian Carmichael struck her as more of a 'giving orders' type, who was more likely to chastise you for doing something wrong than thank you for doing something right.

"You're welcome." She hitched her luggage up on her shoulder. "May I go now? It's been a tiring journey, and I have a lot to do."

"Yes, of course," Gillian said, looking down as she stepped out of her path.

Viola pulled her mobile from her pocket, dialling a number as she strode across the front lawn. The call was answered immediately.

"Hey, I've arrived," she said.

"And is it full of savages as you feared?" The sarcastic voice of her agent, Caroline, came back.

"One at least," Viola replied. She looked behind her to see the woman still standing there, staring in her direction. *What is her problem?!* Their eyes met briefly before Gillian turned and strode away. "I'd barely touched down when I was set upon."

She fell silent as she looked up at the house, the sound of Douglas lifting off behind her echoing off its walls.

"Are you still there?"

"Yes, I — " she said breathlessly, thinking about how this moment should have played out had things not changed so drastically. She pulled the box a little closer, her grip tightening as she tried to push away the thoughts of her mum's ashes within.

"Hey, Viola. Take a deep breath."

Viola inhaled, noticing how clean the air felt as it filled her lungs. "I didn't expect to be here alone, you know."

"I know, and yet, here you are, and you can handle it. Take some time, kick back, relax, and rest that beautiful voice of yours."

Viola inhaled again. "Mmm, I'll try. I'm not sure how much relaxing I'll be doing. Work starts tomorrow."

"Yes, and you hired a project manager for a reason."

"I did," Viola sighed.

"Let them get on with it. Read a book; write one if you need to. Get friendly with the savages if you must, though not too friendly. I'll have your car delivered tomorrow; you can take in some country air. Do some healing, and then we'll get you back to it."

"Okay."

"Keep checking in, won't you?" Caroline asked. "I'll need to hear from you regularly to make sure the savages haven't killed you in some ancient village ritual."

Viola snorted. "I wouldn't put it past them if they are anything like the one I just met."

There was no going back now, Viola realised as she hung up. She rounded the house and opened the front door — or, rather, she only just managed to open it with all the post blocking it. She hadn't been expecting any post yet except junk mail, and this didn't look like junk mail. Setting her luggage down, she picked up the letters, noticing some envelopes were addressed to Gillian Carmichael. Some of the postmarks were weeks old.

Speak of the devil... the postman was walking down the drive. She sifted through the rest, realising they were all for Gillian.

The postman approached her as he ferreted in his bag. "You the new owner?"

"Yes, Viola Berkley."

He looked up and handed her a letter. "As I live and breathe," he said with a smile. "My wife is a huge fan of yours; she'll never believe I'm delivering your post. We even came to one of your concerts last year."

"Thank you. Now these aren't mine," Viola said, trying to change the subject back to the matter in hand, literally. Checking the addressee on the additional letter he'd just given her, she added, "And neither is this one."

"No, they would be Mrs Carmichael's. She's too important to redirect her post like the rest of us mere mortals," he said, adjusting his postbag on his shoulder. "Or too poor," he muttered.

"Well, I don't want them," Viola said, waving them at him to encourage him to take them.

"I am duty bound to only deliver as per the address as I told her."

"Does she still live in the village?"

The postman chuckled. "Oh yeah, she never left." He pointed to the lodge at the end of the drive. "You're neighbours."

Viola's face soured.

"You can deliver them yourself. Or throw them at her. I've been inclined to do that a few times. You should take her cat back to her too," he said, pointing to the side of her at one of the windows. "That's hers un'all."

"Cat?" Viola said, her eyes shooting to the window, where a black cat was sat, watching them with an air of quiet judgement.

She turned back, only to find the postman sauntering up the drive, whistling to himself. He stepped aside to allow a grocery delivery van to pass, it was right on time. She was desperate for a coffee, but with the delivery from John Lewis with her new coffee machine, crockery, and other essentials like bedding not due until later, she would have to wait.

By the time she'd unpacked the shopping and made it to the drawing room where the cat was last seen, she found it curled up on one of the Chesterfield sofas.

"Hello there," she greeted the animal. "How did you get in? Did you sneak in when I wasn't looking?"

The cat opened one eye and then closed it again.

Giving the cat a stroke on the head to gauge its temper, she said, "You're a cutie, aren't you?"

The cat purred.

She ran her hand over the sofa. Although clearly old, they both had a worn-in charm that appealed to her. Discovering the place could come partially furnished had been a pleasant surprise.

"I have to kick you out, kitty," she said, turning to the task at hand. "This is my home now, and I don't think it will go down too well with your mistress if you move in with me."

Brushing her hand over the cat's back, she slipped her other one under it and picked it up, cradling it against her. Grabbing the pile of post on her way out, she carried them both up the driveway, grateful the cat wasn't putting up a fight. It seemed quite content being held, and although she couldn't hear it purring over the sound of the gravel crunching underfoot, she could feel the vibration in her chest.

She'd always wanted a cat, but her penthouse in London wasn't ideal for one, and life on the road made pet ownership difficult. Perhaps having one so close on the property would help her feel more like she had a cat in her life. Reaching the lodge, she pulled the rope hanging from a bell.

"I believe these are yours?" Viola said, handing a pile of letters to Gillian as she opened the door.

"Not content with taking my home and throwing my horse, now you steal my cat?" Gillian said as she took the letters.

Viola let the cat down, and it ran inside. "I'm returning your cat, not stealing it. It was in *my* house."

Gillian sniffed.

Was that the woman's gripe? She thought she had taken her house from her. Technically that was what had happened, but why would she sell her house if she didn't want to? After the postman's comment, Viola was beginning to wonder if it was a financial decision, very likely something Gillian had been forced into. A pang of empathy rose inside her for the woman, but then she pushed it away. This woman was worthy of no one's empathy.

With that thought, Viola gave her a flat smile and turned, calling back, "I'd appreciate it if you'd redirect your post in future."

The woman's financial problems weren't her concern.

CHAPTER 4

Viola woke the next morning to a pressure on her stomach. Peeking through one barely opened eyelid, she spotted a black cat curled up asleep on her.

"Not you again," she groaned. "You're going to get me into serious trouble."

She was of half a mind to shoo the cat off. Instead, she extracted herself from under the duvet and hurriedly dressed under the watchful eye of her new friend. The builders were due to start work today, so she needed to get moving. Just as she finished dressing, the sound of a bell rang through the house. She opened the front door a minute later to discover a man of later years breaking through the seams of a tightly fitted tweed suit.

"Miss Berkley, it is an honour to welcome you to our little village. Or is it 'Mrs'?"

Viola groaned internally. "Miss."

"Major Hargreaves, at your service." He gave a light

nod. "Everyone calls me Major. I wonder if I might discuss a matter with you regarding your land?"

Feeling as if she had no choice, she stepped back and gestured for him to come in.

"Thank you," he said, removing his flat cap as he stepped past her and strode into the great hall, turning into the drawing room without further invitation.

Viola followed.

"Ah, Agatha," the major mumbled. "Fancy seeing you here." He turned to Viola to add, "I didn't realise you'd bought the cat as well as the house."

"I didn't," Viola replied as she entered, noticing the cat had changed location and was curled up on the sofa. It was useful to have a name for her.

The major sat himself down next to Agatha. "I'll cut straight to the point. It's regarding your bottom field. Every summer we hold a classic car show, and I thought I should let you know, out of courtesy, that we'll be doing it again."

"Are you asking me or telling me?" Viola asked, glaring at him as she sat on the sofa opposite.

The major made some noises with his cheeks before saying, "Gillian never had a problem with it."

"I am not Gillian, and this is not her estate."

"No, no, I know that. I was hoping you would appreciate the importance of community activities. I was also hoping you would open the event for us."

Viola flashed him a thinly veiled smile of gratitude for the offer, though she couldn't help thinking it was to give her no other option than to agree to his request.

"It would be nice to have a proper celebrity opening it for a change," the major added.

"Proper celebrity? Who normally opens it?" Viola questioned, intrigued.

"Gillian."

Viola suppressed a laugh. "Is she a celebrity?"

"No," he was quick to reply. "She likes to think she is, being lady of the manor and all that. She also won a point-to-point back in the eighties, and she's been riding on that one ever since. Pardon the pun." He chuckled to himself as his eye glanced over Viola's figure, making her shiver.

"Look, I'm not opposed to the idea of you using the field. I would simply like more information. Could you put a full proposal together so I know exactly what I would be agreeing to? Access, insurance, timings, that sort of thing?"

The major nearly blustered at this, then seemed to think it would be in his better interests to rein in the impulse. "Well… yes. I'll see what I can summon up."

"Good," Viola said, standing up and hoping he would take the hint. "I look forward to seeing what you summon up."

"Yes, of course," he mumbled, getting to his feet.

As she ushered the major out, two elderly women approached the front door, arms linked. The major doffed his cap at them as he passed. One of the ladies was carrying a bunch of vibrantly coloured flowers.

"Miss Berkley, please forgive the intrusion," her companion said. "We wanted to welcome you to the village and give you this spring bloom from our garden to brighten your new home." The woman nudged the other, who was staring at Viola in awe.

"Thank you," Viola said, relieving the woman, who was still gaping at her, of the flowers.

"Don't mind Louisa; she's a big fan of yours. Not that I'm not! I'm more able to keep my wits about me."

Viola smirked at her. "And you are?"

"Elouise," she replied with a soft smile.

"Oh. Two Lous," Viola observed with a laugh.

Elouise's smile widened. "Yes, exactly. Now we won't keep you, Miss Berkley."

"Oh, please, call me Viola."

The woman acknowledged her with a nod.

"Come along, Louisa," Elouise slipped her arm back through her companion's and pulled at her. "Toodle-oo."

Viola couldn't help chuckling at the pair.

The news of her arrival seemed to have spread through the village, likely thanks to the postman. So much for trying to keep a low profile.

As the women disappeared up the drive, Viola pondered what she should do about the cat. Should she put it outside? Return it to Gillian again? It appeared quite intent on staying put. Whatever she was going to do, she needed a coffee first. As she reached the kitchen and put the flowers down, the sound of the bell rang out.

With a deep breath, she turned on her heel and headed back to the front door, already feeling this big house was going to make her fitter. She opened it to reveal a short, middle-aged woman with a light brown long bob and a wide, beaming smile.

"I'm Bridget, from the village."

Viola could see she wasn't going to get any peace until she'd greeted every villager, and now in desperate need of a coffee, the only answer was to invite the woman in.

"Come in, Bridget from the village. Coffee? I was just trying to make one."

"Oh, yes please," Bridget answered with a goofy smile. "I live in one of your estate cottages in the village, so technically that makes you my landlady."

Viola hadn't thought of herself as a landlady. There was a lot she would need to get to grips with as an estate owner, and she didn't feel ready for any of it. At least she had her solicitor to deal with the financial side of things.

Viola stepped back to let Bridget into the porch and found herself following her through the great hall in the direction of the kitchen. It seemed the villagers were more familiar with her house than she was.

"The word around the village is you arrived by helicopter, and you flew yourself," Bridget said as they entered the kitchen.

"Yes, that is true," Viola said, placing two cups under the spouts of the coffee machine and pressing a button.

"Impressive. When did you learn to fly?"

"About fifteen years ago."

"Is it not frightening, being up in the sky alone?"

"I'm not usually alone, though yes… I suppose I am now," Viola's tone dulled.

"I expect after singing in front of millions of people, not much frightens you." Bridget paused. "I'm sorry. You're not supposed to ask famous people personal questions, are you?"

Viola was going to debate asking anyone personal

questions, but Bridget continued before she could even answer.

"Oh, what a posh coffee machine!" Bridget said, admiring it as the last of their rich coffees poured from the spouts. "I've never seen one so big. I'd love something like this."

"How do you take it?" Viola asked, smiling at the woman's enthusiasm. Perhaps the villagers weren't all savages.

"Black, please. We're all delighted to have you here in Kingsford, you know."

"So I gathered." Viola passed Bridget a cup. "I've received quite the welcome already today." She nodded at the flowers resting on the hideous stainless-steel worktop as she took her own cup from the machine. She couldn't wait for the builders to start ripping the kitchen out.

"Oh, are they from Louisa and Elouise? They're beautiful."

"They are. Sadly, I didn't think to bring a vase," Viola said, pushing the box containing her mum's ashes further along the worktop so she could put her cup down. She would need to move her to safety before the builders arrived. "I have a penthouse in London which I still use regularly. I couldn't bring anything from there, and there is only a certain amount you can fit into a helicopter. I've had a delivery of essentials from John Lewis yesterday, but I never thought of a vase as an essential before."

"It is around here. I can lend you one if you like, until you get yourself kitted out."

"Thank you. Everyone is being so welcoming. Well, except for one," Viola groaned.

"You've met Gillian then." Bridget giggled into her coffee cup.

"Yes! She accused me of stealing her house the moment I arrived."

Her mind slipped back to the previous day and the figure of Gillian Carmichael striding across the lawn in her jodhpurs and riding jacket. Her shoulder-length blonde waves bounced with her stride. Viola shook the thought away as she recalled the fury on the woman's face.

"Oh, don't mind Gillian. She doesn't bite. Well, not unless you give her a good reason to." Bridget smirked.

Viola let out an amused breath of laughter; Bridget's sense of humour had caught her off guard. "Is stealing her house a good enough reason?"

Bridget grimaced. "Perhaps give her a wide berth."

They both laughed.

"Gillian might seem fierce," Bridget added, "but she's a pussycat really, once you get to know her."

"I'm not sure I want to get to know her, though having her living at the bottom of my drive and stabling her horse, I expect avoiding her will be unavoidable. Are you friends with her, then?"

"Oldest and dearest," Bridget replied, taking a sip of coffee. "We've been friends since she moved to the village about thirty-five years ago. Which brings me to a favour I need to ask." She worried her lip, then said, "It's just that the flower show — "

"Don't tell me you want my bottom field too?"

"Your great hall, actually," Bridget replied sheepishly. "I'm assuming I'm not the first to ask for a favour today."

"No. Do you organise it then?"

"Gillian does. I just help her with her events between my part-time job as parish clerk. She keeps me busy."

Viola immediately imagined Bridget to be some kind of dogsbody to Gillian and felt a flush of sympathy for her.

"Do you not have a husband or partner?"

"No. I'm a widow." Bridget sighed. "Have been for a long time."

Viola flashed her a sympathetic smile. "Well, I'm sure Gillian couldn't do any of it without you, but you can tell Gillian that if she wants my hall, she can ask me herself."

"Oh, yes, of course," Bridget replied quickly, her mouth twitching as if trying to contain a smile.

"Does she organise everything around here?"

"Pretty much, except the classic car show."

"Ah yes, that would be the major's domain. He asked me to open it."

"Oh, really?" Bridget said, her eyes widening.

Viola raised an eyebrow. "You seem surprised?"

"It's just Gillian does that every year. She'll be furious," Bridget said, her mouth twitching again.

That would be one benefit of opening the car show. Not that Viola wanted to. She wanted to be left alone.

"There's also the annual manor summer ball," Bridget continued, "if that is still going ahead, of course. It's the event of the year, and that would be your job now, not Gillian's."

"My job? As what? *Lady of the manor*?" Viola said, her mouth quirking up at one corner. "I assume that's held in my great hall too."

"Err… yes."

"Is there no other place this ball could be held?"

"Well, it wouldn't be the manor summer ball without the manor."

"That's kind of what I was aiming for." Viola smirked, playfully narrowing her eyes.

Bridget giggled. "Oh, yes. I see. Unfortunately, nowhere in the village is big enough. There's also the summer fete and the harvest festival. The manor is — *was* the centre of everything in Kingsford. The village hall has always been a bit inadequate for Gillian's events, and she's always been more than happy to hold them in the great hall."

I bet she has. No doubt to ensure she controls everything, Viola thought to herself.

"She has — *had* excellent caterers, and her cook was an exquisite baker," Bridget continued.

"I could use a cook and housekeeper. I don't suppose Gillian's would be interested in returning, assuming they haven't gone with her?"

Bridget reached for her handbag and extracted a pencil and a piece of paper. "No, she didn't take any staff. I can give you the cook's number; she was also the housekeeper."

"Even better."

Draining her cup, Bridget stood, scribbled a number on the paper, and pushed it over to Viola. "I don't want to take up any more of your time. I'd best go and give Gillian the news. Thanks for the coffee,"

"Can you take her cat with you? I found her on my bed this morning. It seems as soon as I open a door, she sneaks in. Either that or she morphs through the walls, which would be surprising in a three-hundred-year-old property."

"Four hundred." Bridget said, then rolled her eyes. "Oh, listen to me. I'm beginning to sound like Gillian."

"You're nothing like Gillian, at least from what I've observed," Viola remarked. She noticed Bridget's cheeks flush as she guided her into the drawing room. "Now you stay out, Agatha. This isn't your home anymore," Viola scolded the cat lightly, placing her into Bridget's arms.

The cat eyed her suspiciously.

"May I ask why Gillian sold the estate?" Viola said as she led Bridget to the front door.

"Financial problems," Bridget half whispered. "Her husband, Jonathon, died rather unexpectedly and left her with even more unexpected debt. It seems he'd remortgaged the house and made some bad investments."

Viola felt a sudden pang of remorse. Was that the reason for the woman's attitude? Was Gillian grieving a lost loved one like she was?

"Well, thanks for coming by, and whenever you get a moment to bring the vase, please do," she said as she waved Bridget off.

She was already looking forward to the woman's next visit. Bridget was likeable and came across as kind and harmless, endearing even. She also struck her as a font of all knowledge when it came to the village, and if she was going to be forced into village life, the least she could do was arm herself for it.

The crunch of gravel drew her attention up the drive: Her Porsche Cayman was finally being delivered. Now she could explore the village hidden behind metal — or, as much as you could hide in such a car.

CHAPTER 5

Gillian made her way down the staircase, negotiating the tight turns as best she could with a basket of dirty laundry. It was bad enough having to do one's own laundry, let alone dealing with a staircase as narrow as the back stairs at Kingsford Manor.

The bell rang out as she reached the bottom. Instinctively placing the basket down, she looked at it, picked it back up, and popped it into the kitchen. She may have been living in the equivalent of a rabbit hutch, but standards still needed upholding. Keeping her laundry out of sight was one of them.

"Morning. I hear you've met our new neighbour," Bridget said as soon as Gillian opened the front door.

"Yes, I had a bit of a run-in with her yesterday. How did you know I met her?"

"I've just come from there," Bridget replied.

Gillian's face dropped as she closed the front door. "You visited her before me?"

Bridget bit her lip. "To be honest, it was a force of habit.

It wasn't until the door opened and she wasn't you that I remembered you'd moved."

"Honestly, Bridget." Gillian frowned then, realising her friend was cradling Agatha. "Please tell me Agatha wasn't at the manor too."

Bridget nodded. "Curled up on your old Chesterfield."

"Traitor."

Agatha leapt from Bridget's arms and ran into the kitchen.

"And I expect you still want me to feed you," Gillian called after her. "Come on through, Bridget. Could you pop by again sometime and ask her about holding the flower show in the hall?" She kept her tone as casual as possible, not wanting Bridget to pick up on how desperately she didn't want to be the one asking.

"I've already asked her," Bridget said as she followed Gillian into the sitting room.

"What did she say?" Gillian asked, turning so abruptly Bridget almost walked into her.

Taking a step back, Bridget replied, "That you should ask her yourself."

Gillian's hands shot to her hips. "Well, really! That settles it then. The village hall it will have to be. I'm not going cap in hand to her. She should know her duty to the village. It will fall on her if the show is ruined."

The village hall, although functional, was on the small side, and it failed to meet Gillian's preferred aesthetic for events. A rather unappealing addition to the village from the seventies, its steel girders and flimsy plasterboard walls contrasted starkly to the charm a Tudor hall effortlessly provided.

"What was the run-in you had with her?" Bridget asked.

Gillian sighed, realising she couldn't avoid explaining. "Her damn helicopter spooked Dudley; he threw me off."

"Oh! Were you both okay?"

"Yes, thankfully. I thought I'd give the pilot a piece of my mind about where they could and couldn't park their infernal machine, and it turned out *she* was the pilot!"

"You told her she couldn't park on her own lawn?" Bridget snickered, barely containing her amusement. "Oh, Gillian, how embarrassing."

"Yes, indeed," Gillian sniped, "and thank you very much for your support."

Bridget covered her mouth with her hand. "Sorry, Gillian. It must have been awful. Being thrown off by Dudley, I mean."

"Yes, well, let's have no more talk about it. How was I to know she was the pilot? She accused me of being misogynistic, you know!"

"Mmm," Bridget hummed, still trying to contain her grin. "Oh, you've had your hair done."

"Yes. I thought it was about time I got out a bit more," Gillian confirmed, patting at her waves and grateful for the change in subject. Thinking of that woman made her blood boil.

"Nothing to do with the new lady of the manor to compete with?"

Gillian rolled her eyes. "Absolutely not." The very idea was ridiculous. As if she had any reason to compete — especially with *her*.

"You know who she is, don't you?"

"I don't care *who* she is," Gillian replied, walking over to the window. Picking up her binoculars from a small table, she pointed them at the manor.

"She's Viola Berkley. You know, the classical singer," Bridget said, knocking into the coffee table as she manoeuvred onto the small sofa. "She's very nice and more beautiful in real life. It's funny how television distorts people." Bridget's attention turned to a laptop waking up on the table.

"I can't say I noticed." That was a lie; it was about the only thing she had noticed when she spoke to the woman. Her flowing auburn tresses had caught in the wind, each strand shining like copper in the sun as they momentarily obscured her lightly freckled face and deep brown eyes. When the woman tucked them behind her ear, the sun highlighted the delicate contours of her face.

"You knew exactly who she was," Bridget said, turning the laptop around. "You've got her Wiki page open!"

Pulled from her thoughts, Gillian replied, "I suspected, that's all. Is it just her, or are we to be overrun by screaming children?"

"How far did you read on the Wiki page?"

"Not far. It would take all week to read her accomplishments."

"If you'd made it to the personal life section you would know she's not married and is a lesbian. I certainly didn't see any children."

Gillian dropped the binoculars, and they crashed onto the floor.

"Oh, darn it," she said as she picked them up and

examined them. "They've broken. Good job I have a spare pair."

A rumbling noise sounded outside. Gillian rushed to a tall bureau on the other side of the room and pulled open a drawer. Extracting a new pair of binoculars, she hurried back to the window and directed them at the manor again.

Gillian clutched her stomach. "She's having a skip delivered!" *Why on earth did the woman need one of those? Nothing in there is skip-worthy.* "What was it like when you went in there? Was it as I left it?"

"Yes, it was bare from what I saw. She'd only brought the essentials like a coffee machine."

Lowering her binoculars, Gillian turned to Bridget and glared. "A good teapot is an essential, not a coffee machine. These yuppies have no taste."

"I hardly think you can call her a yuppy; she's not much younger than us, for a start."

"How old is she?"

Bridget's eyes scanned the laptop. "Forty-four, according to Wiki; only eleven years younger than you."

Not as much as Gillian had thought; she'd assumed the woman was in her thirties. Her youthful appearance certainly suggested it.

"Well, you know what these city types are like at any age. They have no understanding or appreciation for the countryside. Arriving by helicopter says everything you need to know."

"How do you know she's from the city?"

Gillian bit her lip before sheepishly answering. "I tracked her flight path; she came from Battersea."

"Stalking her now, are we?" Bridget replied with a hint of amusement.

"I'm simply keeping myself abreast of any newcomers to the village and the threat they could pose."

"Viola seems very pleasant and down to earth."

Overlooking the fact Bridget was on first-name terms with her replacement, Gillian turned her attention and binoculars back on the manor. She could make out Viola striding through the front door. She flicked her long, auburn hair to one side, giving a hint of a tingle in Gillian's stomach. Ignoring it, she watched as a man jumped down from the lorry and approached Viola, who pointed to an area of the drive and then disappeared back inside.

"She needs a cook and housekeeper," Bridget continued, "so I gave her Mrs Johnson's phone number."

"But she's mine!" Gillian cried, as a feeling of betrayal stabbed at her. "Why would you give that woman her number?"

"She's not yours anymore, is she?" said Bridget, with a hint of challenge in her voice. "What reason would I have not to?"

"There's another truck pulling up now. It's Metcalfe's," Gillian snarled, ignoring Bridget's question. "Damn woman is stealing my gardeners now!"

"You never used Metcalfe's; you had your own gardeners."

"And where do you think they went when I sold the manor?" The last three words stuck in her throat.

"Surely, it's good if some of the locals can be reemployed. You wouldn't want them to be unemployed?" Bridget asked, joining Gillian by the window.

"Of course not." She just didn't want Viola Berkley to have another thing of hers. "Are you stopping for tea?"

"No, best not. I'd better head off soon. I promised Viola I'd lend her a vase."

"A vase?"

"Yes. It seems Elouise and Louisa dropped off some flowers as a housewarming gift."

"They haven't dropped any to me," Gillian grumbled, lowering the binoculars.

"You're hardly new to the village, are you?"

Gillian pursed her lips in reply. "Has everyone in the village visited her this morning?"

Bridget nodded at the binoculars. "I'm surprised you haven't noticed."

"As if I have nothing better to do," Gillian exclaimed, cursing herself for allowing housework to distract her from all the action.

"The postman's wife put it on the village WhatsUp group last night. I guess it was inevitable she would have a few visitors."

"WhatsApp, Bridget. WhatsApp."

Bridget pinked. "Oh yes! Of course, silly me. I know the major was there before me. I think he was asking about using the bottom field for the classic car show. He even asked her to open it."

"The damn cheek of it. I've opened it since it began. It's my job." Did that blasted woman want everything of hers? "Did you know she hasn't donated anything towards the restoration of the cricket pavilion? The lads are doing a sponsored run and came round for sponsorship last night. Her name wasn't on the form, and they said they'd come from the manor."

"I'm sure she would have contributed something; she's ever so nice."

"You'd better be off," Gillian replied sharply, having heard quite enough about Viola Berkley. "You don't want to keep the lady of the manor waiting."

"I never have before," Bridget said through a smug grin.

Gillian scowled at her as she retreated. Was there anything left that Viola Berkley could take from her? With her gaze fixed back on the manor, she pondered again why Viola would need a skip. What was she going to be removing? Bathrooms? Her beloved kitchen? Historic features that her yuppy brain couldn't appreciate the true value of? Feeling her legs weaken at the thought of any part of her precious home going in that skip, Gillian looked around her. She was going to need to set up a permanent watching post with a chair, and another pair of binoculars would need purchasing immediately — to have one was to have none!

CHAPTER 6

"Thanks for coming by to check," Viola said, holding her hand out to the planning officer as they reached the front door. She flashed him a smile despite her body itching with anger at his unannounced appearance an hour before, which had interrupted her morning. He was only doing his job; the anger she needed to save for someone else.

"Sorry again, for disturbing you," he said, shaking her hand. "We have to check these things when we get a complaint."

"Oh! It was a complaint then," Viola pushed.

The man bit his lip. "Can't comment, sorry. Thanks for your time."

Viola watched as the man crossed the gravel drive and entered a car parked beside an overloaded skip. Ben, her project manager, appeared by her side at the front door.

"Any idea who reported you?" he asked.

Viola looked at the lodge and noticed the twinkling of a lens in the window. "I have my suspicions, yes."

"I'd best get on. The lads do like an early finish on a Friday, and some of the tiles in that last bathroom are proving difficult to pry up. We'll aim to start reinstalling the kitchen next week," Ben said, turning and heading back into the house.

"Glad to hear it."

There was only so much that could be done with a microwave and a camping stove. After two weeks of ready meals, Viola couldn't wait to have the new kitchen installed. Although she would make some use of it herself, she was looking forward to speaking to Mrs Johnson, Gillian's old cook and housekeeper, later that day. Even if the woman popped in a couple of days a week to clean and prepare some meals, it would be useful.

Right now, though, she needed to deal with Gillian Carmichael.

When there was no answer at the lodge, Viola decided to try her luck at the stables. She found Gillian grooming a handsome black horse in the stable yard. She was dressed in her riding clothes again, and it took Viola a moment to pull her eyes away from the woman's frame as she bent and stretched to brush the horse. She had always been drawn to older women, but this one was a definite no-go despite how attractive she was.

She took a deep breath and focused on her anger as she forced herself towards Gillian.

"I presume you were the busybody who called the planning department," she began.

Gillian snapped around. "I'm sorry?"

"Good." Viola knew damn well Gillian wasn't apologising, merely asking her to repeat herself, but she was taking it anyway. The woman's gaping mouth confirmed her intended offence had landed. "I can assure you, as I did the planning chap who tried to lecture me and my project manager as to what is allowable and what isn't, that all the changes I am making to *my* home do not require planning permission. Or, in fact, anyone's permission, including yours."

Gillian's mouth flapped around some more, so taking advantage of the silence, Viola continued.

"If you'd had the decency to come and ask me what I was doing, I would have been happy to show you. Instead, you prefer to sneak around behind people's backs and report them for things they haven't done."

"I…" Gillian stammered.

"My project manager is adequately versed in historic properties."

"I have legitimate concerns for the welfare of my former home and perfectly serviceable utilities," Gillian snapped, finally finding her voice.

"They may be perfectly serviceable, yet it is not to my taste, and it's *my* home. I would appreciate it if you kept your meddling nose out of my business and away from your window," she asserted with a firmness there could be no misunderstanding.

She could hear Gillian spitting out, "Well, I…" behind her as she walked away.

Viola decided a walk was in order. Her phone rang as she passed the side of the manor.

"Hey, Caroline," she sighed as she answered. Her soothing voice was exactly what she needed right now; she always grounded her.

"Wow, you sound tense. You're supposed to be relaxing in the countryside. You aren't overdoing it, are you?" Caroline's concerned voice replied.

"Relaxing would be a fine thing if the doorbell wasn't constantly going or the builders banging or neighbours sticking their fucking noses in where they're not needed."

Viola reached a bench overlooking the estate and sank onto it.

"Breathe, darling."

"I am breathing," Viola reassured her.

"Fire or air?"

Viola thought before answering. "Air."

"Good. Now, who has the sticky nose, and where are they sticking it?"

"Gillian fucking Carmichael," she seethed through gritted teeth. "The woman who owned this place before me and all but lives in my garden. She owns the lodge at the end of the drive, and I'm sure she's watching my every move. It wouldn't surprise me if she's rummaging in the skip every night."

"Struggling to let go, is she?"

"She reported me to the planning office."

"Remember we all deal with loss differently."

"That may be so — hang on." Viola frowned. "I don't remember telling you her husband died."

"Her husband died!" Caroline exclaimed.

"Yes. What were you talking about?" Viola asked, confused.

"Her losing her house, of course. The poor woman."

Hmm. That was a fair point. Was the woman mourning the loss of her house as well as her husband?

"Why don't you do something to lift your spirits?" Caroline continued.

"If you're suggesting what I think you're suggesting, that is not going to cut it."

Caroline's laughter resounded in Viola's ear. "I was thinking more of holding a housewarming party, though you could try that too. It might work in the short term, so long as you don't think of this Gillian whilst you're doing it."

Viola's breath caught unexpectedly, causing her to cough.

"Oh! Is that your problem?" Caroline purred. "Is she hot?"

"Caroline!"

"I've hit a nerve, haven't I? Why don't you think of her and channel that anger? It would probably make for a better orgasm."

"I'm hanging up now," Viola replied, twisting her lips. "Unless there was a particular reason you rang?"

"No, simply checking in on my dearest friend," Caroline retorted.

"And your biggest meal ticket."

"Oof! Harsh."

"Factual," Viola snarked.

"You know I love you despite how incredibly rich you've made me. In fact, I'm working on something exciting for you, but you need to be fit."

"Oh God, it's not *I'm a Celebrity... Get Me Out of Here*, is it?" Viola shivered. "I told you I will never do that."

"No, of course not. It's early stages right now anyway."

"Good. I need this time off, Caroline, and you promised me nothing until the end of summer."

"I know, I know," Caroline reassured her. "You can hold me to that."

Viola breathed deeply with relief. After years of working with little rest, she needed some time to restore herself, especially after losing her mum.

"How are you getting on with the savages?"

"Well, like I said, everyone wants something. There's been an endless stream of locals visiting; some bring flowers whilst others demand access to my land or my house like it's their birthright. I've only been here a couple of weeks, and I've already donated thousands to restore the cricket pavilion just to get the damn chairman of the cricket club off my back. Even the local reverend has been bothering me about attending church on Sunday. Apparently, I have my very own pew at the front, and he wants me to join some church committee as an honourable member."

"Do people still go to church?" Caroline said, clearly fascinated.

"Apparently. I won't be going. I came here to disappear for a while, but it's like the locals all think I hold some position."

"You do. Lady of the manor," Caroline snarked.

"Oh, don't you start. I wish everyone would leave me alone."

"On that note, I need to head into a meeting."

Viola laughed. "It doesn't apply to you, but yes, go. I need to prepare myself for Mrs Johnson, whom I hope will be my cook and housekeeper."

"I'm glad to hear you'll be getting some help. It looks like a big place, and you don't want to be dusting and hoovering it. We'll never have you singing again."

Muttering her agreement and a farewell, Viola disconnected the call. Taking in her surroundings, she realised how beautiful the estate looked from here. With the manor at the end of the path to the left and the top of the church spire poking above the trees to the right, an expanse lay between, comprising a small valley with a stream and the hill beyond. One could pass the time of day very easily just sitting there — not today, though; there were things to do. She noticed a plaque on the bench as she stood up.

Henrietta Fotherington
Taken too soon. Missed forever.

It was a bit mysterious, perhaps a relation of the Carmichaels. Bridget said they'd lived on the estate for more than four hundred years. Thinking no more of it, Viola returned to the house to await Mrs Johnson, who arrived precisely on time. This pleased Viola to no end; punctuality was an essential skill for a cook, though any previous employee of Gillian's was likely to be well trained or more likely running on fear.

"Come through to the kitchen; it's just being renovated. It will have all the mod cons once it's done," Viola added, hoping selling the kitchen would help persuade the woman to come and work for her.

Mrs Johnson ran a fingertip along the top of an old cast-iron radiator as they passed through the great hall.

Examining the thick layer of dirt on the end of it, she scowled.

Viola felt compelled to justify the mess. "There's a lot of dust from all the work going on. You can see why I'm in need of some help."

Mrs Johnson didn't react, which made Viola a little nervous as she followed her into the kitchen.

"Golly! You've gone to town in here," Mrs Johnson said, looking around as they entered. "Not a trace of the old one. It's magnificent."

"I'm not sure it will please Gillian Carmichael," Viola said, though she inwardly cringed at her own question. She'd been hoping to gauge some reaction for the fallout she might expect when news got around, but what was she thinking? She didn't care what that woman thought anyway.

"Ah yes, Mrs Carmichael," Mrs Johnson replied. "What a woman."

"Yes, indeed," Viola agreed, shaking her head.

"Such a respectful, kind, and generous woman. She's a true saint."

Viola looked at her to see if she was joking. She was aggrieved to find what she could only describe as deep affection in the woman's eyes.

"I have a lot of respect for her. She dedicated her life to this estate, only to lose it thanks to that husband of hers. I never liked him. The loss of a husband like him a woman can quite easily bear. The loss of Kingsford…" She shook her head. "I dare say it broke her heart. Not that she'd admit it. She's nothing but grace and fortitude."

"Really?" Viola couldn't help blustering. "Are we talking about the same Gillian Carmichael?"

Mrs Johnson let out a laugh. "She may have a way about her, but she did her job remarkably efficiently."

"Her job?"

"Yes, running this place. Organising all the village events. You have big shoes to fill."

Viola gulped. "I'm beginning to realise that." How had she signed up for a job by buying a house? It was a job she most definitely didn't want.

"Are you on your own? No husband or family?"

Viola looked at her blankly. The question always came as a surprise to her; she'd been outed as a lesbian after a relationship went sour in her twenties. It also pissed her off every time she was asked if she had a husband. Not only did a woman not need a husband, but some also didn't need or want men at all. She despised the insinuation that a husband was the norm. Why couldn't people say "partner" and stop excluding others? It wasn't difficult.

Perhaps the woman didn't know who she was, though; that would make a welcome change. She'd encountered enough obsessive fans to last several lifetimes.

"It's just I need an idea of how many will be living here," Mrs Johnson prompted her. "It makes a difference when you are clearing up after them, especially the young'uns."

"Oh, right. Yes, of course. It's only me."

Mrs Johnson lifted an eyebrow. "Big house for one."

"Yes, it is." She inhaled deeply, "It wasn't meant to be that way."

"So rarely it is."

"I bought the house for my mum." Viola took in a deep breath. "She passed away recently."

Mrs Johnson's no-nonsense demeanour deflated. "Sorry to hear that, dear. I lost my mum last year. Doesn't get easier, only different. A bit like raising children, I say."

Feeling her eyes beginning to moisten, Viola walked over to the window, minding not to trip on some of the workmen's equipment, which was scattered on the floor. She wasn't expecting it to get easier, but the reminder of the emptiness inside her from her mum's death, not to mention how it was unlikely to leave, sat heavily in her stomach. She needed a distraction. Was a housewarming party the answer?

"I assume you can cater for parties," Viola asked her guest.

"Is the pope Catholic?" Mrs Johnson replied with a laugh.

Viola smiled.

"I'll pop in every Monday, Wednesday, and Friday if you're happy with that, and I can leave you something in the fridge to reheat if you want. Leave a note for Monday if there's anything you particularly like or don't like, and let me know if you need me for anything else."

"Perfect. Thank you," Viola replied, slightly taken aback by the woman. She was sure she was the one who was supposed to be setting terms, not that she was about to argue.

"I won't keep you. I'll see myself out, and don't worry — I've still got my key."

Viola blinked. Should she have changed the locks?

What if Gillian still possessed a key too? Would she be letting herself in like her cat was? She wouldn't put it past the woman to do a bit of snooping; she looked the type.

Mrs Johnson, on the other hand, was mild-mannered and agreeable. She was the sort of woman you knew you could rely on to run a house, which left Viola with a feeling of inadequacy. There was no question of wearing Gillian's shoes, let alone filling them. She wasn't respectful whatsoever; she'd met children with better manners. Was the grief making her unpleasant? It did strange things to people; Viola knew that much herself.

But she had a party fixed in her mind now; planning it would give her something to focus on other than her lacking as lady of the manor. With any luck, she'd be able to piss off Saint Gillian at the same time.

CHAPTER 7

Gillian glared out of her bedroom window at the garish disco lights spilling out from inside the manor. They stood out like beacons against the darkness, pulsating in rhythm with the beat of the music — if the cacophony emanating from within could be described as music.

For thirty-five years, every party at the manor had been meticulously planned and overseen by Gillian herself. Hearing laughter from outside — laughter she had no part in — sent a wave of nausea rolling through her. She pressed a hand to her stomach, steadying herself against the bitter reminder of how much had changed.

Glancing at the clock by her bedside, she noted it was two in the morning. Its faint glow illuminated the glass of water beside it. Small ripples moved through the water, mirroring the vibrations she was beginning to feel in her own body.

The sensation intensified, accompanied by a sound overhead — a helicopter, she suspected, a thought which was confirmed by a bright glow of light passing above. She watched as it flew around to the back of the manor and descended behind it. Hopeful it was collecting guests and signified the end of the party, Gillian returned to her bed exhausted, jealous, and alone.

Shoving earplugs into her ears, she fell back onto her pillow and closed her eyes, pushing all thoughts of Viola Berkley aside. With her eyes shut, she could imagine herself being anywhere in the world, but there was only one place she imagined herself to be — her old bedroom.

A few hours later she wrenched her eyes open at the muffled sound of her alarm. She noticed Agatha at the bottom of the bed as she silenced it.

"Was it too noisy over there for you, too, Agatha?" she asked the cat through a yawn as she removed her earplugs.

Agatha peered at her through slitted eyes.

"I'm surprised you weren't there partying with them, since you practically live there."

Gillian covered another yawn as the cat closed her eyes. She didn't have the luxury of drifting back to sleep like her four-legged, part-time houseguest, no matter how much she wished she could. Duty called, so she pulled herself from her warm bed and dressed for church. She would have to skip riding Dudley this morning — she was in no condition for it — and without the parkland to ride through, she had lost her desire for it at the moment.

The church service didn't help her tiredness. It felt longer than usual, which was always too long, and she almost nodded off twice. Luckily only Bridget appeared to notice, nudging her from her seat beside her.

As the service ended and the usual milling about commenced amongst the villagers, the major approached her.

"Ah, Gillian. I still haven't heard from that Berkley woman about using her bottom field for the classic car show. Would you have a word with her? Tell her how things are done around here?"

Gillian glared at him. "As you no longer require my services to open the show, I have no reason to be involved. I'm sure you can see my conundrum, Major."

His face dropped. "Oh! About that... I thought my asking her might persuade her; you know, cajole her into it. You know we'd want nothing more than for you to open it again, Gilly."

Gillian cringed and shot him a death stare, not only for shortening her name but for trying to flatter Viola Berkley, hoping it would tempt her into opening the show. At least it appeared to have backfired, all credit to the new lady of the manor.

"Good day, Major," she said with a nod. Having spotted Bridget coming back from the toilets in the adjoining chapter house, it was time to make an escape.

"Are you not going?" Bridget asked as she joined her.

"You must be joking; it would be like using the lavatories in the sandpaper aisle at the DIY store. I'll wait until I get home."

Bridget smirked. "Yes, it was a bit. I suppose it cuts costs even more if no one uses it."

As they left the church, Gillian tried to circumvent the reverend. She was in no mood for him today. Her efforts were to no avail.

"Mrs Carmichael," he sniffed. "We did discuss you freeing up the front pew last week, did we not?"

"Miss Berkley is not here, nor has she been here for the last few weeks," Gillian observed. "Nor do we know if she has any intention of being here! Shall we discuss it further if she ever *deigns* to be here?"

The reverend inclined his head, as if sensing from Gillian's tone that now wasn't the time to press her.

Taking that as an agreement, Gillian marched off, closely followed by Bridget.

"Can you believe she hasn't attended church again? If not for us, the manor pew would have been empty for the first time in — "

"Four hundred years!" Bridget interrupted.

Gillian lifted an eyebrow at her friend. "More than four hundred years, Bridget. I'm surprised we couldn't feel all the Carmichaels turning beneath us in the crypt. The major has been on at me about the classic car show. For someone who hasn't been here long, Miss Berkley has caused a lot of disruption. She needs to understand her duties if she's to be lady of the manor."

Gillian covered a yawn with her gloved hand as they approached the gate.

"You sound like you need to go back to bed," Bridget stated.

"Mmm," Gillian agreed. "Did the party not keep you awake all night?"

"No, I left around eleven."

Stopping dead in her tracks, Gillian growled out, "You… attended her party?"

Bridget kept walking, oblivious at first; then she

slowed and turned back when she noticed Gillian wasn't beside her. "Yes. I was surprised not to see you there. Although I suppose you and Viola didn't exactly hit it off, did you? There were quite a few famous people there. I had a lovely chat with one of the Spice Girls. Not sure which one, though."

"Anyone else from the village there?" Gillian sniffed. "Actually, I don't wish to know."

Bridget bit her lip and replied softly, "Should I not have gone? Is it considered sleeping with the enemy?"

"You're fifty-four, Bridget. You don't need my permission to attend a party." Gillian felt like adding that it was exactly like sleeping with the enemy but refrained. Bridget was free to do whatever she chose to do; she just wished she wasn't getting quite so friendly with that damn Berkley woman.

"In that case, I had a great time," Bridget said with a grin. "The music level was more suited to the younger generations, but Mrs Johnson put on a wonderful spread as usual."

Gillian shuddered at the thought of what had gone on inside her beloved manor house. Full of drunk and drugged-up riffraff in all likelihood. "They were respecting the building, weren't they?" she asked cautiously.

"Oh yes, but — " Bridget hesitated.

"But what?"

"I accidentally walked in on two people getting rather into it on one of your old Chesterfields."

Gillian's hand went straight to her mouth. She regretted ever leaving the sofas there. If only the lodge was bigger, she could have taken them with her. She should have found the money to put everything into storage to save it getting soiled.

"You should see her new kitchen," Bridget continued.

"I don't want to know."

"It's beautiful," Bridget said, a smile forming on her face.

"I said I don't want to know," Gillian sniffed.

Bridget looked down. "Sorry, Gillian."

"You know she had the gall to come and lecture me in the garden the other day? Accused me of nosing in her skip."

Bridget laughed. "Are you telling me you didn't?"

"Once doesn't count. I happened to notice the kitchen fireplace was in it."

"You hated that fireplace!" Bridget protested. "Your mother-in-law put that in during the seventies."

"That's not the point," Gillian stated. "She's throwing away the nation's heritage."

Bridget laughed. "She's doing it a service. There's a much nicer one in its place now. It's far more in keeping with the building."

Gillian scowled and chewed at her lip. "I'll walk back through the estate today. Alone."

She was quite done hearing about the party and her house being torn apart. It broke her heart. Why had she not left instead of moving herself in full view of the place she wanted to be? She was torturing herself. When she had decided to move into the lodge, it was with the naive idea that, somehow, she would get the manor back. The more time passed, though, the more she realised it was unlikely to happen. Changes were being made to her house — it would always be hers in her heart — and she couldn't do anything about it. The person making those changes wasn't even living up to the role she'd taken on. Did the woman not realise she was taking on a job, not simply buying a house?

Waving goodbye to Bridget, Gillian opened the gate onto the footpath that crossed the estate. She needed to clear her head, and there was only one place she could do that properly: on her bench. As she steadily climbed the small incline and it came into view, to her horror she could see it was already taken.

∼

Viola leaned back against the bench and closed her eyes, filling her lungs with the spring air. It didn't make her feel better, even with the soothing scent of blossoms filling the air; her worries still lingered as much as her headache. She'd only drunk three glasses of wine at the party, but combined with the noise and lack of sleep, it was enough to give her that hangover feeling.

Her thoughts of the previous night churned inside her, refusing to be swept away by the tranquillity of her idyllic surroundings. The laughter and chatter around her felt hollow, unable to fill the void left by the absence of her mum.

She could engage in the superficiality of small talk and lose herself in the rhythm of the music, yet deep down, the loneliness persisted. A silent ache echoed in the depths of her soul. Amidst the crowd, she felt isolated, trapped in a bubble of grief while the world carried on around her.

With a tired sigh, Viola opened her moist eyes, only for them to fall on Gillian Carmichael. She was marching towards her in a fitted tweed blazer and navy trousers that hugged her figure with infuriating elegance. What did that woman want now?

Viola groaned internally as she realised there may be some strong words coming about last night's noise levels. Perhaps by some miracle, she was coming to apologise for sticking her nose in with the planning department. She groaned again when she realised how hot she found Gillian in tweed.

"You weren't at church again," Gillian accused her, taking the seat beside her on the bench.

Again? Someone's keeping count. She wasn't sure whether to feel flattered or stalked.

"Why would I be at church? I'm not religious," Viola replied flatly. So much for tweed. She was annoyed with the woman after only one sentence had left her mouth.

"What has religion got to do with it? I'm not religious either; none of us are. If pressed, you would find the reverend isn't either. Church is not about religion — well, not in a small village like this, it isn't."

"Forgive me if I always assumed it to be so. What is it about then?"

"It's about community."

Viola raised an eyebrow, "Community?"

"Yes. It's more of a social club than anything, especially for an ageing population like Kingsford. It brings the villagers together once a week. They can talk about what ails them, how they need help fixing something, that the shop is stocking a new brand of cereal. It is the wheelhouse of any small village."

Viola was dying to point out that it sounded like the only reason Gillian was going was for the latest gossip, but she didn't have the strength.

"It allows us to care for each other," Gillian continued, hardly drawing breath, "and provide when one of our own is in need. What if none of us bothered to attend?" She shook her head in disgust as she added, "The manor has never failed to be represented in more than four hundred years. It's tradition. Your absence is breaking down the very fabric of society."

Viola had been accused of a few things over the years; breaking down the fabric of society was certainly a new one.

She blew out an exaggerated sigh. "And there was me hoping you were coming to apologise."

"For what?" Gillian barked. "What reason would I have to come to you to apologise?"

"For sticking your nose into my business," Viola insisted, wondering if the woman was being deliberately obtuse or if she'd forgotten their previous altercation.

Gillian stuck her nose in the air. "The Kingsford Estate is everyone's business. It's our business when you don't clean out the lake and it clogs up and runs into the village. It's our business when you let dead wood hang off trees over the lanes and it hits our vehicles." Turning to Viola, her tone hardened. "Being lady of the manor involves more than parting with money to buy a building. It's a way of life. A privilege. A role. You have a duty — "

"I am sick of hearing about my duty," Viola replied sternly, wishing she could shout at the woman yet unable to summon the effort it would take. "How I need to open this or organise that and give my property over for some event."

"Now look."

"No, you look," Viola snapped, sick of the woman's rudeness.

Gillian pulled herself back, as if it was the first time someone had ever stood up to her.

"I don't care that you were once lady of the manor or whatever," Viola replied, anger rippling through her voice. "No one has asked me; they've told me. This is my estate, and I won't have people telling me what I should be doing with it. What are you even doing here? This is private property. You old-guard elites think you are entitled to swan about wherever you like. You don't own Kingsford anymore; it's mine." Taking a quick breath, she added, "Can't I have any peace?"

"This is a public footpath," Gillian was quick to reply.

Fuck. Viola was at a loss for words. How did she not know that? Her solicitor had mentioned one. She'd assumed it was somewhere else on the estate, not practically leading past her house.

"And as for peace," Gillian continued, "I assumed that would be the last thing on your mind considering the number of people in attendance last night and the level of noise you were making. Holicopters circling in the small hours, keeping us all awake. No consideration for the villagers."

The main appeal of the party had been to piss off

Gillian, yet in the cold light of day and with her head aching, Viola was regretting the party even more. Pissing off Gillian was one thing; having to deal with a pissed-off Gillian was another. The mild hangover was making her feel worse about everything. It always amplified her fears and anxieties, which was part of the reason her mum had stepped in all those years ago and helped her out. She'd stopped her partying, her excessive drinking, and put her on the right path. Her mum hadn't been gone long, and already she'd slipped back into bad habits.

Viola felt her eyes begin to sting, and she pushed the thoughts away. Crying in front of Gillian Carmichael was not on the agenda. She'd never hear the end of it. Thankfully Gillian started up again, her vitriol providing a surprisingly welcome distraction.

"Why even come to the countryside if you intend to make noises like that? It should be kept in the city. True peace is found in the morning birdsong or giving a neighbour a lift to the hospital or having one's cook prepare a meal for someone in need. Even in collecting the fruit from the estate and making preserves for the villagers and throwing them a *civilised* ball once a year to give them something to look forward to. Holding a jumble sale so others might enjoy items we have lost our love for, or a book club to encourage reading and stave off loneliness and boredom.. You youngsters have no idea what it is to be old. I wouldn't presume to understand it myself, of course, but I see it when I care to look."

The woman was baffling. She seemed to genuinely care about the community — provided she was the one in control. Gillian had devoted her life to a role she believed was intrinsically linked to ownership of the manor. Losing her home meant losing the identity and status she'd spent years cultivating. Viola couldn't see how a building could define a person's worth, let alone their status in society. Gillian, however, clearly did, and clung to what she'd lost with a conviction Viola would never comprehend.

"If you must know, it was a present to my late mum."

Gillian frowned. "Late…?"

"Yes." Viola took in a deep breath. As she let it out, she added, "She died suddenly, two weeks after I bought Kingsford for her."

Silence hung in the air until Gillian finally spoke. "It was never your intention to live here?"

Viola shook her head. "Not full-time."

"Why not put it back up for sale then?" Gillian pressed.

"I'd paid deposits and contracted work to be carried out. She may have only visited twice, but Mum had a strong vision for Kingsford, and I wanted to make that happen, despite her not being here to enjoy it." Gillian's face appeared to curl at the mention of changes being made, which annoyed Viola further. "Now you see why I am here. When, really, I would rather be anywhere else," she added firmly.

"I know grief," Gillian said, nodding her agreement.

Anger and sadness pushed their way forward inside of Viola. "What do you know about it?" The words erupted sharply from her lips. "Your husband died a few months ago, and you appear to grieve only for your damn manor. Isn't that a little heartless?" Viola's eyes filled with warm, unbidden tears, and she made no effort to hide them. She was tired of hiding behind a facade of strength, and it would do Gillian Carmichael good to see what effect her cruelty could have on someone. Viola sniffed as she wiped her eyes with the backs of her hands.

Then Gillian did something Viola wouldn't have expected. Reaching into her pocket, she extracted a cotton handkerchief and handed it to Viola. Surprised though she was, Viola took it and wiped her eyes, noticing the letters GC embroidered onto one corner. Who even used handkerchiefs these days, let alone embroidered ones? As her eyes cleared a little, Viola noticed Gillian's hands were twitching and her body fidgeting in her seat.

"I'll... erm..." Gillian mumbled and then stood.

Viola watched in surprise as the woman hesitated, her words trailing off into an awkward silence as their eyes locked. Her gaze lingered on Viola, a little too long for her comfort, the crackling tension causing her to hold her breath and her heart to pound in her chest. It was as if Gillian was studying every detail and imperfection until she finally turned and walked away.

Viola's eyes followed the infuriating woman as she strode down the path. Noticing a hint of jasmine coming from the handkerchief, she placed it under her nose. Inhaling deeply, she smiled as a sense of calm washed over her from the pleasant scent — the scent of Gillian.

Although she was grateful for the gesture, she couldn't help feeling a little apprehensive at the prospect of facing Gillian again to return the handkerchief. The thought of seeing the woman again filled her with even more conflicting feelings, even a hint of longing. She quickly tucked the handkerchief into her pocket and pushed all thoughts of Gillian Carmichael from her mind.

CHAPTER 8

A wave of nausea hit Gillian's stomach as soon as she woke the next morning. She'd hoped the lack of sleep from the previous night would have seen her off to a deep sleep, but instead she'd tossed and turned, playing over her altercation with Viola.

She couldn't blame the woman for buying the manor; it was Jonathon's fault it was on the market. She also couldn't blame her for not meeting the standards required of her. Not everyone was born for the role the way she was.

A pang of regret sat inside her too. She hadn't intended to make the woman cry. It had pained her to witness it, and it had weighed on her since. She may have had a firmness about her, but she hoped she never strayed into heartlessness as Viola had suggested.

Offering comfort didn't come naturally to Gillian. Emotions were an unknown territory for her, and the idea of reaching out felt foreign and uncomfortable. A stiff upper lip was her motto, a shield against raw emotions. It hadn't stopped her wanting to offer solace to ease the woman's suffering, though. The unfamiliarity of the urge confused her, and the instinct to retreat had won out in the end.

There had been something attractive about Viola in that moment of vulnerability. Something was captivating about the woman, full stop. Was it her strength and determination to fulfil the vision of her late mother despite how raw her grief must be? It couldn't be anything else; she wouldn't let it be anything else. Gillian simply admired strength wherever she saw it.

In the past, Gillian had grappled with grief. It was a suffocating shadow that had threatened to consume her when death took away her soulmate in her late teens. The pain was relentless, a constant ache that left her hollow inside. She was given no emotional help from the person she needed it from the most — her mother.

In her darkest moments, Gillian found a flicker of resilience inside her, a stubbornness to endure. Endure she did, but she was never the same again. She packed her identity away and pushed herself forward, set on building a new life and a new relationship with grief. She had vowed never to let it pull her down again. With little affection for her late husband, his loss had been bearable. The loss of the manor and the added magnetism of the woman who owned it, however, were beginning to lift the lid on a hard-won battle from the past.

With Bridget due for elevenses, she needed to buck up her ideas, yet her body was failing her. Whatever dark cloud weighed on her brain was weighing over her body too. Removing her silk pyjamas, she scrutinised her slender frame in the mirror with a critical eye for its traitorous imperfections. Who would even want her body with all its ridges and furrows, marked by the passage of time and the trials of life? Would it ever find fulfilment from what it desired? Could she even allow it to? Shaking her head, she breathed out hard, pushing the thoughts away as she dressed.

Her darkened state must have remained with her, for by the time Bridget arrived later that morning, it was the first thing she commented on.

"You look rather glum today," she said, not even clearing the front door. "Are you coming down with something?"

"Sit yourself down," Gillian said, directing her to the sitting room. "I'll make the tea, and then I can fill you in."

She needed to prepare better for answering the front door. When Bramingham was around to answer it, she had had a few moments to ready herself, slipping on a hostess's face and looking ready to welcome whoever entered. It was a skill acquired over the years. She may have felt born for her role, but she had been ill-prepared for it in the early days. Her mother-in-law was well versed in being lady of the manor and had taught her well. She learned quickly, driven by the fear of being looked down on in Jonathon's social circles.

"I had another run-in with Viola Berkley," Gillian admitted as she placed a tea tray on the table in front of Bridget a few minutes later. "It left a rather bad taste in one's mouth."

"Oh, Gillian," Bridget said as she took a cup and saucer

of steaming hot tea. "You two should really try to get along; you are neighbours, after all. Why don't you go over and apologise? Clear the air."

"Apologise?" Gillian choked out. "That's a bit extreme. I said nothing that didn't need saying. I'm not even sure it was me who made her cry. She appeared contemplative when I got there."

Bridget narrowed her eyes. "And at that point, you decided to raise your issue? She has just lost her mother."

Gillian squirmed under Bridget's scrutiny, struggling to justify her actions even to herself.

"What was your problem anyway? The party?" Bridget's question lingered, her eyes fixed on Gillian, whose expression at the mere mention of the word must have given her away. "Was it the noise or the fact you weren't invited?" Bridget took a sip of her tea before adding, "For what it's worth, she didn't seem to be having a good time."

"It's not about the party," Gillian replied, thankful her friend didn't push for an answer to her second question.

Did she feel snubbed by the lack of an invitation or put out that the woman invited Bridget? Either way, she didn't appreciate the reminder that Bridget had attended. Or that her approach to the situation may have been less than considerate. She always prided herself on her consideration for others. When it came to Viola Berkley, though, she struggled.

"Bridget, do you think I'm heartless?" Bridget's floppy jaw and gaping mouth said everything, leading Gillian to add with some mild trepidation, "You can be honest."

"Really?"

Gillian nodded and braced herself.

"I guess at times you can be" — Bridget's eyes flickered around the room, avoiding contact with Gillian's — "a little insensitive to others."

She was about to react, but noticing a hint of regret on Bridget's face, she took a deep breath instead — only to hear Bridget continuing on.

"If you tried a different approach, you would get a different reaction. You tend to bulldoze and — "

Gillian raised her hand to stop her. "That's enough honesty for today; thank you, Bridget." She'd heard more than she needed. She wasn't even sure why she was discussing it with her — perhaps hoping it would ease some of her guilt — but it wasn't working. If anything, it only made her feel worse.

Bridget was right in one respect: If she and Viola were going to be neighbours, then they needed to find a way to get along. Despite her irritation at seeing the younger woman possess everything Gillian longed to reclaim, she felt an inexplicable draw to her. With a curiosity she could barely admit to herself, she had started watching Viola's performances on YouTube, finding herself completely immersed in them. She reasoned with herself, attributing her fascination to the captivating voice of the singer, who possessed a knack for drawing in her audience. Shaking thoughts of Viola away, she focused on her guest and their plans for this year's flower show.

When they had finished their tea and laid out plans, Bridget excused herself. She was due to play bridge after lunch with Louisa and Elouise, a tradition the three of them and Gillian had in the past upheld every week. Since losing the manor, though, Gillian refused to host the game in her pokey lodge. There wasn't enough space for a table, and she'd be damned if she was playing at the kitchen table. The fewer people who saw the less-than-ideal conditions of her current living situation, the better.

Even though Louisa and Elouise offered to host up at Kingsford House, Gillian couldn't face the humiliation of playing in someone else's home. She was a hostess; it was her role. She didn't know how to be a guest. Bridget had informed her they made up a fourth by having Louisa persuade their cleaner to play, so she assumed she wasn't even missed.

Feeling the need for a walk and fresh air to lift her mood, Gillian devoured a quick lunch and headed out. She allowed her feet to carry her wherever they pleased. If she happened to bump into Viola along the way, then so be it.

Her feet led her to what had become a familiar route through the village to the church and back to the bench overlooking the estate. A place that held memories of peace, and echoes of unresolved emotions. She sat, unsure exactly what she was doing there yet unable to resist the pull that drew her to it. Was part of her hoping to find Viola after all?

∽

Viola stared out the kitchen window at Gillian Carmichael as the heat from her mug warmed her hands. It was the third afternoon in a row that she'd parked herself on the bench since their previous meeting.

Taking a sip of coffee, she contemplated whether she'd been too harsh in snapping at the woman when all she'd said was that she knew grief. Everyone dealt with it differently, so who was Viola to judge and measure that? It wasn't comparable to her feelings of loss, nor should it be. People processed it in their own unique way.

Her phone vibrated on the worktop, interrupting her thoughts. The illuminated screen read *Caroline*. Viola picked up, grateful for the distraction.

"Sorry I haven't checked in," Caroline said immediately. "I've been up to my lady balls at work. How was the party? I'll make the next one, I promise."

Viola sighed. "Not sure there will be a next one."

Caroline tetched. "That bad?"

"Let's say it did little to lift my spirits."

"Sorry to hear that. What are you up to today?"

"At this exact moment, I'm watching Gillian Carmichael sitting on a bench in my garden."

A confused-sounding Caroline questioned her further. "Can she do that?"

"Technically, yes. As it's on the public footpath that crosses my land, she has every right to sit there."

Viola wondered if she only had a right to pass through her land and not sit there for hours.

"And why is she there?" Caroline asked.

"I'm trying to figure that out myself. Last time we spoke, she…" Viola trailed off, catching herself before admitting that Gillian had brought her to tears. That wasn't entirely accurate, though; those tears had already been brimming before their conversation. All Gillian had done was give her a push over the edge. "We didn't exactly see eye to eye," she finished lamely.

Viola caught sight of the handkerchief Gillian gave her, now sitting on the worktop clean and folded, ready to be returned. She briefly contemplated stuffing it through Gillian's letterbox and never speaking to her again.

"Maybe she wants to apologise?" Caroline suggested. "For whatever it was you didn't see eye to eye on."

"Mark her territory, more like," Viola said, turning her attention back to Gillian, who hadn't moved an inch since she'd appeared there half an hour ago.

"Afraid she'll pee up the bench?"

Viola scrunched her face. "Eww." Over Caroline's laughter, she added, "You're probably not wrong, though. I wouldn't put it past her to mark everything she thought was hers. Which is basically anything that is now mine."

"Then go and reclaim your bench."

She thought back to the plaque she had seen on it and pulled her lips to one side. "I'm not sure it's mine to reclaim."

"It's on your land and therefore your property. If she wanted it, she should have taken it when she moved out."

Caroline made a good point. Why hadn't Gillian done that? There would be room enough in her small garden for it.

"Perhaps it wasn't only the bench that meant something to her, but also its position," Viola pondered.

"Yes. Not satisfied with crossing your property, she wanted to sit down and enjoy the view." Viola hummed in thought as Caroline continued, "Sounds to me like she's trying to get your attention."

"What?" Viola's forehead furrowed. "Why on earth would she want my attention?"

"Maybe she fancies you." Caroline chuckled.

Viola spat out a laugh. "Gillian Carmichael is as straight as they come. In every respect. The only reason she'd want my attention is to tell me everything I'm doing wrong as lady of the manor."

Her gaze landed on the enormous box of expensive chocolates from the major. Even after she'd agreed to let him use her field for the classic car show, he was still bestowing her with gifts, eager to persuade her to open the event. Her latest and most emphatic refusal must have done the trick; he hadn't bothered her since. At least Gillian talked to her straight; she wasn't a suck-up. It was refreshing. She didn't care who Viola was; she treated her like anyone else — maybe even worse than anyone else.

"You know, of all the people I've met since I've been here, Gillian is the only one who hasn't sucked up to me," she observed. "In fact, she's been actively hostile."

"I fear you will have to get along if you're neighbours," Caroline stated. "I'm sorry, I must fly; I have a meeting with a rising pop star in an hour. I'll impatiently await my invite to your new digs."

"Oh, yes, of course, you must come," Viola urged, realising it was remiss of her not to have invited her to the manor already. "Let me know some dates; it's not like I'm busy here."

"I'll put my assistant right on it. Perhaps you can invite

Gillian to dine with us. I find it's always better to dine with the enemy."

Viola let out an agreeable hum, even she wasn't entirely sure anymore that Gillian was the enemy.

Having put Caroline's mind at ease that she was okay and more or less keeping herself distracted, her eyes fell back to the bench. Gillian was still there and still didn't appear to have moved. Curiosity got the better of Viola, enough to pull on a jumper and head outside.

As she approached the bench, she noticed that Gillian was now seated almost sideways, with one leg resting on the seat and her elbow propped on the back. A flutter of something stirred in Viola's stomach at the sight of the woman. She took a deep breath to steady herself as she arrived.

"Mind if I sit?" she enquired, her tone polite.

"Be my guest," Gillian replied, gesturing to the space beside her. "Even though it's your property."

Viola hesitated, then replied, "I feel this bench might belong to you, though." Noticing Gillian's glance at the shiny, gold plaque screwed to it, she asked, "Who was Henrietta, if you don't mind me asking?"

It took a moment for Gillian to answer, and when she did, a deep breath was behind it. "A friend."

Viola recognised the distant gaze in Gillian's eye, the subtle tremble in her voice, and the flicker of tenderness on her face as a smile curved the edges of her lips. She sensed that Henrietta had been something more — yet that couldn't be true.

"I'm sorry if I suggested the other day that you didn't know grief. I can see now that you do."

Gillian looked down and placed her hands together in her lap.

"I may not grieve for my husband… but I have grieved for others. I've learned enough to know that if you let it, grief will eat you alive."

"It doesn't always come for us when someone close dies, does it? You can be sure the guilt at the lack of it follows, though."

A simple nod was all Gillian offered.

Viola decided to continue, hoping that sharing something personal might make her open up a bit. "When my dad died some years ago, I couldn't mourn his loss. It was no loss, only relief. He was an alcoholic. He'd turn up at concerts where I was performing and demand access to my dressing room. I let him in. At least he was contained there; otherwise he would make more of a nuisance of himself elsewhere. Most of the time he would pass out on the sofa. Other times he could get violent, demanding money. I always refused. I wasn't going to be party to his problem. I offered to pay for clinics where he could get himself sober; he showed no interest."

"And where was your mother during this?" Gillian demanded, speaking up at last.

Viola blinked, surprised by the sharp edge in her voice.

"My parents split up when I was in my late teens. I'd left home at that point anyway. They only stayed together that long for me." Viola let out a sigh. "I wish they hadn't bothered. Mum met someone and remarried; Dad sank into a hole of self-pity, lost his job, and started drinking. I don't think she realised how far he had fallen, even though I tried to tell her."

"Sometimes we can only see the truth with our own eyes," Gillian said, her earlier sharpness replaced with a calm, reflective tone.

Viola looked at her and smiled. "Yes, we do… and she did when he was hit by a bus, having walked in front of one in a drunken stupor. She came to the hospital to support me. It was a little too late; he never regained consciousness. Like I said, all I felt was relief that he had died. She could see it and realised how bad things were… how much she'd let me down."

"What happened after that?" Gillian asked with curiosity in her eyes.

"I pushed her away and focused on work. It stayed that way for a long time. She would reach out to my agent occasionally to make contact. I continued to ignore her. In my early thirties, I got in with a bad crowd and ended up abusing alcohol myself. Like father, like daughter, I guess, although on a much different scale. I never fell as deep. You would have thought I would avoid it, yet in a way, I was drawn to it. I was in a downward spiral." Viola shrugged. "I thought it held the answers, but all it did was affect my performances."

Viola wasn't sure why she was telling Gillian about her past. She'd spent a lifetime keeping things in, only sharing them with Caroline and her mum. A gut feeling reassured her that Gillian wasn't the type of person who would broadcast something shared in a private moment. She struck her as the type of woman who kept a lot inside and cared deeply about what others thought.

"My agent at the time wasn't happy and threatened to drop me if I didn't pull myself together. He arranged —

without my consent — a meeting with my mum. I thought I was meeting him for coffee, and instead, she was there. My mum's husband had not long passed away, and she wasn't in a great state herself. Over time, though, we became a strength for each other. I was something else for her to focus on, and she gradually sorted me out."

Gillian scoffed. "I hope you dropped the agent."

"I did. I have a great one now. Caroline is supportive. She encouraged me to come here and take some time out."

"Not too long, I hope?"

"Is that a compliment of my work, or are you sick of me already?"

Gillian's face dropped.

Viola nudged her playfully. "It's okay. You don't have to answer that."

Hearing Gillian's sigh of relief brought a smile to Viola as they sat in silence, taking in the serenity of the estate. The woman was a bit of an enigma. Viola realised she was enjoying her company — even if she wasn't saying much, which was a first. In their previous exchanges, Viola had been hissed at, growled at, and shouted at, but something about the bench — or the estate itself — seemed to disarm Gillian, maybe even soothe her.

"I'm sorry," Gillian suddenly said. "All that can't have been easy."

"It wasn't," Viola replied, surprised to hear words of sympathy from her. "As you see, I survived."

"I'm sorry about your mother too."

"Thanks."

"I didn't grieve mine," Gillian said so quietly that Viola wondered if she knew she'd spoken the words.

Viola hesitated to probe deeper. She was unsure how the woman would react, and part of her didn't want Gillian to leave. Despite the curiosity burning inside her, she decided to change direction.

"Can I ask why you didn't take this bench with you? I'm not saying you should have," Viola added quickly, not wishing to get Gillian's back up by being misunderstood. "I'm asking if you'll share with me why. Is it the view?"

"It belongs here," Gillian replied softly. "Like many things."

"Like you?"

Gillian's face twitched, making Viola wonder if she might have pushed her too far.

"You're not just grieving a building, are you? You lost a lot more."

"I've lost everything," Gillian said, her voice carrying a hardened edge. It softened slightly as she continued, "It isn't the first time, and I don't expect it will be the last."

Viola wondered if she was referring to Henrietta.

"For what it's worth, I'm sorry for your loss. Even if I'm partly responsible for it."

Gillian stood, leaving Viola angry at herself for taking the conversation too far.

"Someone else would have bought it," Gillian answered begrudgingly. "I can hardly hold you responsible. I'm… I'm sorry if I've made you feel like you are."

Too surprised to respond to Gillian's apology, Viola hesitated before asking, "Will you be back tomorrow?" careful not to sound accusatory.

"Will you be calling the police if I am?" Gillian asked, her words laced with a hint of defiance.

Viola laughed out loud at Gillian's suggestion. "No, I thought it might be nice to continue this conversation; that's all."

"Possibly," Gillian replied, her hardened face softening again, almost into a smile. "I may be washing my hair."

Viola couldn't refrain a smirk as Gillian headed down the path to the church. She also couldn't stop herself admiring her backside as she went.

CHAPTER 9

Gillian opened the front door of the lodge to discover the major on the doorstep with his fist clenched as if he was about to knock.

"Ah, Gilly, there you are." A bunch of flowers appeared from behind his back.

"Major," Gillian replied with an annoyed sigh. Ignoring the flowers she stepped out and closed the door firmly behind her.

The major took a step back. "You're looking lovely. Off anywhere nice?"

"No," she replied flatly, not wishing to elaborate.

The major was always overly friendly. Even when Jonathon had been alive, he would sniff around her like a dog on heat. Jonathon found it amusing, probably because he could see how uncomfortable it made her.

"Can I help you with something, Major?"

"Yes. That bloody Berkley woman! She's refusing to open the car show. Isn't that exactly what these celebrities are for?" Not waiting for an answer, he continued. "She hasn't done anything for the village, not like you do, Gilly," he said, voice dripping with saccharine sweetness.

Rolling her eyes, Gillian set off down the path, the major at her heels.

"Although," he called after her, "she put up the money for the new cricket pavilion."

Stopping abruptly, Gillian turned to him. "Pardon?"

"She… put up the money… for the… cricket pavilion," the major hollered slowly in her direction.

Gillian glared at his audacity to assume she was deaf. "The whole restoration?"

He nodded. "Will you do it?" His thick, white brows and crinkled eyes twitched with anticipation.

"What?" Her mind was elsewhere, thinking of Viola and the fact that she had done something remarkable for the village — something more than she could offer it now.

"Open the car show. You always did a wonder — "

Not wishing to hear him grovel further, for fear it may make her vomit, she answered swiftly. "I'll do it on two conditions. One, stop calling me Gilly, and two, never bring me flowers again."

He stiffened. "Oh, of course, Gilly — I mean Gillian. See you Saturday then."

The man was of his time. Sadly, he didn't realise that time had long passed. As he bumbled off through the estate gates, she smiled, pleased to have her job back.

Viola's words, "It would be nice to continue this conversation," played over in Gillian's head as she made her way through the garden of Kingsford Manor. Armed with what was essentially an invitation from Viola, she didn't think she would mind if she crossed through the garden, rather than taking her usual route past the church.

A red kite circled above her head as she sat in her usual spot on the bench. She'd installed it shortly after arriving at Kingsford, to mark a brief chapter of her life that, despite her desire to move on, deserved to be remembered. It became her sanctuary, a place to unburden herself from the thoughts that weighed her down — memories of the past, reflections on the present, and fleeting hopes for the future. Anything she needed to unload, she brought to the bench, and it absorbed it all. It was her space to breathe away from the often-hectic pace of life inside the manor house.

There was no way she was going to move it when she left. It belonged there, and with it being on the public footpath she knew she would be able to sit on it whenever she wished with little issue.

Jonathon didn't even ask who it was dedicated to when the bench was installed. She was grateful in a way, not to have to lie. The bench had seen better days. Although it was made of oak and kept well maintained over the years, it was still a few decades old and had weathered many harsh winters in its time.

Making herself more comfortable, she stretched out her legs and wondered if Viola would appear at some point. Her gaze wandered frequently along the path to the house as she sat looking out over the fields. The changing seasons always brought a new perspective, unveiling new growth and subtle changes, altering the landscape before her eyes. It had served as a reminder over the years to soldier on in difficult moments. She needed that reassurance now more than ever as she floundered in the unknown.

After thirty-five years of a stale marriage and now into her autumn years, she couldn't help wondering what the future held for her. Was she destined to live in the lodge until death rang the doorbell? She certainly felt too old for any more changes in her life. Change in nature was generally a positive thing, showing growth and maturity. Losing her home, however, left her broken-hearted and put her right back where she had started out.

Recalling her words to Viola the previous day, she hoped this was the last time she would lose everything; not that there was much left to lose, apart from her health. The only person she had ever loved had departed this world long ago, and with her, she had lost her identity. Clawing her way back to civilisation, she had formed a new one only to lose it all over again. She needed to get it back; it suited her, and she liked it. Life just wouldn't be the same without the manor.

She caught a small smile on her lips as she thought of their conversation. The woman was growing on her. She had gumption, especially in choosing to take on the estate when the easy option would have been to put it straight back on the market. To then create her mother's vision, despite her loss, was admirable, and Gillian found herself admiring Viola. She was impressive in other ways too — learning to fly a helicopter, not to mention achieving significant success in her career.

Viola's openness about her past the day before had stirred an unexpected feeling in Gillian, something she could only liken to pride. She was not one for apologies, but she felt better having given one. She could count on a single hand the number of times she had apologised for something. It helped that she was rarely in the wrong.

Viola's understanding of the guilt that could be felt when one didn't grieve resonated deeply in her. Gillian felt guilt over Jonathon's death too, not only from the fact she had spent her life pretending to be happily married but also from the relief she no longer needed to. He'd been part of her life for the majority of it, and they had shared the occasional good times.

Perhaps she had never given Jonathon the chance he deserved. It was hard when he wasn't who she truly wanted. In the end, she was relieved she hadn't opened her heart to love again. The only real grief she felt was for how her life might have unfolded had she been brave enough to pursue a different path. That would have meant no Kingsford — not that it was hers now.

"Not washing your hair then?" Viola's voice came from behind her, making Gillian jump.

"I found time to do it this morning," she said, watching Viola take the seat beside her.

"Lucky me," Viola said, her face pinking a little.

Gillian couldn't help smiling at Viola's comment as she held out a folded handkerchief to her. She acknowledged it with a nod.

"Do you not have a dog or something?" Viola asked, settling back against the bench. "I thought you country folk all owned one."

"I never could get along with them; they are too needy for attention. A husband was quite enough. I have the cat — I *had* the cat."

"You still have a cat." Viola laughed. The gentle nudge she gave Gillian took her by surprise, making her lips tighten into a smile. "Although I am considering charging you for her bed and board when she sleeps over."

"I'll be sure to pass your invoice onto her," Gillian retorted. "And you do know that *you* are country folk now." She narrowed her eyes as she took in Viola's grey jeans and light blue hoodie. "Not that anyone would be able to tell by your attire."

"Ouch," Viola said. "Coming for my clothes now, are you?"

"Well. You could play your part a little more… authentically."

Viola raised an eyebrow. "Could you help?"

"I can direct you to a decent country outfitter not far from here," Gillian replied with a light laugh.

"Why don't you come with me? Give me a guiding hand?"

"I'm sure they can serve you adequ — " Noticing Viola's face fall in what Gillian could only interpret as disappointment, she realised she was looking to her for advice. "On the other hand, perhaps I should. To make sure."

A smile bloomed across Viola's face, giving Gillian a warm flutter in her chest. It led her to question when she'd started caring about how Viola felt.

"Thanks," Viola replied with a grin as she closed her eyes and arched her head back into the sun.

Her long, auburn waves cascaded over the back of the bench. Gillian couldn't help herself and stole a glance at the graceful curve of her profile whilst the opportunity allowed.

Viola radiated that annoying natural beauty that many women craved. Those who possessed it often failed to recognise it within themselves since women were conditioned to focus on their flaws rather than celebrate their natural appearance.

Her smooth, lightly tanned skin showed no signs of ageing, a stark contrast to Gillian's complexion. She likely maintained an extensive and expensive beauty routine to help. Having invested in similar efforts in her forties, Gillian had come to the sobering realisation by her fifties that there was no denying the inevitability of ageing — at least not for her.

Mirroring Viola's posture, Gillian allowed herself to bask in the warmth of the sun's rays and the soothing melody of the birds twittering in a nearby bush. They remained that way, in peaceful silence, until they were interrupted by the sound of a miaow. Agatha jumped between them, looked at both women in turn, and then climbed onto Viola's lap.

Gillian had expected to feel jealousy, but to her surprise, she only felt happy for Viola. "She trusts you," she said, reaching out and tickling the cat's head, feeling the vibration of her purr.

Viola tickled Agatha under the chin. "I trust her."

Agatha stretched up, touching her nose to Viola's. Gillian smiled at the bond forming between them amidst their recent upheavals.

"I can even forgive a cold, wet nose," Viola said, wiping her own with her sleeve.

"It must be difficult being famous, knowing who to trust," Gillian said softly.

"I've only trusted two people in my life," Viola said with a sigh. "One of them has left this world."

"You trusted me with a lot yesterday, and I'm only your annoying neighbour."

"You are the only person who doesn't want anything from me — except my house." Viola grinned. "You've told me all the ways in which I'm failing and how I should be doing this and that, but you don't want me to do it. You want to be doing it. You don't see me as Viola Berkley, world-renowned classical musician; you see me, Viola, who is squatting on your property. It's refreshing. You're refreshing."

Gillian could feel her cheeks burning as she tried to battle against the pull of her lips. Viola chose that exact moment to look straight at her, just as her mouth gave out and creased into a smile. Typical.

Their eyes locked as Viola said, "Give me one person in this world to pass the time of day with who doesn't want me for my body or my money."

With her cheeks continuing to burn, a wave of heat swept over the rest of Gillian, along with a wash of guilt for her previous admiration of Viola's beauty. Rationale kicked in as she told herself she was simply admiring her, not ogling. With their awkward silence beginning to linger, Gillian decided to move the conversation elsewhere.

"I was thinking, You could dedicate a bench to your mother."

"Are you trying to move me off your bench by any chance?" Viola teased.

"Not at all. I know from experience that there is something therapeutic in dedicating a bench to a lost loved one. I still come here to reflect and attempt to leave my thoughts here each time."

Viola tilted her head in question. "And that works?"

"Not exactly. Not to begin with anyway. There is no way around grief; it's a process, and you can't bypass any stages," Gillian affirmed, her voice carrying the weight of experience.

The sound of sniffling drew her to look at Viola. Tears were rolling down her cheeks. A pang of guilt hit Gillian in the stomach as she watched her companion wipe her tears with the back of her hand.

"Sorry," Viola said, taking a deep breath. "It just hits sometimes. Often when I least expect it."

"Here," Gillian said, passing her the handkerchief. "Keep it. I think you might need it more than me. I have plenty more."

"Thanks," Viola said, wiping her eyes with the handkerchief. "I just feel so alone."

"I'm here," Gillian said, doing her best at adopting a soothing tone, "and trust me, I'm not going anywhere."

Viola laughed through her tears. "Is that some sort of veiled threat?"

Gillian grinned. "Perhaps." Pointing at a small group of trees on the horizon, she added, "You see those trees over there? I planted them. Well, I instructed the gardeners to. The hedgerows in front I added to encourage more wildlife. I would have done more with the surrounding area if Jonathon hadn't sold it all off. So much of the historic Kingsford farmland was lost to intensive agriculture, much of the South Downs too. The chalk grasslands mostly disappeared when the sheep did. There are only the rabbits left to encourage the likes of the milkwort to flourish. Humans have been impacting the landscape for centuries; we aren't the first, and we won't be the last."

Spotting a bird, Gillian pointed at it. "The skylark is the most prolific bird in the South Downs, and it's only here because the first farmers relieved the land of its beech and yew trees. It's ground-nesting and avoids trees where it knows predators lurk. It was only by removing the trees that we gained the botanical tapestry we love and fiercely protect today. The South Downs is the oldest manmade habitat in England, you know?"

"This place really flows through your veins, doesn't it?"

Gillian turned to find Viola looking at her with a tenderness in her eyes. A rush of something new spread through her chest, a feeling she could only describe as comfort — unexpected but welcome.

"Mmm. I've done what I can to protect it over the years. Instead of mowing the entire lawn, I left the edges to wildflowers and into the meadows beyond. I planted more shrubs on the borders of the garden and added climbers. Jonathon didn't have much love for Kingsford; he saw it as a chain around his neck. He left me to style the house and garden over the years. Not that he noticed any of the changes I made."

Her face dropped as she recalled all the times she had tried to impress Jonathon during their early days, only to give up.

"You've done a wonderful job with it," Viola said. "It was the garden that drew Mum to the manor, plus her love for the area and the nature here, especially the skylarks. She grew up in the South Downs so it was always close to her heart. She said she could see herself on the patio, G & T in one hand" — her voice began to break — "taking in its beauty."

As Viola's tears began to flow again, Gillian's hand twitched, hesitating as she debated whether to offer some comfort. Physical touch didn't come naturally to her; it was a language she hadn't practised. She folded her hands in her lap instead, opting for silence. She believed that sometimes sitting beside someone was enough.

On the rare occasions when Gillian's emotions overwhelmed her, she cried alone, hidden away from the world. She knew how isolating that experience could be. There were so few people with whom one felt safe enough to shed tears in their company. Viola was correct about needing one person to pass the time of day with. There was always Bridget, but with her it wouldn't pass so quietly.

In those moments of sorrow and isolation, she had longed for what she was having right now: sitting with someone in silence, feeling at peace whilst taking in the world around them, admiring the landscape together, seeing it and appreciating it in different ways.

In all the years of her marriage, she could count on one hand the number of times she and Jonathon had sat in the garden and passed the time together. Could she have had that with someone — a woman even — had she allowed herself to? Gillian felt a warm, wet tear roll down her cheek and quickly wiped it away, though this drew attention from where she least wanted it.

"Are you okay?" Viola asked, dabbing the handkerchief against her own cheeks.

"Yes. Yes, of course," Gillian snapped as she wiped her face again to ensure all traces of her tears were gone.

"Why are you ashamed to show emotions, Gillian?" Viola asked, point-blank. "It's not something to be embarrassed about. What's wrong with showing that side of you to the world?"

"It's weak," Gillian replied curtly, her jaw tightening.

"Being vulnerable is a strength, not a weakness. It's the greatest measure of courage. Who told you it was a weakness?"

"I... I was never encouraged to show emotions. It was actively discouraged," Gillian admitted, her voice faltering.

"By your parents?" Viola pressed, her gaze searching Gillian's face for the truth.

Gillian shrugged. "My mother. My father worked away."

"It's not healthy to cloak yourself in walls, Gillian. What are you hiding behind them?"

"Nothing," Gillian snapped. "You don't know me. Nobody does."

Viola's jaw fell open and worked silently before she settled on, "Because you don't let them."

"I would only disappoint." She wanted to get up and walk away, yet some invisible force held her down in her seat.

"Wow. That's quite a statement, Gillian. May I ask why

you never grieved your mum?" Viola asked, caution in her tone. "What did she do apart from teaching you some seriously unhealthy emotional practices and low self-esteem?"

For the moment, Gillian ignored the bald face of the question and pondered her answer. How could she give it honestly without giving away a part of herself she'd hidden most of her life? Leaning forward she rested her elbows on her knees. Would it be so bad for someone to know? Someone who felt safe? She shook her head at her thought only for a voice to point out there was little chance of judgement by someone who was in some respects similar to herself. It was Hen's voice, encouraging her on.

"I…"

Words were failing her even if she wanted to say them. How could the loss of someone still affect her so long after? It was ridiculous, irrational even. Feelings were irrational. The warmth of Viola's hand radiated into her back, and her leg pressed against her.

When had she gotten so close?

Viola leaned forward, mirroring her. Her hand slipped into Gillian's, sending a wash of adrenaline through her like butterflies.

"Trust me, Gillian."

How could she not tell this woman anything she wanted to know? Her bold eyes and soft, encouraging smile were like magnets. Part of her needed someone to know her, to see her, to have someone remember the real Gillian when she left this world. She found her mouth opening, and before she knew what was happening, words were flowing freely as if pulled from her by some invisible force.

"Hen was a natural rider. I wasn't always." Gillian smiled remembering her first lessons. "Her parents ran a riding school, so she grew up around horses. She was bought her first pony at two. We became friends when we were fourteen, and I became… infatuated with her, you might say. She was everything I wanted to be and everything my mother wanted me to be. She was clever and talented. We became inseparable over the years, and my… infatuation turned into something more. I couldn't have been more surprised, though, when she kissed me one day."

The memory of Hen's soft lips meeting her own on that warm summer day brought a smile to her face. It had been her first kiss, and she could still recall every detail as if it happened yesterday — if she allowed herself.

"How old were you then?" Viola enquired.

"Sixteen. Hen never saw seventeen."

"What happened to her?"

"A low-flying helicopter spooked her horse in the yard, and he threw her off."

Gillian watched as Viola's face paled, her lips twitched as if she was unable to decide whether to grimace or speak. She held her expression steady as Viola scanned her face, perhaps hoping she would say she was joking.

When Viola finally spoke, her voice was quiet, hesitant. "That's… awful."

Gillian sighed inwardly and decided to move on. This wasn't about making Viola feel bad for the situation she had created when they first met, even if the true consequences may have only just sunk in for her.

"Hen knew not to remove her riding hat before she dismounted, and yet she did. It was a hot day, and we'd been for a ride. I was the only one with her. She lay there, unconscious… I couldn't rouse her." Gillian inhaled deeply, finding herself breathless. A squeeze from Viola's hand sent warmth through her. It gave her the strength to tell the story she hadn't shared with anyone else. "Her parents were out. My mother arrived to pick me up moments after Hen fell. She called an ambulance from the house — we didn't have mobile phones back then, did we?"

"What happened next?" Viola asked, shifting in her seat.

"They took her to hospital. I forced my way into the accident and emergency room, only to reach her as the doctors stopped trying to resuscitate her." Gillian swallowed hard at the memory. "They allowed me a few minutes with her."

There was a heavy silence, broken only by the occasional measure of birdsong.

Then Viola took a slow, even breath. "I'm so sorry," she murmured. "That must have been horrendous."

Gillian took a breath, too, and exhaled. "I kissed her goodbye at the very moment my mother stepped through the curtain."

Viola's eyes widened. "Oh."

"Mmm. I didn't expect her to find a parking space so quickly. Our relationship was already pretty strained by then, and yet this was a turning point. She never looked at me the same again, even with my insistence that it was a platonic kiss goodbye to my best friend. It seems we hadn't been as careful as we had thought. She'd begun to suspect something, and she chose that moment, as Hen lay dead in that hospital room, to tell me how I sickened her, how she was glad Hen was dead, how I needed to forget about her and start being a proper young lady."

Viola grimaced. "And did you?"

Gillian nodded, embarrassed to admit it. "I was broken. I realised if I stayed in line and did as I was told, it would be easier for everyone. I didn't have the strength to breathe, let alone fight my mother. She kept me alive, even if I wasn't living. I thought she would be satisfied when I married Jonathon; instead she went on to eye our marriage with suspicion. In a way, it was a relief when she died. I no longer needed to look over my shoulder, worried she might say something and bring my house of cards falling down. Looking back, there was nothing to fear. For all her faults, one thing my mother wasn't was stupid. She knew my being at Kingsford would benefit her too. She would have been a fool to speak up and suggest our marriage was anything other than genuine. It didn't stop her worrying, though, and jibes over the years about the lack of grandchildren and suggestions I wasn't the motherly type didn't help. In the end, she took my secret to the grave. Only she knew what I felt for Hen."

"How long have you been keeping this in?"

Gillian didn't answer. She didn't want to say *forever*.

Viola's hand squeezed hers again as if she sensed the answer. "And you haven't told anyone since?"

She shook her head, still unsure why she let herself

open up so completely to Viola. She was like a vampire, sucking everything from her, and she'd surrendered it to her willingly.

"Not even Bridget?"

Gillian shook her head again.

"Do you not trust anyone either?" Viola's voice was heavy with sadness as her eyes appeared to search Gillian's for a glimmer of truth.

"The one person who knew *me* rejected me," Gillian said, her voice trembling. "Can you blame me for never wanting to open up again?"

"No. No, I can't."

"My mother's cruelty taught me something about people, and I knew I could never be that person again. When I moved here, I dedicated everything I had to Kingsford and the village, helping wherever I could. I know my manner and approach may not be everyone's cup of tea, but I get things done. I make a difference — or, at least, I did."

"You still do. Only you get to decide when to stop. You can't let this place define you. You're so much more than it; so much beyond it."

Gillian sighed, deflating a bit. "Whatever I am, I'm all alone and losing direction for my next chapter."

"You're not alone," Viola said softly. "I'm here for you, too, and I won't be going anywhere either." She quirked a smile before adding in a soft, teasing tone, "I'm sorry to disappoint you."

Gillian didn't feel disappointed. She was about to voice that when Viola removed her hand, leaving a cool sensation against Gillian's skin. She instantly missed its weight and comfort.

"Now that you've told me your darkest secrets, are we still going shopping?"

Were they her darkest secrets? An *mmm* escaped Gillian's mouth in answer to herself.

"Great. How's Saturday?"

Realising she'd inadvertently agreed to that day, she replied quickly, "Can't. I'm opening the classic car show." Gillian blushed as soon as she realised how eagerly she'd spoken.

"Good. It's your job. That's why I refused, amongst other reasons. So… Sunday?"

"This isn't the city, you know. Shops close around here on a Sunday."

"Monday then?"

Out of excuses, Gillian nodded. She liked how desperate and persistent Viola was to tie her down to a date. Okay, not a date exactly, merely a meeting to assist her in finding her country attire. She would need to carefully consider how to dress Viola's body in tweed, finding the best way to compliment her figure. It was the least she could do. Her body was beautiful, with gentle, subtle curves. Tweed would look fabulous on her.

"Thanks for the chat," Viola added as she stood, pulling Gillian from her thoughts whilst presenting the very shape that occupied her thoughts.

"Oh… anytime," Gillian stuttered.

"I can't fix your past, but I can sit with you whilst you work on repairing yourself," Viola said with a warm smile.

Gillian opened her mouth to object to the need to repair herself. She was perfectly fine, or she had been until Viola coaxed the past out of her. She searched for a sense of regret, only to find a surprising feeling of lightness inside instead. "Likewise," she finally replied.

Viola gave a nod of acknowledgement. "See you tomorrow then?"

Gillian nodded and watched as Viola walked away. It took her a moment to realise she was caressing the hand that Viola had held. An urge forced her hand to her nose, and she inhaled, finding a faint, pleasant aroma, a natural musky scent that was becoming so familiar to her.

What on earth had gotten into her?

CHAPTER 10

*V*iola smoothed down her knee-length, floral summer dress and unbuttoned the top two buttons of her cardigan as she waited at Gillian's door. Realising her actions weren't something she'd have done when she thought Gillian was straight, a flicker of disappointment settled over her.

She told herself that Gillian having been in a relationship with a woman an eternity ago didn't mean anything. She'd recently lost her husband, and although she didn't appear to be grieving him, it didn't mean she would be ready to seek out anything new.

She was about to fasten the buttons when Gillian opened the door, looking resplendent in a long, V-neck, navy dress with a large, brown leather belt tied at the waist and matching sandals. She took Viola's breath away, leaving her head feeling fuzzy.

"Ah, it's you," Gillian said, her voice sharp with surprise. She pulled the door closer to her side, narrowing the opening as though guarding a secret within. "You're early."

"Nope. Bang on time, in fact," Viola replied, quickly recovering herself.

She could make out the faint sound of music coming from another room as Gillian looked at her watch. She recognised the song instantly.

"I thought you'd toot or something," Gillian replied, her eye unmistakably giving Viola a good look-over.

"I find it best not to toot; it rather draws unwanted attention," Viola replied, trying not to be snarky.

"Oh, yes, of course. I guess that explains your comically sized hat and sunglasses."

"I don't go anywhere without them. Am I coming in, or should I wait in the car?" Viola asked, sensing Gillian was uncomfortable with her seeing inside the lodge.

"Erm, yes, I'll be out in two minutes," Gillian said, closing the door.

"Okayyyy," Viola said to herself as she retraced her steps to the car.

Gillian appeared five minutes later and slipped into the passenger seat. Viola wasn't about to tease her about her poor timekeeping; instead, she decided to be bold and say what she was feeling. After their conversations the previous week, she felt brave enough to tackle Gillian head-on.

"Are you embarrassed about your home?" Viola asked as she drove through the iron-gated, pillared entrance.

Gillian's head whipped around so fast Viola was sure it would have given her whiplash.

"What do you mean?"

Viola wasn't sure she could make herself any clearer. Deciding it would be best to ignore the question and try a different approach, she said, "I live in your old house, remember? I know where you come from. Having a small house isn't anything to be embarrassed about. I wasn't exactly born with a silver spoon in my mouth either."

"You weren't?" Gillian questioned, sounding a little more relaxed.

Viola shook her head as they drove past the village green and the new cricket pavilion. A large sign was being erected on the back of it. It read *The Berkley Pavilion*. Viola shrank into her seat, hoping it would escape Gillian's notice. The laughter that filled the car seconds later said it hadn't.

Viola groaned. "I asked for my donation to be anonymous."

"This is a small village. Nothing is anonymous," Gillian replied, still unable to contain her laughter. "They couldn't have made that sign any bigger if they tried."

Gillian's amusement faded as they left the village, but unable to resist a playful jab back as she stopped the car at a crossroads, Viola turned to her passenger with a mischievous glint in her eye and asked, "Were you enjoying my voice?"

"Sorry?" Gillian's expression turned puzzled.

"I thought I heard my cover of 'Bring Me to Life' playing when I walked in."

"Oh... erm..." Gillian's cheeks tinged with pink. "Bridget brought it around last week and left it."

"Left it playing?" Viola teased lightly as she drove off. She enjoyed poking fun at her new friend — if she could call Gillian that. This time, however, she could see her comment had made Gillian somewhat flustered as she fanned herself and then lowered the window. Hoping to put her at ease, she added, "You don't have to answer that. Something I do want to know is if the classic car show went well?"

Gillian let out a dry laugh. "Let's see, everyone was disappointed to find me — yet again — opening it instead of the A-list celebrity they'd been promised."

Viola grimaced.

"And then there was the speech the major asked me to read." Gillian rolled her eyes. "I drew the line at thanking Viola Berkley and the Kingsford Estate for the use of the land. I couldn't quite stomach that. So, no, I wouldn't say it went well, at least for me."

"Oh… sorry."

"It's not your fault," Gillian replied with a resigned sigh. "It's the major's, for overpromising and delivering a spectacular anticlimax."

"I wouldn't call you an anticlimax," Viola said, looking over at Gillian with a smile. The subtle shift in Gillian's posture made Viola press on. "Why do you give so much to the village?"

The reply came quickly. "Duty."

"You're not the queen, Gillian."

Gillian turned to Viola as if she was about to dispute that fact, then answered, "No, thankfully. I am very much alive."

"You know what I mean."

"I do, and you've given a lot too. The Berkley Pavilion

didn't come cheap," Gillian said, biting her smirking bottom lip.

Viola snorted. "Thank you for the reminder."

"Of the name or the price?"

"Both!" She grinned. "I wanted to make a good first impression, that was all. It got them off my back... at great expense."

"I know. They have been pestering me for a new one for years. My policy is always to make do and mend." A grin formed on Gillian's lips. "You know the old one was perfectly serviceable."

A realisation dawned on Viola. "Oh! Have I been had?"

"Let's say they saw an opportunity and took it." Gillian laughed and then covered her mouth. "It will only add to the appeal of the village... as long as no one looks at the back of it."

Viola glared over her sunglasses at Gillian's smirking lips. "If you find it distracting, how about you focus on navigation instead? Where am I going?"

Taking direction from Gillian, Viola turned down the high street of a gorgeous historic market town ten minutes later. It was typically laid out with a moot hall at one end and car parking down the middle of the road. Both sides of the street housed rows of shops in quaint Georgian buildings.

"Market day is on a Wednesday, so we shouldn't have difficulty parking." Gillian pointed to a shop further down on the left, aptly named 'Country Attire'. "Park as close as you can to that."

Viola drove the Porsche into a space outside a row of

shops, squeezing them between a yellow car and an old blue camper van.

"It's nice being out, doing something normal," Viola said as she exited the car. "It's something I don't get much chance to do. The hat and sunglasses are great, but you draw more attention wearing them in the winter."

A woman with long, brown hair appeared from the dry cleaner, arms laden with more clothes bags than any human could be expected to carry.

"Here, let me help you," Viola said, racing forward to help her as a bag slipped off the top of the pile.

"Thanks. My wife has a lot of dry cleaning."

"Then you should tell your wife to come and help you." Viola laughed.

"Oh, I would if she wasn't working away," the woman said with an affectionate smile. "Would you mind opening the passenger door for me, please?"

The woman nodded at the light blue camper and handed her a key.

"Of course," Viola replied, retracing her steps between the vehicles. "You have a sweet camper," she added, opening the door and taking a quick nose inside at the cute interior and what could only be Laura Ashley curtains.

"Thanks," the woman said as she laid the bags over the front bench seat. She took the key from Viola and jumped in herself, manoeuvring over the dry cleaning to the driver's seat. "Thanks for your help."

"Anytime," Viola said, closing the passenger door and joining Gillian, who was watching them from the pavement. "Do you know who that was?"

Gillian shook her head.

"Sydney Mackenzie. Beatrice Russell's wife."

"Who?"

Viola gawped at that. "You haven't heard of Beatrice Russell? World-famous actress, stunningly beautiful?"

"Should I have?" Gillian replied with disinterest.

Viola laughed. "Had you heard of me? You know, before I came here and stole your house from you."

The twitch at the corner of Gillian's mouth told her she took the remark as it was intended — playful.

"I listen to Classic FM and Radio Four. What do you think?"

"Hard yes. Sydney helped write Beatrice's autobiography, back when she was her PA."

"She married her PA! That's a bit inappropriate, isn't it?"

"Let me not to the marriage of true minds admit impediments. Love is not love — "

" — which alters when it alteration finds or bends with the remover to remove," Gillian finished.

"You know Shakespeare?"

Gillian shot a look of incredulous disbelief over the top of her sunglasses.

"Of course you do," Viola answered herself.

"Sonnet one hundred and sixteen," Gillian called back as she marched ahead.

"Yes, anyway," Viola said, jogging a little to catch up to Gillian, "Beatrice's autobiography was a bit last minute and completely took the shine off mine. Not that I minded. Sydney's book was great; she writes fiction now."

Gillian stopped outside the door to Country Attire. "You have an autobiography?"

"Yes. I'm surprised you haven't read it since you are such a fan of my music," Viola said with a twitch of an eyebrow.

That earned her another icy stare from Gillian as she lifted her sunglasses onto the top of her head. Though she had expected it to leave her a little cold, Viola found herself oddly aroused by its intensity.

"You seem a bit young to have an autobiography."

"I'm forty-four."

"Exactly," Gillian deadpanned.

"I only did it to get the truth out. There are so many lies published by the media, and being a private person only seems to make them thirstier for blood."

"Perhaps I'll pick up a copy."

"I could give you some spoilers… over lunch? Not that there is much left to tell." Viola suggested, holding the door open for Gillian. She held her breath as she waited for an answer, realising it might be a step beyond where their relationship was at this moment.

"That would be agreeable," Gillian answered.

Viola noticed Gillian was trying hard to hold in a smile as she brushed past her and into the shop, her dress accentuating every curve of her body. It left Viola with a sense of something pleasant sweeping through her stomach.

"Are you coming?" a voice demanded.

Viola couldn't ignore the subtle edge of authority in Gillian's tone or how it made her pulse quicken. There was a confidence about her that both challenged and intrigued Viola, drawing her to the woman. "Yes," she replied, rolling her eyes with a smile as she followed behind.

It was like stepping back in time to an old haberdashery shop; the air even held that scent of the past you get when you sniff an old postcard or photograph. Large wooden display cabinets covered the walls, each one brimming with ties, cufflinks, caps, and scarves. Alongside them stood rails of tweed jackets and check shirts, exuding a timeless elegance.

Gillian appeared to know the staff quite well and rattled off some instructions, which sounded more like orders, to meet her requirements. Viola was surprised when she requested everything in her exact size — a lucky guess, she assumed.

She was ushered into a changing room, where Gillian's arm appeared at random intervals through the curtain with another piece of clothing for her to try. She matched the garments as best as she could and presented herself to Gillian, who then instructed her on which shirt to match with which pair of trousers or jacket.

The result was a stunning ensemble: a dark-green herringbone tweed jacket and trousers paired with a matching waistcoat and crisp, white shirt. The earthy tones complemented her auburn hair, creating a look that exuded class and sophistication. She noticed Gillian's gaze was fixed on her, perusing what felt like every inch of her body and causing Viola to inhale a deep breath.

Gillian suddenly looked away, reaching out to the shop dummy beside her, where her fingers fumbled to take a tweed cap from its head. "Here, try this."

Viola took it and placed it on her head, grateful that it contained her hair.

"Perfection," Gillian whispered so softly Viola wasn't sure if she was meant to hear.

She flashed a smile anyway, which only seemed to make Gillian stumble and reach for a rail of jackets to steady herself. She must have needed lunch.

∼

"I have a confession to make," Gillian said, taking a sip of Sauvignon Blanc, as they ate lunch in a sunny, quiet spot in a pub garden. "I *was* listening to your music this morning. It seems I lost track of time when you arrived."

"Oh, you are a fan then?" Viola's tone was teasing again.

Gillian wasn't going to rise to it; she wanted to answer honestly. She needed Viola to know how she felt about her music. How it made the hairs all over her body stand on end, sent shivers through every part of her, and lit something in her core that burned. She deserved to hear it; she was extremely talented.

"Your voice is... beautiful," was all that came out when she opened her mouth, and she cursed herself for it.

Viola's eyes twinkled as she sipped her orange juice. Her smile was stretched so wide Gillian was sure she wouldn't be able to drink, but somehow, she managed. It left her wondering how much bigger her smile would have become had she found more words than *beautiful*.

"Thank you for saying that. Am I right in thinking

giving compliments isn't something that comes naturally to you?"

Gillian groaned internally, placing her knife and fork on an almost empty plate. The woman had a knack for pinpointing people's vulnerabilities and exposing them, much as Gillian herself tended to do. She didn't appreciate it when the tables turned on her, though.

"As much as I wasn't encouraged to show emotion, I wasn't taught to compliment either."

"And yet sometimes you can't help yourself, like just now," Viola teased, stealing a chip from Gillian's plate.

"Apparently," Gillian replied dryly, realising it was something about Viola that made her say these things.

She watched her companion with a smile as she reached for another chip. Her carefree nature and disregard for etiquette were refreshing in a way. She recalled Viola referring to her as refreshing the previous week. Perhaps the two of them were a breath of fresh air for each other.

After they agreed it was time to head back, they made their way into the pub, where they argued over who would pay the bill. Viola won by being quicker to pass her card to the barman, insisting she owed Gillian for accompanying her and pointing out it was she who had invited her to lunch.

"You never gave me a proper answer as to why you do so much for the village," Viola said as they reached the car two minutes later.

There she was again, looking for honest answers, pushing for truths.

"I believe I answered: It's my duty." Feeling Viola's

eyes on her across the roof of the car and sensing she wouldn't accept that, Gillian countered with, "Why do you sing?"

"It's who I am," Viola replied as they entered the car.

"Kingsford is who I am. Well, it was."

Viola nudged an elbow at Gillian. "Hey, I told you not to let it define you."

"Some things are easier said than done."

"You once said you lost everything. Do you really think that's true?"

"Yes," Gillian replied softly as she clicked on her seat belt.

"You have a house; you're respected in the community."

Gillian laughed. "You have to be respectable to be respected."

Viola's eyebrows shot up. "What on earth does that mean? You are respectable."

"If people really knew me, they wouldn't see me the same way." Gillian sighed and looked out the window.

"I see you, and I think you are respectable."

"You're different. You're like me."

After a pause, Viola replied, "You mean because you like women? It kind of sounds like internalised homophobia to me. That can be a very lonely place."

That assertion knocked Gillian back on her heels. Was she ashamed? She didn't know who she was. She'd spent most of her life hiding, pushing herself into a box to quash parts she didn't like, putting on a performance to display what was left so it was palatable to other people. She had grown up in a different era; it was what you did to get by.

"I've been lonely my whole life… except for a brief time, with Hen."

"Maybe that's why you do so much for the village, to feel less lonely. Surely Bridget is good company."

"Bridget is my rock, yet we are worlds apart in some respects. Sometimes it can feel more isolating when you are surrounded by people who don't understand you… if you know what I mean."

Viola nodded. "I do. I've never felt more alone than I have singing onstage in front of hundreds of thousands of people. It's quite a transition to go back to the dressing room. To begin with, there was only me. Then Mum."

Gillian watched a smile tug at Viola's lips as she started the car's engine and began reversing onto the high street.

"She was there when I sang with Elton, for the queen and the pope. She even came to the front lines with me to sing for the troops in Afghanistan."

"I'm sure she was very proud."

Viola's smile fizzled away, replaced with a touch of melancholy which matched her tone. "I'll have to get used to it being me again."

"Have you not performed since she died?"

"No. I cancelled a few performances. I can't put off returning to work for too long, though; people might forget who I am."

"I doubt that," Gillian replied.

Viola's face pinked as a small smile returned, only to disappear again. "Before I go back, I need to rediscover my creativity."

"'We are all born artists; the problem is staying one.'"

"Picasso?"

"Indeed," Gillian confirmed, impressed Viola knew. "Self-doubt and fear crush creativity."

"Mmm," Viola mumbled. "I haven't even written anything since Mum died."

"Give it time. I'm sure you will get there."

"I came here to hide from the world. I'm not sure I'm ready to return to it yet."

"Why are you hiding?" Gillian murmured.

"Oh, grief, exhaustion, stress, anxiety…" Viola sighed. "How long have you got?"

"All day," Gillian replied, looking across at her.

Viola responded with a soft smile. "I'm supposed to be here to rest. To find some peace in the countryside."

A thought struck Gillian suddenly, one which made her slightly queasy. "And I came at you with all your faults and failings."

"You sure did," Viola answered with a resigned tone. "It's fine. I happily admit I'm out of my depth. I had no idea what I was taking on with the estate, and you weren't the only one pointing things out. Honestly everyone has been very kind — if a little pushy. I only wanted a quiet spot in the countryside."

Gillian let out a light laugh. "I'm not sure there is such a place."

"I can quite believe that now. How was I to know that the village would have such demanding residents? Mum was the type of woman to embrace it, encourage it even. She would have found great company here, lots to keep her busy. She was full of excitement to be moving to Kingsford; she'd never lived in a place as grand."

"You suggested earlier that you weren't well off,"

Gillian said, hoping to find out exactly what that meant. One man's poverty was often another man's wealth.

Viola nodded. "We lived in a small house when I was growing up. A two-up two-down, you might say. We lived hand to mouth as my dad was drunk most of the time, and he couldn't hold down a job. I came from nothing with only my voice. I managed to secure a place at the Royal Academy of Music; it was upwards from there. I learned to only rely on myself to succeed."

Viola had worked hard to get where she was, she deserved the manor. All Gillian had done was pretend to be someone else and in love. Did she deserve any of it? Was that why she spent her life doing countless things for others? Because she believed she needed to pay for her life in some way?

"And succeed you did," Gillian assured her. "Despite your upbringing."

"I often wonder what it would have been like to have a 'normal' upbringing. A happy family. Then I wonder if I would be where I am now."

"You mean was it your adversities that got you this far?" Gillian clarified.

Viola nodded.

"I often wonder the same. Where would I be now if Hen hadn't fallen that day? What life would I have lived, and who would I be? Her death changed me; it was a catalyst that propelled me into Jonathon's path. I lost so much only to gain Kingsford; losing it has been like losing Hen all over again." She took a breath as she remembered why she never talked about these things. It was bloody difficult. "The feeling of loss never truly fades, does it? It lies dormant, waiting to resurface. At least this time it feels more like an old friend paying a visit rather than a fire consuming me from within."

"Our lives have multiple paths, all with multiple destinations. We can't walk back along them, only accept the path we have walked. As hard as that feels sometimes."

Gillian swallowed hard. "Some days impossible."

"Sometimes a new path can lead us to good. I know Mum was very happy with Stephen, her new husband. I wish she'd left my dad sooner, but then she might not have known Stephen. Or she might have met someone else who wasn't good for her. They made the best of their time together, and then fate brought Mum back to me when I needed her and she needed me. I believe everything happens for a reason. We may not even choose the path we walk; we find ourselves on it one day and hope it's the right one. If it's not, it may be there to steer us to the right path in the future. A path can even be a test."

"Hmm, maybe," Gillian mused as she stared out the side window at the hedgerows flying past.

"I will always be grateful that my mum and I reconnected," Viola continued. "Unlike my dad, she never wanted any money from me. She never asked for a penny, not once. Kingsford was my gift to her. I wanted her to rest, enjoy some time in one location for a change, tend the garden, and pot some plants. My life is hectic; she couldn't keep touring with me, especially overseas, and I knew I needed to learn to survive on my own again. Little did I know I would literally be alone again."

Gillian noticed Viola's hand reach under her sunglasses as if wiping a tear away.

"Sounds like a lonely place at the top. Do you not have groupies, or whatever they call them these days? No girlfriends?"

"I don't think the type of groupies you are thinking of exist anymore; not quite in the same way, anyway. As for girlfriends… I've been too scared to let anyone in. I've never quite managed the whole long-term relationship thing. The few people I dated lost interest once they saw how little time I could give them."

Gillian nodded her understanding, even if the concept was alien to her. She would have loved for Jonathon to have been around less; it would have been perfect. Her thoughts turned to the woman beside her and how she would feel if she was around less. A tug in her chest took her by surprise.

Viola pushed a button on the dashboard, and music began to fill the car. Gillian immediately recognised it as one of Viola's songs, which her driver then proceeded to sing along to. Hearing the real thing only a foot away from her created an even more visceral reaction than hearing the song at home. The warmth and passion that exuded from Viola as she sang made Gillian's body tingle from head to toe. She rubbed at her arms, hoping the hairs would stand down before Viola noticed her goosebumps.

"I wasn't expecting a live performance," Gillian said as the song ended.

"It's the least I can do for you taking me shopping. Are you cold? I can turn the climate control up," Viola said, noticing Gillian rub her arms.

Gillian stumbled, unsure whether to agree that she was cold or admit the effect Viola's voice was having on her. Why was it so hard to get the words out? She didn't normally have a problem being honest; it was simply easier when the tone was negative rather than positive. She wondered why that was.

"Oh! Did I do that?" Viola asked.

Gillian was about to deny it, then found the words, "Your voice seems to have an effect on me," coming out instead.

The resulting smile that formed on Viola's lips lit up her face. A smile crept onto Gillian's, too, knowing that smile had come from her words. Viola really was incredibly beautiful.

"Singing is about all I can do, so, sorry, not sorry, I guess," Viola said.

"And fly a helicopter! That's rather impressive."

"Yes, that too. I'm sorry it took you by surprise."

"I may have overreacted."

"You didn't, considering your history," Viola remarked gently as the car pulled up outside the lodge. "Here you go; you can make an escape."

Gillian didn't feel like she wanted to, yet her hand naturally reached for the handle and opened the door. "Thank you for lunch."

"Thanks for helping me out with the outfit."

"It was my pleasure." Gillian felt her face flush as she realised how pleasurable their time together had been.

"We should do it again," Viola said. "Soon."

Viola's suggestion caught Gillian off guard, as much as she approved of it. "Erm, yes. That would be agreeable."

As she shut the door, she noticed the window going down, and Viola was leaning over from the driver's seat. Her breath caught at the eyeful of cleavage Viola was accidentally revealing.

"If I don't see you before Sunday, please ensure you take the Kingsford pew and get that damn reverend off my back. Tell him you are representing Kingsford; the lodge is part of it after all, and if he doesn't like it…"

"Yes?" Gillian said, peeling her eyes up, to Viola's face.

"You can deal with him, I'm sure," Viola winked.

Gillian smiled at Viola's confidence in her ability to handle the situation and at the thought of retaining her pew. She was right; the lodge was a part of the estate, despite having different owners — though she very much hoped she would see the owner of the manor before Sunday.

CHAPTER 11

Much to Gillian's annoyance, she did not see Viola for the rest of the week. With arrangements for the summer flower show in full swing, she and Bridget were busy trying to work out how to fit everything into the village hall. It was proving to be a challenge, and its success would hinge heavily on the British weather playing ball — something no one should or could rely on.

She spent the last hour of the church service going through the plans in her mind, making sure everything was in order and checking they hadn't forgotten anything. She needed to keep herself busy or she would nod off, and that wasn't a good look, especially not from the front pew. Keeping her thoughts occupied also helped her to avoid eye contact with the reverend over her seating position; there were only so many smug smiles you could give a person.

Finally emerging into the warm, bright sunshine — a

stark contrast to the cold, dark, dreary church — Gillian approached the reverend.

"Ah, Reverend, wonderful sermon today, and always so easy to hear from the front pew."

The reverend opened his mouth to speak, but Gillian continued before he could get a word out.

"You know, my friend Viola pointed out the other day — after we'd luncheoned together — that the front pew is a Kingsford pew, and as Kingsford Lodge is technically within the boundaries of the estate, she insisted I should make use of it."

The reverend's mouth closed again as the colour drained from his face.

Where once she would have enjoyed waiting for a reply, an apology even, she found herself moving away. Enjoyment came from other places now, like passing the time of day with a good friend. Her mind went to Viola as her eye caught Bridget's. A pang of guilt kicked her in the stomach. She could have two friends. She'd spent the last four days with Bridget yet found herself missing the quiet company of Viola — more than she could explain.

Bridget joined her, accompanied by Mrs Hawkins.

"Mrs Carmichael," Mrs Hawkins said, "I was hoping Dudley might be able to use these carrots. They are a little past their best, but I don't suppose he minds."

"No, I don't suppose he will," Gillian replied, taking the carrier bag she was offered. "Thank you."

As Mrs Hawkins walked away, Bridget whispered, "She's the second person who's asked me this morning if there will be a ball this year."

"If anyone wants to know, then they should ask me."

"You mean Viola?" Bridget corrected her.

"Oh, yes," Gillian replied curtly, frustrated that at times her mind allowed her to believe nothing had changed. Each time the realisation left her with a cold emptiness in the pit of her stomach.

"I'll leave you here today, Bridget. I'm going to walk back through the estate and sit for a while."

"Good idea. You deserve a rest after the last few days we've had. I'll pour myself a glass of wine and finish reading my book."

"You do that; you've earned it, too," Gillian said, tapping Bridget on the arm as she headed to the gate which led to the Kingsford Estate footpath.

Gillian didn't have much time to read fiction. Her younger self wouldn't recognise her today; her head had always been in a book, usually a classic like a Brontë or Austen. Although they were good books, she found over time that she wasn't comfortable with them. She stopped reading romance entirely after meeting Hen, to then fall into an Austen book, only to realise it more resembled the Forsyte Saga.

Heterosexual romance left a bad taste in her mouth. The gendered power imbalance was inescapable, and the objectification of women didn't sit right with her. The inequality was plain uncomfortable. Jonathon had persuaded her to try Agatha Christie's books, which she found surprisingly enjoyable. They were also a good talking point when they ran out of anything else to discuss, which was frequent.

The air was warm and moist as she made her way up the hill to the bench. A distant rumble of thunder told her she wouldn't be enjoying some peace on it for long. She would take what she could get; if she'd learnt anything in recent months, it was to take nothing for granted.

Stopping near the bench, she watched the once–bright blue sky darken as thick, grey clouds edged closer. Out of the corner of her eye, she noticed movement. Viola was striding towards her, dressed in her new tweed trousers, white shirt, and matching waistcoat. The sudden pounding in her chest made Gillian wonder if it wasn't only the woman's voice that sent pleasant shivers through her.

Viola's shirtsleeves were rolled up to her elbows, and her auburn hair was tied in a ponytail. It induced the same weak feeling in Gillian's legs that she had felt in the outfitters, followed by the same thought: What did Viola look like… underneath it all? She pushed the thought away again, as she had done in the shop. It wasn't appropriate, and she wasn't that person anymore. She needed to uphold her image in the village. Getting weak over a beautiful mezzo-soprano was not on the cards.

It wasn't like beautiful women hadn't caught her eye over the years; she'd just learned to ignore herself and suppress everything. She was good at it, and the aged population of Kingstord with its lack of temptations had helped — until now anyway.

Swallowing hard, she recollected Viola standing in her doorway earlier that week, wearing a short summer dress with one too many cardigan buttons open. A wave of nausea followed as she recalled Viola hearing her voice resounding through the lodge and catching a glimpse inside. Finding out later that Viola came from a poor background at least made her less self-conscious about her current living conditions.

Exasperated that, yet again, she had failed to keep the thoughts at bay, Gillian let out an audible sigh, only to realise Viola was beside her already.

"Are you okay?"

"Yes, just a little out of breath," Gillian lied, looking back down the embarrassingly small incline.

"Have you come from church?"

"Yes. The front pew specifically," Gillian said with a hint of mischief as she took her usual seat on the bench.

"Excellent."

"You'll be pleased to know I only gloated a small amount."

Viola grinned as she took the seat beside Gillian. "Good. You know the reverend offered me a committee place. I politely declined. Should I send you as my representative for that too? I assume it was yours once?"

"No, thank you. I find I'm quite content without the pettiness of it. Leave them to it, I say."

Viola nudged her. "Well done, you."

It caught Gillian off guard, but knowing Viola felt comfortable enough to do that filled her with delight. A wet spot of something landed on her hand. Large drops of rain began to fall, thick and heavy.

"Shall we finish this conversation back at mine?" Gillian asked.

Not waiting for an answer, she got up and strode up the footpath. She wasn't ready to be parted from Viola quite yet. As she reached the back door of Kingsford

Manor, she stopped to check if Viola was following, finding her right behind.

"You know this is my house," Viola said, lips tight in a smirk.

Gillian looked around. "Oh. Yes. Sorry."

"Don't be. You strike me as a creature of habit. I'll give you a period of grace. Are a few years enough, do you think?" Viola flashed her a cheeky grin as she opened the door and stepped into the back hall.

Gillian's lips tightened as her eyes narrowed. She wasn't sure that would be enough time, but she wasn't about to voice it.

She hesitated a moment before crossing the threshold. It was her first time entering the manor since losing it. When she searched for a feeling, she found that only numbness remained. She couldn't be angry at Viola for having the manor now, and being angry at Jonathon was pointless. It didn't stop her from wanting it back, though.

Viola disappeared into the cloakroom, emerging with a towel in hand. "You're soaked," she said, reaching out and dabbing Gillian's chest with the towel.

It was an unexpected yet pleasant sensation. She could feel the warmth of Viola's rhythmic breath against her wet skin, which made her pulse surge. Their eyes locked until Viola stepped back, holding the towel out to Gillian.

"Oh, sorry. I didn't — "

Gillian, momentarily thrown off, managed a quiet, appreciative "Thanks," her voice barely more than a whisper as she took the towel. Viola offered an awkward smile before scurrying into the kitchen.

Running the towel across her chest and down her arms,

Gillian slipped her shoes off, patting her ankles and the tops of her feet. It wasn't the first time she'd been caught in a downpour on a summer's day. Hanging the towel on a radiator to dry, she went through to the kitchen, where nothing could have prepared her for what she was met with — especially as she had forgotten at that moment that Viola had renovated it.

Gone was the harsh stainless steel, which had been replaced with chic, sage green, custom cabinetry in a classic Shaker style, complemented by an oak herringbone floor and dark marble worktops. A large island inlaid with modular Gaggenau cooktops dominated the centre of the room.

"This is exquisite," Gillian gasped.

"It's Clive Christian."

Gillian knew the name well; she'd dreamt of having a Clive Christian kitchen. Necessity had led her to stainless steel rather than oak when she had refitted it, and although she'd come to love it over the years, it hadn't stopped her from pining for something like this.

Moistness creeped into the corners of her eyes. At first, she couldn't pinpoint why she was feeling emotional — it was just a kitchen, after all — but the new one represented change, a strikingly visual one in this case. She missed the old interior, or at least everything it symbolised, now a lost era. Still, she had to admit she was thrilled to see a kitchen that finally matched the building's grandeur — especially the new marble fireplace, a definite improvement over the original.

Gillian pushed a pang of jealousy away; she didn't

want or need those feelings now. Viola had created a masterpiece where she was unable to.

"May I?" Gillian gestured to what appeared to be a large cupboard.

"Knock yourself out."

Gillian opened the doors to find oak racking in the doors that held spices and shelves as well as drawers. "It's remarkable. Functional, elegant."

"It is. Why don't you have a peek through there?" Viola urged, pointing at the door that led to the dining room.

Hesitant at first, Gillian found her feet and forced them across the kitchen. It would be rude not to look despite the fear of what she might find holding her back.

Gillian's mouth opened as she discovered the room was unchanged.

"I don't have anything fancy when it comes to tea, I'm afraid," Viola called out from the kitchen.

"You kept it the same," Gillian said as she returned to the kitchen.

"Sometimes new isn't best, and when it comes to a table, you need something loved and used. I like to eat meals in there, even when it's only me."

"I used to spend a lot of time in there, too," Gillian said with a smile. "It's such a bright room compared to the front of the house."

"You see now? I'm not a total heathen. Much of the place remains as you left it. I may have also improved a couple of bathrooms."

Gillian tilted her head in concession. "They needed doing."

"What can I get you to drink?"

"Assuming Earl Grey is off the table, I guess I could lower myself to a coffee in that fancy machine of yours." She nodded at a Sanremo coffee machine.

"I only bought that until the kitchen was finished. This is what I use now," Viola said, heading straight for the row of sleek appliances built into the kitchen cabinets. "That one will become a backup."

Viola opened a drawer underneath what looked like a water dispenser and took out two mugs. On closer inspection, Gillian could see it was a coffee dispenser, not a water dispenser. She spotted a Gaggenau logo, the same brand stamped across all the integrated appliances.

"How do you take it?" Viola asked, placing a mug underneath the spouts.

Not being a coffee buff, Gillian racked her brains. "However it comes is fine."

Her eyes fell to the kitchen island, noting something she hadn't expected to see.

"A wine cooler?" Gillian said, her tone questioning.

"Yes."

"I assumed you didn't drink."

"Why?" Viola asked, passing a steaming cup to her.

Gillian hesitated before saying, "Your past addiction. You drank orange juice at the pub."

"Abuse, not addiction. There's a big difference. I didn't drink at the pub as I was driving, and it was lunchtime."

"Oh, yes, of course." Gillian lowered her head, wishing she hadn't mentioned it at all.

"Not that it's not okay to drink at lunchtime," Viola clarified, placing another cup under the spouts and pushing a button. "I have boundaries now, and it helps me to have a better relationship with alcohol. I used it in the past to help with my problems. Not that it helps of course, it just masks… takes the edge off, for a short time at least."

Taking her cup from the coffee machine, Viola gestured to a breakfast bar overlooking the parkland. "Shall we? I find this is my favourite place to sit now."

"I think it would be mine, too," Gillian agreed as something brushed against her leg, making her jump. Agatha launched herself onto the breakfast bar and proceeded to walk up and down it. "Oh, Agatha, where on earth did you come from?"

"I ask her that daily," Viola said, sounding a bit vexed. "I'm careful when I open the doors, and I don't leave windows open. It's a bit of a mystery."

Agatha continued her procession along the breakfast bar, ignoring anything in her way.

"Sorry." Viola reached out to pick up Agatha, who was having none of it and scurried off out of reach.

"Don't be. Technically she's still my cat, even if she has moved out. Or not moved out. Whichever." Gillian's forehead furrowed.

"I get you," Viola assured her, patting her arm and then leaving her hand resting there.

It was warm and soft against Gillian's skin, a gentle touch that shot a wave of comfort through her. It wasn't unwelcome, yet it stirred feelings again in her that she didn't want to think about, let alone deal with. It made her wonder why Viola was still touching her. She was quite hands-on at times, though recalling those situations it was more likely to be a supportive gesture. The tender nudges, playful smiles, and little digs she couldn't ignore. Could they be construed as flirting, or was she so out of touch that she was reading too much into it all?

"Honestly, this kitchen is a work of art," Gillian said, hoping to turn her internal monologue off by talking over it.

"My mum chose the style and helped a lot with the layout," Viola said, looking behind her. "It's gutting that she never got to see the finished article and only saw it on a screen. It evokes a lot of memories from her final days." Her voice faltered. "It's beautiful because it's hers, but it's also a constant reminder that she's gone."

Gillian realised then that the kitchen was a tribute to Viola's loss, with each carefully chosen detail serving as a silent echo of her mother's influence, now immortalised in its grandeur. It wasn't just a kitchen; it was a space that held grief and love in equal measure. For all her own grief over what had been lost at Kingsford Manor, Viola was mourning, too — just differently, if not deeper.

"You've made it into something that keeps her here with you."

Viola nodded. "Sometimes, I imagine what she would say, what she would think seeing it in person."

"I'm sure she will be looking down on it from somewhere and that she would find it as enchanting as we do," Gillian said.

"You believe that?" Viola asked, eyebrow raised.

Gillian pondered the question before answering, "No, not at all."

"Then why say it?"

"I thought it might bring you some comfort," Gillian

said with a shrug. "Perhaps I've been going to church too often."

"Sounds like it. Thanks for the thought, though."

Gillian picked up a book from beside her and examined it. "What are you reading?"

"A romance," Viola answered, sipping from her cup.

"I wouldn't have taken you for a romance reader. Don't you find the power imbalance in those kinds of books a bit distasteful?"

"That's the best bit. The ice queen boss being forced to melt by her assistant."

"Ice queen, eh? Then the assistant is a man. Romance has come a long way."

"No, they are both women." Viola grinned. "It's a sapphic romance."

"Sapphic?" Gillian blinked in confusion. "Not lesbian?"

"In this case, it's a lesbian and a bisexual woman, so yes, sapphic."

"Things really *have* come on."

"Where have you been these past decades?"

"In here, out there." Gillian nodded out the window. "It has been some time since I've wandered into a bookshop. I don't remember seeing a sapphic romance section. I'm sure I would have remembered."

"They have whole book shops dedicated to LGBTQ+ books now. You won't find so much in the larger retailers, mainly youth or new adult offerings from traditional publishers. You need the indie presses and authors. I do a lot of travelling, and I'd go mad without it. I often listen to audiobooks too. Can I take it that you only read heterosexual romance?"

"Once upon a time. I became sick of female characters being developed just enough to serve the role of the love interest, only to then become an appendix of a man."

Viola nodded her agreement. "It is so much more difficult to get them right. Queer romance is gentler, more balanced, and less aggressive. The characters are often portrayed as equals, with less emphasis on traditional power dynamics or roles. I find it makes the relationships feel more authentic and relatable. I could lend you one if you like?"

"I don't think that's necessary," Gillian stammered, though she couldn't deny she was more than a little intrigued.

～

Viola could see in Gillian's face that she was a little intrigued by the concept of a sapphic romance book; even so, she wasn't about to push it on her. She was still baffled that Gillian was completely unaware of an entire industry, one that she might take pleasure in.

It wasn't as if she knew exactly what Gillian's sexuality was; she had once mentioned being like Viola. That didn't necessarily mean she was a lesbian; she could be attracted to women as well as men, or 'people' as she preferred to see it. She wasn't sure any woman could be in a relationship with a man for that long if she were a lesbian — but then, this was Gillian Carmichael. Viola wouldn't put anything beyond her abilities.

Until she heard otherwise, she decided that Gillian was likely to be bi or pansexual and that she herself would assume nothing concrete. Knowing Gillian, though, Viola didn't think she would be into labels. The woman had spent most of her life pretending to be someone else; she likely didn't know who she was anyway. It didn't stop Viola from feeling like Gillian's eyes were hungry for something more than lunch when they were inside the outfitters. She had stared so intently at her that she felt like she was being undressed.

Who knew, though? Maybe Gillian really liked tweed.

"The rain has stopped. I'd better check on Dudley," Gillian said, draining her cup and stepping off her stool. "Thanks for the coffee. It doesn't compare to Earl Grey, yet it was perfectly palatable."

"Noted. I'll get some in… for next time."

Gillian's smile was unmistakable despite her attempts to hide it as she made her way through to the back hall. It may have arisen, though, from the mention of Earl Grey rather than the potential for a future invitation.

The towel on the radiator reminded Viola of their earlier moment when she had patted it against Gillian's wet chest. She cringed as she replayed it in her mind, wondering what she'd been thinking. The truth was, she hadn't thought at all. She was caught up in the heat of the moment. Her gaze had inadvertently lingered on Gillian's chest, and in a momentary lapse, she had reached out to dry it without fully considering the situation. Their brief eye contact, followed by her quick retreat, only added to her unease.

Watching Gillian slip into her shoes, Viola couldn't

help wondering how she had perceived the gesture. She had seemed at ease when entering the kitchen, and no awkwardness had followed.

Pushing the thoughts aside as Gillian headed to the door, Viola realised she would be gone in a moment. "Could I come with you? I haven't managed to look around the stables, and I'd like to meet Dudley. Properly, anyway."

Viola blushed a little as she recalled the altercation with Gillian at the stables following her unexpected planning meeting.

"Of course," Gillian replied as she picked up a bag of what looked like carrots beside the door.

Viola hadn't noticed it before, being too distracted by Gillian and the rain. Slipping into her boots, she asked, "Why do you have a bag of carrots?"

"They're for Dudley. Mrs Hawkins from the village shop occasionally has some past their best. He's not as fussy as her customers."

"I made the mistake of nipping in the shop the other day." Viola chuckled as she held the back door open for Gillian.

"Mistake?"

"Oh, everyone was perfectly nice; it's just a few customers conducted a loud conversation with the woman behind the counter about the manor summer ball."

"The villagers aren't very subtle, especially when it comes to anything important to them," Gillian said as she led them around the side of the manor. "Bridget mentioned this morning that people were asking."

"Does it mean that much to people?" Viola asked, her tone full of curiosity and concern.

"It's the event of the yea — was the event of the year, I mean," Gillian replied, her voice trailing off as she corrected herself with a hint of frustration.

Viola caught the solemn look on Gillian's face. She didn't want people to miss out on something meaningful to them. She also couldn't face organising it. "Is there nowhere else it can be held?" she asked, trying to offer a practical solution.

Gillian sighed, her gaze dropping to the crunchy gravel underfoot. "There is nowhere spacious enough, and I don't think it would have quite the same feel were it not to be held at the manor. It's more than a location; it's about the tradition and the memories tied to it."

Viola nodded; she could understand that.

"The last party I organised was a bit unruly," she said, sticking her hands into her pockets.

"So I heard. A summer ball has a better class of attendees. It's all very civilised."

"I wouldn't even know where to start with a ball."

"Is that the issue, organising it? You aren't opposed to the concept?"

"I'm not opposed to the idea of anything if people ask rather than demand or assume." Viola noticed Gillian tilting her head in acknowledgement as they walked along the path towards the stable. "I only threw the housewarming party to feel less lonely. It didn't exactly require much organising. I asked Mrs Johnson to put on a buffet and order drinks; a friend was the DJ. I put the word out to some friends and acquaintances, and they put the word out to theirs, it seems. You heard the rest."

"There is far more planning than that required for a ball, and anyway, I thought you came here for a bit of peace."

"There is a difference between peace and loneliness."

"They've always been much the same to me," Gillian replied softly. "Until recent weeks anyway."

Viola stole a glance at Gillian and noticed a smile twitching at the corners of her lips. What did Gillian mean by that? Was she insinuating that since they were spending more time together, she felt at peace but not lonely? Viola's heart squeezed until she realised it couldn't be that. As desperate as she was to ask, she refrained. She was happy to push Gillian in some respects; that comment, however, felt too personal to intrude on. Instead, she decided on something she knew would bring an even bigger smile to the woman's face.

"If I agree to a ball, would you organise it? It's way beyond me, and I can't help thinking the role of lady of the manor is far more suited to you than me anyway."

Gillian's eyes shimmered as they approached Dudley, whose head was poking out of his stall door.

"It is. I mean, it's all I'm qualified and equipped for, and I'd like my job back."

"Is that a yes then?" Viola clarified.

"Yes," Gillian answered, her eyes crinkling as a smile swept across her face.

It made Viola's heart squeeze again. *What was that?*

Gillian turned away from Viola, putting her attention back on Dudley. Viola suspected she didn't want her to see the joy on her face. The woman seemed intent on hiding all her emotions, even the good ones.

"Are you sure it's not too late to organise everything? Summer is practically here."

"Not for me. I can organise a ball in my sleep."

Viola believed that. She copied Gillian in how she touched the bridge of Dudley's nose. Not having grown up around horses, she was unfamiliar with them and found them a little intimidating.

Dudley appeared gentle enough, though, and she watched in awe as he rubbed his muzzle affectionately against Gillian's shoulder. He seemed enamoured with her, and Viola found herself beginning to feel the same way.

"There's just the four stalls?" Viola asked, taking them in and immediately noticing they looked a bit worse for wear. She hadn't paid them much attention when she chewed Gillian's ear off about the planning officer.

"Yes. You could hire the others out and make an income. The structure needs a bit of work first, though."

"How lax of the previous owner," Viola teased.

Gillian narrowed her eyes at her and then smiled. "There is good money to be made from livery. Jonathon was never in favour of it. It was part of my plan for the estate when he died. There's room for eight stalls if you convert the garages. Subject to planning, of course."

"I wouldn't wish to upset the neighbours; they are very sensitive to change," Viola said with a playful twitch of her head.

"Ha," Gillian retorted, pulling two carrots from the

bag, which she placed at her feet to stop Dudley nosing further into it. "Here."

Viola took the carrot Gillian offered and watched as she fed hers to Dudley.

"Keep a flat palm as much as you can. If you offer up fingers, they'll likely be eaten. Not on purpose, I might add." Gillian placed an arm under the horse's neck and pressed herself to the side of his head. "Dudley wouldn't hurt a fly intentionally. Would you, boy?"

The horse spotted the carrot in Viola's hand and pushed forward, making her take a step back.

"It's okay," Gillian assured her, stepping behind her.

She could feel Gillian's hands press lightly onto her shoulders and encourage her forward.

"Lay your palm flat and offer it to him." Gillian was so close it sounded as if she was whispering into her ear, making Viola almost forget to breathe.

Gillian gently guided her arm towards Dudley, who leaned down and pulled the carrot into his mouth with his soft, furry lips. It tickled Viola's hand, causing her to smile.

"Is Dudley safe, or is the stable liable to fall down and injure him?" she asked as Gillian stepped back from her and around to Dudley's side. "I wouldn't want to find myself in court for being neglectful."

"He's fine. I wouldn't home him in an unsafe environment for convenience."

"Of course, sorry," Viola replied sheepishly, realising too late what she must have insinuated.

Gillian looked down and scuffed her shoes against the cobbles. "I don't think I've properly expressed how grateful I am that you've let me keep Dudley here."

"You could repay me with lessons," Viola suggested cheekily.

"Riding lessons?" Gillian glanced up, a smile tugging at the corner of her lips.

"Yes. I've always wanted to learn to ride, and as you can see, I need to become a little more comfortable around horses."

"I'm sure I can help you with that."

Their eyes met across Dudley, and a shared smile formed between them. Viola wondered if she was the only one who could feel a spark of excitement in her core.

"I should get back. Before the heavens open again," Viola nodded at a dark cloud moving overhead. She stroked Dudley's nose. "It was nice to meet you, Dudley. I hope we see more of each other."

As Viola walked away, Gillian's voice called out.

"I'll be in touch soon… about arrangements for the ball. And your lessons."

Viola turned and walked backwards slowly. "I look forward to it."

Very much so.

CHAPTER 12

Gillian checked her watch.

"Am I keeping you from something?" Bridget asked from the sofa with a teasing smirk.

Time was passing more quickly than she realised. Bridget's arrival at the lodge two hours prior to finalise the plans for the flower show on Saturday felt like it had only been five minutes ago.

"Oh no… I… yes, I do have an appointment."

"You should have said," Bridget replied. "We can finish this up tomorrow."

"It completely slipped my mind." That was a tiny lie. It was all she'd thought about that morning until Bridget had arrived and she became distracted.

The doorbell echoed from the hall. Viola was early. Again. Gillian scooped up her paperwork, pleased that Bridget was doing the same.

"Who is it?" Bridget asked.

Gillian contemplated not telling her until she realised that the two of them seeing each other was unavoidable.

"Viola. I asked her to pop over to discuss some initial details for the ball. We need to get a date set as soon as possible."

"Good idea. I'll never know how you managed to persuade her when the two of you have been drawing daggers," Bridget said with a smirk as she filled her bag with her notes.

"We have come to an understanding, that's all," Gillian replied sharply.

"Well done, you, for being the bigger person. You know, the gossip in the village is that the two of you left together the other day in her car."

"We don't listen to idle gossip, do we?"

"No, Gillian." Bridget smirked. "Unless we started it."

"Exactly." Suddenly realising what Bridget said, she glared at her. "We don't spread gossip. We merely keep people informed." She held a guiding hand towards the sitting room door.

Taking the hint, Bridget left the room, leaving Gillian to glance around to make sure everything was in order. She wasn't overjoyed at the prospect of showing Viola her minuscule home. There would never be a good time, but having visited the manor for coffee, it was only polite to reciprocate.

She made her way through to the hallway to find Bridget sitting on the bottom step of the stairs, tying her shoelaces.

Viola knocked on the door again, and Gillian opened it with a raised eyebrow. "You're early. Again."

"I'm on time actually," Viola chortled back.

"It's always polite to be five minutes late. Therefore, being on time is arriving early."

Viola frowned at her playfully as she entered. "This isn't the nineteenth century, Gillian."

"Indeed, it is not. Thank you for that sad reminder."

"And if it were, then any time the lady of the manor wished to call on one of her subjects, she could, and not be reprimanded for it," Viola teased.

"Subjects! I suppose then *I* should be grateful we're not still bound by such archaic customs."

Viola grinned. "Modern times have their perks. Like the freedom to be early without judgement."

"And to remind others of their outdated etiquette?" Gillian questioned with a smirk.

"Precisely."

Bridget appeared beside them, having put her shoes on. Gillian had forgotten she was still there.

"Oh! Bridget. Sorry, I didn't realise you were here," Viola said.

Bridget smirked at the two of them. "I'll leave you two to it. Thank you for agreeing to a ball, Viola. The village is abuzz with excitement."

"My pleasure and thank you. I assume you'll be helping organise it."

"I will." Bridget beamed. Looking Viola up and down, she added, "Oh, do you ride?"

"No," Viola replied, adjusting the sleeve of her jacket. "Gillian is teaching me."

"Oh, is she?" Bridget said in a tone that danced on the

edge of curiosity, a faint smile tugging at the corners of her lips.

"Yes, well, run along, Bridget," Gillian said impatiently. "I'm sure you have some calls to make."

Bridget shimmied past Viola and stepped outside. "Yes, of course."

"Run along? You make her sound like a child. Or worse, a dog," Viola said sharply, as soon as Gillian closed the door behind her.

"Do I? Oh," Gillian said quietly.

"Yes."

"It's just my way. I don't mean anything by it."

"Do you ever consider how your words might sound to others?"

Gillian acknowledged what she was saying with a straightening of her lips. She hadn't, but something in Viola's voice said she should.

She turned her attention to Viola's outfit, which comprised beige jodhpurs, a white shirt and her tweed jacket. Her hair was tied back in a ponytail, revealing a long neck.

"You certainly look the part," Gillian said, immediately thinking she looked more than the part. She was breathtaking.

"I know how fuss — fastidious," Viola quickly corrected herself at the raise of one of Gillian's eyebrows, "you are about people dressing appropriately for the task at hand."

"I'm not entirely sure about the trainers," Gillian said, furthering Viola's point. "I'm sure I have a pair of boots that you can borrow."

"I was hoping you might. Do I get to see any more of your home?"

"Oh. Of course, come through." Gillian led her through to the sitting room.

Viola surveyed the room for a long moment before pronouncing it, "Cute."

"More cosy than cute," Gillian said, "and not in a positive sense."

"It is cute and cosy," Viola pressed, taking in the room. "Sometimes I dream of having a smaller house again. The manor wasn't meant for me alone, and it's a big place to rattle around in by yourself. I've never lived so rurally before; it can be quite scary at times, particularly at night."

"You are perfectly safe. It's safer here than the city. People that aren't meant to be here stand out a mile away. Tea? I have coffee, but I don't recommend it. It wouldn't live up to your high-end expectations."

Viola hesitated for a moment, then answered with a smile. "I'll have whatever you're having, thanks."

When Gillian reappeared with a tea tray, she found Viola looking at some framed photographs on the windowsill. A pair of binoculars sat beside them.

"You have a good view of the manor from here," Viola said, quickly turning her attention out the window.

"Yes," Gillian answered, setting the tea tray on the table.

"I don't think I appreciated how difficult it must have been for you, moving from there to here. Every day seeing the manor from your window — sometimes at remarkably close proximity through a pair of binoculars."

Gillian's face blushed as she joined Viola by the window, only for her to flash a teasing smile.

"Sorry, I don't mean to make light of your loss. I'm envious that you have such an attachment to a place. I've never stood still long enough to form one to anything."

"Does that include people?" Gillian asked.

Viola looked back out the window and let out a sigh. "Yes, I suppose it does. Until recent years anyway, when I grew close to my mum. Even that didn't last."

"You once said you never had a long-term relationship."

"It's hard enough to find friends to trust, let alone lovers. You never know if the next person will kiss and tell, so you tend to avoid it altogether."

All Gillian could think was what a waste it was. This woman deserved to be cherished and loved every day, to feel the warmth of genuine affection and the joy of being deeply desired. It was heartbreaking to imagine her spending all those years in solitude, her beauty and spirit unnoticed and unappreciated, missing out on the intimate connections that bring meaning to life. Viola deserved more than simply existing; she deserved to be seen and adored.

Her thoughts fell back to herself. Didn't she deserve this too? Having experienced this with Hen, if only for a short time, she knew how wonderful it felt. She also knew how it felt to lose it. Maybe they were both better off alone in the world.

"Anyway, enough of my depressing personal life," Viola said, taking a seat. "Fill me in on the plans for the ball. I've got some ideas too."

"You do?"

"I was thinking we could do a casino-themed night."

"Casino?" Gillian questioned, sitting opposite her. "Gambling?"

Viola's face lit up. "Yes, if you like."

Gillian didn't like it at all. She wasn't convinced the villagers would either. Change wasn't something they embraced. They knew what they liked, and they preferred it to stay that way.

"We could set up a few card tables, maybe a roulette wheel, even hire professional dealers. Think James Bond, licence to thrill."

Gillian poured tea into a fine bone china cup and handed the saucer to an excited Viola.

"I'm not sure how it would go down with the villagers; they like their traditional ball. They are creatures of habit."

"Like you," Viola said, giving Gillian a questioning look over her cup.

"Perhaps. We have a particular way of doing things around here."

"Then let's try something new. If it doesn't work, then you can blame me. Technically, it's my event. You can say you advised against it and that I was having none of it, and I'm not. We can keep the tables to one end so as not to interfere with the dancing or whatever else you do at one of your balls."

Viola's enthusiasm was infectious. Not to the point that Gillian would agree it was a good idea yet enough to want to please her. If a casino night was what she wanted, and she could pass the buck if it was a disaster, it could be a win-win.

"I'm sure that whatever you do you will make a success of it," Viola pressed. "You are *Gillian Carmichael*, and I would never bet against you."

Gillian's face burned, from both her words and the hopeful smile Viola was giving her.

"Okay, Casino Royale Ball it is then."

Having settled on a date, they agreed Gillian would send out a save the date via the village's WhatsApp group, following it up with formal invitations later that week. Time was of the essence to get everything organised, and it was the only supply she was short on.

Until the forthcoming flower show was over, Gillian wouldn't be able to do much more than to get the invitations out and book the casino tables. She felt Viola's eyes watching her as she scribbled on a notepad a list of things that needed attending to. It was good to have some direction again that involved the manor.

"You really know what you are doing with all this," Viola said as she watched her.

"It has been my job for thirty-five years."

"I'm glad I'm not the one doing it. It's so overwhelming."

"If it helps, I could unburden you further," Gillian proffered casually as she looked up.

Viola narrowed her eyes. "How?"

"Direct any requests or demands on the manor to me in future. I'll deal with it all for you."

"Like a kind of social secretary?"

"If you like." Gillian shrugged.

"I can't help thinking it's me doing you a favour here."

Gillian laughed. "I think we could agree it would be a mutual favour. No villagers knocking on your door."

"Hmm. Then let me thank you with dinner, say Friday at seven?" Viola proposed, her eyes hopeful.

The invitation took Gillian by surprise. "That... would be... lovely," she stammered.

"Great! You can meet my friend and agent, Caroline. She's staying for the weekend."

"Oh," Gillian replied, taken aback at how disappointed she felt knowing it wouldn't be just the two of them. "Oh, how nice," she added quickly.

It would be interesting to meet someone close to Viola; she might be able to gain more insights into the woman.

"Shall we ride whilst there is a break in the rain?" Gillian suggested, keen to impress Viola with more of her skills. "I'll pop up and change."

∽

Viola watched as Gillian demonstrated how to tack up Dudley, her hands deftly adjusting the straps and buckles. Her movements were precise and practised, her fingers strong yet gentle.

There was something undeniably captivating about the way she moved that turned the heat up inside Viola. Gillian's focused expression, the enthusiasm that lit up her face as she explained each step, only heightened her heart rate. She was completely captivated by the vast knowledge and passion she was exuding, particularly whilst clad in a pair of jodhpurs.

Having equipped Viola with riding boots and a hat,

Gillian turned to teaching her the correct way to mount and dismount. She noticed a hint of surprise in Gillian's eyes when she managed it easily. Although the thought of feigning difficulty for some extra "assistance" certainly crossed her mind, she found herself genuinely wanting to impress Gillian instead.

Gillian reached up and took her hand, adjusting the reins. "There. Now relax."

Viola slumped, causing Gillian to press her hand firmly into Viola's lower back.

"Don't slouch."

Repositioning again, she found Gillian's hand on her side.

"Relax your hips."

Being touched by Gillian every time she got it wrong was not exactly going to entice her to get it right.

Viola adjusted her posture, feeling more secure in the saddle. "Like this?"

"Exactly," Gillian confirmed. "We'll start by walking to the paddock to get your body used to the seating position and movement. Keep your heels down and close to him; feel his rhythm beneath you. To start moving, squeeze your legs together. To stop, pull back on the reins lightly. Try it."

Viola took a moment to absorb the instructions, then pressed her legs in. Dudley began to walk, and a laugh of delight escaped her lips.

"That's it," Gillian encouraged, following beside her. "You're doing great. Now, to steer him, gently pull the reins in the direction you want to go."

Viola practised steering, marvelling at how responsive

Dudley was to her commands. Each successful turn boosted her confidence a little bit more.

"You're a natural," Gillian said, clearly impressed. "Keep your back straight and those heels down. Imagine a line running from your head through your spine to your heels. It will help you maintain your balance."

As they reached the paddock behind the stables, Gillian went ahead and opened the gate.

"To maintain a steady pace, keep a light, consistent pressure with your legs. If you want to speed up, squeeze a little harder. Always stay relaxed."

Viola did as instructed and found that Dudley obediently followed her command as he began to trot.

"Remember to look where you want to go, not down at Dudley."

Viola nodded and looked up. Gillian continued to provide her with tips and corrections as she moved Dudley around the paddock. With every passing minute her confidence in guiding the beautiful beast increased. After half an hour Gillian suggested they head back to the stables.

"Dudley is a great horse to learn on. He's a gentle giant," Viola said, leaning forward in her seat and patting him affectionately whilst Gillian closed the gate behind them.

"He's my best friend. I find horses more tolerable than people," Gillian said, her tone thoughtful as she walked beside them.

"Why?" Viola asked with curiosity in her eyes.

Gillian paused, gazing at Dudley with a fond smile. "Horses are honest," she began. "They don't hide their feelings or intentions. If they're happy, you'll know it. When they're scared or uncomfortable, they'll show it. There's no deceit, no hidden agendas. With people, it's often hard to tell what's going on inside their heads. With horses, what you see is what you get."

Viola considered this, nodding slowly. "I guess that makes sense. It must be nice to have that kind of straightforwardness."

"It is," Gillian agreed. "And there's something incredibly calming about being around them. They live in the moment, responding to what's happening now, not worrying about the past or future. It's a good reminder to do the same."

Viola smiled. "There's a kind of purity in their nature."

"Exactly," Gillian said, her eyes meeting Viola's. "Horses are majestic and intelligent. They can teach us a lot about trust and patience. They're always willing to trust and give us their best despite many of them having been poorly treated or having negative experiences with humans. They're still willing to let us sit on their backs where they are most vulnerable."

Viola hummed her agreement.

"They force you to be patient and regulate your emotions," Gillian continued. "Dudley was always my calm amongst the storm of an often-hectic life. We are patient with each other; we have an unbreakable bond."

"I can see that," Viola replied, a pang of jealousy hitting her.

"When we ride, I forget everything except the powerful rhythm of his hooves beneath me, pounding against the earth as the cool wind blows through my hair. The sense of freedom is exhilarating when we move together as one, both perfectly attuned to each other's slightest cue."

"It sounds magical. I've long admired those people in the movies, cantering across a field, hair blowing in the wind. How long would it take to teach someone to canter?"

"Quite a lot of lessons. Going off how well you've done today, I think you could pick it up sooner. It's not only about knowing how to make the horse canter; you need to build a relationship with it and be prepared to deal with any problems at that speed."

Viola nodded, knowing it would take patience.

"I could take you for a ride if you like. Let the wind blow against your face if that's what you're looking for," Gillian suggested as they stopped outside the stables.

Viola's face lit up. "You could?"

"Yes," Gillian said, stroking Dudley's nose and wiping some dirt away from his eye.

"Now?"

Gillian laughed. "You are keen. How about I take you on one of my regular routes around the estate? Before I sold it, I mean."

Viola narrowed her eyes and grinned. "The recent horseshoe prints would have nothing to do with you then?"

"They would not," Gillian replied, hiding her grinning lips behind her hand. "Jump down and I'll remove the saddle."

Viola dismounted, stumbling as her feet hit the ground. Before she could right herself, Gillian's arm wrapped tightly around her waist.

"Careful," Gillian murmured, her voice low and close, the grip of her hand firm against the rough fabric of Viola's tweed jacket. Even through the layers, the warmth of her touch seemed to burn straight through to Viola's skin, leaving her breathless.

"Thanks," she gasped, managing a shaky smile as Gillian released her. She stepped back with an almost reluctant slowness.

With the saddle removed, Viola recovered as Gillian busied herself in the stable. She emerged with a riding hat perched on her head and a small set of steps in hand.

"We'll have you up front; you're a little smaller than me." She placed the steps beside Dudley. "Here. I wouldn't like your chances of mounting this time without the stirrup to help you."

Viola thought she was probably right as she climbed the steps.

"How do I…"

"Take hold of his mane to balance and lift your leg over," Gillian instructed.

Viola did as she was told, gripping Dudley's mane and swinging her leg over his back. She could feel the warmth from the horse beneath her as she adjusted her posture. Seconds later, Gillian was sat behind, her legs pressed against her, holding her firmly in place. The sudden closeness took Viola by surprise; she hadn't fully appreciated how much intimacy the ride would bring.

"Are you okay?"

"A little nervous," Viola admitted.

Gillian chuckled softly, the sound soothing Viola's nerves.

"Relax. Let Dudley and me do the work."

Viola took a deep breath, trying to steady her racing heart. She could feel Gillian's arms around her as she gripped the reins. The warmth of her body radiating against her back felt comforting yet exhilarating.

"Hold on tight."

With a gentle nudge from Gillian, Dudley started moving, the rhythm of his gait quickly setting in. Viola focused on the motion, matching her movements to Dudley's. Every movement of the horse amplified her awareness of Gillian's body against her. The proximity was intoxicating, heightening every sensation in her body as they moved as one.

They reached a large open field beside the paddock, and Viola could feel Dudley's powerful muscles moving beneath her as Gillian transitioned them smoothly into a canter. She held his mane to steady herself, careful not to pull it and hurt the creature as the wind whipped through her hair. Squinting against the rush of air, a smile spread across her face as the steady, comforting, powerful thud of Dudley's hooves matched the rapid beating of her heart.

"How are you feeling?" Gillian's voice was close. Her warm breath against Viola's ear caused goosebumps to prickle all over her skin.

"Amazing!" Viola called back, trying to keep her voice steady despite the swirl of emotions. Every brush of Gillian's body against hers, every shift and movement felt charged with an electricity she couldn't ignore.

As they picked up pace, the landscape around them blurred into a tapestry of greens and blues, the world narrowing to the three of them. Viola found herself hyperaware of every detail: the strength of Gillian's arms and legs rooting her to Dudley, the steady rhythm of her breathing, their shared laughter that dissolved into the wind. She wished the moment could last forever.

"You're doing great," Gillian murmured, her voice low and reassuring.

Her words sent a shiver through Viola as each stride of Dudley's canter bound her closer to Gillian in ways she was only beginning to understand. She wondered if Gillian could sense the turmoil inside her; if she was feeling what she was feeling.

Gillian's arms and legs tightened around her as they descended a hill, anchoring her securely. Viola leaned back into her, feeling protected and connected in a way she hadn't anticipated. As she surrendered to the moment, trusting Dudley and Gillian fully, the tension within her began to ebb.

Dudley settled into a steady trot and Gillian's hold on her softened. All remaining stiffness in Viola's body melted away. Passing the paddock, Gillian's arms gradually loosened, finally releasing completely as they arrived at the stables.

"That was incredible," Viola replied, her heart pounding for reasons beyond the ride. The thrill of it, combined with the closeness to Gillian, made it difficult to focus on anything else.

"I'm surprised you find it so exhilarating; surely it can't compare to flying a helicopter?"

"Flying a helicopter is its own kind of thrill. It puts you far from nature, looking down on it rather than being at one with it. You move over it rather than through it. You don't experience the scents or the wind," Viola said thoughtfully. "Like an observer, not a participant."

Gillian nodded. "When you're on a horse, you're part of the landscape. You feel every movement, every change in the terrain. You smell the earth, the grass, the trees. You hear the sounds around you, not the roar of an engine. There's nothing quite like it."

"It's like being truly connected," Viola said, more to herself than to Gillian.

The vibration of a soft hum from Gillian's agreement resounded against Viola's ear.

"For reference, I don't mind you riding around the estate. As long as it's only you. No hunting parties."

"I never allowed that sort of thing on the Kingsford Estate," Gillian said, her voice laced with indignation. "All wildlife is — *was* welcome here."

"I'm surprised. I took you for the traditional type. Tooting your hunting horn and everything," Viola teased as they stopped outside the stables.

"I am. However, there are some traditions I can't get behind, and killing defenceless animals is one of them."

Gillian shifted behind her, landing gracefully on the ground. She turned and gestured for Viola to do the same.

"Your turn," she said with an encouraging smile.

Viola took a deep breath, gripping Dudley's mane as she carefully swung her leg over his back and slid down his side. Gillian stepped closer, her hands reaching out to steady her as she landed.

"That's it," Gillian said, her hands lingering on Viola's waist a moment longer than necessary.

"Thanks," Viola replied, her voice slightly breathless as

she savoured the warmth of Gillian's touch. Their eyes locked, and for a second, neither of them moved. Only the sound of Viola's breathing filled the space between them.

Gillian blinked and stepped back suddenly. "It is I who should be thankful. You don't know what it means to be able to continue to ride the estate."

"I think after today, I do. Thank you for the lesson and that wonderful ride."

Gillian smiled, the warmth reaching her eyes. "Any time."

"I'll hold you to that," Viola said with a grin. She patted Dudley affectionately. "You did great, boy."

Dudley snorted, seeming to enjoy the praise.

"I'll see you Friday," she said, "for dinner. Don't be late."

"Only the required five minutes," Gillian quipped.

"That will be acceptable," Viola replied, smirking as she walked away from the impossible woman she couldn't seem to get enough of.

CHAPTER 13

Viola stuffed the last remnants of a chocolate muffin into her mouth as she sat at the breakfast bar. Mrs Johnson spent the morning baking a selection of sugary delights in anticipation of Caroline's visit, and she was unable to resist scoffing one with her coffee as an afternoon treat.

Her eyes tried to focus through the rain-splattered window to the horizon, where she and Gillian had ridden only days before. The memory of that ride was vivid in her mind — the thrumming of Dudley's hooves; the wind against her face, blowing through her hair; and the comforting presence of Gillian behind her.

Viola sighed as she traced a finger along the glass, following the trails of raindrops as they joined together and lost their battle against gravity. The landscape outside was a stark contrast now. Even softened by the rain, it held the same allure, stirring a desire inside her to be back there with Gillian.

An unmistakable vibration pulled her from her

thoughts. Caroline was arriving in the helicopter she had booked for the weekend. Clambering from her stool, she made her way to the back hall and opened the door as the helicopter touched down on the grass.

She waved at Caroline as she emerged from it and beckoned her inside. The tall woman, in her late fifties, carried herself with an athletic grace. Her dark brown fringe fell into her eyes before she flicked it away with a practiced gesture, causing her high ponytail to swing from side to side.

"V, this place is beautiful, even in a downpour! The photographs do not do it justice," Caroline said as she reached the door, shaking water droplets from her coat before stepping inside. "You've bagged yourself a stunner."

"It is rather," Viola agreed, pulling her into a warm hug.

Caroline pulled back after a moment, a hint of regret in her eyes. "Bad news, I'm afraid. I need to be back in London tomorrow for an urgent meeting. Sorry."

"Oh. I'd booked us Sunday lunch," Viola said, her shoulders sagging." I was going to fly us there."

Caroline scrunched her face. "We have tonight, and then you can fly me back to Battersea."

Struggling to disguise the disappointment on her face, Viola nodded her agreement. She was looking forward to showing Caroline around the estate. She waved at her regular pilot, Douglas, as he walked across the lawn to the front of the house, briefcase in hand. Like clockwork, she could make out the distant sound of crunching gravel coming from the front of the house as his car arrived to collect him.

"Come on in," she said, shutting the back door and taking Caroline's coat. "I'll give you a whistle-stop tour before our guests arrive for dinner."

"Guests?"

"Yes," Viola confirmed as she hung up the coat. Noticing a draught coming from the cellar door beside her, she pushed it closed with her foot. "Gillian will be joining us and Bridget, her friend. She lives in the village too."

Caroline frowned. "Gillian. Gillian Carmichael?"

"Yes." Viola laughed.

"The self-same woman you've done nothing but moan about since you got here?"

"I've got to know her a little since then."

Or more likely a hell of a lot. She knew more about Gillian than anyone did, even Bridget. Knowing things about people didn't exactly translate to knowing them. In this case, though, she had a good idea of who Gillian was, and the butterflies circling her stomach from thinking about her told her she liked what she saw.

"You would have to get to know her a lot to invite her to dinner. Hang on. Didn't you say she was hot?"

"No, I recall you suggested she was hot. And yes, I have got to know her, and she's teaching me to ride." Noticing the cheeky grin forming on Caroline's face, she quickly clarified. "A horse, Caroline! Goodness. It's so easy to talk to her. She doesn't see me as a celebrity; she sees me as me. We seem to click in an odd way." Viola stopped, realising she may be overly justifying her new friendship.

"I for one am glad you have found a *friend*. Just don't

get too comfortable or you won't ever want to go back to work. You are, after all, closing the Proms in September."

Viola groaned audibly. She had forgotten. In fact, she'd forgotten entirely about work, living quite contentedly in her Kingsford bubble.

Caroline tilted her head in response. "We agreed it would be a good way to ease you back in."

"I know. Will you be there?"

"I can't, V. Sorry. I'll be in L.A."

Viola felt the pangs of loneliness that had recently subsided rise inside her again. This would be her first performance without her mum. There would be no one to help her prepare. No one she could practise the songs to, even though it was ingrained in her, as they all were. There would be no one there for her when she came offstage, to chill with and enjoy a glass of something. A wave of panic swept through her as she realised there was no longer anyone to moderate her, to keep her on track, to keep her accountable. Her mum's voice sounded in her head: 'One and done.' It was something she always said in the dressing room when they enjoyed a celebratory drink.

"Are you okay?" Caroline asked, catching her eye.

"Yes. Only it's my first performance without Mum," Viola answered, inhaling a deep breath.

Caroline placed her hands on Viola's shoulders, looking her straight in the eyes. "You will be fine. You are magnificent. You can do this," she said, pulling her into a tight hug.

Viola forced a smile and took another deep breath as she returned the embrace. She could do this; she needed to. Although her mum was no longer here, she could still do it for her, keeping up with the routines they made. She wasn't going to let her down.

As Caroline pulled back, she patted Viola's chest gently. "She's in here. You won't let her down."

Viola wiped her eyes, which were filling with tears. "I won't."

"Now come on," Caroline said, putting an arm around Viola. "Show me all the exciting nooks and crannies. There better be a priest hole hiding somewhere, or I will be extremely disappointed."

"I gave the place a good search when I moved in, and the only things I found were some old paintings in the attic."

"We can ask this Gillian of yours."

"She's not my Gillian," Viola disputed, as much as she liked the sound of it.

"Yeah, yeah," Caroline countered as they left the room.

Following a tour of the manor, Viola showed Caroline to a guest room at the back of the house, where the windows offered sweeping, uninterrupted views of the estate.

The sound of pans clattering from the room below signalled Mrs Johnson's arrival to prepare dinner, so Viola left Caroline to settle in and retreated to her own bathroom, where she sank into a hot bath. She relished the calming embrace of the water as she thought about the evening ahead. She was excited yet nervous to see Gillian again, and her mind wandered to what she might wear to dinner. She wouldn't be short of beautiful dresses, having spent decades as a hostess.

After her bath, Viola selected a chiffon maxi dress that

she knew would show her figure off to her advantage. Its rich, deep green hues contrasted with the auburn waves she'd teased into place over her shoulders. Taking a moment to admire herself in the mirror, she felt a sudden surge of confidence. Secretly she hoped it might catch Gillian's attention.

Refreshed and ready, she made her way to the great hall, checking her watch to see how long it would be before Gillian would arrive. She began to hum a riff that popped into her mind from nowhere. It had been a while since that last happened. Her humming turned into a soft, melodic singing as she descended the stairs. When she noticed Caroline at the bottom looking up at her, she stopped.

"Don't let me stop you," Caroline said with a wide grin. "It's good to hear you singing again. I don't think I've heard this one before."

"It just slipped into my mind," Viola admitted. "I haven't felt the urge to write anything new since Mum died."

"These things come back to us when we are ready. Sometimes a good break is all we need." A corner of Caroline's mouth twitched into a smile. "Or a new muse."

Viola scowled at her playfully. "That's enough, thank you."

"Shall we crack open the champers?" Caroline said, deftly changing the subject by nodding at a bottle and four glasses on the banqueting table.

"You'll have to wait. It's rude to start before the guests have arrived. They are quite fastidious about etiquette around here."

"The savages know about etiquette?" Caroline said, recoiling in faux shock.

"Yes, more so than you it seems."

"I suppose there must be one downside. Otherwise, this place is really something."

"You like your room then?"

"Like it? I love it. It will be difficult to get me out of it in the morning, more specifically that spa bath. Did the house come with all the furniture? My four-poster bed must be hundreds of years old."

"Probably about four hundred, which is how long the Carmichaels owned it."

A knock at the door echoed into the hall, sending butterflies through Viola from head to toe.

"That will be our guests."

Viola opened the door to find Gillian in an elegant, off-the-shoulder, V-neck, full-length black gown with a slit up to her thigh. It revealed ample amounts of cleavage, which Viola struggled to tear her eyes away from.

"Gillian, wow." Viola blinked, realising the last word had let itself out.

"Wow, indeed." Gillian gestured to Viola as she entered the porch.

"Oh, thank you," Viola replied, feeling her cheeks burn as she smoothed down her dress and flicked a curl of hair back over her shoulder.

She approached Gillian, placing her hands on her bare upper arms and giving an air kiss to the left and then the right cheek, where she lingered. Her cheek was still grazing Gillian's as a hint of her perfume caught in her nose. It was different to Gillian's usual jasmine scent; this was much heavier, with hints of patchouli and musk. It, like the woman herself, was intoxicating.

A polite cough sounded from behind, making them both jump. Bridget was standing at the threshold.

"Oh! I didn't realise you were coming, Bridget," Gillian said, pulling back abruptly. "How lovely."

"Am I here to make up the numbers?" Bridget asked, her voice teasing, though a flicker of uncertainty crossed her face, as if she wasn't entirely sure she wanted the answer.

Viola felt a pang of sadness for the woman. "No, you most certainly aren't," she said, reaching out to her and guiding her inside.

She air-kissed Bridget as well and took her shawl, which was covering an old-looking floral-printed dress. The woman had likely given up trying to look glamorous next to Gillian, or perhaps couldn't afford to compete. As Viola hung up the shawl on a peg, the echoes of clicking heels warned her that Caroline was approaching.

As predicted, Caroline appeared, squeezing herself into the small porch. Taking a brief look at both ladies, she held out a hand to Gillian. "You must be Gillian. I'm Caroline. I've heard so much about you."

Viola was rapidly regretting inviting her to stay.

Gillian's soft smile in her direction and question of "Oh, really," did nothing to help her growing anxiety at what the rest of the evening might hold.

Caroline nodded. "Viola doesn't stop talking about you. I was sorry to hear of the loss of your husband, and of course this delightful building."

"Thank you," Gillian replied. "I'm bearing it as best I can."

"Let's go through to the great hall for some champagne before we all suffocate?" Viola said, feeling short of breath suddenly. "Dinner will be served shortly."

She gestured for Gillian and Bridget to go through ahead of her. As they passed, Caroline greeted Bridget, then extended an arm, lightly catching Viola to hold her back.

"You definitely didn't notice how hot she was when you were having these little chats with her?" Caroline whispered once the two women were out of earshot.

"No," Viola lied, hoping she sounded at least a little convincing.

"Bull. Look at her, she's a goddess. All you do is talk about her on the phone."

"Oh, okay, I'm attracted to her. So what?" Viola hissed. It felt great to say it out loud finally, to someone. To admit it to herself even.

"Ha! See? What a shame she's straight."

"Mmm." Viola looked down. Any further response than that and she would likely give something away.

"Mmm? Is that it? Spill. Now."

It was impossible to hide anything from Caroline, especially when she was glaring at her so intently.

"I can't," Viola replied with a shake of her head.

"Can't? Or won't?" Caroline pushed.

"I promised. I can't say anymore," Viola whispered.

"You haven't said anything except 'mmm' and then grinned inanely."

Had she? *Shit*.

"Your face always gives everything away." Caroline smirked. "Especially when you are smiling like the Cheshire cat."

"For fuck's sake, Caroline. Look, I can't say anything. She trusts me," Viola whispered. She then made her way into the great hall to end the conversation.

"Okay, I won't make you break a trust," Caroline said quietly as she followed behind. "I'll assume — from looking at her — that her uptight cute butt is overcompensating for something, and she might not be as straight as she makes out."

Viola glanced at Gillian's perfect backside across the hall, her gaze lingering longer than intended. She quickly averted her eyes, feeling a flush of heat in her cheeks again.

∾

"Why didn't you mention you were invited?" Gillian whispered to Bridget as they entered the great hall.

"Why didn't you?"

"In case you hadn't been."

"Likewise," Bridget countered.

Gillian pursed her lips. The likelihood of a scenario where Bridget was invited and she not was highly improbable.

A tightness gripped her throat as she took in her surroundings. She'd only made it as far as the kitchen when she stopped for coffee with Viola and hadn't been into the great hall itself since that last day. It felt like an eternity ago.

"Are you okay?"

"Yes, of course," Gillian replied, her tone sharper than intended. Catching the look of disbelief on Bridget's face, she softened and admitted, "Well, maybe it is a little unsettling to be back."

"It would be," Bridget said, placing a comforting hand on her arm.

Gillian turned, looking for her host, only to see her enter the hall with Caroline. Viola was breathtaking. The sight of her at the door overwhelmed Gillian, leaving her unsteady on her feet. Now, she watched as Viola walked towards her, the dark-green fabric of her dress shimmering under the chandelier. It was magnificent; the colour accentuated her rich hair, and the low V-neck drew Gillian's eye down to her cleavage, leaving her feeling guilty for peeking.

The sound of phone alerts pinged, pulling Gillian's attention away. Her hand shot into her bag as quickly as Bridget's went into hers to retrieve their phones.

"I do apologise," Gillian directed at Viola, knowing how impolite it was to be checking her phone. "It's the flower show tomorrow, and a minor leak in the roof of the village hall was brought to our attention this morning."

Bridget looked to Gillian, having read the message. "Oh, Gillian, what do we do?"

"How bad is it?" Viola asked, approaching Gillian with concern.

"It appears that the minor leak has become a major leak. It was rotten, and we now have a hole in the roof."

"Will we have to cancel the show?" Bridget asked.

"I don't know. The weather looks awful again

tomorrow, so the village green isn't an option. We may have to."

Gillian looked to Viola. She didn't want to ask, but with months of hard work put in by the villagers, she knew she must.

"Look, why don't you hold the flower show here?" Viola said with a shrug. "I won't be around tomorrow anyway as I'm flying Caroline back to London. Mrs Johnson can let you in early; she'll be clearing up from tonight."

Gillian pressed her hand to her stomach at the offer only to realise it may not have been genuine. Viola may have sensed she was about to ask and decided to get ahead of her. Either way, she couldn't say no. "Are you sure?"

"Yes," Viola said, placing a hand on Gillian's arm. "Now let's have some champagne. You both look like you could use a glass… or two."

"Thank you," Gillian mouthed, taking a glass from Viola.

The soft smile she received in return nearly stole her breath. She bit back her own grin, taking a small sip of champagne to cover it. Feeling strangely light-headed already, she knew she would need to limit her alcohol intake this evening if she was going to be in any fit state for her early start.

"We should go through to the dining room," Viola said, gesturing to a door off the great hall. "I was informed that dinner will be served promptly at seven thirty."

Gillian smiled with fondness, remembering Mrs Johnson's strict schedules.

Viola directed them to their seats, placing Gillian beside herself.

Although the usual small talk commenced over dinner, Gillian found it difficult to focus on, or engage, in it. Memories from the afternoon she had ridden with Viola resurfaced, as they had done many times over the last few days. With the woman sitting next to her, it was difficult to ignore them and push them away this time. The soft sound of laughter from Viola at a joke Caroline had told reminded Gillian of her enjoyment as they rode across the fields. Her laughter had been so genuine, so infectious.

Gillian recalled pressing into her back as she held the reins, supporting herself with her legs, grounding Viola to Dudley as his powerful hooves propelled them through the fields of Kingsford. The sensation of Viola's body against hers as it tensed and relaxed during their ride lingered in her mind, as did her scent.

"You're very quiet this evening," Viola said, her voice low.

Noticing Caroline and Bridget were engaged in a conversation about the logistics of organising a concert, Gillian replied, "Am I?" She took the last bite of a particularly delicious lemon torte and placed her fork down. Mrs Johnson had outdone herself.

"Unusually so. You normally have an opinion on most things," Viola teased.

Gillian narrowed her eyes at her host, following it up with a tightening of her lips.

"Is it being here?" Viola whispered, leaning forward.

"No," Gillian swiftly denied. Noticing Viola's raised eyebrow, she realised she couldn't fool her. "Okay, it is a little strange. I'm sure it's something to which I will become accustomed."

Viola's expression softened; her eyes filled with understanding. "I, for one, am glad you are here."

A warming sensation spread through Gillian's body. "Me too."

The conversation shifted back to the table, with Bridget probing Caroline on the ins and outs of being an agent to some of the country's top musicians.

With the cheeseboard wiped clean, Viola suggested they go to the drawing room for drinks. Gillian was so close behind her that she noticed a light freckling on her bare shoulders, as delicate as the ones on her face. Her skin looked soft and inviting, captivating Gillian's attention until they entered the room and an unexpected change in the atmosphere pulled her attention away.

A new fabric adorned the windows, and matching cushions were scattered on the Chesterfields. Light and modern, it brought a refreshing feel to the room, a stark contrast to the dark, oppressive atmosphere that had once filled the room. Gillian felt a twinge of nostalgia mixed with a feeling of unease. She traced her fingers along the arm of the familiar Chesterfield, its leather smooth and cool under her touch.

Bridget's hand rested on her shoulder, offering a brief, reassuring squeeze. Gillian nodded in acknowledgment, appreciating the silent support of her friend, who had an uncanny knack for understanding her lately. The small yet grounding gesture reminded her that she wasn't entirely alone, even in this unfamiliar version of her own space.

Bridget took a seat next to her as Viola placed herself

on the other sofa opposite Gillian. Caroline admired the room, popping her wine glass onto the mantelpiece.

Looking at the fireplace, Gillian realised the painting above it was different.

Viola seemed to notice and said, "I found that in the attic and thought it was rather thought-provoking. I hope you didn't leave it by accident. I assumed it was one of the items you wanted to leave with the house."

"No, not at all. Sorry, I should have thrown it away rather than leave it up there. Jonathon had a brief compulsion of wasting money on hideous, worthless artwork."

She remembered telling Jonathon that she had thrown it out, along with the other paintings he bought, when in truth she had stashed them away in the attic. They might be junk, but the frames were reusable, and this one particularly was so old and beautiful that she hoped she might be able to repurpose it in the manor one day.

"I'm glad you didn't throw them away. I rather like this one," Viola said, giving the artwork of a woman stabbing a man in the back an admiring eye.

"That reminds me, Gillian," Caroline said. "Are there any priest holes in the building?"

"Not to my knowledge. I wouldn't expect there to be either, considering the Carmichaels were Church of England," Gillian replied, her tone clipped.

"Oh, yes, right." Caroline's fingers fidgeted with the stem of her wine glass.

"So, Viola," Bridget added quickly, "how did you and Caroline meet?"

It felt like an odd question to Gillian; she made it sound like they were a couple.

Caroline walked behind Viola and placed her hands on her shoulders.

"Now that is a story that we can't disclose. Let's just say a famous singer brought us together."

"That's a shame," Bridget said. "We love a bit of gossip, don't we, Gillian?"

"We certainly do not," Gillian scowled.

Her eyes shot to Viola, embarrassed she might think her a gossip, only to see Viola lift her hand to her shoulder and tap on Caroline's hand. It took her by surprise and made her shift in her seat. Was she reading everything wrong? Were Viola and Caroline, in fact, a couple? Viola spoke affectionately about Caroline. She also said she didn't trust anyone enough to have a relationship, a long-term relationship more specifically. Could it just be sex? The thought unsettled her more than she liked. What did she care about who Viola had sex with? Even so, the idea gnawed at her.

Caroline collected her glass from the mantelpiece and sat next to Viola. "So, Gillian," Caroline said. "I understand you're organising the summer ball for Viola?"

Slipping her shoes off, she tucked her feet onto the seat and leaned an arm against the back of the Chesterfield, her body turned towards her friend. The sight of Viola and Caroline's easy intimacy stirred feelings of jealousy inside her.

"She has kindly bestowed me that favour." She glanced at Viola with a knowing look; Viola returned it with a playful glint in her eyes.

"Doesn't that make her your boss?" Caroline sniggered.

"Oh, yes. It kind of does, Gillian," Bridget put in with a mischievous grin.

Gillian coughed on her wine, just managing to speak as she recovered. "It's purely voluntary. I can withdraw services at any time."

"I'll do well to remember that," Viola shot back with a wink that made Gillian cough again.

"When do we get to hear you sing again, Viola? Any performances planned?" Bridget asked.

Gillian noticed Viola's face fell flat at the question. She remained silent, and Caroline answered for her.

"She is singing at the Proms in September."

"Oh, exciting! I'll be sure to watch."

Viola mustered a smile for Bridget, though Gillian could see it wasn't genuine. She caught Viola's eye and gave her a soft smile, receiving one back.

Bridget yawned and covered her mouth quickly. "Sorry. I'm afraid I'd better head off," she said, draining her glass and standing. "I need to prepare some signs before I go to bed to redirect people from the village hall. There won't be time in the morning."

Viola leaned forward to place her glass on the table, the movement inadvertently offering Gillian a glimpse down the neckline of her dress. The curve of her cleavage was impossible to ignore. Gillian's eyes darted away as soon as she realised she was staring.

"I'll see you out, Bridget," Viola said, her dress sweeping around her, showing off her attractive shape as she passed Gillian.

Gillian watched as they left the room, a flush creeping up her neck.

"It must be strange for you to be here, with someone else as hostess?" Caroline said as soon as they were alone.

"I bear it the best I can," Gillian admitted. Her voice was tinged with wistful resignation as she glanced around the room, taking in the familiar yet altered surroundings. "I spent years making this house a home. Every corner, every detail was a part of me. Seeing it now, it's like looking at a stranger wearing my clothes. Not that Viola hasn't done a good job," she conceded.

Caroline gave her a sympathetic smile. "Viola has a distinctive style, that's for sure."

It left Gillian feeling like a relic of the past, an echo in a building she once ruled.

"She seems quite taken with you... as a friend," Caroline continued. Her tone was neutral, yet her eyes were probing.

Gillian looked away, unsettled by where the conversation was going. It felt rather like Caroline was marking her territory. "Does she?"

Caroline nodded, her gaze still fixed. "She speaks fondly of your time together. It's good she has you... to guide her, especially with the ball."

"Mmm. I'm always happy to help a *friend* where I can," Gillian replied, her voice carefully controlled as she looked back at her.

Caroline opened her mouth to speak again, just as Viola appeared in the doorway.

"I'd best head off too," Gillian said quickly.

Having had more to drink than she intended and

spending the entire evening battling waves of jealousy over the manor and Viola, she was beginning to grow weary of maintaining a cheerful front.

"Of course," Viola replied.

Gillian directed a nod in Caroline's direction as she joined Viola by the door. "It was nice to meet you."

"Likewise. I do hope we meet again."

"Caroline seems nice," Gillian said as she and Viola walked back through the great hall. "She's obviously good for you. I'm happy for you both."

"Happy for us?" Viola chuckled. "You make us sound like a couple."

"Are you not?"

"Good god, no," Viola replied. "Older women are my type, yes, but not Caroline. Plus, she's into men."

"Oh," Gillian replied, relief washing over her at the confirmation, only for a tightness in her stomach to grab hold at how much it meant to her.

As they reached the porch, Viola turned to Gillian. "I hope everything was to your liking this evening."

"Oh, everything was perfect," Gillian assured her, the words feeling heavy on her tongue. "You've done an excellent job."

Viola's eyes sparkled with gratitude. "Thank you. That means a lot coming from you. Thank you for coming."

"I appreciate the invitation — and for saving my skin with the flower show. Might I see you tomorrow?"

"I hope I'll return before you finish."

Gillian couldn't contain her smile as she stepped outside. "Well, good night."

"Good night."

As she turned to leave, Viola called out, her voice carrying a note of uncertainty. "Oh, Gillian?"

Gillian swivelled quickly on her stiletto. "Yes?"

"It's just… I have the helicopter for the whole weekend and a table booked for lunch on Sunday at a rather delightful restaurant in the Surrey Hills. Would you join me?"

"I'd love to."

"It was for Caroline and me, but with her "

"I said yes," Gillian cut off a flustered Viola.

"Oh, great," Viola replied, lowering her head and kicking at the gravel. "Knock for me at about eleven thirty?"

"I look forward to it," Gillian replied, turning and continuing the precarious journey across the gravel drive in her high heels.

When she put her key into the front door of the lodge a few minutes later, she gulped, realising that Viola meant she would be flying them to the restaurant. She pushed the thought from her mind. First, she needed to get the flower show done and dusted; then she would worry about that.

Stepping into the lodge, she blew out a deep breath. She couldn't deny the excitement bubbling inside her at the thought of lunch with Viola. It mingled with a complex array of emotions that Viola stirred within her. There was an undeniable pull, a magnetic force that drew her closer to Viola despite her best efforts to remain detached.

She also couldn't ignore the way her heart quickened around Viola, the way her thoughts kept drifting back to their time together. It felt like more than a friendship, yet admitting that, even to herself, was a step she wasn't ready to take.

CHAPTER 14

Gillian knocked hard on the door of Kingsford Manor. Stepping back, she wondered if it would ever get easier with time, if the pain of her loss would ever subside. Each visit brought back a flood of memories and, with it, an ache in her chest that felt as fresh as the day she left.

She took a deep breath and steadied herself. Spending so much time in the manor the day before, organising the flower show and welcoming the guests had all felt so natural. After clearing up she'd almost taken herself upstairs for a shower until Bridget reminded her she no longer lived there.

Viola opened the door with a smirk. "Gillian! Fashionably late, I see."

"Indeed. I hope I'm dressed appropriately. I wasn't sure what one wears for a helicopter ride crossed with a posh lunch."

Gillian smoothed her hands over the soft fabric of her

navy midi dress, the delicate spray of white blossoms creating an elegant contrast against the deep blue. The v-neckline dipped just enough to reveal a hint of cleavage as the hem swayed gently in the light breeze around her knees.

"Unlike a horse, it doesn't come with a uniform. You look perfect."

"Thank you. You look… lovely too," Gillian said, admiring a little too intensely Viola's white shirt tucked neatly into a pair of blue chinos.

"Thanks. I'd rather be in a summer dress like you, but it's not very practical for flying a helicopter, and the matching footwear wouldn't work."

Gillian watched Viola reach for a grey linen blazer hanging on a hook and slip it on. Her bust was testing the very edges of her shirt as she stretched her arms through the sleeves and pulled her hair out from the collar. It did nothing to help Gillian's composure, especially in the warm sunshine. Fanning herself with her hand, she tried to think of anything to distract herself.

"Err, you were back late yesterday. I thought you were just dropping off Caroline."

"I was. I thought it would be best to give you some space. The last thing you needed was me breathing down your neck. I wanted you to be comfortable to do your thing."

"Thank you. I appreciate it," Gillian lied. She was disappointed that Viola hadn't made an appearance during the show, even though she would have felt like a spare part and only served to distract Gillian. "And thank you again for coming to my rescue."

"You're welcome. Did it all go okay?"

"About the same as it always does with Elouise and Louisa picking up most of the prizes, much to the annoyance of the rest of the villagers. If only everyone would put in the same time and effort as those two do at Kingsford House, then they, too, may hold a rosette."

"Sounds controversial."

"It always is, but I brook no questioning," Gillian said firmly. "My decision is final."

A smile danced on Viola's lips and her eyes shone as she stepped outside. "Oh, I bet you don't."

Gillian's face flushed at her impish tone.

"Let's walk around to the back. I've already locked up everywhere else," Viola directed as she closed the front door and locked it.

"Everyone was very grateful to be back here, especially when we were besieged by rain," Gillian said, following Viola through the garden. "You've made yourself even more popular amongst the villagers. You know, if you wanted to stump up for the renovations on the village hall, I'm sure we could arrange a name change to Berkley Hall. We could go a step further and change the village name to Berkley."

Gillian felt a nudge in her side, sending a pleasant tingle through her.

"Ha ha! I suppose you can turn your attention to arrangements for the ball now?"

"Yes," she confirmed with a smile. "Although everything is already booked."

"Efficient as always."

"Fail to prepare — "

"And prepare to fail," Viola finished. "Trust you to quote that."

Gillian grinned at how well Viola knew her already. Her grin disappeared as the helicopter came into sight on the lawn. She gulped at the thought of being in it and thousands of feet in the air at any minute, with nothing else between them and the ground.

She pushed the unhelpful thoughts aside; they only added to the anxiety of having lunch with Viola. It wasn't as if she hadn't already had lunch with her, and yet something was making her heart race and her stomach a little queasy. She made a quick job of convincing herself it was simply the helicopter.

"Right, shall we?" Viola said, opening the door for Gillian and offering her a hand.

"Thanks." Gillian took her hand and stepped into the cockpit. She navigated her way around a stick — the steering gear, she presumed — and sat down.

"Buckle up while I do the walk-around."

Gillian did as instructed as Viola shut the door and disappeared. Taking in her surroundings of levers, buttons, and screens, Gillian wondered what they all did. When Viola reappeared, she climbed in beside her, lifting a clipboard and iPad from her own seat. Gillian watched as she wrote on the clipboard and tapped at her iPad, interacting with the screen and touching buttons on the instrument panel and above her head. Her hands and feet moved to the pedals and controls, pushing and moving them as if testing them out.

Viola put on a headset and passed one to Gillian. "Put this on so we can hear each other. I need to check you are secure." She pulled at the straps on Gillian's harness and inspected the buckle. "I need to check the door too." She leaned around Gillian, her body brushing against her as she stretched to look at the lock.

Gillian instinctively pulled herself back, holding her breath as Viola leaned closer.

"Okay, we're all good to go. Ready?" Viola asked, popping on her sunglasses.

Gillian nodded as she exhaled, feeling her heart rate pick up as Viola's musky scent lingered in the air and she realised how much she was taking in. It did nothing to help her nervous disposition.

The helicopter's rotors began to spin, sending a gentle vibration through the cabin. As they lifted off the ground, a sense of weightlessness washed over her. The noise of the rotors was a constant, throbbing hum, filling her ears through the headset as she focused on the view outside.

Viola looked impressive as she manoeuvred the helicopter, her hands steady on the stick. Her focus was steadfast, scanning the instrument panel, fingers making minute adjustments to the controls as the rotor blades whirred rhythmically, slicing through the air with precision.

Gillian peered down out of the window as the helicopter ascended smoothly, the buildings below became smaller and smaller. She placed a hand on her stomach, feeling a little queasy. When she took a deep breath, it didn't go unnoticed.

"Everything is fine," Viola said through her headset. "I'm a good pilot. Trust me."

Gillian nodded. She did. Even though she'd never fully

trusted anyone besides herself, she had complete faith in Viola's abilities.

They remained silent during the flight, with Viola occasionally talking to someone Gillian could only assume was air traffic control. She took the opportunity to admire the breathtaking view of the South Downs, with its undulating surface covered in a patchwork of woodlands, hills, and fields. She felt an incredible sense of freedom as if she were detached from the world below, soaring effortlessly through the air.

They couldn't have been in the air more than ten minutes before they began descending. The weightlessness gave way to a slight pressure as the landscape below loomed larger.

Gillian stole a glance at Viola; her concentration never wavered as she skilfully navigated their descent onto a large expanse of grass in front of a Victorian mansion.

As Viola commenced what appeared to be shutdown checks, Gillian took the opportunity to collect herself. She automatically moved the sun visor, hoping to find a mirror, then felt foolish as she remembered she was in a helicopter. When Viola was finished, she shot around to Gillian's side and opened the door for her, holding out a hand to assist her.

"Enjoyable? Or are you ordering a taxi to take you home?" Viola asked, as they joined the path from the lawn to the restaurant.

Gillian thought before answering. "It was tolerable, I suppose." She hadn't exactly enjoyed it, but it hadn't been as bad as she was expecting. Like a plane, the takeoff and landing had been the most terrifying, but they were over swiftly.

Viola's forehead furrowed as her eyebrows lifted playfully. "Only tolerable? Maybe I should call you that taxi."

"I'm sure I can find it tolerable and still request a ride home." Gillian grinned.

"Let's see how you behave in the restaurant first," Viola teased, nudging her shoulder into Gillian's. "It's Michelin-starred, so none of your rudeness or I'll call you a taxi myself."

There was a time when she would have objected to such a statement, yet now, she found herself smiling at Viola's gentle teasing.

A doorman greeted them at the entrance to the restaurant and led through several oak-panelled corridors with high, ornate, moulded ceilings and crystal chandeliers. A waiter seated them at a table overlooking the lawn and the helicopter.

They exchanged awkward smiles as they took their seats at the beautifully laid table for two. Not wishing to add to the giddiness she was still feeling from the helicopter ride, Gillian ordered an orange juice from the waiter when he returned a few minutes later.

"Would you prefer something stronger?" Viola questioned. "Please don't feel like you can't partake because I'm not."

"I'm feeling a little light-headed from the flight," Gillian replied, hoping it was simply that and had nothing to do with the beautiful woman across the table, who was currently removing her blazer. A hot sweat washed over her, and she picked up the menu to fan herself. She needed to get a grip. Feelings like the ones Viola just caused were a thing of the past and needed to stay there. "So," Gillian continued, desperately trying to think of something to distract herself, "flying… is it even called flying if it isn't in a plane?"

Viola raised an eyebrow at her.

Gillian could have slipped under the table and never come out. Why did she say that? Why was her brain all mushy?

"I suppose we could call it 'helicoptering' if you think that works better. Traditionally it's called flying."

The heat searing through her intensified from embarrassment. "Oh yes. Of course."

"Are you okay, Gillian?" Viola said as she tracked the ever-faster-moving menu. "You look a bit red."

Gillian put the menu down and stood up. "Yes, fine, thank you. I'll just nip to the…" She trailed off, spotting a directional sign for the lavatories.

Grabbing her handbag, she headed towards it. Her head was heavy and her mind fuzzy. Reaching the toilets, she stood in front of a mirror and took deep breaths. She desperately wanted some cold water on her face. Knowing it would ruin her make-up, she settled for washing her hands instead.

A woman appeared from one of the cubicles and their eyes met in the mirror. The woman, who bore a vague familiarity Gillian couldn't place, flashed her a smile. Gillian returned it and focused on washing the soap off her hands as the woman washed hers. Catching a brief look at her in the mirror, Gillian noticed she was still smiling to herself. She looked genuinely happy and at ease.

Gillian tried to recall if she had ever felt like that in the previous years — or decades even. What did one have to do in life to have such a smile on one's face? She recalled the brief moment when she had thought the manor was all hers; she had felt genuine happiness then, until it was ripped from her clutches.

Throwing her damp towel in the laundry bin, she turned to leave, giving a final glance towards the still-smiling woman. Navigating her way back to the table she racked her brain, trying to place her.

"The dry cleaners," Gillian muttered as she retook her seat opposite Viola. Their drinks had arrived, so she took a refreshing sip of orange juice.

"Dry cleaners?" Viola asked, a questioning eyebrow raised.

"I saw a woman in the lavatories. I couldn't place her at first, but now I realise she's the woman you helped with her dry cleaning."

"Oh, Sydney Mackenzie?"

Gillian shrugged, unable to recall her name.

"I wonder if she is here with her wife," Viola said, her eyes darting around the restaurant.

"Ah, yes, the famous actress," Gillian said dryly, recalling that Viola had mentioned her before. "Is this considered a celebrity hangout then?"

She watched Viola, who was now straining her neck to get a look at everyone. It was an interesting notion that even people who were celebrities could fluster at the sight of a "bigger" celebrity.

"It's a Michelin-starred restaurant. If it's not celebrities, it's wealthy people who see themselves as celebrities. Ah, look, over there." Viola nodded behind Gillian.

Gillian turned to look, only for Viola to hiss.

"Try and be subtle about it! Celebrities always know when someone is staring no matter how much you try to hide it." Viola threw her napkin to the side of Gillian's chair. "Oops, careless me. Could you get that for me?"

Burying the urge to suggest Viola herself was being less than subtle, Gillian pushed her chair back with a grin and picked up the napkin. Lingering for a moment, she looked behind her. She spotted Sydney and arched a little more to get a look at her supposedly stunningly beautiful companion, if she recalled Viola's words correctly. Maybe that was the reason for Sydney's immovable smile.

Did Gillian need to find a new love for herself? No one was likely to want her, penniless and on the wrong side of fifty; any beauty she retained was bound to fade in the coming years. Without the manor she wasn't likely to be moving in the right circles to pick up an eligible bachelor; she wasn't likely be moving in any circles anymore, and there was no man in Kingsford she would touch. Frankly, there wasn't a man anywhere she would want to touch.

Leaning a little further, she could feel her balance tipping unfavourably. Before she could grab the table to steady herself, she fell onto the floor. Grappling quickly to get up as her face flushed with heat, she looked towards Beatrice Russell to see if she'd noticed, only to find piercing blue eyes glaring back at her. The woman held a certain presence about her, although she looked a bit up herself for Gillian's liking. She soon turned her attention back to Sydney.

Realising the entire restaurant was silent and staring at her tempted Gillian into running from the room. Instead, she sat back down only to find Viola was visibly shaking with laughter behind the drinks menu. Two brown eyes appeared over the top of it.

"Yes, I'm fine, thank you," Gillian growled whilst holding a false smile on her face, which she directed at the other clientele to reassure them all was well.

"Sorry, I'm going to need... a minute," Viola said, holding a finger up, unable to keep her mirth restrained.

Gillian cast her eyes heavenward. "When you are quite finished."

Viola took some deep breaths, blowing each one out slowly. "Did you get a look at her during your pirouette? She's very beautiful, isn't she?"

"She is, but she has nothing on yo — " Gillian bit her bottom lip and then quickly added, "You, for example, or even her wife. You are both plain and simple."

Raising an eyebrow, Viola questioned, "Plain and simple?"

Gillian waved a dismissive hand. "Oh, you know what I mean."

"Oh no, you'll need to explain that one." Viola smirked.

"I mean that there is more beauty in the subtle, the understated, and the quietly profound; a quiet allure that whispers to you gradually and invites rather than demands your attention. It possesses a kind of grace that lingers in one's mind."

The soft curve of Viola's smile and the gentle sparkle in her eyes were an exact example of the details that captivated Gillian, a beauty that grew deeper with every glance.

"Good save, and thank you, I guess."

Taking a gulp of her drink, Gillian immediately regretted not having asked for something stronger. The waiter returned to take their lunch order; Gillian was grateful for the interruption and the opportunity to change the subject once he left.

"Tell me, what made you want to learn to fly?"

"I spent a lot of time being flown around in a plane," Viola explained. "I'm not one for chartering a private jet for myself, so I would always fly commercial. I got fed up with the cancelled flights, sitting around in airport lounges. I thought there must be a better way of getting around. I can have a helicopter to me within half an hour at Kingsford and be in Paris in an hour and a half. I can't completely avoid planes for long hauls, but helicopters work well for getting around once I'm there."

"Why not hire a pilot?"

"Where's the fun in that?"

Gillian shrugged; she couldn't argue with that.

"I considered buying a helicopter, then realised it's too much hassle to keep and maintain. Now I have one at the touch of a button. The company I use is happy for me to fly anything I'm licensed for. When I toured Australia, Mum came with me, and I hired a helicopter to get us both around. She loved it."

"Can I ask how she died?" Gillian asked cautiously.

"An aneurysm. She was all alone in my penthouse at the time." Viola gazed into the distance and repeated softly. "All alone."

Gillian found her hand reaching forward and resting on Viola's. She was about to withdraw it, then forced herself not to. She could offer some sympathy without it meaning anything.

"They said she didn't stand a chance, even if I had been there. Nothing could have saved her; it was a ticking time bomb."

Viola's gaze drifted to the window as Gillian's thumb unconsciously stroked her hand.

"Can I ask something else?" Gillian said, breaking the silence.

"Full of questions today, aren't we?" Viola replied, returning her attention with a tone laced with teasing amusement.

Gillian narrowed her eyes slightly, a hint of a smirk playing on her lips as she tilted her head. "Just curious."

"Go on," Viola encouraged.

"I was going to ask how your parents took you being a…"

"A lesbian?" Viola finished for her with a raised eyebrow.

"Yes." Gillian hadn't quite been able to get the word out herself.

"Initially it was quite a shock as they read about it in the newspaper."

Gillian's face dropped in horror. "Oh."

"I guess you missed that."

"I'm not one for newspapers. Jonathon always read them. I made good use of them in the cat's litter tray."

"That's definitely where they belong." Viola laughed. "My dad was too drunk to care about anything, and my mum was shocked, more so that I hadn't confided in her."

"How did your coming out make it to the newspaper?"

"I didn't come out. I was forced out."

Realising her hand was still on Viola's, Gillian patted it and withdrew it. "I'm sorry."

"My girlfriend at the time…" Viola stopped as if trying to find the right word. "Let's just say I don't think we were a good match, and as with these things, you don't find out until it's too late. She wanted more from our relationship and thought she was owed some status from being my girlfriend, without a thought of how it would affect me. This was a long time ago; the world was a different place, yet… I still don't think we have progressed that much."

Gillian hummed her agreement as Viola continued.

"I refused to come out. I didn't want my sexuality to become the focus of my career. I'm a singer who happens to be a lesbian, not a lesbian singer. She decided I needed a bit of a push and leaked it to the media. She arranged for photographers to be outside a restaurant she took me to on our first anniversary, then kissed me in full sight of them."

Gillian grimaced.

"She denied all knowledge of setting it up," Viola continued. "I later found out through another friend that it was her, and I ended it."

"Couldn't you deny it, claim it was a platonic kiss?"

"I wasn't going to lie; I wasn't ashamed of who I was. I just didn't trust others to be able to see past it. I was right, and my career took a knock for a few years. I worked hard, put all my energy into it, and it became less of an issue eventually. Old news, you might say."

"I can see why you've avoided relationships. It must be hard to trust again after that."

"It is hard to get past that kind of betrayal. That's when I began a relationship with alcohol instead. It was easier than with people; at least you knew where you were with it. Looking back, it would've been easier to avoid both, but with alcohol, you knew what it cost you; you knew how you would feel the morning after. Everything was quantifiable."

Gillian nodded. It made perfect sense.

"Whilst we're asking questions," Viola said, leaning back as the waiter placed their plates down, "what got you into horse riding?"

"My mother's insistence. I was quite resistant to begin with."

"Why?"

Gillian took a deep breath as she put her napkin on her lap. It felt silly to admit it now. With Viola's eyes fixed and demanding, she answered truthfully. "I was scared of them."

"Really?" Viola said with a hint of surprise.

"Yes, really," Gillian echoed back.

"Sorry, it just seems odd when you are such a natural with Dudley. What made you overcome your fear?"

"Hen. I saw her passion for them. She trusted them, and I trusted her."

Viola smiled. "Why was your mum keen for you to learn to ride?"

Gillian hesitated as she stabbed a new potato with her fork. Was she about to reveal her whole past, to Viola? She knew she was in safe hands. The most she was likely to receive from her was some light teasing, which she secretly found enjoyable. "You must have heard the term 'Fake it until you make it'."

"Of course. I was guilty of a bit of that in my early career."

"My mother lived by that… with good reason. Not that I appreciated it at the time. My current position has forced me to become humble in some respects, and I can see she was trying to do her best."

"What were you faking exactly?"

A reassuring smile from across the table encouraged Gillian on.

"Our position in society. My father was a successful man, and we were comfortable by the day's standard. He was an accountant — until he went through a breakdown. I would say he recovered, but he was never the same again. He couldn't work as an accountant anymore; he struggled with any work, to be honest. He managed to get a job working for the council as a bin man; it worked for him. I remember him telling me he found peace in the simplicity of a physical task. The fact it would knock him out at the end of a shift no doubt helped."

Viola's eyebrows lifted as she took a sip from her glass. "Oh."

"I didn't even care that I got teased at school for it. I was happy that he'd found some peace. My mother, on the other hand, wasn't someone to disappoint, and being married to a bin man wasn't what she had planned. If that wasn't embarrassing enough for my mother, one day he up and left. She was mortified — not that he left, more so about what the neighbours would think."

Viola nodded. "Being a single mum in those days wasn't the done thing."

"Exactly. For a while, she claimed he'd got a job working away. When he never returned to visit, it became harder to keep up with the lies. People notice things, and they gossip. We moved to an area where people didn't know us, and she claimed she was a widow. There was a whole new set of people for her to impress."

"Did that help?"

"Moving didn't stop us being poor. That's something that follows you everywhere. Even into your bed when you're freezing because you can't afford heating. I was entitled to free school dinners at school, but my mother was too embarrassed to allow it. She didn't want the other children telling their parents we were poor. I got a lunchbox with barely enough to feed a pigeon. She would rather her child went hungry than lose face."

"God. I'm sorry, Gillian."

"It didn't help that she would buy things we didn't need, with money we didn't have, to impress people she didn't even like."

"Is this how you met Hen?"

Gillian nodded, swallowing her mouthful before answering. "Riding lessons were her attempt to mix me with what she called 'the right sort of person'. Hen's parents owned the riding school."

"Ah, yes, you mentioned that before. You didn't meet her at school then?"

"No. Hen was a day student at a nearby private school. No matter how much my mother wanted to pretend, she couldn't afford private school fees. She would tell people she wanted me to have a more natural upbringing and to learn to socialise with people from all walks of life. She supported our friendship, urging me to spend time with Hen's family and join them for weekend events when I was invited. She hoped Hen would 'rub off' on me."

Viola smirked and then covered her mouth. "Oh, sorry, Gillian."

A smile edged onto Gillian's lips as she realised what she'd said. "You know how that ended and how mortified she was when she found out about us. She believed she had caused it by pushing me towards Hen in the first place."

"I don't think it works like that. It's not the common cold."

"Precisely. We were two people who got along, a little too comfortably for my mother's liking. I was her ticket out of poverty, if only I would marry someone respectable. Hen, she…" Gillian sniffed and swallowed, trying to regain control of herself.

"Hen, was never part of *that* plan?" Viola finished for her.

"No." Gillian dabbed the corner of her eye with her serviette as she pretended to wipe her mouth. "I may have lost Hen, but that's one thing she left with me: a love for horses. After university, for which I was awarded a scholarship, I got a good job in PR. The salary was good, and I saved every penny to buy a horse."

"And that led you to stable the horse at Kingsford?" Viola questioned.

"Yes, where I met Jonathon. I rather fell on my feet as my mother said — repeatedly. At the age of thirty he was in danger of becoming a professional bachelor. As soon as he showed an interest in me, I encouraged him. I didn't stop to think about things like love. He made me laugh — to begin with, anyway. We got married before the end of the year. I believe he loved me to begin with, but over time I felt more like a prize he'd won and wanted to show off. I was fond of him, of course, but to me, he was an escape from poverty. I didn't need love then. I needed to not be poor. I'm not the first and I won't be the last to marry for those reasons."

Viola nodded her agreement. "Everyone has a different motive to get married."

Gillian smiled as she tucked into her sea bass, grateful for Viola's understanding rather than judgement of her actions.

"We worked well together for a time; then bitterness and resentment kicked in as we got older, and we grew apart. The money flowed less, and my looks… well, I wasn't twenty anymore."

"Gillian, you're still beautiful. I couldn't help noticing the photographs of a younger you on your windowsill. All you've done is blossom more."

Goosebumps tingled down every extremity of Gillian's body at her words. "That's kind of you to say — "

"It's the truth," Viola pressed. "I'm sorry for what I said to you, about being wealthy and entitled. Well… the wealthy bit. If I'd known about your backgrou — "

"It's fine. You didn't know. I haven't exactly been living in poverty since then, so yes, I have become a bit entitled. None of this is to go any further," Gillian said, reaching out and tapping the table.

Viola placed a hand on top of Gillian's. "Everything you say to me stays between us. I would hope the same goes the other way around too."

"Yes, of course."

Viola gestured between the two of them. "This is a safe space; you can tell me anything."

"You've heard it all now," Gillian said, retrieving her hand as she realised she was enjoying Viola's soft hand and caressing fingers a little too much.

"You seem embarrassed to have come from a poor background."

"I built a life at Kingsford, crafted it over decades. It would wipe away my last shred of dignity if people were to find out now. I would be a liar, an imposter."

"Is it not time for the real Gillian to step into the limelight and reveal who she really is?"

"No, I'm not sure it is. I've already lost so much; I can't risk losing the last remnants of my life."

"Do you even like this Gillian, the one you've crafted?" Viola asked, placing her knife and fork down on her empty plate.

"I don't dislike her. I've grown used to her over the years," Gillian replied, with a hint of defeat. "I had to."

"Like an old, worn-out pair of slippers that don't quite fit right?"

Gillian glared at Viola. "They may be worn, but they still fit comfortably."

"Yet they no longer support you properly."

"They still aren't ready to be discarded into the waste," Gillian bit back, hoping to stop the conversation in its tracks.

Viola had said Gillian could tell her anything, and she had, leaving nothing out. When had she become the person Gillian confided everything in? There was nothing left to share; Viola knew it all, from her unhappy childhood and marriage to her first love.

After they both declined dessert, Viola insisted on paying the bill. Gillian couldn't exactly argue with her. Having seen the prices on the menu when they had sat down, she'd calculated the maths in her head. She wasn't normally one for accepting handouts, but on this occasion she was happy to relent. It helped that Viola was extremely insistent that it was her treat.

As they were getting ready to leave, two women sat at a table behind them. One proceeded to speak to the other in a concerned voice about a Labrador with an upset stomach.

"He's probably eaten something he shouldn't have," the other woman replied nonchalantly. "It wouldn't be the first time."

"I'll call Freddie and check on him in a bit," came the reply.

"That's all you want to hear about whilst you're dining," Gillian said with a roll of her eyes, grateful they were leaving.

Viola frowned. "I know that voice." She turned and looked at the woman. "Arte Tremaine, is that you?"

The woman twisted around in her seat and then stood.

"Viola?"

Gillian watched as the two women embraced, feeling slightly jealous at their ease and close contact.

"What are you doing here?" Viola asked. "Last time I saw you was in Italy."

"I live in the area now. My gran died, and I took over her hotel."

"How sad. You aren't teaching anymore then?"

"I am," Arte confirmed. Turning to her companion and smiling, she added, "My wife, Charlotte, runs the hotel side of things for us."

Gillian and Viola nodded at her, receiving a smile and nod in return.

"Congrats."

"Thanks," Arte replied. "I have an art studio onsite in one of the old barns. If your mum needs a bit of respite, send her my way."

Viola looked down. "Mum passed away a few months back."

"Oh, I am so sorry," Arte said, rubbing Viola's upper arm.

"Thanks."

"You must be bereft without her."

Viola nodded. "I'm finding my way, day by day. Oh, this is my friend, Gillian Carmichael. I moved to the area recently, too, into Gillian's house, actually."

Gillian smiled at Arte, glad to finally be acknowledged.

"Oh, are you two an item then?" Arte asked.

"No," Gillian replied, her tone perhaps a bit too sharp and immediate.

"No," Viola reiterated with a gentle laugh. "Gillian

unwittingly sold it to me. She lives in the lodge now, so technically she's my neighbour too. It would be great to catch up sometime."

"Here, take my card." Arte reached into her phone case and extracted a business card.

"Thanks. I'll text you my number. I hope your dog is okay."

Arte rolled her eyes. "Rodin's a walking dustbin. He never learns."

Viola chuckled. "It was lovely to bump into you."

"And you," Arte said, taking her seat.

"How do you know her?" Gillian asked as soon as they were out of earshot.

"Mum and I spent about six months living in Italy whilst I was touring there. She broke her ankle on some cobbles the day after we arrived, so I rented a place in Rome for her to recuperate and act as a base for us. Arte lived in an apartment next door. She helped enormously, checking in on Mum when I wasn't around. They got on like a house on fire, and she taught Mum a bit of art to keep herself occupied. Mum turned out to be a natural at painting."

Viola's phone vibrated. "It's Caroline. I'd better take this, sorry."

"I'll meet you outside," Gillian said, nodding at the lavatories.

As she made her way towards them, she looked back at the two women to see them embracing Sydney and Beatrice like old friends. *What a small world.*

On her return, she found Viola outside.

"Everything okay?" Gillian asked as Viola hung up her phone.

"Caroline has booked *Country Life* Magazine to come and do a photoshoot of me at Kingsford later this week."

"That's a bit short notice, isn't it?"

"There was a cancellation. I was on the list, and Caroline agreed. She thought it would help keep me in the public eye while I've been taking a break from work."

Gillian frowned, and noticing the scared puppy look on Viola's face, a flicker of fury burned inside her. "I thought the idea was for rest and recuperation. Does Caroline not understand you aren't ready?"

"She believes there is only so much rest one needs. She doesn't want me to be out of the limelight for too long, and I get that. It's sweet that you worry for me, but this and the Proms will ease me back into work. Can I ask a favour?"

"Of course."

"Would you be there?" Viola asked softly.

"Me? Why?"

"For one, to support me… as my friend."

Gillian smiled at the word.

"Two, for authenticity," Viola continued.

"Authenticity?"

"I'm not you, Gillian. I don't have wardrobes full of country outfits, and I don't understand the demands of the countryside as you do. I worry I won't look the part without someone who knows how to look the part being there. Sorry if it's too much to ask. Don't answer now. Let's get home, and you can answer when you are ready. I assume you are coming with me and not taking a taxi?"

Gillian narrowed her eyes. "I'll risk it."

Viola grinned, looped her arm through Gillian's, and led them to the helicopter.

Was it too much to ask? For a friend to support another friend? Is that what they were, friends? The question sat in her mind as they flew back to Kingsford, Gillian now feeling more at ease in the cockpit and more comfortable with a person than she'd been in a long time. She already knew her answer, yet it would do no harm to make Viola wait — at least until they landed.

CHAPTER 15

Viola pressed her hand to her stomach. Nausea had lingered since Caroline's call about *Country Life* publishing an article on her. She'd never felt nerves like it, not even when she was performing for thousands of people. There were always a few butterflies beforehand but nothing like the last few days of feeling sick.

She knew why: Her performances she was prepared for; *Country Life* she wasn't. How could she be? She wasn't exactly a true model of what they were looking for. She was a wealthy woman who had bought a house in the South Downs and knew nothing of 'country life'.

She'd already spoken with the features editor earlier that week. The call came unexpectedly, leaving her no time to ask Gillian for support, so she answered the editor's questions honestly and concisely. Caroline had briefed the editor beforehand, suggesting that the article touch on Viola's time away from the spotlight and her journey through grief. The editor promised she could look over the article before it was published, but it was the photographs that concerned her the most.

With the photographer due any minute, there was nothing more she could do to prepare. Mrs Johnson had deep-cleaned the previous day, so all she needed now was Gillian's steady presence to hold her together, in the way only Gillian could.

The thought made her smile as she remembered Gillian toppling off her chair at the restaurant. Although she had managed to stifle her laughter behind the menu, Gillian's glare suggested she didn't fully appreciate it.

Viola was looking forward to seeing her again; it had been too long for her liking. Although her feelings for Gillian confused her, she was equally baffled by her behaviour. Was she overanalysing everything, thanks to Caroline's influence?

Having questioned her agent about her hands-on behaviour at their dinner together, she admitted that she'd tested the waters to see how Gillian reacted. Viola hadn't even noticed Gillian shifting uncomfortably, and yet Caroline had. When she disclosed that Gillian asked outright if they were a couple, Caroline of course gloated. The relief that crossed Gillian's face when she learnt they weren't couldn't be mistaken, but why? It wasn't possible that Gillian had any interest in her like that, surely. Maybe she didn't like Caroline and was relieved they weren't an item.

A knock at the door made her heart jump into her throat. When she looked at the time it was ten minutes before anyone was due. Gillian wouldn't be early, would she? Opening the door confirmed Viola's thought — no, she would not.

A short, balding man in his fifties or even sixties, with an unkempt beard, held his hand out. "Miss Berkley, a pleasure. I'm Colin, the photographer for *Country Life* Magazine. You are expecting us, I believe."

"Yes, come on in," Viola said, standing back for him to enter. Two young men followed him carrying equipment, then a young woman with what looked like a make-up bag. "Go through to the hall."

"Mind if we have a scout about?" Colin asked as he passed.

"Be my guest."

She contemplated calling Gillian to say the crew were early, only to hear gravel crunching up the drive and the woman herself marching down the drive toward her. All attempts to rein in her smile failed; nothing could contain her relief at the sight of Gillian.

"Typical," she said as she approached. "I heard them arrive… early."

She didn't catch the rest of Gillian's words; her imagination took over, urging her to silence the woman with a kiss and throwing Viola completely off balance in the process. "Are you well?" Gillian asked as she entered the porch.

"Nervous," Viola replied, though she realised her nerves were already dissipating.

Gillian faced her. "Don't be. I'm here now." She hung her handbag on a peg, extracting a notebook and pen. "I took the liberty of making a few notes."

"Great," Viola said as she led them through to the great hall, where her visitors were busy erecting equipment and setting up laptops on the banqueting table.

"Miss Berkley, I need you in make-up, and we need to discuss your outfit." He stopped to look at her, his eyes casting over her white shirt and blue chinos, which made her uncomfortable. "Actually, no need. What you are wearing is perfection."

She turned to Gillian — after all, it was her creation — only to find she was looking her over too. Her eyes lingered, thoughts seemingly miles away. This time it didn't make her feel uncomfortable; it made her feel all kinds of things — hot, sweaty, breathless, light-headed. She wasn't sure how much longer she could push away those feelings, to keep telling herself that they were nothing, that she wasn't falling in love with Gillian when that was exactly, precisely, completely, and utterly what she was doing.

"Gillian, this is Colin the photographer, and this is my — "

"Coffee, black, two sugars, dear. We had an early start," he said, giving Gillian nothing more than a cursory glance.

"I'll make that for you," Viola offered, noticing a slightly contorted appearance fall over Gillian's face.

"You are her PA?" Colin questioned Gillian with a crumpled forehead.

"I am not," Gillian scoffed. "I used to own Kingsford Manor, and I am here to support Viola in its presentation."

"That's what we're here for," he replied abruptly. "Now Viola, have you got an old tea set we can use? Anything will do as long as it's old."

Fearing her modern mugs wouldn't cut it, she looked to Gillian, hoping for help.

"And that is precisely why I am here," Gillian cut in, giving a satisfied lift to her chin. "I'll be back shortly."

Viola flashed her a smile as she passed her, mouthing a thank you. As Gillian had said, this was exactly why she had asked her to be on hand; she was the sort of woman who could find a solution to anything.

Gillian returned, carrying a heavy cardboard box, just as the make-up artist was adding the finishing touches to Viola's cheeks. Viola caught Gillian doing a double take at her, sending butterflies fluttering through her entire body.

Gillian turned pink and looked away, placing the box on the table and lifting tissue-paper-wrapped objects from inside. "Erm... do we need to fill it with tea?" she asked, her voice unsteady.

"We don't bother with that, dear." Colin laughed.

Viola cringed as Gillian visibly twitched at the word 'dear'.

"The camera can't see what's inside, can it?" he added.

Gillian's face twitched, probably at the lack of authenticity, which was amusing, considering her lack of it.

"Right, we'll have our first shot in the drawing room; those Chesterfields are perfection. Then we'll have one in the study with that beautiful desk," Colin barked. "James, set up the tea set."

One of the young men jumped to attention and approached Gillian, tentatively taking a cup and saucer from her. The items rattled a little as they passed between hands.

"I'll take them through for you," Gillian said, retaking them. "You can carry the teapot, with both hands."

"Good idea." James grasped it, taking considered steps towards the drawing room.

"Still nervous?" Gillian asked Viola as they followed.

Viola gulped, then nodded, feeling unsettled again.

"You must have done photoshoots before."

"Yes, of course, in gorgeous dresses with my hair glammed up. It's a far cry from this, being me."

"Imagine you're performing; exude the same confidence."

She was performing, just not in her natural habitat. This was tantamount to faking.

Colin looked around the room at the lights set up by the other young man, who had been introduced as Matt, and made minor adjustments to their positions. "Something is missing," he said, scratching his beard. "Can we get a fire lit? Add a bit of atmosphere?"

Viola looked to Gillian to ask for permission, only to realise it was her house. "Of course."

After several failed attempts by James to get a fire going, Gillian took over, and in seconds a fire was roaring in the hearth, much to the surprise of everyone except Viola.

Taking a seat on the Chesterfield where Colin directed her, Viola was immediately pounced on by the make-up lady who made some finishing touches. She began to feel a little claustrophobic with the heat of the fire radiating onto her and hoped she wasn't going to sweat through her shirt before the end of the shoot.

Colin crouched by the door, putting himself at eye level

with his camera as he directed her on how to hold the cup and saucer. She realised she was pulling a fake half smile and tried to change it, only to fail miserably.

"Look natural, like you've lived here for hundreds of years. Not you obviously, your ancestors."

Wondering if Colin would survive the comment, Viola's eyes drifted to Gillian, who stood by the door. Fury darkened her face. As their eyes met, Gillian's expression softened, making a smile form on Viola's mouth.

"Yes, that's it. Perfect." Colin took several photographs and then stood behind James at a laptop where they whispered until Colin shouted, "Okay, everyone, let's move to the next shot in the study."

The small room, by Kingsford's standards, housed a beautiful antique desk and shelves crammed with old books.

"Have you got some old family photographs we could use?" Colin asked, taking in the room. "Ideally sepia if you have any that old. They would look great on the desk."

She didn't. Her photographs extended to one of her mum taken shortly before her death, which sat on the mantelpiece in the drawing room. Whether there were some in her mum's belongings in storage, she wouldn't know until she was brave enough to go and sort through everything.

"I'll be back in five," Gillian said with an exasperated breath.

Viola's stomach tightened. She hoped this wasn't all too taxing for Gillian. She returned a few minutes later with a handful of old framed photographs Viola recognised from her sitting room in the lodge. It probably wasn't the time to ask after the identities of the sitters. Considering Gillian's childhood issues, she assumed they were members of Jonathon's family.

"Thank you, dear," Colin said, selecting two that looked similar in age, one of a man and the other of a woman.

"I am not a four-legged woodland creature, so do not address me as such," Gillian snapped. "The word is steeped in ageism and sexism, as are you, and it underscores your lack of respect. I'm not here to fit into whatever outdated assumptions you have about who deserves to be taken seriously. If you wish to address me, drop the 'dear' and use my name, Gillian, and speak to me with the respect you would give anyone else."

Viola found her hands clapping together, but upon receiving a glare from Gillian she stopped her applause immediately. All Colin could muster was an awkward nod before quickly moving on to directing the shot.

He positioned Viola so that she was leaning back in the chair with her feet on the desk, reading a copy of *Country Life*. Gillian's face was a picture. It wasn't as if Viola wouldn't clean the desk after. By the time they finished the set of shots, though, Gillian was nowhere to be seen.

When they reconvened in the great hall, Viola was relieved to see her sitting at the table. It wouldn't have surprised her if she'd left.

"I don't suppose you have a cap for that outfit," Colin enquired. "Maybe a walking staff? Pet dog?"

"I have a cat - well, Gillian has a cat. I'm sure it will be around here somewhere."

"Not quite the look we're going for. What about a

horse? You must have one of those," Colin said, his tone implying a touch of impatience.

Viola turned to Gillian, eyebrows strained, silently asking for help.

"Let me guess — *Gillian* has one of those," Colin answered for her, his sarcasm as unwelcome as ever.

"Indeed, *Gillian* does," Gillian replied coolly.

Realising this would require another change of trousers, Viola slipped away, returning five minutes later in her jodhpurs.

Colin gave her a once-over. "Have you not got a proper riding jacket?"

Viola looked at Gillian again, just as the woman rolled her eyes.

"I'm sure I have a jacket in the wardrobe from when I was younger — and thinner — that might fit you well."

As Gillian made to leave, Colin called out, "Could you show James where the stables are so he can set up?"

With a huff she left with James in tow, then returned with a shapely black velvet jacket that fitted Viola like a glove. She could have done without it in the hot summer air which currently suffocated Kingsford.

"Perfect," Colin said, admiring Viola. "Are you sure this isn't really your house, Gillian?" He chuckled.

Viola cringed, bracing herself for a response.

"It most definitely is not my house," Gillian snapped.

Colin pulled himself back and straightened his face. "Where's this horse then?"

Gillian marched outside, followed by everyone else. As Viola caught up to her, she realised she would have to ride

Dudley. As if sensing her unease, Gillian placed a hand on her back as they walked.

"I'll suggest we go into the paddock; at least it's familiar. Remember everything I taught you."

Viola nodded. She could walk Dudley around the paddock; she'd done it before.

The crew busied themselves arranging their equipment while Gillian tacked up Dudley. Agatha emerged from the stable and stretched. Approaching Dudley, she rubbed her head and then body against his leg. It surprised Viola that he didn't react. Instead, he lowered his head and appeared to nuzzle the cat's side, pulling on her heartstrings in the process.

"I'll stay close by in case you need me," Gillian whispered as she gestured for Viola to mount.

"Thank you."

Once mounted, she retraced the steps they had taken during her lesson. Gillian opened the gate ahead of her, then closed it once everyone was through. Colin called out directions, asking Viola to position Dudley in a certain spot for the 'perfect light' and 'perfect backdrop'.

She was sure Dudley was completely biddable; unfortunately, she failed to instruct him correctly, and the pressure made her more flustered. Every time Gillian stepped forward to try and assist, Colin called for her to get out of the shot.

"Left — no, not that left. The other left," Colin barked.

"I'm trying," Viola said through gritted teeth, biting back a sharper reply.

After fifteen minutes, Colin called time, and they returned to the stables, where Jason immediately held a laptop in front of Colin. Viola could only assume they were analysing the photographs of her and Dudley.

"We'll have to work with what we've got," he grumbled.

"You asked if I owned a horse, not if I could ride one," Viola said, jumping down, pleased to see Gillian close at hand should she need her.

"I assumed all country folk rode, regardless of horse ownership," Colin retorted.

The smile on Gillian's face as she removed Dudley's saddle didn't escape Viola's notice. She'd let her have that one.

"We could do with another external shot," Colin said. "Have you got some sort of outdoorsy vehicle? Although that car in the drive is very nice, it's not befitting the look we go for at *Country Life*. I thought I spotted an old Land Rover on the way in; that would be perfect."

Gillian rolled her eyes. "Give me five minutes."

"Thank you, Gillian," Viola called after her, wondering at what point the woman's patience would give out and she would snap completely.

"Calls for a wardrobe change, I'm afraid," Colin said, gesturing with his arm that they return to the house. "Reset on the drive," he called to his crew.

By the time Viola had changed back into her country attire, complete with her tweed cap, Gillian's Land Rover was in front of the house. This time she was more comfortable than in the previous shot. Standing beside a vehicle was more natural to her than riding a horse.

It appeared to suit Colin better too. He snapped away as she posed around the car.

"Perfect!"

If the man said perfect one more time, she may have to injure him.

"It suits you," Gillian said, nodding at the Land Rover as soon as Colin called the shot.

"It suits my outfit, not me."

Gillian smirked. "True."

"We'll take some extra internal and external shots, pop a drone up, and then we'll be out of your hair," Colin said, appearing beside them.

"Great."

"I understand you'll be at the Proms next month," he said, seemingly attempting to make conversation.

"Yes."

"My wife and I are going this year."

"Oh," Viola said, a little too questioning. Colin wasn't the type of man she would have expected to attend the Proms.

As if picking up on her confusion, he said, "It's not my thing, but the wife loves it. She's been badgering me about going for years. At least I'll know someone on the stage."

Viola gave him a quick smile as he walked off; it soon disappeared at the reminder that she'd have to go back to work soon and leave Kingsford for a while.

"Drink?" Viola asked Gillian as they walked toward the manor, assuming she could use several.

"Yes, please!"

Viola was about to tell Gillian to take a seat as they entered the drawing room only to notice her collapsing onto the nearest sofa. It brought a smile to her face at how relaxed Gillian was around her, or was it the house she felt at ease in? Viola poured a small measure of whisky into a glass for herself and then what she considered to be a normal measure for Gillian.

"Thank you for today. I wouldn't have managed it without you… and your Chesterfield… your tea set, photographs, Land Rover, horse, and riding jacket, which I must remember to give you back."

"Keep it. It fits you better than it will ever fit me, and as for the rest, let's not make a habit of it," Gillian replied with a neutral tone, as she took the glass Viola offered her. "There is only so much humiliation I'm willing to take — even for you."

"Thank you, and I'm sorry. I shouldn't have asked for your help today," Viola said, letting out a quiet sigh as she sat beside her, realising just how much she had asked of her.

"It's fine," Gillian said with a wave of her hand. "I enjoyed giving the photographer a piece of my mind at least."

Viola smiled. That moment had been the highlight of her day. Everything else only reinforced her feeling that she didn't quite fit in at Kingsford.

"I don't feel I belong here," she said. "I feel like a fraud. You know I paid a contractor, whom I don't even know and don't remember employing, hundreds of pounds the other day for trimming hedges. I have no idea if I even own them. He said he did it every year."

"Ah, Wakes & Sons. Yes, that is legitimate, and crucial work I'm afraid."

"Good to know. I'm a city girl, out of my depth, hoping I don't drown. I'm not sure I deserve Kingsford."

"What are any of us deserving of? That tea set belonged to Jonathon's family, and you might have noticed the photographs were of his grandparents. Sometimes we must borrow a bit of someone else's history to get us through. I didn't have to be rich to live here, and you don't have to know about the countryside to deserve to live here. You'll pick it up, and if you need help in the process, you only have to ask."

"Thank you," Viola said, flashing her a tender smile.

"It's me that needs to thank you. I always hoped it might be me making an appearance in *Country Life* one day. Not that they would have reason to feature me, but I always thought Kingsford deserved some exposure. It has that now, thanks to you."

Viola smiled, pleased that Gillian hadn't found the day to be all that bad.

"Sorry he thought you were my assistant."

Gillian shrugged.

"If it's any consolation, you made the best assistant." Receiving a scowl from her companion, Viola added, "Okay, okay. Top up?"

"No, thank you. It's been a long day, and I need a clear head for tomorrow. Bridget and I have ball business to attend to; it's not far off."

"Anything I can help with?" Viola asked. "I must admit to feeling a little guilty leaving it all to you."

"It's what I do best. Enjoy the evening."

"I'm sure I will."

Even though she trusted Gillian's abilities, she couldn't help feeling nervous about what awaited her at the manor ball. Underlying it there was excitement, though, mainly at spending more time with Gillian.

Draining her glass, Gillian stood. "I should head off."

"Thanks again," Viola called.

Gillian flashed her a smile, and with that she was gone from the room, leaving a slightly empty feeling inside Viola that she was beginning to experience every time she left.

CHAPTER 16

Viola pushed her lips together, compressing her red lipstick. It was the final touch to her appearance, complementing her off-the-shoulder, crimson, satin gown. It was the end of a busy day setting up the great hall for the evening's ball and the beginning of what was likely to be a long evening.

Gillian had left an hour ago to get ready, leaving the place in a still silence that deepened with every passing minute. Watching Gillian in her element filled her with pride and a little of something else; competence was sexy, after all.

Gillian had spent the whole day directing people from behind her clipboard, making minute changes that always worked no matter how pedantic they might have appeared. Unsuspecting men were barked at as to the correct placement of the casino tables they were delivering, and with the authority Gillian carried in her tone, no one dared to disagree with or question her. She knew exactly what she was doing and excelled at it. With

Bridget running around as her right-hand woman, they made a good team in bringing everything together.

Nerves tingled through Viola's extremities, not just for Gillian and the significance of the evening, but for something deeper. She didn't doubt everything would go smoothly; she knew it would. It was the thought of spending the entire evening with Gillian which made her stomach flutter.

Her phone vibrated, the name *Arte* appearing on the screen.

"Hi, Arte," she said, answering it. "How are you?"

"Great thanks. It was good to see you the other day."

"Yes, it's been too long."

"Look, this is a bit of an odd one." Arte paused for a moment before continuing. "I noticed you in *Country Life*; I've got a copy. You looked most impressive."

"Oh, ignore all that; it was so embarrassing. Everything in the photos practically belongs to Gillian."

"Including the artwork above the fireplace?" Arte questioned quickly with concern in her tone.

"No. Why?"

"I suspect it could be a lost painting, and it could be valuable. I couldn't believe it when I saw it."

"Lost? What does that mean?" Viola asked, concerned she was about to get a knock at the door from the authorities.

"That it's slipped off the radar, the art world has lost track of it. I'm not saying it's stolen or anything," Arte reassured her. "Charlotte called a contact of hers at the Courtauld Institute in London. They want you to take it over to them to look at it properly. It's quite hard to tell from a photograph. It looks like it could do with a clean."

"Yes, it's been in the attic at Kingsford along with some others."

"I'll send you the details for Charlotte's contact if that's okay. You should follow this up. Regardless of the value, finding a lost painting has significant importance in the art world."

"Yes, of course," Viola assured her, similarly intrigued to learn more about its origin.

"And if it does turn out to be something, please let me know. Immediately."

"Of course. What do you think it could be?"

"It has the style of Artemisia Gentileschi, a seventeenth-century artist. There are several of her works whose whereabouts are unknown, presumed lost."

Viola smiled at the name. "Is your name a coincidence or…"

"Yes, I'm named after her," she replied with enthusiasm, only for her tone to become immediately serious again, "I'm going to text you the details right now."

"Okay, thanks for your call, Arte, and thank Charlotte for me."

"I will. Do take any others it was with. Who knows what else you might have? Please keep me posted."

"Will do. Thanks, Arte," Viola replied as she hung up, feeling slightly sick yet excited.

Her phone vibrated to alert her to Arte's text. She ignored it, deciding to enjoy her evening and deal with it all in the morning. She would wait until she knew something concrete before mentioning it to Gillian. She certainly didn't want to distract her from the evening's event.

Making her way downstairs, the riff that popped into her head the night of their dinner came to mind again. Humming it aloud, she found the notes flowed effortlessly, and even lyrics came to mind. She paused by the grand piano in the great hall. The polished surface gleamed under the soft lighting, beckoning her to play.

As she ran her fingers over the keys, the piano's rich tones filled the hall, blending with her voice in a harmonious duet. Lost in the moment, Viola forgot everything around her as each note seemed to rise from the depths of her soul. It wasn't until she heard a soft, appreciative hum that she noticed Gillian standing beside her.

"I did knock," Gillian said softly. "It's a beautiful song," she added, her voice filled with admiration.

Viola's smile wavered, feeling both proud and a little vulnerable. "It's new. It came to me a few weeks ago, the first in a long time. Every day, I keep my vocal cords in good shape using other people's work, but there's nothing quite like working them on your own songs."

Gillian stepped closer, her eyes fixed on Viola with an intensity that made her heart race. "You have an incredible gift, Viola. Don't let it go silent."

The sincerity in Gillian's words struck a chord deep inside. She nodded. "I won't." Viola stood, her eyes tracing the elegant outline of Gillian's figure, which was accentuated by her silky, strapless black dress. The low cut at the front didn't escape her notice either. "You look incredible."

"Thank you. You look…" Gillian's usually hardened expression softened, melted away even, as she struggled to find her words. "…exquisite. As always," she remarked with a warm smile.

Viola's heart felt like it stopped beating. Her lips parted, drawing in a deep breath that filled her lungs and rebooted her brain. "Thank you."

"I thought you might go for a tuxedo."

"I considered it, briefly." Viola grinned. "It's difficult to get me out of a dress."

Gillian lifted an eyebrow as the corners of her mouth twitched. "Is it now?"

The flirtatiousness in her voice encouraged Viola's response. "I guess it depends on who's trying," she said, her own voice low and teasing. The pinking in Gillian's cheeks discouraged her from going any further. She didn't wish to make her uncomfortable. "You're early. That's not like you," she added, only to be met with a sly grin.

"I am not a guest, so technically I cannot be early. Anyway, I thought it was best, in case others put in an early appearance. I didn't want to abandon you, and I thought the band would need cajoling from their van." Gillian turned at a noise from the porch. "And here they are."

Five men dressed in tuxedos filed in and went to the far corner of the hall, where their instruments were set up. Mrs Johnson appeared from the kitchen carrying two buckets with champagne bottles nestled within. Two waiters carrying trays of fluted glasses followed behind.

Checking her watch, Gillian reached for a set of nearby light switches. With a few clicks, the chandeliers dimmed, and the soft wall lights created a warm and inviting atmosphere.

"I hope people come," Viola whispered, her nervousness rising again.

"Of course they will," Gillian replied with unwavering confidence. "Don't underestimate the pull of the main attraction."

Viola raised a curious eyebrow. "And what exactly would that be?"

Gillian leaned in, a playful smirk tugging at the corners of her mouth. "You, Viola. You."

Viola's arms tingled with goosebumps as a shiver ran down her spine — a mix of nerves at her guests' expectations and the thrill of Gillian's playfulness. She tried to mask her reaction until the warmth in her cheeks betrayed her. "I'm not sure I'm ready to be the star of the show," she admitted.

"Be yourself. That's more than enough."

Viola felt a wave of reassurance wash over her, though the flutter in her chest remained. "You make it sound so easy," she murmured, half to herself.

"Remember who you are, how hard you've worked, everything you've achieved," Gillian replied, her tone encouraging yet firm. "Trust me, Viola, you deserve all the attention. They're here for you. And I am too."

Viola couldn't help smiling, her nerves slowly giving way to calm just as a knock from the front door resounded. "Well then," she said, taking a deep breath, "we shouldn't keep them waiting."

Gillian tilted her head. "We?"

"They are as much your guests as mine. I mean, you invited them, not me. I don't even know most of them."

"Then we greet them together."

Viola felt Gillian's hand slip around her back, resting on her hip and guiding her to the front door. It felt good there, like it belonged.

Half of Kingsford appeared at the door, and the other half was further down the drive. Relief washed over Viola as the great hall filled to the band's tune and faces filled with delight at the casino tables. What she hadn't counted on was every guest having a copy of *Country Life* in hand, ready for her to sign.

Having satisfied them all with a signature on the cover, she took herself off to a corner of the room, hoping to disappear for a while. She watched Gillian mingle with the guests, her laughter feeling like a soft melody that carried through the room and tightened her chest.

She was a striking contrast to the woman Viola had come to know over the past few months. This was not the Gillian who was in the throes of navigating the challenges of her new life with a subdued demeanour. This was the confident, commanding, and self-assured figure who had made such a lasting impression on her from their first encounter. It was as if she was stepping back into a role she was born to play — a performer on her own stage. This was Gillian in her natural habitat, a place where she felt at home and where her true essence shone brightest. Gillian was not merely acting; she was embodying the role she thrived in.

As the evening wore on, Viola couldn't take her eyes

off her. Despite dancing and chatting with everyone, Gillian didn't falter once; it only appeared to energise her. The locals looked to be enjoying themselves, too, with free-flowing alcohol and a myriad of games to keep them entertained. It stemmed Viola's nerves to see everyone relaxed.

The major caught her and coaxed her into a dance. As soon as they stepped off the dance floor, her eyes were searching for Gillian. He was launching into a story about his latest classic car purchase when a welcome hand pressed against her upper arm, gently tugging her away and rescuing her from any further conversation.

"You don't mind if I steal her, do you, Major?" Gillian asked, not waiting for an answer.

Viola flashed him a polite smile of appreciation for the dance, only to notice his tongue practically hanging out. His gaze had locked onto Gillian, eyes sharp and hungry, like a predator stalking its prey. A flutter of anger and jealousy stirred inside her as Gillian steered her towards Elouise and Louisa. She pushed the feelings away, knowing it was unlikely Gillian felt anything for him except contempt.

Viola felt Gillian's guiding hand slip away as they stepped out of the crowd and joined the two women. Gillian angled herself towards Viola before taking a deliberate step back, creating a sudden distance between them. It felt odd, especially after how close they'd been before everyone arrived. Why was Gillian pulling away now? Viola's mind raced for an explanation. Was she trying to avoid giving the impression that they may be more than friends to the villagers?

"Are we enjoying ourselves, ladies?" Gillian asked.

Elouise nodded. "Louisa and I love a bit of gambling, don't we, Louisa?"

"Indeed," Louisa agreed. "Viola, this is a masterpiece. The best party we've been to in years." She stopped, looking at Gillian as she bit her lip.

"Actually, this was all Gillian's doing," Viola clarified.

Both women looked visibly relieved. "In that case, Gillian, you have outdone yourself."

The two Lous excused themselves quickly at waves from friends.

"See?" Viola said. "The villagers do embrace change. You should give them more credit."

"I don't believe they are ready to embrace all change," Gillian countered, "and not the particular change you are insinuating."

Viola conceded the point. Accepting a change in the ball's theme was hardly the same as embracing someone they'd always seen as heterosexual as something else, even though it should have been.

She sighed, wishing Gillian could be herself, whoever that was. Instead, she was a butterfly in a jar, and Viola wanted to set her free. But whilst Gillian clung to these rigid ideas of how people should behave, she never would be free. She allowed herself to be shaped by the opinions of others, and in a close-knit society such as this — one she'd been part of for decades — breaking free from that would be no simple feat. It would require something worth risking it all for, something strong enough to tip the balance against her fears. Viola couldn't help but wonder and hope that she could be that something — that *someone*.

Gillian admired Viola's body as it moved gracefully around the dance floor. The more formal music she planned for the evening had given way to more modern tunes, as requested by several of the younger villagers. The older generations were politely covering their yawns with their hands; she knew they would be making excuses to leave soon.

Viola caught her eye and smiled, making Gillian's heart skip a beat. As the song ended, Gillian took the opportunity to speak to Viola.

"May I suggest you thank everyone for coming? It will allow the older villagers to make their escape and anyone under sixty to let their hair down a little."

"Good idea."

Viola nodded and headed off to the staircase as Gillian strode over to the band to stop them from beginning a new song. Bridget joined her, her cheeks were flushed as they always were after a couple of drinks passed her lips.

"Everything is going swimmingly, don't you think?" she exclaimed with a little bounce, her excitement bubbling over.

"Yes. Perfectly so." The word reminded her of the annoying photographer from *Country Life*. She smiled at the recollection of giving him short shrift.

"You seem to be enjoying yourself. You and Viola are getting along like a house on fire."

"What's that supposed to mean?" Gillian replied sharply.

Bridget recoiled. "Nothing."

Gillian felt instant regret and squeezed Bridget's arm. "I'm sorry, Bridget. I'm rather tired."

The chink of a champagne glass filled the air, and the room fell into silence. Gillian made her way towards the staircase as if drawn there by a force. Bridget followed behind.

"May I have your attention, everyone?" Viola called out.

All eyes turned to Viola immediately, including Gillian's; they didn't want to be anywhere else. She was captivating. The room seemed to dim around her, leaving only her figure illuminated. Her curls cascaded over her shoulders, catching the light in a way that made them shimmer with life.

Viola didn't speak right away. She didn't have to. Her presence was enough to hold everyone in a silent, shared anticipation. When her lips finally parted, her voice was soft yet strong.

"I won't keep you from your merriment for long, but I couldn't let the evening pass without thanking you all, not only for coming this evening, but for welcoming me so warmly to your wonderful little village."

Everyone cheered.

"I also can't go without thanking Gillian and Bridget for organising everything this evening. Some of you may have noticed my skills lie elsewhere, so I couldn't have done it without them." Viola raised her glass in their direction. "To Gillian and Bridget."

"Gillian and Bridget," echoed around the great hall.

"Now don't let me keep you. Please top up your glasses and get spinning on the roulette wheel."

Viola descended the stairs, where she was immediately embraced by Bridget. Gillian took the opportunity to wipe the corner of her eye. As the band kicked back into action with something more lively than before, Bridget pulled their host towards the dance floor.

Taking a couple of steps up the staircase, Gillian scanned the crowd, only to realise what she was doing. Jonathon was dead; she didn't need to keep an eye on what he was up to or with whom. Not that she would ever have stopped him. She turned a blind eye to his subtle and often less subtle escapades out of necessity.

After his mother died, she had feared he might divorce her and trade her in for a newer model. He would never have done it whilst she was alive. Divorce wouldn't have been welcomed by her, she was fond of Gillian — they were cut from the same cloth, it turned out. Jonathon cared deeply for his mother, and he wouldn't have wished to disappoint her.

Once she was dead, though, Gillian couldn't rest on her laurels as she had done. She believed that if she let him pursue whatever he was seeking, she would be safe. Trying to stop him, she knew, would only breed resentment.

They both knew the role she should play, and she played it flawlessly, ensuring her position as the irreplaceable lady of the manor. She also knew him better than anyone, knew his likes and dislikes, his quirks and whims. Starting over would take effort, more effort than she believed Jonathon would be willing to make.

She looked up at his dead ancestors on the walls, as much ancestors to her now as they ever were his. Living in a place for so long, and a place like Kingsford, sank into your bones; it grew you like soil grows a plant. Without it, she was wilting.

As the evening wore on, Gillian found herself constantly drawn to Viola's side, their interactions charged with a tension that neither openly acknowledged. Every glance felt like it carried a deeper meaning, a silent conversation understood only by the two of them.

When in conversation with others, she did her best to distance herself from Viola, mindful about what the villagers may construe from physical closeness. Although she was drawn to Viola in ways she could hardly comprehend herself, the last thing she wanted was people reading too much into their friendship.

"Gillian?" Viola's voice cut through her thoughts.

"Yes?" Gillian blinked.

"I was asking if you'd like more wine," Viola said, a flicker of concern in her eyes.

"Oh, no, thank you," Gillian replied, trying to steady her voice. "I think I've had enough for tonight."

"Are you okay? You seem a bit distracted suddenly. Is everything all right?"

Gillian nodded, grateful for the concern yet feeling the weight of her emotions pressing down on her. "I'm fine, just a little tired from a long week. I need some fresh air. Excuse me."

Taking a moment alone to gather her thoughts, she stepped out into the garden, where the cool night air brought some welcome relief. She stared up into the vast expanse of the sky, filled by a universe of infinite stillness and endless possibilities. Here she was, nothing but a particle of it, feeling that something — someone — was pulling her towards a future of impossibility.

She wondered if Viola felt the same pull. If it was growing stronger every day as it was for her. She could feel parts of her that were once buried deep inside her trying to resurface. Forcing out a long breath into the cold air, it swirled around in front of her like a mist and dissolved into the darkness. As irresistible as Viola was, Gillian needed to ignore, control, and even fight these feelings.

Behind her, she could hear the door open and then close softly. She turned to see Viola standing there, the look of concern on her face making her even more beautiful than usual.

"Gillian, are you sure you're okay?" Viola asked, stepping closer.

"I'm fine, honestly," Gillian replied, though her voice betrayed her inner turmoil.

Viola reached out, touching her arm. "If something's bothering you, you can tell me."

Gillian looked into Viola's eyes, seeing the genuine concern there. The tension between them was almost palpable, a mix of unspoken feelings and unresolved emotions. *Be strong*, she told herself.

"It's... this place, memories of evenings like this," Gillian began, her voice trembling. "It's hard to see everything changing, to see someone else in a role I used to fill."

She stopped herself from adding that it was even harder that it was Viola now fulfilling that role, someone she admired more than she should. It would be easier if she could go back to disliking her.

Viola's expression softened, her grip on Gillian's arm tightening. "I understand. Don't forget you're still important here, Gillian. More than you know."

Gillian swallowed hard, feeling a lump in her throat. "Thank you. That means a lot."

The night air wrapped around them like a comforting embrace. Gillian knew she couldn't avoid properly addressing her feelings forever. For now, though, she was content to stand beside Viola, sharing a moment of quiet understanding, friendship, and companionship.

"Holding parties like this was a big part of your role, wasn't it?" Viola asked.

Gillian nodded. "I've felt more like my old self than I have in months." Looking up at the manor she added, "About now I would be crawling upstairs to my bed. Instead, I'll be walking to the end of the drive."

"I understand how difficult it must be, but you are mid-journey to somewhere new. It seems a shame to look back rather than forward."

Gillian wasn't so sure she was moving forward or even if she wanted to. She couldn't go back, but the pull of the past was strong. She felt trapped in a halfway house suspended between the past and the future, unsure which direction to take.

"Change can be good," Viola continued. "It challenges us. It's my first performance soon without Mum. I have to get through it; I don't have a choice. I'm sure once I have, I will be stronger for it."

These last months with Viola around, although

challenging at times, felt easier, particularly in recent weeks. Was she serving as a distraction from her problems? Tonight held the atmosphere of old times, a reminder of her previous life, which was unexpected. She had prepared herself that it would feel different with Viola as hostess, but it hadn't. The ball carried the ambiance of any other party she'd thrown at the manor.

She looked to Viola; her face was solemn and deep in thought, no doubt about her upcoming performance. Her expression didn't appear convinced she would be stronger. Should she offer to accompany her? Viola needed to get through it; it didn't mean she should do it alone. She was about to offer until she remembered Caroline. Would she be going?

"Would you come with me, as my guest?" Viola said, seeming to read her thoughts. "You'll have a whole box to yourself. Caroline can't make it."

"Oh."

"I hope it's not too much to ask of you. Especially after the magazine shoot, and then tonight." She quickly added, "You could bring Bridget… if you didn't want to be alone."

"No, I don't mind coming alone."

"That's a yes then?" Viola questioned, a tone of hope in her voice.

"Yes, of course. I'm here for you. As much as you are for me."

"Thank you, Gillian," Viola replied, placing her hand on Gillian's upper arm and shooting a pleasant warming sensation through her in the process. "I know I shouldn't be nervous; it is my job after all, but it's been a while, and things are different now. I don't just mean Mum. I've been enjoying my time off… late mornings, late evenings." She paused, then added coyly, "Spending time with you. My workload only increases from here."

The thought of Viola returning to the world that demanded so much of her, of a space growing between them again, made her chest tighten.

"I'll still be here," Gillian reassured her.

Viola's hand lingered a moment longer on her arm, sending the gentle warmth deeper into her skin, into her thoughts.

"I know," Viola whispered, her gaze unwavering as their eyes locked.

There was a vulnerability in Viola's stare that Gillian wasn't used to seeing. A rare glimpse beneath the composed surface she always presented to the world.

Gillian felt suddenly overwhelmed, and her throat tightened. "It's late. I'd best be getting back. I don't want to turn into a pumpkin," she said with a grin as she stepped back. "I'll head back from here rather than coming inside."

"Thank you for a wonderful evening," Viola said. "You really do know how to throw a party, not that I ever doubted it."

Gillian smiled. "This was all your idea, remember?"

"But you made it happen."

"Bridget and I made it happen."

Viola conceded with a smile and reached forward, embracing Gillian in an unexpected hug. "Good night, Gillian."

With their bodies pressed together, it took her a few

seconds to respond, but she placed a hand on Viola's back and patted it. An urge to pull Viola tightly against her body betrayed her initial reservations.

Nevertheless, she resisted. Pulling herself back, she said, "Good night, Viola."

She turned, relieved to be creating some distance, not only from the pull of Viola but from the reminder that Kingsford Manor was her home, her heart, and she wanted it back — along with the life she held so dear.

CHAPTER 17

*V*iola hummed as she paced the length of her dressing room. The motion helped burn off some of the bubbling nervous energy that always surged through her before a performance, making it easier to focus once she started her breathing exercises. It was a trick her mum had suggested when she first accompanied Viola to performances.

She smoothly transitioned to lip trills, feeling the familiar vibrations loosening her vocal cords. The Proms always tested her patience; waiting for her turn to perform made the anticipation build even more. Although this was her third time attending, tonight was special. It was her debut at the Last Night of the Proms, and it was an honour few in the world received.

Sinking into the sofa, she closed her eyes and inhaled deeply, taking in the silence with every breath. Her mum would always leave the room whilst she carried out the final part of her warm-up. It was easy to think she was on the other side of the door now, waiting for the call to come back in.

Emotions were trying to rise inside her again, but she knew she couldn't let them win. With her make-up redone once already, she didn't think a second request would go down well. Her thoughts needed directing anywhere except to her mum's absence and her impending performance.

Her mind drifted to Gillian and the text from her saying she had arrived and found her seat. Rehearsal timings and her appointment with Arte's contact at the Courtauld Institute meant she had needed to be in London ahead of Gillian. She ensured her safe arrival by sending Douglas to pick her up. She hoped she was enjoying herself, even if she was alone, hundreds of feet above her.

Gillian appeared to be more content with her own company; she had likely become accustomed to it in a marriage like hers. Even though the woman surrounded herself with people by organising this event or that, Viola couldn't help feeling Gillian sought out people as a distraction rather than for their company.

She had exuded confidence at the ball, spending time with people and moving amongst them with effortless grace. Gillian had perfected the role of hostess over the years. Her enjoyment came from other people's enjoyment. She was a social catalyst, a connector, a facilitator, and the curator of experiences. Everything she did was to showcase her talent and ensure other people's happiness.

Although Gillian would be the last person to admit it, she was a generous, caring person, giving her time and skills for nothing to benefit others. Butterflies fluttered inside Viola, even if she could feel her breathing exercises were doing their job. Thoughts of Gillian brought them to the surface again.

Despite the success of the ball, by the end, it looked to have beaten Gillian. Her forlorn manner before she departed had left a bittersweet taste in Viola's mouth. A lot had changed for Gillian that year; it was bound to take a toll on her.

Was she asking too much, expecting her to organise the ball in her old house and then partly host it? She had tried to make the effort to host herself, but it didn't come as naturally to her as it did to Gillian. It was simpler to let her take the spotlight. Pushing her aside would have only made things worse in the end. Gillian had said how difficult it was to see someone in the role she once held. Knowing her sadness came from that aspect of their friendship was a heavy weight to bear, but Gillian was intelligent enough to realise if it wasn't Viola filling that role, it would be someone else.

Was it worse for Gillian now, being friends with that person? Would it have been easier if they hadn't become friends? The thought made her feel a little queasy, and she exhaled slowly. She didn't even want to be friends with Gillian; she wanted more. Her heart was screaming at her when they said good night at the ball — to reach out, to kiss her. She couldn't do it. It was a step too far, and she wasn't going to risk what she'd already built with Gillian.

Her phone rang, rattling against the glass table as it vibrated. When she answered the video call, Caroline's face filled the screen, framed by a backdrop of blue sky.

Caroline lifted her sunglasses and squinted. "I was hoping to catch you before you go on to say good luck."

"Thanks. Looks hot there."

"It is. I could quite happily move to L.A."

"Don't even think about it."

Caroline laughed. "Speaking of hot countries, I can finally tell you what I've been working on. I think you're going to love it."

Viola held her breath with trepidation about what her agent had up her sleeve.

"A two-month tour of Australia. It will take you through until Christmas."

"Oh, great." She forced a cheerful tone, though it felt hollow. After her last tour in Australia, she'd been eager to return, but now that it was happening, the timing couldn't be worse. The idea of travelling halfway across the world, away from Kingsford and Gillian, left her feeling more subdued than excited.

"I'm glad you are upbeat about it because I wanted to run the idea of rolling it into a world tour next year, after Oz."

A knock at the door told her that time was up, without a moment to digest what Caroline said and what it meant.

"Sorry," she begged off, "I've been called. I'll call you back tomorrow."

"Make sure you do."

Viola ended the call and took a deep, steadying breath as she rose to her feet. Taking a quick swig from her water bottle, she gave herself one final look in the mirror. Satisfied, she straightened her shoulders, opened the door, and began the walk to the stage — alone.

She tried to focus her mind on her performance, not on the empty space beside her where her mum's once-steady presence had offered final words of encouragement. Even now, Viola could hear her mum's voice telling her to 'touch their hearts.' It was something she would often say before Viola stepped onto the stage.

The sound of the audience applauding the performing musicians echoed as she reached the stage entrance. The conductor, a talented woman she'd worked with on several occasions, appeared from the stage with someone she knew to be a pianist. He shook her hand and strolled off down the corridor.

The conductor took a quick sip of water from a bottle passed to her by an assistant and gave her a nod of reassuring acknowledgement as Viola continued to ignore the empty space beside her. Taking her cue from a man with a headset, Viola blew out a steady breath and made her way onto the stage, followed by the conductor.

The audience roared into a deafening applause again as they passed the orchestra, some even rising to their feet in a standing ovation. As she made her way to the centre of the stage, she glanced upward, squinting against the glare of the stage lights. Her eyes searched the boxes close to the stage, where she knew Gillian was seated.

Any remaining nerves dissipated as she spotted the outline of Gillian, who was standing and clapping along with everyone else. Viola was unable to make out any details, but her overall image and smiling face were enough to lift her spirits. She wasn't alone. Gillian was with her, and standing beside her was her mum. In spirit, anyway.

The atmosphere changed, and an astounding silence that only came from halls like the Royal Albert settled in. Thousands of people surrounded her, their eyes fixed on her in anticipation. A subtle nod to the conductor signalled that she was ready, and with that simple gesture, the orchestra came to life, the first notes swelling into the air as she joined them in perfect harmony.

She could do this.

～

Gillian sat in the silent darkness, utterly mesmerised by Viola's performance. The grandeur of the Royal Albert Hall faded into insignificance as her voice filled the space with what the programme informed her was 'Liebst du um Schönheit', accompanied by the BBC Symphony Orchestra.

Viola's commanding presence on the stage, in a strapless, light pink, sequined dress that sparkled under the lights, was a sight to behold. Her tone was both powerful and delicate. Gillian could feel it pressing against her chest as each crescendo sent shivers down her spine. Softer moments pulled her deeper into the performance as if she and Viola were the only two people in the room.

The sheer control Viola possessed over her voice was staggering. It effortlessly shifted from bold and commanding to soft and tender, weaving the emotions of the song through every rise and fall of the melody. A feeling of possessiveness washed over Gillian. This was her Viola… her friend… her… what was she? At the very least, she was a woman who was making her eyes leak with her words and her voice.

She reached for a tissue and dabbed her eyes. Since Viola had entered her life earlier that year, Gillian had been swept up in a storm of emotions she hadn't felt in ages. She felt vulnerable, her focus was slipping, and she was utterly distracted. Viola awakened something deep within her, a persistent pull that left her breathing unsteady, her thoughts tangled, and her heart racing in ways she couldn't fully grasp. And now, watching her perform, it was as if every emotion had been amplified to its breaking point.

The final notes lingered in the air, followed by a pregnant pause before the eruption of thunderous applause. Gillian found herself unable to move, her breath caught in her throat. Viola did more than sing; she left everyone, including Gillian, awestruck.

The entire hall was whistling, cheering, and waving flags. It made Gillian's eyes water with pride, and she was grateful she hadn't gone heavy on the mascara. Viola thanked the conductor, then spread her arms wide to the orchestra, who stood and took a bow. Gillian realised that this wasn't simply a performance. It was Viola in her truest form, baring her soul through the song. For Gillian, it was as if she were seeing a different side to Viola. This was Viola the performer, and she was astounding.

She disappeared for the next couple of songs, returning for two more before the interval and two more after. Her final performance of 'Rule, Britannia!' brought Gillian to tears yet again. As the music faded and the audience erupted into another deafening round of applause, she was sad to see Viola leave the stage again.

Following the National Anthem and the finale, 'Auld Lang Syne', a steward appeared behind her. "Gillian Carmichael?"

Gillian nodded, unable to find her voice.

"Miss Berkley has asked me to take you to her dressing room. If you'd like to follow me?"

The steward led her down numerous staircases, the upmarket decor gradually changing into bland, cold corridors that disappeared into the distance. Despite their cavernous quality, they were crammed with people and instruments.

What should have been a few moments to calm her nerves served to increase them. With Viola rehearsing in London the past week, an unsettling distance had formed between them, one which Gillian disliked. Although they exchanged the occasional message, she felt obliged to leave Viola to her work.

The steward stopped outside a door and knocked. A sign next to it read 'Viola Berkley'. Receiving an immediate invitation to enter, he opened the door for Gillian. She thanked him and stepped inside.

Viola was pouring champagne into two glasses.

"Well?" she asked.

"You were… phenomenal," Gillian breathed.

"Thank you. Have a glass of champagne with me," Viola said, bringing one towards her.

Gillian was still battling the adrenaline pumping through her body. Champagne was unlikely to help, but she wasn't going to refuse.

"Thank you."

They clinked glasses.

She noticed in Viola's manner that she, too, was still riding the waves of adrenaline from her performance. There was an undeniable glow about her, an excitable energy that radiated from her, illuminating her face. She took a sip from her glass and placed it on the table. Turning her back to Gillian, she pulled her hair to one side.

"Unzip me, would you? I must get out of this dress before I suffocate."

Gillian located the zip and pulled it down, immediately realising Viola was braless. As she reached the bottom, a pair of light pink knickers revealed themselves.

"Thanks," Viola said, making her way towards the door. With her back to Gillian, she let her dress slip to the floor and stepped out of it effortlessly. Before Gillian could process what was happening, Viola unhooked a dressing gown from the back of the door and slipped into it.

Caught off guard by the sudden intimacy of the moment, Gillian found her pulse quickening as she tried to steady herself. Viola, seemingly oblivious to her effect, picked up her glass from the table, gestured for Gillian to sit, and then settled beside her.

"Thank you for being here. You don't know how much it meant to me to see you before I began."

"It was my pleasure, I assure you," Gillian replied with a smile, happy to influence such a sublime performance. "Your first song was beautiful. German, I presume?"

"Yes," Viola confirmed.

"I didn't know you spoke it."

"I don't. It's only a few words when you look at it. It's easily taught."

"What is it about?" Gillian asked, still wondering what was the meaning of the words which had affected her so much.

"It warns against the attraction of superficial values like riches, youth, and beauty. Mahler composed it based on a poem by Ruckert, 'If you love for beauty'. He wrote it to his wife."

Viola broke into song:

If you love for beauty, Oh, do not love me!
Love the sun; She has golden hair.
If you love for youth, Oh, do not love me!
Love the springtime; It is young each year.
If you love for riches, Oh, do not love me!
Love the mermaid; She has many shining pearls.
But if you love for love, Oh yes, do love me!
Love me always, I shall love you evermore!

Gillian smiled, her skin tingling from her private recital.

Viola leaned towards her, hand outstretched. "You have an eyelash."

Frozen to the spot as her heart pounded in her chest, all Gillian could do was take Viola in as she drew near. The scent of her perfume and the fold in her dressing gown revealing her bare breasts were overwhelming her senses.

Viola's fingers brushed against her cheek. "Your eyes are a little red too."

Gillian's body tensed at her touch. Her head was foggy,

heavy even, as she desperately tried to relax. "It was an emotional performance."

"Think of that," Viola said, trying to remove the eyelash. "I made Gillian Carmichael cry. And she didn't even know what I was singing."

"Please don't mock me," Gillian replied, her tone hard.

Viola levelled her face with Gillian, her hand pressed against her cheek. "I'm not mocking you. I'm in awe of you. You are a remarkable woman."

Gillian tilted her face away. "I hardly think so."

Viola placed her other hand on Gillian's other cheek and pulled her back. "Then why can't I take my eyes off you? Why can't I stop thinking about you? Why does my heart scream every time we are apart?"

Their eyes met in an unwavering stare that felt like forever. Gillian's lips parted to reply, but she had no idea what they would say. She wondered if Viola was going to kiss her. She realised how much she wanted to be kissed, devoured even, by the woman in front of her. Unable to resist any longer, her hand reached for the back of Viola's head and pulled her into a kiss.

Viola's eager mouth sent a rush of warm tingles shooting through her body like she had never felt before. Her breath caught as the sensation spread, intensifying with every movement of their lips, awakening something deep within her. Every touch was electric as the world around them melted away, leaving only this intense, undeniable feeling that consumed her entirely

The words from the song of riches and beauty filled her head as Viola's tongue came searching for hers. When she watched Viola on that stage, she had wanted to claim her for herself. Was that not for her riches and beauty, her success, her celebrity? Were her feelings superficial and lustful? They were most definitely lustful. She couldn't deny that as her tongue tangled with Viola's.

But even as desire coursed through her, her thoughts were clouded, her head aching with confusion and guilt. What was she doing kissing Viola? Her mind and body battled in desperation to find answers, to find a way to let her animalistic instincts have what they desired.

All she could think about was Kingsford, that Viola owned it and she didn't. She could hear the villagers whispering about her and see them pointing at her, judging her. Judging her for who she was and what she wanted, Kingsford, and not the person who owned it, even if that wasn't true.

Nothing felt right. Every moment longer of Viola's lips, her soft warm breast that she was caressing without realising, felt like she was using her. Everything screamed at her to stop.

She pulled back. "I'm sorry. I can't." She forced herself to her feet as Viola pulled her dressing gown around her. "I shouldn't have…" Gillian trailed off as she looked back at Viola. What was she thinking? One slip and their relationship had changed. She grabbed her bag and made her way toward the dressing room door. As she opened it, she couldn't bring herself to look back, swiftly closing it behind her.

Damn her weakness. The emotions of Viola's performance had overrun her, and her near-naked body barely hiding behind the dressing gown had tempted her. A warm rush rose again inside her at thoughts of Viola's allure, her desire for her. She pushed them down, desperate to get control of herself.

Looking for an exit sign, she found one directing her back the way she'd come only ten minutes before. That was a time when everything was fine, when she had a lid on her feelings. A voice in her brain mocked her: "You were never in control."

Needing air, she opened a door, not noticing until it was too late that it was the stage door. Camera lights flashed as she stumbled down the steps onto the path, gasping for breath. Once the photographers realised she was no one of interest, they stopped, allowing her to pass through them. All she could see was the looks they were giving her.

"You all right, love?" one of them asked as she stumbled on the curb.

Righting herself, she quickened her pace to get away, grateful she had opted for a hotel within walking distance of the Royal Albert Hall and not a room in Viola's penthouse. She knew she would need distance from the woman who was making her feel things she hadn't felt in decades. She couldn't trust herself or her feelings, and now they proved untrustworthy.

A voice in her head spoke over her thoughts: "You want her. You need her. You desire her." She pushed them aside, only for images of their kiss to fill her mind. The woman had taken everything from her, and now she was coming for her heart.

Her feet carried her at such a pace that the fallen early autumn leaves danced around her, their yellowing hues catching the glow of the streetlights. How was it nearly autumn already and she hadn't noticed? Everything was more noticeable when she owned the manor. She had been more attuned to the seasons then. Now she felt disconnected, lost once again in a wilderness of emptiness, much like the life she'd known before Kingsford. She had let Viola distract her from it all.

Her thoughts turned to Viola in the dressing room. She'd left her there, all alone after her big performance. How would she be feeling, having been walked out on without so much as an explanation?

A sick feeling rose in her stomach. Gillian stopped in her tracks. What if Viola continued drinking? What if she didn't stop? Should she go back? She pushed herself forward. It wasn't on her if Viola chose that path. She could only control her path; that was the only way she could convince herself to keep walking away from the hall, away from the person who, not long ago, she had disliked and now couldn't get out of her head.

CHAPTER 18

Gillian looked out over the parkland of Kingsford Manor from her usual spot on the bench. The sunshine warmed her face, but a cold breeze swept around the rest of her, reminding her summer was gone. She wanted to make the most of the estate whilst Viola was still away. Given how she had left things in the dressing room, she wasn't sure under what circumstances their paths might cross again—or if she would still be welcome. Part of her wanted to avoid it as long as possible. A light cough sounded from behind, telling her that her time was already up.

"I'll go," Gillian said, making moves to stand.

A hand on her shoulder stopped her. "Please don't. May I join you?" Viola asked, sitting beside her without waiting for an answer.

"Sorry, I thought you were still in London. I didn't hear a helicopter."

"I came back by car last night."

The awkward silence that commenced wasn't going to

get any less uncomfortable, so Gillian decided to address the issue head-on. She was a 'tear the plaster off in one swift movement' kind of woman.

"I must have hurt you, I'm sorry. I didn't want that. I just can't be… that. I'm not like that anymore."

"It hurts, yes," Viola admitted. "Was it unexpected that you kissed me first? Yes, very. That you ran? No." She paused, then added, "I know you didn't mean to hurt me, but it would have been good to have at least talked about it."

Gillian's head dropped as Viola continued.

"I've wanted to kiss you for a while and refrained. I feared it would make you run, and I was right. I didn't want that either. If you don't want to talk about it, or can't, then we won't. I will ask what you meant by 'like that'. You often talk in terms that sound a little homophobic. You once even struggled to get the word 'lesbian' out of your mouth."

"I don't have a problem with gay people," Gillian muttered as she shifted in her seat.

"I'm sure you don't have a problem with other people being gay, but I get the impression you believe we are somehow inferior. It's okay for others to be 'like that'; you just don't want to be seen as that yourself. Am I right?"

"I understand my feelings," Gillian replied firmly. "Accepting those feelings is a hurdle; acting on them is Herculean."

"You did act." Viola's tone was firm, firmer than Gillian had ever heard it. When she chanced a glance at the younger woman, her eyes coiled with some unknown emotion. "You kissed me, and I felt you, Gillian. I felt all of you. I felt what you wanted."

"Wants and needs are different. I need to uphold my standing in the village. I've already fallen too far."

"And what?" Viola snapped. "Acknowledging your feelings for me would lead to you being where? At the bottom of the Kingsford social hierarchy?"

"I've already acknowledged my feelings. As you say, I kissed you," Gillian answered. "As for taking it any further, that I cannot do. I built a life here, a life I could only once dream of, and I lost it. I cannot bear any more losses."

"Loss! A life with me would be a loss," Viola said, turning away from her.

"I didn't mean…" Gillian trailed off, unable to make sense of her thoughts.

Viola turned back, eyes blazing with anger as she glared at her. "What did you mean? That you're ashamed to be with me. Is that why you kept your distance at the ball? Standing apart from me in conversations to prevent us from appearing too close. Is that it?"

Despite recoiling in her seat at Viola's tone, Gillian tried to pitch her reply with composure. "I was merely standing back to give you space to host. I was all too aware it wasn't my position. I am also aware that at such events I can too easily take over." She refrained from adding that she was worried if she stood too close to her, everyone would be able to read her face and see how much she longed for her.

"I thought you would enjoy it, and you seemed to."

Viola's tone softened, much to Gillian's relief. "You were in your element at the beginning of the evening."

"I was. That's the problem. It served as a reminder of everything I lost, how far I've fallen."

"Fallen? Is that how you see it?" There was a touch of empathy in her voice. "Your circumstances have changed, that's all. Your house has less square footage, and from what I understand, there isn't any *less* money in the bank."

Gillian's face dropped as Viola continued.

"These are all superficial, materialistic things that don't even begin to measure your worth or who you are."

"My position as lady of the manor was not materialistic. Maybe it is you who underestimates the position you hold now."

"It's just a name, Gillian," Viola said, her voice brimming with frustration.

"Like award-winning musician?" Gillian bit back.

"Yes, exactly like that. It's a label people put on me, not something I put on myself. I'm Viola, and I can sing. You are Gillian, a generous and caring woman who can organise like no one else. That is your value, who you are and what you do. Not that you even show this to the world; you hide it, preferring to show a woman who's hard and closed off. Doesn't it take an enormous amount of effort to play this part? To be someone you aren't?" Viola took a deep breath. "Let people see the real you, the one you have shown me these past months," she urged gently.

"I've only lost focus the last few months. I need to get it back," Gillian replied firmly.

"And I'm guessing that is my fault, this loss of focus?"

Gillian kicked at the gravel under her feet, feeling she was losing a grip on the conversation as well. "That's not what I said."

"You didn't need to. I can read between the lines. I want you to be you, and I want to be with you. I can make you happy." Viola paused, then ventured, "I believe I do make you happy."

Gillian rubbed the side of her mouth, fearful that Viola would notice the tiny smile that rose in one corner of it. Viola did make her happy, but the lifestyle she was offering didn't. They could stay friends; Viola could still be in her life and make her happy, regardless of a label that didn't fully capture the complexity of their connection.

Viola reached out and touched Gillian's leg. "When was the last time someone ravished you, Gillian? Properly, I mean. The last time you were touched by someone you wanted. Stripped and taken until you were breathless and shaking."

Gillian's breath hitched, her body tensing as the question cut through her like a knife. Its bluntness made her heart race and her skin prickle with a flush of heat as she struggled to maintain her composure. Her gaze dropped, her eyes focusing on a stone on the path as she grappled with the flood of emotions. The intensity of the question made her feel exposed, her mind caught between discomfort and a rush of forgotten yearning.

"Never then," Viola said decidedly when Gillian failed to answer. "Why let other people's view of you hold back your happiness? Do you really care what they think? Do their opinions matter so much to you that you are willing to push who you are aside?"

Gillian didn't know how to reply. She cared what other people thought. She always had done.

Viola took a deep breath and continued. "Another thing your mum taught you: to live your life by other people's rules. We live in a different world now, and it's time you caught up to it. You've stuffed yourself away at Kingsford for an eternity, and it's suffocated you."

The problem was, part of her still felt like a child, deeply craving her mother's approval. All those memories of things she'd said, cold remarks, put-downs, they were still resting on the surface of her skin and the edges of her soul.

"You let your guard down around me, and I don't think you do that with anyone else… probably not even Bridget. I see the real you, Gillian. The one you've kept hidden, the one you still hide from everyone else except me."

"I'm not sure how to be her," Gillian replied, her voice faltering. "I'm even less sure I want to be her."

"You are her! This other Gillian, the cold one who protects herself, that's not you. That's someone you created to stop yourself from getting hurt. You don't need to protect yourself, not with me."

"And everyone else?" Gillian's voice cracked.

"Does that really matter? Honestly."

She'd suppressed the possibility of a life like that thirty-five years ago. It wasn't so easily unpacked like a suitcase after a holiday.

"You need to work out what makes you happy because all I see is a woman who has spent a lifetime trying to make others happy, your mum, your husband, even this goddamn village. What about you? Where does your happiness come into it? What does it look like?"

"Making others happy makes me happy."

"What bullshit. You were taught to serve others to fulfil your happiness; the two are exclusive. You can do things for others and seek additional happiness elsewhere. Would you be happy if your gravestone read, 'Died happy by making everyone else happy'?"

Gillian didn't answer, couldn't answer. Making others happy was all she knew. It was her safety net, her place in her community; her small world where everything made sense, where she could get on and do and shut everything else out that was scary, unknown, and unwalkable.

Viola pushed on. "If you only had six months to live, Gillian, what would you do with them? Attend a Women's Institute meeting, organise a coffee morning, sit through a sermon?"

She'd never given that question a moment's thought. She believed contemplating one's mortality was best avoided.

"I'm not going to push you into this," Viola said. "You have to come willingly."

She wanted to; she just didn't know how. Feeling Viola's growing frustration, she tried to be honest, whispering, "I can't go back."

Viola grabbed her hand. "You wouldn't be going back. You would be moving forward, to a place you should have always been. We spoke a lot about grief. Do you not think part of you is grieving an alternate life you could have lived?"

"I didn't live it, and it's too late now," Gillian snapped,

frustrated by all her questions. She pulled her hand from Viola's,

"It's never too late," Viola urged. "Too late is when you take your last breath, and you are some ways from that point."

"Can't we go back to the way we were?" Gillian pleaded.

"I'm in love with you." Viola sighed. "I don't think I can, no."

Gillian's heart leapt at her initial words, only for it to drop and shatter. Her chest tightened as if she'd been punched. She stared at Viola, searching for a glimmer of hope in her eyes. All she saw was a resolve that was both heartbreaking and final.

"We can't — " Gillian started, her voice faltering. "We can't just throw everything away."

Viola's expression softened, though her eyes remained firm. "It's not about throwing things away, Gillian. It's about being honest with ourselves. I love you, which makes it harder to be around you and not with you. To watch you deny yourself some true, raw happiness in life… it's not for me."

Gillian swallowed hard, trying to process the weight of Viola's words. She reached out a hand, but Viola stood. The space between them felt impossibly wide. "What happens now?" Gillian asked, her voice barely a whisper.

Viola took a deep breath. "I will return to work. You should get back to what you do, to what is most important to you — avoiding your unhappiness by living vicariously through everyone else's happiness. Christmas is on its way. I'm sure you must have something to organise. I'm sure that will make you happy. I hope it's enough for you."

With that, Viola turned, her footsteps on the gravel fading until silence surrounded Gillian, and she was left with only her thoughts. Those thoughts told her she wanted to sweep the woman up and kiss her, but it was too much, too far from what she knew. Too far from what was safe in her already uncertain future.

CHAPTER 19

Viola sipped at her coffee, ignoring the voice suggesting she add something stronger to it to help her situation. She knew by now that wouldn't make anything better.

Staring out of the kitchen window, she contemplated calling Caroline. She needed to talk to someone, and there only was Caroline for that purpose. Forty-four years old with the sum of one friend — who was technically her agent. Her friendship with Gillian had proved it was possible to make new friends past forty, though. Should she be more trusting? She sighed. People weren't trustworthy; her past proved that. But Gillian was different — a smile reached her lips — so very different. She'd never met anyone like her before. To say she was unique was an understatement.

A pain tugged inside her. Now she'd lost her. Had she pushed too hard? Expected too much? Asked for too much? She only wanted the best for Gillian, for her to find herself and be free of the shackles she seemed so willingly enslaved to.

She knew coming out wasn't an easy task. It wasn't even something she had found the courage to do herself. Someone else did it for her in the end. It may have hurt at the time, but she didn't regret it. Being true to yourself is vital for a healthy body and mind. She couldn't imagine what living as someone else your entire life would feel like.

All she felt now was lonely, almost as lonely as she had been when she first arrived at Kingsford. She thought the feeling had left her or lessened at least. Now she wondered if Gillian had helped mask those emotions or distracted her from them. It had been many months since her mum passed away, and her body and mind were getting used to her not being there; that much she felt. That pain resided deeper inside her now.

Now there was a new pain sitting on her surface. Her body and mind had been growing used to someone else being there, but now she was gone too. Why was she foolish enough to allow it to happen? She tried to be kind to herself, to tell herself she couldn't have predicted this, that she would fall for the unobtainable in the wake of her grief.

The countryside had grown on her, too, but for a city girl, its vast contrast left her yearning for the buzz of urban life. As much as she appreciated its tranquil charm, the absence of familiar sounds and scents made her long for the bustling streets and the familiar pulse of London. Was it possible to be suffocated by nothingness? Clean air and silence? Maybe she should sell up and go back to the city, forget all about Gillian Carmichael.

As a tear rolled from her eye, she picked up the phone and called Caroline. She sniffed away her emotions as she picked up the call.

"I was about to call you," Caroline greeted her. "We need to discuss the idea of extending the tour. Are you up for it? I've had a huge amount of interest across the States. I can have you there as soon as January. I need a hard yes as I need to get the team on promo ASAP. We'll start on the West Coast and end at Carnegie Hall, then move on to Europe in the spring."

Viola smiled at her use of the word 'we', knowing Caroline wouldn't be there, leaving it all to the tour manager. Maybe it would be best to keep busy until she could get over Gillian. Some distance between them would help. A few thousand miles should do it.

"Sounds great," she found herself saying before she could think any more about it. "Let's do it."

"Excellent. I'll start the ball rolling. The reviews for the Proms are all positive. Returning to live performances will please a lot of your fans."

"Mmm," Viola hummed.

"Are you okay? You were happy with your performance, weren't you?"

"Yes, all that was fine. It was in the dressing room when Gillian kissed me that things started to go awry."

A spluttering, gargled noise, followed by a coughing sound, came down the line.

"She kissed you?" Caroline finally said, her tone hovering between shock and fascination.

"Yes. Then she ran away."

The sound of Caroline sucking in a breath came down the phone, followed by, "Oh."

"Mmm," Viola murmured again, the memory of Gillian's taste mingling with champagne lingering on her lips, not to mention how hard she had fought to resist the temptation of finishing the bottle alone.

"Have you spoken to her since?"

"Yes. She wants us to be friends."

"Ouch."

Viola sensed the vibration in her throat coming to hum again. She stopped herself, knowing it was a numbness coming over her and taking her power of speech. She needed to think clearly and act. To look after herself; protect herself.

"I'm thinking of selling Kingsford. It was always meant for Mum; I was only ever going to be here on and off. It's too painful to stay; it would be easier to be in love with Gillian somewhere else entirely. Australia is beginning to feel like the perfect destination."

"How does Gillian feel about you selling?" Caroline asked, confusing Viola with her concerned tone.

Viola huffed. "What has it got to do with her?"

"Considering you are selling to run away from her, and it's her house, then I'd say it's got everything to do with her."

"I'm not running away, and it's not *her* house!" Viola's voice sharpened, the words escaping before she could stop them. She paused, trying to regain control of her emotions.

"You know what I mean," Caroline insisted.

She did. Kingsford would always be Gillian's, regardless of who owned it.

"Have you told her you are considering it at least?" Caroline continued.

"No. It only just came to me, and if I will be touring a lot next year, it makes sense. I should leave whilst the pain is so strong." Looking out the window, she added thoughtfully, "This place sucks you into its little universe, and I'm not sure it ever spits you back out again. It would have been perfect for Mum."

"Don't let me stop you. I need you back at work," Caroline said, adding more cautiously, "Surely if you sell, then Gillian will be at the mercy of someone else. Someone who may not be as sympathetic to Kingsford as you have been."

"Is that my problem?" Viola sniffed.

"I thought you cared about her. Perhaps even loved her."

"I do, but I can't dictate my life around some of her emotions while she ignores others. She's doing everything she can to push them away." Realising how much frustration was in her voice, Viola took a breath, only to find her voice wavering as she continued. "I can see how she feels about me. She says it with her eyes, even if she won't admit it."

There was a soft sigh on the other end before Caroline's voice came through, filled with quiet sympathy. "You know you can't force these things. If it's meant to be, it will be. You must give her space and hope she comes around."

"I know." Viola sighed. "I said as much to her." Her phone vibrated against her ear to indicate another call on the line. A glance at the number set her heart racing. "I'm going to have to phone you back. The Courtauld Institute are calling about that painting."

"Which painting?"

"The one I hung up that Gillian disliked," Viola confirmed.

"What did they want with it?"

"I hope I'm about to find out. I'll call you back." Viola hung up and accepted the incoming call before she lost it.

"It's Georgina, from the Courtauld Institute."

"Hi," Viola replied.

"We've looked at your painting and carried out some sympathetic tests."

"Great," Viola said, gripping the phone. "What's the conclusion?"

There was a brief pause before Georgina spoke again, making Viola nervous. "Have you heard of the artist Artemisia Gentileschi?"

"Only recently, from Arte, Charlotte's wife. Seventeenth-century artist, right? Not bad for a woman in that era."

"Correct. She was very much a modern woman in a patriarchal world. A lot of her early work ended up attributed to male artists or even her father as their styles were similar, so we've only recently begun cracking open the world of Artemisia in some respects. She came to England in the 1630s and worked alongside her father in the court of Charles I. Seven paintings by her are recorded in the inventories, and only one was thought to survive. Following the king's execution, we suspect that many were sold off and scattered across Europe. Another similar painting was recently discovered in the store at Hampton Court Palace, having been attributed to someone else. This painting holds a CR brand. Any idea what that means?"

"No," Viola said, eager for the woman to continue.

"Carolus Rex. King Charles, Charles I specifically, in this case. It was one of the lost paintings. We've uncovered a CR branding under a couple of layers of backing material of your painting. It was very faint, but the imaging techniques we use revealed it."

The penny dropped, and Viola quickly asked, "You think mine could be one of these lost paintings?"

"From what I've seen, I'm one hundred percent sure. Some notable experts on Gentileschi's work have looked it over. We all agree it is an original. We tested some flecks of paint and one in particular interested us called lead antimonate yellow. It's an unusual pigment particularly associated with her work. The nature of the painting, with the young woman stabbing the man in the back, is very much her style, I'm afraid to say. A lot of her work depicts very dramatic scenes, some very violent towards men. She was raped as a young woman, and men aren't portrayed favourably in her art. She was quite the feminist. You own a very important piece of art. Thank you for bringing it to our attention."

"What do I do now? Is it still mine, or should it be returned to someone?" Viola asked, realising she was completely clueless when it came to such things.

"No, it's yours. It's lost, not stolen. We'd like to know more about the provenance, but there is no doubt about what it is."

"Do lost paintings often come with a provenance?"

"Yes and no. Some lost paintings aren't actually lost but misattributed and have a provenance. With a painting that has disappeared completely, like in this case, provenance is trickier. Where did you find this?"

"It came into my possession with a house purchase; they were left in the attic. I do know the previous owner; it was her late husband that bought it."

"It's so often the case that these paintings come to light following deaths and house moves. I expect she will want it back." Georgina chuckled.

"I expect so too," Viola agreed.

"I can put you in touch with someone who can help you with everything. He's a renowned art dealer and has experience with paintings of this level of importance."

"Thanks," Viola said, massaging her temples as she tried to take everything in. "That would be great. How much is it worth? Thousands?"

"Millions, more like. Although the lack of provenance could affect the price."

Taking a moment to absorb the enormity of the figure, her thoughts went to the other paintings. "Are the other paintings worth anything?"

"No. There was nothing of value amongst the rest, unfortunately. I wouldn't call any art worthy of the bin, but in the case of those…" She let out a light chuckle. "I can see why they were left in the attic. The Gentileschi on the other hand, someone missed a trick."

"Indeed." Viola smiled, thinking of Gillian's disdain for it just because her husband had bought it.

"We're happy to temporarily store the Gentileschi here

if you wish. I'm assuming you don't have insurance since you didn't know what it was."

"No, I don't. I would be grateful if you would, thanks."

The thought that Gillian had likely thrown the painting in the attic, where it lay discarded for however long, made her shudder.

"No problem. When you've decided what you want to do with it, we can arrange transportation. We can also prepare it for sale if you want to go down that route, as it needs some cleaning and restoration."

"Thank you," Viola answered, trying to keep track of the conversation even as her head was buzzing with it all.

"One last thing. The painting will garner interest from the media and the art world. Are you happy for us to announce its discovery and handle any PR?"

"Please do."

"We'll keep your name out of it," she confirmed.

Having said goodbye to Georgina, she dialled Caroline, who answered immediately.

"And?" came the immediate demand.

"Erm, it's an Artemisia Gentileschi."

The line went quiet. Viola checked her phone to make sure they were still connected. Caroline eventually spoke.

"Seriously?"

"Yes, have you heard of her?"

"Of course." Caroline scoffed. "You know, she has quite a story."

"My contact at the Courtauld Institute mentioned she was raped."

"Yes, by a family friend. Her father took him to court for damages done to his 'property'; she was then tortured to make sure she was telling the truth. The case was found in her father's favour, but the perpetrator never served his five-year banishment from Rome, and in the end, she was the one who left."

Viola rolled her eyes. "Typical."

"What are you going to do? Sell it?"

"I can't. It's not mine, is it?"

"Whose is it?" Caroline questioned.

"Gillian's. You think she would have left it in the attic if she knew what it was?"

"I guess not, no." Caroline paused, then continued, "You know what this means?"

"No," Viola replied, not having had a second to think about anything.

"If you do sell Kingsford, Gillian could be in the market for a new home, or an old one. A Gentileschi could be worth a fortune."

"Millions, according to my contact," Viola corrected.

"There you go then. Gillian will be overjoyed. Everything will be as it should."

How would everything be as it should if she didn't have Gillian?

"I better go. I need to digest this and work out what I'm going to do."

If the summer ball and the photoshoot for *Country Life* had taught her anything, it was that Gillian belonged at Kingsford Manor. Viola had spent months trying to shake off the guilt that buying the place crushed Gillian even when the wheels had been in motion long before she purchased it from her. It was Gillian's circumstances that had led to the loss. If she'd known about the painting, then she wouldn't have lost anything. The thought of never having met her hit Viola hard in the chest.

Opening her phone, she searched through her emails from the solicitor. There was one document she needed to check — the covenant placed on the property when she bought it. In it was a schedule with an itemised list of contents to be included in the sale which were to remain with the house in the event of any future sale.

She skimmed through it. Not seeing what she was looking for, she gave it another more thorough check. There was no mention of paintings in the attic; the twelve listed she could place in the house. Gillian must have viewed them as garbage not to list them. If the Gentileschi wasn't amongst the paintings on the covenant, then legally they passed into her possession upon the sale. Morally, however, they belonged to Gillian.

Her mind raced with possibilities. Gillian would be able to afford to buy the estate back if she decided to sell it. There wasn't any choice other than to sell it; Kingsford Manor must be restored to its rightful owner. If she couldn't convince Gillian that she should find peace with herself, she could at least help restore order to her life.

As for herself, she would make a quiet retreat into the shadows. She had no intention of sticking around whilst Gillian insisted on play-acting in her own life. She would miss Kingsford Manor and its quirky little village, but now it served as a reminder of how she didn't fit in. She'd come to see through the changes her mum envisaged, and they had been accomplished. She'd dragged the building out of the last century, where Gillian left it — along with herself — to languish, and she'd allowed it to breathe.

Picking up her phone again, she dialled Walter's number. She would have to make sure everything was in order before speaking to Gillian. Despite needing some distance from the woman responsible for the sharp, gnawing pain in her broken heart, Viola knew that their paths were going to cross sooner than she expected.

CHAPTER 20

A knock at the door made Gillian jump. She rubbed her eyes as she got to her feet to answer it; her eyelids were heavy and dry from staring at the wall for the past hour. Her mind was running in circles, caught in an endless loop of thoughts of Viola and how things had ended between them. It clung to her like lead, pulling her down and making her limbs feel heavier with every step she took towards the door.

Why couldn't these feelings go away? Why did they have to surface in the first place? They did nothing but cause problems. She'd succeeded in keeping them at bay for so long, and now they had decided to betray her with Viola. She was sure, given time, they would dissipate, and Viola said she would be away with work soon. As much as she would miss her, some space would do Gillian a world of good.

She answered the door to find Viola standing there, her hands stuffed in her pockets and her jaw tight.

"Viola… what are you doing here?" Gillian asked, her grip tightening on the door handle.

"Can we talk? It's not about us. I won't go there again. I promise," Viola said, her voice quieter than usual yet carrying a weight that made it impossible to ignore.

It took Gillian a moment to reply; the flutter in her chest was doing nothing to help her. She stood back. "Come in."

As Viola entered, Gillian noticed the wide berth she gave her, stepping around her and into the sitting room. She followed, taking her usual seat as her visitor paced the room.

Gillian's eye caught the clothes horse, laden with drying clothes in front of the window. She hadn't expected guests today and wished she'd left it in the kitchen, out of sight. She eyed it with quiet irritation as it reminded her of what she'd been reduced to.

"Will you not sit?" she asked, gesturing to the chair opposite.

Viola sat without answering.

"Is everything okay?" Gillian asked, beginning to worry.

"I'm leaving Kingsford," Viola said bluntly. "I'm selling up. It's for the best. Plus, work will take me away for a while."

With confusion and disbelief bubbling inside her, Gillian tried to process Viola's words as she continued speaking. Her sentences spilling out in a breathless stream.

"It will give us some space. You some space, I mean. I don't need space. Sorry, I promised I wouldn't mention that — "

Gillian's frustration boiled over, her voice cutting through Viola's rambling like a sharp blade. "If you're leaving because of me, then I'm not sure how you thought you'd avoid mentioning us! Will you at least vet the buyer, or will you sell it to the highest bidder and damn us all to hell? Don't forget the covenant — everything I left must stay with the manor!"

Viola's eyes widened, hurt flashing across her face. Gillian wasn't sure if she cared anymore.

"Everything?" Viola said, her voice laced with bitterness. "Including the priceless lost Gentileschi painting you left in the attic? Or would you like that back too?"

"What?" Gillian leaned forward. "What do you mean?"

"If you would give me a minute to explain why I'm here instead of jumping down my throat, I'll tell you. The painting you despised appeared in the *Country Life* article; remember, I hung it above the fireplace. Arte spotted it, and to cut a long story short, the Courtauld Institute currently have it. They say it's a lost painting by Artemisia Gentileschi."

Gillian couldn't contain her laughter at the foolish suggestion. "It can't be. Jonathon was always picking up old forgeries, hoping they were originals. Do you know who she is?"

Viola rolled her eyes. "I am well versed by now, yes."

"It would be worth a fortune."

"Yes, it is," Viola replied flatly. "Millions, apparently."

Gillian opened her mouth to speak, but nothing came out. Her mind was whirling again. Viola didn't appear to be joking; there was an unfamiliar gravity to her demeanour and serious lines etched on her face.

"Thankfully it wasn't itemised on the schedule, so legally, it's mine."

"You *legally* own the painting?"

"Yes."

Too restless to sit anymore, Gillian stood and began pacing the room. The answer to all her problems had been right under her roof all along. How could she have been so blind? The loss of the manor was entirely her fault, and now, with the painting discovered, Viola owned that as well. How could such a thing even be possible? The thought sent a surge of anger and confusion through her, making her tremble.

"That's a good thing. My solicitor said if it formed part of the covenant we would be in a sticky situation. As it isn't, and it is mine, I have asked him to draw up a formal document confirming it was passed to me with the sale of the estate… and that I am now giving it to you."

Gillian turned and stared at Viola in disbelief.

"If you sell the painting, it will give you more than enough money to buy back the estate. You can have your material possessions back and everything important to you — including your title. I hope they make you happy."

She ignored Viola's dig. As much as she wanted it all back, she wouldn't accept charity.

"I can't accept such a *gift*."

"I'm not *gifting* it to you, Gillian. I'm returning *your* property to *you*. If you wish to have it back."

Their eyes locked.

"I do," Gillian replied softly, unsettled by the formality of their conversation.

"Good. It's rightfully yours regardless of legal ownership, and I can put that right. I'll have my solicitor get in touch with you, and he'll give you some contact details for people who can help you sell it. He can then arrange the sale of the estate back to you, once you've sold the painting. Is the price I paid you acceptable?"

"You don't want more?" Gillian questioned, her brow furrowing. "You put a lot of work into it."

"Work you didn't approve of, so no, it doesn't feel right to increase the value," she said with a firmness Gillian didn't feel she could debate. "Here is my solicitor's card."

Gillian took it, her fingers brushing against Viola's. The brief contact sent a jolt through her as she examined the name and number.

"Thank you," she murmured, feeling grateful and yet uneasy.

"Maybe we can walk back along a path after all. You can return to where you belong. A time before…"

Was she about to add the word 'me'? Her forlorn expression spoke for her. Gillian wasn't sure she wanted to return to exactly where she had been, though she possibly wanted to be somewhere close. She wasn't even sure she could regret everything that had passed. It had brought Viola to her door after all, even if she was about to exit back through it.

"I appreciate you bringing this to my attention." As she spoke, she realised how formal she sounded too. Was this what they had been reduced to? "Where will you go?"

"First back to my flat in London, and then I'm heading

to Australia for a tour. I'll head over early, acclimatise to the heat… and being alone again."

Gillian's stomach tightened as they fell into silence. It was hard enough coming to terms with the thought of Viola leaving Kingsford, let alone being on the other side of the world.

"When will you be back?"

"Around Christmas time."

Gillian nodded.

"Then I'll head to America after the new year until the spring, then onto Europe."

"I'm happy for you, that you have a packed schedule. Something to keep you busy."

"Me too. The distraction will be… welcome," Viola replied quietly, with a strained smile.

"I didn't mean for things to end like this," Gillian admitted. "To drive you away. I will miss our chats and our odd little adventures together."

Gillian took the short nod from Viola as agreement as the room filled with stifling tension.

Viola broke the strained silence by clearing her throat. "May I ask a favour?" Her tone was polite, distant, devoid of emotion, like she'd given up on the world.

Gillian looked at Viola, forcing herself to meet her gaze. A sadness shimmered in her eyes. Gillian's body tensed as a surge of guilt and helplessness washed over her. "Of course," she replied, her voice soft yet cautious, bracing herself for what was coming.

Viola hesitated, her fingers lightly tapping against the arm of the chair as though searching for the right words.

"Would you look after the place for me until the sale goes through?"

Gillian blinked, feeling a sharp pang at the thought of Viola leaving. She nodded, trying to mask the disappointment that threatened to surface. "Yes," she said, her voice steady despite the knot forming in her throat. "I'd be honoured."

Viola's lips twitched into what may have been a small, forced smile. Gillian couldn't be sure; it disappeared almost as quickly as it came. "Thank you," she replied, her tone formal and guarded. "Feel free to use it as you need."

Gillian nodded whilst a million thoughts raced through her mind. Was this how things were going to end between them? So stiff, so painfully polite?

Viola sat forward in her seat. "If you need anything or have questions about the sale — "

"Yes," Gillian cut in, hopeful she may suggest calling her.

"Then contact my solicitor; he will handle everything." Viola's voice wavered slightly, as though she, too, sensed the finality in her words.

Gillian opened her mouth to speak, to say something meaningful. All that came out was a quiet, "Okay."

The formality of it all — the businesslike tone, the solicitor — made the emptiness in Gillian's stomach grow. She wanted to ask if this was goodbye, if Viola truly planned to disappear from her life as abruptly as she'd entered it, but she couldn't find the courage to say it aloud.

Viola stood. "I suppose that's everything," she murmured, making her way to the door.

Gillian followed her through to the hall, skirting

around her to open the front door even when she knew by opening it she was helping Viola step through it and leave.

"Goodbye, Gillian," Viola said, her voice distant, as though she was already half gone.

Was that a final farewell? Her way of saying they wouldn't be speaking again? The question sat heavily inside Gillian as Viola stepped outside onto the path.

Before Gillian could muster a response, Viola turned and walked away, her pace brisk and determined. Gillian stood frozen, watching Viola's hands lift to her face. Was she crying? A wave of uncertainty hit her, tightening in her chest. She wanted to call out something, though what words she didn't know.

She stared down the empty path long after Viola vanished from sight, her gaze lingering on where she'd last seen her. Slowly, she closed the door, her fingers absentmindedly grazing her cheek as she felt something on them. Realising her eyes were damp, she brushed them with the back of her hand.

She retraced her steps to the sitting room and collapsed back into her seat, the weight of the past thirty minutes crashing over her. Had Viola's visit happened, or was it a dream? She was about to regain everything she wanted, yet instead of the relief or excitement she imagined, an unsettling hollowness lowered onto her chest, meeting the nausea which rose from her stomach.

~

Viola wiped her eyes as she closed the gate of the lodge behind her, the weight of her emotions pressing down on her harder than she cared to admit. She'd promised herself that once inside, she would keep her feelings in check, compartmentalise, but that was easier said than done. Gillian made her feel things even when she tried not to. She did so even when she was angry, which she clearly had been when she realised she was mistaken about Jonathon's painting — and, worse, that she held no rights to it at all.

She could see the confusion and fury in Gillian's eyes, yet beneath there was something deeper that tugged at Viola. It was the way Gillian's voice stiffened, her tone deliberately neutral, as if she were trying to mask how much she cared; the way her mouth opened to speak only to close again as if she were holding back words she didn't dare speak.

Exhaling slowly, she walked the well-trodden route down the drive. The tension in her body and the knot in her chest reminded her how complicated things had become.

"Ah, Viola," came Bridget's voice, making her jump. "I was coming to invite you to tea next week."

She hadn't even noticed the woman walking towards her. A quick, subtle dab of her eyes was in order; unfortunately, it didn't get past Bridget's notice.

"Are you okay? I've seen many people leave Gillian's crying, even done it once or twice myself. I never expected you to be among us."

"I'm leaving Kingsford, selling up," Viola said quickly, hoping it would be enough to divert her.

"Oh. I'm sorry to hear that." Bridget blinked, then eyed Viola with curiosity and concern.

"I have a tour of Australia until Christmas, and then I'll be in America for a while after the new year, followed by Europe, so, you know, lots to keep me busy. Plus, it's all a bit too much living in the countryside; this place is a lot of work. I love it, and I find a strange kind of peace here, even if I miss the city, but I mainly find burden and responsibility."

"Might you visit occasionally, for peace, without the burden and responsibility?" Bridget asked gently.

"I don't think so." Viola looked towards the lodge, then wondered if Gillian was looking out at them through her binoculars. She turned back to Bridget, who was staring at her with a softness about her eyes.

"You know, when she first came here, she didn't speak much about her past. I never questioned her about it. I assumed she would talk about it if she wanted to, but she never did. I got the impression she didn't think much of her mother."

Viola nodded.

"She might not let people in, but it doesn't mean we can't see in. She isn't that good at hiding things. She's only human — don't tell her I said that." Bridget smirked. "She and Jonathon were never Cinderella and Prince Charming, you know, yet somehow, they made it work. I saw her eyes drift enough times to women to get an understanding of the truth. At first, I thought she was admiring their fashion, but I sensed it was more the shape of what lies beneath that enraptured her."

Unsure how to respond, Viola remained silent. She couldn't confirm anything; that would be outing Gillian.

"I've noticed that same look directed at you recently.

You seem to have awoken something in her. Which is remarkable, really," Bridget added, "considering there was a time she blamed you for everything."

Viola smiled, knowing the impact she had made. Not that it changed anything. "She's too proud."

Bridget placed a hand on Viola's arm, her expression calm yet firm. "She always was. Give her time. Leave her to understand what she's missing. People come to terms with themselves in their own way."

Viola sighed and nodded as uncertainty filled her eyes. "I hope so," she murmured. "For her sake."

"I know it's not something we can ask of you, but I urge you to sell the manor to someone who will be sensitive to Kingsford... and its inhabitants." Bridget glanced at the lodge.

Unsure exactly how much of Gillian's future financial situation she should disclose, Viola decided less was best. Like her sexuality, it wasn't for her to mention.

"I promise you, only someone Gillian approves of will buy it."

"Thank you," Bridget replied, exhaling a breath. "I'll miss you."

"I'll miss you too. Keep in touch, won't you?"

"I will," Bridget answered, reaching forward and hugging Viola.

With a rub of Viola's shoulder, Bridget flashed her a smile, and they parted, walking their separate ways. Viola was going to miss her. Bridget was down to earth, honest, and someone grounding for Gillian, whether either of them realised it or not. She knew how to read her friend like an open book, never missing a beat.

Feeling the need to lift her spirits, she headed to the stable. Dudley would cheer her up. As she approached his stall, he whinnied at her, stretching his neck over his door.

"Hey, Dudley."

His lips twitched as Viola stroked his nose.

"I haven't got anything for you, I'm afraid. You just get me today. I hope that's enough."

He snorted, scattering a puff of warm breath into the cool air.

"I'm going to miss you, almost as much as I'll miss your annoying mistress. I was looking forward to spending more time with you."

A tear ran down her cheek at the realisation she wouldn't see the horse again. She wanted to leave as soon as possible in hopes it would ease her pain, but the thought of not being at Kingsford caused pain too. She knew she must force herself to leave, but it didn't make it any easier to do. She needed to heal away from here and come to terms with not being enough for Gillian to push herself out of her comfort zone.

Dudley nudged against her hand as she stroked him. Taking out her phone, she wrapped her arm under his neck and pressed her face to his. She smiled, thinking back to when she felt a little afraid of him. Dudley nuzzled against her shoulder as she took a selfie.

"Bye, Dudley."

Pulling herself away she gave him one last stroke on the nose and walked away. The sound of his feet stamping against the stable floor made her tears flow again.

As she neared the manor, she blinked through her blurry vision and could make out Agatha in the distance.

Wiping her sleeve across her damp eyes, she caught sight of the cat weaving her way around the far side of the building. Curious, she followed at a careful distance.

When she rounded the corner, she arrived just in time to see a tail flick out of sight, vanishing through a cellar window. Noticing a small pane of glass missing — just large enough for a cat to slip through — she crouched down, leaning closer to peer into the shadows below.

"Agatha."

From somewhere in the darkness, a small, rather disgruntled meow echoed back.

"That's how you've been getting in," she groaned, realising the cellar door, which never closed properly, didn't have a faulty catch at all. Someone was using it to sneak inside unnoticed. She was going to miss the quirky little cat too.

As she stood, her eyes caught the bench where she often sat with Gillian. She approached it, hesitating before finally taking a seat. The memories rushed back — Gillian's smiles, their shared honesty, the way her presence felt both calming and electric. Viola would never regret getting to know her; those moments had shaped something in her.

As for falling in love with her, that she might regret. Gillian Carmichael wasn't the kind of person you could forget easily, no matter how hard you tried. It scared Viola the most — knowing no matter where she went, part of her would always feel tethered to Gillian.

CHAPTER 21

TEN WEEKS LATER

Gillian walked down the drive towards the manor, a box of china under one arm. It was a huge relief that the sale of the painting had gone smoothly, allowing the contracts to be completed as winter set in. It was the time of year when the building looked most regal; it was often draped in a blanket of snow with the flickering lights of the fires inside casting a warm glow through the windows. Today there was neither snow nor lights, only a quiet stillness.

Her pace slowed as she neared the familiar facade, each step feeling heavier. It loomed larger than ever, its walls holding stories that refused to fade. She had thought she would be ready, but now standing here, on the cusp of entering the life she thought she had left behind forever, uncertainty gripped her.

Agatha followed a few paces behind. Perhaps she was eager to return home without the threat of eviction by an irritable mezzo-soprano. To Viola's credit, since they had become friends, she appeared to have accepted the cat's wandering ways, allowing Agatha to come and go as she pleased.

Friends. The word cut through Gillian. She couldn't even describe them as that anymore. The emptiness inside her served as a daily reminder. The only contact she'd made with Viola since she left was through their solicitors, although she saw her once — or believed she did. On the day of the auction, when she looked around the very crowded room, a pair of sunglasses and a baseball cap stood out to her. She was sure it was Viola. Following the auction, there was no sight of either a baseball cap or sunglasses, and there was no Viola.

Turning to see if Agatha was still following, she noticed the cat was retracing her steps back along the path. Something Viola once said came to mind: *Our lives have multiple paths, all with multiple destinations, and we can't walk back along them, only accept the path we have walked.* She also admitted later, *Maybe we can walk back along a path after all.* Looking down at her boots as they crunched into the gravel, Gillian realised she was literally walking back along her path.

The thought of getting the estate back had once felt all-consuming. Viola may have distracted her from those thoughts for a time, but they were always there, lingering under the surface. They lessened over time, as she became used to her new life or at least grew to accept that her return may never happen. The anger that had once resided inside her was no longer there; she was unsure when it had left her.

Unlocking the porch door, she placed the box inside and locked it again. Before going inside, she needed to do something and made her way to the church.

Wending her way through the churchyard she searched for Jonathon's grave. Having forgotten its precise location, she realised she'd not visited it once since the funeral. She found what she was looking for, though, thanks to the clean headstone standing out like a beacon amongst older ones. Standing beside it, she dangled the keys off her finger, over Jonathon's grave.

"I got it back," she whispered, her voice barely audible against the rustle of the wind. The sound of her words made her recoil.

What was she doing here? Had she really come to gloat over a grave? A pang of nausea rose in her stomach. She took a deep breath, willing it to fade, but the unease lingered. Looking around, she noticed the other graves. Each was carefully tended, adorned with fresh flowers that brought vivid bursts of colour to the grey headstones. Jonathon's grave was bare, with no flowers, no signs of visitors, only the cold, hard stone and earth.

Her fingers tightened around the keys as she stood there in the silence, wondering what she'd become. Their marriage had been far from perfect, but Jonathon did share Kingsford with her. He'd allowed her to fall in love with it, probably all the while knowing it was the only reason she stayed.

She hadn't exactly entered the marriage honestly. If anything, she was the one who had manipulated him into believing they were something they weren't and that a happy future together was possible, all at a time when her love for Hen was so strong and her loss so raw. The need to escape her mother was so present, so urgent, as was her hatred for herself. She had been desperate. Could she blame herself for the actions she had taken? Could anyone? She left the grave feeling empty, a sensation she was growing accustomed to since Viola left.

As she walked back, a dream from the previous night came to her. She was in a rowing boat beside the bank of a lake in the dead of night. Jonathon helped her in and then pushed it away from the bank. She begged for him to pull her back, but he ignored her, so she floated around the lake with no direction and only the light of the moon to guide her. Viola appeared on a bank in the distance, waving at her, beckoning her and telling her to use her oars. When she hadn't got any closer to the bank despite what felt like a night of rowing, Viola suddenly appeared in the boat beside her and helped her row. By the time she got to the bank, she was alone; Viola and Jonathon were both gone. It had left her in rather a panic when she woke.

Arriving back at the manor, she stepped into the porch, where she removed her coat and boots. It wasn't her first time there since Viola left. She had gone in to turn on the heating once the temperature dropped. Today was the first time she'd been in, though, since retaking possession of the property.

Picking up the box of china, she made her way to the

great hall, where the familiar scent of aged wood hung in the air. It carried traces of Viola too, and while part of her wanted to push it away, another part of her ached for it to linger. The grand piano she had left behind would serve as a permanent reminder of her.

Her footsteps echoed against the stone floor, amplifying the stillness in the cool, draughty air. It was quite the contrast to the warm, intimate, cosy lodge she'd grown fond of. The vastness of the space felt oppressive now; it was something she'd never experienced before, but the void carried a weight. It was all hers, every inch of it, but she was still directionless. This wasn't how she'd imagined it would be, standing in this grand space with everything she'd ever wanted. She should be feeling more — more excitement, elation, drive. Instead, the same hollow ache resided within.

Everything would feel better after a cup of Earl Grey, and with Bridget due soon, she needed to get a move on. Gillian carried the box to the kitchen, setting it on the smooth marble worktop. As she unpacked the delicate china mugs and teapot, her gaze wandered around the room. Viola's renovations really were impressive.

Her eye caught the window, where the two of them had enjoyed coffee together. Where she had discovered sapphic romance, a quiet passion that had blossomed over the last few months — not that she had told Viola as much. Exploring these stories was something she would keep private, a place where she would lose herself in worlds that felt foreign yet familiar.

She removed the kettle and filled it with water. Leaving

it to boil she made her way to the drawing room and pulled back the curtains. The painting that had always hung above the fireplace was back where it belonged. The thought of Viola rehanging it for her before she left made Gillian smile. It was more suitable for the space than Viola's choice, not that she regretted her fishing it from the attic — that she would be forever grateful for. She wished she'd been able to thank Viola in a better way and that things could have ended differently between them, not as abruptly as they had done. As she sparked a fire to life in the hearth, a voice echoed from the hall.

"Coo-ee. Anyone home?" Bridget's head appeared around the drawing room door.

Yes, Gillian was home, but it didn't feel like she was.

"Come in," she said. "I'll fetch some tea."

Five minutes later she found Bridget nestled in her usual seat as she entered with a tray of tea and biscuits. Sitting opposite her friend, it felt as if the last year hadn't happened. Except it had. A lid she'd closed tightly enough that it would need a crowbar to open had flown off in Viola's presence, and Gillian had struggled to put it back on.

Bridget tucked into the biscuits and began to fill her in on the village gossip. Gillian's attention flickered, her thoughts drifting elsewhere as she struggled to stay engaged in the conversation. She didn't care that the major had passed out on the village green that morning from too much revelry at the Fox and Hounds last night or that prices were on the up again in the village shop or that a house in the village was for sale. She didn't care for any of it.

"You get to climb back into your own bed again tonight," Bridget said, her tone bright but edged with concern.

The comment caught Gillian's attention, striking a chord against the thoughts she'd been wrestling with. She had considered moving back in or at least spending a night there before they finalised the paperwork, but something held her back. She'd told herself she would wait until it was official and the estate was hers again. With that time finally arriving, something still didn't feel right.

"Hmm," she mumbled.

"You don't sound keen."

"So much has happened since I last slept there," Gillian ruminated. "I'm not sure it will feel the same."

"Did you expect it to, after almost a year away? A lot has changed. You've changed; there are probably more changes to come." Bridget sat back in her seat and stirred her tea. "You know," she said, setting her spoon on her saucer. "I've been thinking a lot lately; about life, I mean. How short it is. You blink, and Christmas is around the corner again, and suddenly you're wondering if you've been living at all."

Gillian looked up from her cup, her expression guarded but intrigued. "You're not usually one for philosophical thoughts," she remarked, trying to keep her voice steady. There was something in Bridget's words that made her uncomfortable.

"I have my moments." Bridget shrugged slightly. "You know I envy you. You have the manor back, a chance to start afresh, a whole new direction if you wish. We only get this one shot, don't we? One life. Seems a waste not to live it honestly, don't you think?"

Gillian's smile faltered as a weight pressed on her chest. "I suppose we all make compromises," she said, her tone more defensive than intended. "It's part of life."

Bridget tilted her head, watching her with a knowing look. "Compromises, yes, but not about the big stuff. Not about who we are at our core." Her tone hardened. "That's not something we should shrink away from. What's the point of living if we spend it pretending? Doesn't that rob us of any real happiness?"

Gillian tensed, crossing her arms, trying to shield herself from the conversation. "Not everything's that simple. It's not always about 'living your truth.' There are people involved. Expectations. Life is complicated."

Bridget nodded, her voice softening. "It is. Life is messy, and people… they can be even messier. You can't bury who you are forever. Not without it eating away at you."

Gillian's pulse raced. Was Bridget talking about her? Did she know? No, she couldn't possibly. She swallowed hard, forcing herself to remain composed. "People don't simply accept change," she said quietly, uncertainty creeping into her words.

Bridget leaned forward, her tone steady and unyielding. "Just because you don't accept change doesn't mean others don't."

Gillian glared at her, speechless.

Bridget took a sip of tea and then started up again. "I know that hiding pieces of yourself, the most important pieces, will slowly break you down. You wake up one day wondering how you ended up living a life that doesn't even feel like yours." She paused. "I mean… that's how I'm sure people would feel if they were living a lie." Bridget stood and reached for the teapot. "I'll fetch us some more tea."

Living a lie. The words caught Gillian unawares, tightening her chest as Bridget left the room. Her gaze dropped to her lap, her fingers tracing the rim of her cup. She'd never considered herself a liar, certainly not in the way she conducted herself. Was any part of her life not a lie? The thought lingered, unsettling her, as she replayed the moments where she'd tucked away her truth, piece by piece; hiding the part of herself that scared her most.

The past months with Viola had been when she felt most true to herself and happiest. Since Viola had left, she'd gone through the motions, keeping herself busy — anything to avoid the quiet moments when her thoughts crept in. She hoped the more noise she made, the less she'd hear her heart breaking. Yet no matter how many tasks she took on, no matter how loud her world became, it didn't stop her from feeling it. The ache was always there, lingering beneath every distraction, reminding her some things couldn't be drowned out.

Now she was alone, truly alone in her core. She'd felt alone most of her life; even if she never was — she was always surrounded by people — it was her choice to emotionally isolate herself. Choosing solitude was easier; it was a form of control. Now, with loneliness thrust upon her, it felt different. Stifling, even suffocating. There was always Bridget, her constant companion. Was that enough when someone who made her feel whole, visible, and complete was out there?

Viola was always unapologetically herself, and she thrived because of it. Gillian wondered what that kind of freedom must feel like — how liberating it would be to live without fear of judgement. Viola once feared that judgement, too, until she was outed. Her story was splashed across tabloids and dissected in the public eye, only to be forgotten a day or two later when some other scandal emerged to entertain the masses.

Her thoughts wandered back to the dressing room, to the moment she couldn't resist and had kissed Viola. Tingles rushed through her as she let herself relive it — the feel of Viola's soft lips against hers, the taste, the undeniable pull of desire between them.

As quickly as she allowed it, she forced the memory away, and with it, a wave of nausea swept over her. The unsettled feeling lingered, leaving her unsteady. It was a sense of being out of sync with herself, as though something inside her was shifting and she wasn't sure how to set it right again.

It was a feeling she'd only experienced twice before: when she lost Hen and the manor. She knew Hen would never return; the manor, however, was back in her hands. Viola's words sank through her: *You can have your material possessions back, and everything important to you — including your title. I hope they make you happy.* She didn't feel happy; only thoughts of Viola gave her any surge of happiness, and now she was on the other side of the world.

Although Gillian had regained her identity as lady of the manor, she wasn't feeling the peace it once brought her. It didn't give her the strength she once felt either. Did happiness not reside in bricks and mortar — or in her case sandstone and mortar — as she once thought?

The manor was now an empty shell full of echoes of happier times. If it wasn't being enjoyed, having memories made inside it, what was the point of it? It wasn't a family home anymore; it hadn't been for decades. It was a meeting space and a good one at that. She needed to make something out of it, let it breathe, and let herself breathe. She recalled Viola saying Kingsford was suffocating her. Had they been suffocating each other? She loved it dearly. The estate was part of her; it ran through her blood. Maybe it was time for a different relationship with it.

Having walked back along the path to the manor, she didn't feel she'd arrived at the place she had left. Was she walking along a new path to a previous destination, one that was unchanged, unlike her? Was she in fact not wilting without Kingsford, as she had once feared, and instead metamorphosing?

As much as she didn't want to admit it, she had changed during her time in the lodge, and all her attempts to forget about Viola had failed too. The lodge and the manor were full of memories of her, as was her heart. She had fallen for the mezzo-soprano, and nothing felt right now that she was gone.

"Are you okay?" Bridget asked, as she re-entered the room and set the teapot down on the table.

"Yes. We have work to do, Bridget, you and I."

Bridget's eyes lit up instantly. "We do?"

"We'll organise a New Year's Eve party for the village, the first event of many to come for 'Kingsford Manor

Estate'. Now there are funds, I want to pay you for everything you do and give you a title. 'Events manager' suit you?"

"Great, and what about you?"

Gillian paused, then answered with a newfound resolve, "I don't need a title."

CHAPTER 22

Gillian rummaged through the crowded assortment of coats hanging in the porch. Locating her own at the back, along with her scarf, she wrapped it around her neck. As she pulled the long, black wool coat over her heavy arms, the weight reminded her of how tired she was. Her whole body ached, exhausted from a day of preparations, the culmination of a month of organisation.

Although tempted to slip away to bed, she knew it would be bad form to leave her own New Year's Eve party before midnight. A quick check of her watch revealed one more hour of loud music to endure. That was assuming everyone departed once the clock struck twelve, which was never guaranteed. It also meant one final hour in which Viola might still arrive — if she was coming.

With a deep sigh, Gillian pushed open the front door and stepped out into the darkness, making her way around to the back. The cold air bit against her cheeks and nipped at her stockinged legs, exposed by her knee-length dress. She didn't care; it was refreshing to feel something other than the numbness and emptiness.

Reaching Hen's bench, Gillian sat and gazed up at the stars in the clear, moonlit sky. They twinkled, as though watching over the world below, where everything shifted and moved in an endless dance. Her breath puffed out in small clouds, vanishing into the cold air — much like the passage of time — ushering in a new year, whether she was ready or not. What would it hold for her this time? Only one thing was important to her now, like she would suffocate without it.

A light in the distance caught Gillian's breath. She stared at it, hesitant to hope, but it was too low to be a star and unmistakably moving. The familiar deep, rhythmic thumping — a sound unheard at Kingsford in months — echoed through the air, growing louder and louder as it neared. It wasn't until the lawn was flooded with light and the helicopter began to descend, that she finally dared to believe Viola was here.

She watched, entranced, as the helicopter lowered itself to the ground in the distance. Silence followed as the blades stopped and the lights went out. Her ears pricked, listening for changes that would signal Viola was heading into the manor. She would give her some time to greet everyone before making an appearance — not wanting to compete for Viola's attention in a crowd. Footsteps coming down the path told her she wouldn't need to vie for Viola's attention.

"I knew I'd find you here." Viola's voice broke through the shadows, making Gillian's heart race.

"How?" Gillian asked, her lips pressing together in a faint smile.

Viola sat beside her, her face lit by the glow of the moonlight. "I first thought something was off when I saw flashing coloured lights coming from within the manor. It was when I stepped from the helicopter and heard 'Come On, Eileen' blaring that I knew you'd be outside. If you were outside, where else would you be other than here?"

A warm sense of belonging spread through Gillian, catching her off guard. Viola didn't just see her, she understood her to her core — understood her patterns, her habits. She let out a quiet sigh, leaning into the comfort of Viola's presence.

"It's not your usual repertoire," Viola continued. "What happened to Mozart?"

"It was Bridget's suggestion. I thought it might be good to try something different," Gillian said, her voice barely masking the uncertainty within her.

"I can hear enough to tell me that everyone inside is having a great time."

"They are, and that's what matters," Gillian replied with a smile, adding casually. "A lot has changed since you left."

"Looks like it," Viola said, shifting herself around to face Gillian. "Speaking of which, I forgot to leave this for the landing lights." She held out a small remote control.

"It just proved useful, so keep it — just in case you need it again," Gillian couldn't help but notice the smile on Viola's face as she put it into her pocket. It pulled a similar smile to her own lips. "How was Australia?"

"Warmer than here."

"That's not difficult." Gillian tightened her coat around her. "Otherwise, a success?"

"Yes. Very successful. A sellout tour. No falling onstage. Couldn't have been better."

Gillian nodded, knowing it would be. She took a silent deep breath, aware that more needed to be said than simple pleasantries, and it needed to come from her. "I'm glad you came." Her voice was little more than a whisper. "I wasn't sure you would."

"I wasn't sure either," Viola replied.

Gillian fidgeting with the sleeve of her coat. "I missed you." She met Viola's eyes, noticing an unmistakable smile on her face that brought hope to her heart.

"I missed you too."

They shared a lingering look, smiling as the unspoken was finally beginning to surface.

Viola shifted, her eyes searching Gillian's face. "So… what else has changed apart from the music?"

Gillian could hear the unspoken question beneath Viola's words. She knew exactly what Viola wanted to know. Why was she invited? Her throat tightened, and she feared the words might refuse to come. The fluttering in her stomach threatened to consume her as unformed words tumbled through her mind. Closing her eyes she pushed everything away and spoke from the heart.

"I find myself missing something that I can't seem to live without," she started, her voice trembling slightly. "When you left, you took a part of me with you. I tried to convince myself I could go on, that I didn't need you. I tried to bury everything, to forget, and I can't. No matter how hard I've tried, I keep coming back to you. It's like there's this emptiness inside me nothing else can fill — not even this place." She looked down, twisting her fingers together. "I don't expect anything from you, but I can't keep pretending. I needed you to know the truth."

Gillian's heart pounded in her chest, her pulse resounding in her ears as she waited for Viola's response.

"I didn't think you noticed when I left," Viola replied, her tone flat and emotionless.

Gillian turned to her. "I heard the helicopter leave. I didn't know it was the last time until they came to collect your car." A feeling of loss rose inside her again until she realised Viola was beside her. She had come. But how did she feel? That was her burning question. She looked at Viola, eyes searching for any hope. "I knew the moment you left I would regret it, but I wasn't ready. Plus, I knew I could never be with you whilst you owned Kingsford. People would think I was only after one thing. I didn't want that. Then I got it back and hoped it would fill the void you left… and it didn't. How could it?"

"Fair point." Viola grinned.

"I realised I'd lost more than woodworm, stone, and mortar. I lost you. As much as I wanted Kingsford, I realised I wanted you in it more than I wanted it back for myself."

Viola raised an eyebrow. "Really?"

"Yes. You know, I don't even live there anymore," Gillian remarked, with a hint of amusement.

"What?"

"Turns out I prefer the lodge. I might have been able to afford to buy Kingsford, but it doesn't run itself. Do you know how much I can charge for exclusive use for a weekend or a wedding? We have five bookings for the coming year. We have events, residential weekends, and retreats lined up."

"We?" Viola probed.

"Yes, myself and Bridget. Finally, I can pay her for all the work she does."

"Wow, things have changed." Viola paused before continuing, her voice pensive. "I never expected anything from you either, you know. I just needed you to be living your best life. That's all I wanted for you. I thought I could help with that. I can't imagine how you've felt hiding yourself away for so long, and I get it. I do. I would probably still be hiding if I hadn't been outed, though I assume it's easier when you have someone by your side, holding your hand."

"Will you be by my side… and hold my hand?" Gillian asked cautiously. Her heart raced as she immediately regretted posing the question, fearing the possibility of an unfavourable answer. Until she heard a definitive "no" there was always hope, however faint.

"Of course," Viola answered with a smile. "Did you ever doubt it?"

"Yes. I thought I may have pushed you away too far."

"I didn't go far."

"You went to the other side of the world!" Gillian exclaimed.

"In body, yes." Viola chuckled. "In my mind and soul, I was here with you — sitting here, passing the time of day as we once did."

It was everything Gillian wanted to hear until she realised Viola's assurance was vague. Seeking clarification, she asked, "What does this mean, precisely?"

"It means I want to be with you, Gillian." Viola's chuckle turned to full-blown laughter. "I want to navigate this strange and sometimes cruel world with you. I want to sit on this bench with you and pass more time, though ideally not in the middle of the night in the freezing cold."

Gillian felt Viola's hand slip into hers. It was warm, sending a gentle surge of comfort through her, easing a lingering tension inside her, as if thawing something within. The softness of her skin was soothing, and it filled Gillian with strength.

"That's if you're sure you're ready," Viola said, her brown eyes searching Gillian's face. "Because these last months…" She paused, swallowing hard, as if the words themselves were too heavy to bear. "They haven't been easy. They've been hell. I couldn't just turn off my feelings for you. Believe me, I tried. I threw myself into work, thinking that if I could just keep moving, keep busy, maybe I'd find some kind of relief. But work didn't help. It just reminded me of Mum. I thought about her, about how much I miss her, and then…" She let out a shaky breath. "Then I thought about you. About us. And it was like grieving all over again, only this time it was for something I thought I might still have but couldn't touch."

Viola's voice cracked, her composure breaking under the weight of her confession. "I ached, Gillian. For you. Every single day, I ached. And I still do. I ache like part of me is missing, like I'm constantly reaching for something that isn't there."

She hesitated, and then her next words came out

quieter, almost pleading. "I don't want to feel like that anymore. But I need to know, before I let myself hope again — are you ready? Can you let me in this time?"

Gillian squeezed her hand, not having fully appreciated the turmoil Viola would feel. She'd underestimated the strength of her feelings, just as she had underestimated her own. She recognised what Viola said; she'd been feeling it, too, these past months.

"I ached for you too. I know I can't fight myself any longer and that I can't bear to be without you a moment longer," Gillian answered, looking down as she added, "As for the rest, I'll need some help to navigate it."

"I'm here." Viola squeezed back, her touch grounding yet gentle. "You don't have to put on a brave face for me. I want to see the real you — the vulnerable, beautiful parts that you hide away from everyone else. You've shown me pieces of you, and now I want to see the rest."

A newfound courage welled up inside Gillian. "I want that too. I want you to see all of me. No masks. No pretence. I want to see all of you too."

"Sounds like we have a deal," Viola said, shuffling closer until their legs touched.

"A deal?" Gillian raised an eyebrow, a hint of amusement in her voice. "Is that what we're calling it?"

"Absolutely. An unbreakable pact to be our truest selves with each other. To be honest, raw, and open, no matter what."

Gillian nodded, a smile spreading across her face as Viola's leg pressed against hers. "I think I can manage that. Be warned — it might not always be pretty."

"I'm counting on it," Viola replied, her voice steady

and her gaze unwavering. "Because I know that with you, every part of it will be real. And that's all I've ever wanted. Someone real in this superficial world."

"And how do we seal this 'deal' of ours?" Gillian replied, her lips curving into a mischievous smile.

"I can think of one way," Viola said, closing the gap between them.

As Viola leaned in, Gillian closed her eyes, her heart pounding. She'd pictured this so many times since the last time they'd been this close, no matter how hard she'd tried not to.

Viola's lips were tentative at first, their coolness barely brushing against Gillian's, yet it was enough to send a ripple of heat through her. Her breath caught, and instinctively, her mouth parted. She needed more of Viola.

As their lips met again, this time with certainty, a rush of emotions made her moan. It seemed to encourage Viola as Gillian felt her hands on her waist, tugging their bodies closer together. She slid her fingers into Viola's hair, savouring what softness she could feel between her cool, numb fingertips.

As their kiss deepened, she allowed herself to relax into it, focusing on the feel of Viola's mouth and her inquisitive tongue. Even though there would be other moments like this, at least she hoped there would, this one she was going to savour. She may have been anxious about all the other aspects of being physical with Viola, but kissing wasn't one of them. It felt safe kissing; it was what she and Hen had done, but that was all.

Her stomach tingled with nervousness as she realised there was no going back. She couldn't allow herself to hide again; as much as the future scared her, there was no closing the lid on these feelings. She would need to find a way to let them breathe, to let them define and shape her. Meeting someone in life was hard enough; to have those feelings reciprocated was even more unlikely. For two worlds to collide at that same time felt like an impossibility, yet it had happened, on this very bench.

Feeling Viola's hands move from her waist, Gillian found them cradling her face, where her cool fingers grazed her cheeks, and tucked a stray strand of hair behind her ear. Her touch was gentle yet possessive, anchoring them as their lips met again, this time with a raw, undeniable urgency. Gillian leaned in, wrapping her arms tightly around Viola's back, pulling her closer, as if the space between them was too much to bear.

The sound of counting down echoed in the distance. "Five… four… three… two… one…" was followed by cheering.

"Happy New Year!" Viola said, pulling back from their embrace.

"Happy New Year!" Gillian replied, looking at the horizon as it lit up with fireworks launching into the sky.

They leaned back against the bench, Viola resting against Gillian's shoulder as they held hands. "I'm so happy you could get Kingsford back," she said. "It always suited you more."

"It did." She knew it suited her even more now than it ever had done. Turning it into an events business had given her some direction when she felt lost. The manor now fulfilled a purpose, and so did she.

"What do we do now?" she asked slowly.

"I'm hoping you might have a room for me."

"You can have your old one upstairs," Gillian offered.

"Great, thanks."

The flat response from Viola told her that it might not have been exactly what she was hoping for.

"Although it doesn't sound like you'll get much peace," Gillian said, hearing the music start up again. "I'm not sure what time they will keep partying until. You could join them… I'm a little tired myself."

"I think we both know I didn't come here for a party."

"Oh?" Gillian said, keeping her tone casual.

"No." Viola looked up at Gillian. "I came for you… all of you."

Gillian's heart quickened at the intensity in Viola's eyes. There was something about the way she looked at her, as if she could see straight through all the carefully constructed walls, right into her core.

For so long, Gillian had kept everyone at arm's length, convinced that no one could truly see or understand her, but here was Viola, looking at her with a sincerity that stirred something deep within. The noise of the distant party faded into the background, leaving Gillian feeling like they were the only two people in the world, and that was all she needed.

"Why don't you come to the lodge for a nightcap?" The widening of Viola's eyes suggested to Gillian she'd hit the right mark. "Until it quietens down. We could talk some more."

"Of course." Viola nodded.

Gillian shivered, the cold air finally penetrating through to her skin.

Viola rubbed at her arm. "Get yourself inside. I'll grab my bag from the helicopter and meet you at the lodge."

"Don't be long," Gillian said as she stood, grateful she would have a few moments to regroup. She was unsure what Viola was expecting from her invitation and even more unsure of what exactly she was offering.

∽

Viola had no intention of being long. She was practically running to the helicopter to retrieve her bag. A nightcap with Gillian Carmichael was not something you strolled towards, especially not after a kiss like the one they just shared.

Their dressing room kiss had ignited a fire within her, and its fleeting nature left her hungry for more. She didn't only want the taste of Gillian — she wanted all of her. Every wonderful part of her. Yes, Gillian could be frustrating, with her rigid, old-fashioned ways, but those had grown on Viola, becoming part of what she now found so endearing.

It was Gillian's insistence on keeping things exactly as they always were that gave her a sense of stability, a sense of home. That passion for order, for the familiar, was so distinctly Gillian — and Viola wouldn't have it any other way.

It was something she herself had never experienced growing up, even in adulthood, so she could understand Gillian defending it. The quirks that once exasperated her were now the very things that made her heart ache for more. That made her long to uncover every part of the woman behind the guarded exterior. She expected there was even more that lay hidden away, more vulnerability that Gillian hadn't let her see yet, and she couldn't wait to unwrap it.

Grabbing her bag from the co-pilot seat, she headed around the side of the manor house, where its windows glowed with a warm, golden light. Making her way onto the drive, she stopped and looked back. The flickering of the fire in the great hall cast a cosy, orange light that embraced the entire house. Shadows danced across the glass as figures moved inside, their laughter and voices creating a welcoming hum. Even the walls seemed to vibrate with energy.

She smiled to see it alive, imagining this liveliness to be the house's natural state over the last few decades, with Gillian at the helm, orchestrating gatherings, presiding over lively soirées, making sure everything was precisely as it should be. A light caught her eye and pulled her from her thoughts. Realising it was the front door opening, she strained to see who it was as a voice came through the darkness.

"You came!"

"Bridget, hi. Yes. Here I am," she replied, approaching her.

"And? Was it worthwhile coming as I told you it would be? I heard you land some time ago. I'm assuming you found who you were looking for."

"Yes, I did," Viola replied with a contented smile. "Thanks for the encouragement and keeping me posted."

"She was very down after you left. I hoped getting this place back would at least put a spring in her step. It did the opposite. So I took the opportunity to sow some seeds of thought."

"It helped. Thank you."

"Are you coming in?"

"No." Viola looked towards the lodge. "Gillian's tired, and apparently we have more to talk about."

"Gillian, talk? That's a new one."

Viola smirked, although her eyes carried a hint of seriousness. "Bridget, can I ask you something?"

"Of course."

"Could you run this place on your own? If Gillian wasn't here."

"I could run it better if she wasn't." Her hand shot to her mouth as if trying to stuff the words back in.

Viola laughed; she'd missed Bridget. "It's okay. I won't say anything."

Bridget smiled and lowered her hand. "I've been her right-hand woman for thirty-odd years. I've got used to my place in Gillian's shadow. We make a good team."

"Isn't it time to step out of her shadow?

"Oh, I'm happy with my position as second-in-command," Bridget said coyly.

"But you're a flower waiting to bloom, Bridget." Viola reached forward and squeezed her arm. "It's time you bloomed. Can you? For her sake as much as your own."

After a pause, Bridget replied, "I think I can." She pulled herself up straight and nodded. "Yes, I can."

"Then you know what to do. I'd best not keep her waiting."

Bridget laughed. "No." Her voice turned more serious.

"Thank you for coming. For her sake as much as your own."

Viola flashed Bridget a smile, acknowledging her throwing her own words back, and walked at double pace towards the lodge. Slipping her freezing hands into her pockets, she couldn't help wishing for the climate she'd left behind in Australia.

A text from Gillian had made it easier to leave the country when her tour finished. Albeit on the formal side, Gillian's request 'for your presence should you have availability to attend a New Year's Eve's party at Kingsford Manor,' made her smile and filled her with hope.

It was her first time hearing from Gillian since she had left for Australia. She'd seen her from a distance, though, having returned from Australia in the middle of her tour to attend the auction of the Gentileschi. She wanted to make sure the painting reached its estimated value, allowing Gillian to proceed with buying the estate. Truthfully, it wasn't simply about the sale. She couldn't help herself. It was an opportunity to catch a glimpse of the woman she missed and for whom she ached, whose company she craved to her core.

In the end, the final bid far exceeded the estimated value. Gillian's face as the gavel went down showed pure elation and relief. She could relax a little knowing Gillian would have more than enough money to follow any dreams she envisaged for Kingsford. The pain that hit her as she snuck out of the auction house knowing any dreams Gillian might have didn't include her was more than she could bear. By the evening, she was on a flight back to

Australia to finish her tour, all alone and regretting ever returning to London.

Now there was only sheer joy in her heart. She was back at Kingsford, with the familiar sound of gravel crunching under her feet as it had done many times before. It was a place that was dear to her, even more so now she didn't have the responsibility for it, and to top it off, she had just kissed Gillian Carmichael — properly.

Lurking in the back of her mind was a fear of the future and whether they could make it work, but as she reached the lodge, she spotted Gillian through the sitting room window and set those worries aside. Love always found a way. Her being here proved that.

Noticing the door was ajar, she let herself into the warm hall as her heart thudded in her chest. She was full of hope that the night may still be young, and she might be able to kiss Gillian Carmichael again — improperly.

CHAPTER 23

"Whisky?" Gillian called out from the kitchen, hearing Viola enter and rustle about in the hall.

"Please," Viola answered back.

She poured Viola a small measure, assuming she wouldn't want any effects from it except the flavour. Topping up her own glass, she quickly downed it, refilling it once more as Viola appeared coatless and bootless in a figure-hugging, floral-patterned, knee-length dress with black wool tights. It was a look that suited her perfectly.

"Thanks," Viola said, reaching for the glass Gillian offered her. Looking around, she smiled as realisation dawned. "Is this your old kitchen from the manor?"

Gillian froze, realising Viola wouldn't know about her recent refurbishments. Or that she had bribed one of Viola's builders to save some parts of the old kitchen for her to repurpose in the lodge. She was nothing if not resourceful, and her homemade shortbread was a winner with him.

"Waste not, want not, and all that." She shrugged, rubbing her cold hands together.

"When did you…? You know what, I don't want to know." Viola looked around, examining the kitchen. "It looks good in here. The quarter of it you managed to fit in. Oh, and there's my coffee machine."

"You left it behind."

"I did. I thought you could probably make use of it somewhere. I didn't expect it to be here, though. Do you really prefer living here?"

"To be honest, I'm at an age where I want to be warm without it bankrupting me." Turning on the hot tap she held her icy fingers under the flow, hoping for relief.

Viola smiled. "I expect this place is great for that. It's very snug."

"It is. Living in the manor alone is very different to when you have staff and a husband."

"Yes. It wasn't something I considered when I moved in. I found it quite scary at times." A grin formed on Viola's lips. "You know what got me through?"

Gillian shook her head as Viola stepped closer and ran her hands through the warm water too.

"I always knew you were up the drive, on guard at my gate, watching over me. Plus, I thought no one would dare cross your path, and they would have to cross it to get to me."

Gillian let out a laugh at the suggestion. Drying her hands on a towel, she passed it to Viola. She had sobered up from her earlier glasses of champagne in the bracing air, but she was beginning to feel a little tipsy again from the whisky.

"Technically there is an access point in the bottom field out to the lane, so…"

Viola threw the towel on to the work surface and put her finger to Gillian's lips. "Oh, you can keep your technicalities."

"Can I?" Gillian gave a flick of her eyebrows and decided to lean into Viola's sudden playful nature. "And where precisely should I keep them?"

"You must have a drawer where you keep your binoculars," Viola said, removing her finger. "No doubt with some tape measures and a copy of *The Highway Code* or something."

Gillian smirked. She did have two tape measures in the same drawer as the binoculars in the bureau. There may even be a copy of *The Highway Code.*

Viola shot her a questioning look. "You have such a drawer, don't you?"

Gillian gave a nod, unsure if that was a positive thing in Viola's eyes or not.

"God, you're hot."

That sounded positive. Hearing Viola say those words, with a tone that sounded like pure desperation, sent a shot of desire sweeping through her. Her fixed gaze made Gillian's legs weaken, and she leaned back to steady herself against the worktop. Viola took a step closer, her eyes hungry, as if they were devouring every inch of her — or they were about to.

"So hot."

"Am I?" Gillian looked down, unsure that was true.

"You have a beautiful body, Gillian," Viola assured her.

"For a fifty-five-year-old? Oh, wait, fifty-six-year-old. Today is my birthday."

Viola smirked. "Seriously? The first day of the year. Always ahead of everybody else."

"It appears that way." Gillian shrugged as a smug grin fell over her face.

"Well then, happy birthday, and you have a beautiful body, full stop. It's made even more beautiful by what's inside."

She felt Viola press her right hand to her chest. She knew Viola was indicating her heart, but part of Gillian wanted her hand on her breast. As quickly as the thought came, Viola's hand was there, causing Gillian to inhale a sharp breath.

"Is this okay?" Viola asked, giving a reassuring smile.

Gillian could only nod, exhaling slowly to calm herself. Finding her voice, she said, "It's been a long time since anyone has touched me, let alone like that." Her voice was nothing more than a breathy whisper, thick with vulnerability and yearning.

"It's okay. We can go at your pace. It's been a long time for me too."

Gillian nodded again, excitement and fear sitting on her surface. Viola's wandering fingertips did nothing to help as they stroked the exposed skin of her chest. She knew her low-cut, black dress was revealing; its plunging neckline exposed enough to draw an interested eye. She felt the light, teasing pressure of Viola's thumb sliding lower, slipping under the delicate silk of her bra. The feel of it brushing against her nipple sent a surge of tingles through her and set her heart racing.

"Mmm." Gillian closed her eyes, feeling light-headed from her touch.

Viola suddenly closed the gap between them, pressing their bodies firmly together, causing a gasp to escape Gillian's lips as arousal flooded her.

The teasing thumb slid back out of her dress, and Viola's whole hand grasped her breast, squeezing hard. An unexpected swirl of pleasure and pain shot through Gillian as Viola clamped an erect nipple between her fingers. As her head arched back in pleasure, Viola's mouth leapt upon her exposed neck, light kisses becoming firm and eager.

Unsure what to do with her hands, she placed them around Viola's waist, where they instinctively slid down to her backside. Her fingers explored the shape of her, caressing and kneading with a hunger to match the kisses being placed on her neck.

"Should we take this upstairs?" Gillian asked, noticing how giddy everything was making her and how much she wanted to be lying down for this level of intimacy.

"Are you sure you want to take this further?" Viola asked, placing kisses on Gillian's chest. "There's still time to turn back if you aren't ready."

She could hold nothing back from the woman who had stolen her heart and held it captive, leaving her utterly vulnerable. "There is no time; no time I want to be without you. I want you to ravish me."

Viola's eyes shimmered. "That I can do."

Taking Viola's hand with a faintly nervous smile, Gillian led her upstairs to the small landing. There were only two doors, one for the bedroom and one for the bathroom, and there was a time it would have embarrassed her for Viola to see it. Now she didn't care; even with a manor full of doors, she knew the number of them didn't matter.

She squeezed Viola's hand, checking she was real, and received a squeeze back. Her tiredness had completely left her, replaced by adrenaline and love for Viola. As she led the way through to the bedroom, the wooden floorboards creaked under their feet.

"It will soon warm up," she said, closing the door behind them and switching on an electric heater.

"We can warm each other up," Viola replied.

Gillian flashed her a nervous smile even as her stomach tingled with anticipation.

"We don't have to do anything," Viola said gently as if reading Gillian. "We could get under the duvet and cuddle and see how it feels. Take it slowly."

Appreciating the gesture, Gillian reached for Viola and pulled her into her. It would be easier to say what she needed to impart without looking at her. "I've never… you know… with a woman."

Viola pulled back. "Not even with Hen?"

Gillian looked down. "No. We were young. We never partook in anything more than what we would call 'heavy petting'."

She felt a pressure on her chin, and then Viola's finger was lifting Gillian's head so that she could peer into her eyes.

"It's nothing to be ashamed of, and there's nothing to be embarrassed about. I've never slept with a man." Viola shrugged and twisted her lips. "I couldn't care less, and I don't suppose you do either."

Gillian shook her head. She didn't care about anything that came before, only the present and the future.

"See? Now, can I help you out of that dress?"

Gillian turned her back to Viola and pulled her hair to one side. She was grateful for the new, matching black silk underwear she wore beneath. At least she didn't have to worry about Viola seeing her in something old and frayed.

She could feel Viola's presence close behind her, her breath grazing her skin, making her quiver. The fine hairs on her arms prickled as the zip lowered. Pressing her hands across her stomach, she gripped the fabric as if it were a shield. Embarrassment began pooling in her chest, but beneath it she felt something stronger — trust. She trusted Viola, and she wanted her to see all of her.

Instead of letting the dress fall with her back to Viola, she took a deep breath and turned to face her. With her heart pounding, she allowed the fabric to slip from her shoulders. It cascaded to the floor in a soft, deliberate surrender, leaving her bare in every possible way. Gillian watched the expression on Viola's face. There was something intimate and grounding about watching her eyes trace her body and witnessing firsthand the impact she made.

"Wow. You are breathtaking," Viola said, brushing her hand over Gillian's belly.

Gillian watched as Viola stepped back and lifted her dress over her head. Dropping it to the floor she removed her tights. Her gaze swept over Viola's body, unable to resist taking in every detail. The simplicity of her plain, black knickers and bra was a stark contrast to her own fancy lingerie.

She suddenly felt overdressed, as though she had tried too hard. Her lace and silk were making her feel exposed. There was something magnetic about Viola's understated beauty, the effortless way her milky skin glowed, the gentle curves that invited touch. Everything about her was natural. Viola didn't need lace or satin; her allure came from something deeper, something more genuine and authentic. Gillian's fingers twitched, needing to reach out, to close the space between them.

"If you don't like them, they're removable," Viola teased.

Sensing her face may have been conveying the wrong message, Gillian smiled. "No, not at all. I was thinking how comfy they look and how beautiful you are."

Viola flushed, a soft chuckle escaping her. "Even in these? I didn't exactly plan on showing anyone my underwear tonight — not that I have many fancy alternatives."

"Nor did I… plan on it," Gillian replied, her voice softening. "Yours look more comfortable and practical. I just tend to choose this kind of underwear out of habit."

Viola's eyes studied her with an intensity that made Gillian's breath catch. "Is it a layer of protection? Something that gives you confidence and makes you feel empowered?"

Gillian paused, taken aback by Viola's insight. She realised there was more to it than she'd ever acknowledged. The layers they both wore, it seemed, were more than simple fabric. "Perhaps."

"Then *perhaps* it's time to remove it," Viola suggested, raising an eyebrow.

Gillian nodded, her heart still hammering in her chest. With one swift movement, Viola reached around and unclipped her bra, easing it down her shoulders and adding it to the growing pile of clothes on the floor. The cool air brushed against her exposed skin, making her shiver. Noticing the desire in Viola's eyes, tracing her breasts as if memorising every detail, sent a sudden surge of heat through her.

She froze as Viola's hands grasped her breasts, cupping and caressing them; the warmth from them radiated against her skin. A light whimper escaped as she exhaled, only to draw in breath again as Viola toyed with her nipples. It sent an unexpected surge of emotion through Gillian, moistening her eyes as she realised she'd never felt so complete.

As Viola leaned towards her, Gillian met her halfway, and their lips crashed together, warm, wet, and greedy for more.

"Tell me to stop… if you want me to," Viola muttered between kisses.

"I don't want you to stop," Gillian whispered as her fingers unclipped Viola's bra.

Viola let out a playful chuckle, the sound vibrating between them as she slid the bra off and tossed it aside.

"What's so funny?" Gillian questioned as her eyes roamed over Viola's bare breasts.

Viola's eyes sparkled with mischief as she leaned closer, her voice breathy against Gillian's ear. "I always imagined you to be a bit bossy in the bedroom."

"You thought of me like that?" Gillian said, feeling momentarily vulnerable, only for the feeling to fade as arousal washed through her.

"Yes, along with all the things I wanted to do to you if I ever got my hands on you."

Gillian's stomach tingled at her words, but her thoughts took over, distracting her. Why wasn't she bossy? Why was she so nervous? She'd done it before. The anatomy was different yet not unfamiliar. Why was she letting her nervousness hold her back from devouring the woman in front of her? Viola was safe, she wasn't judgemental, and she could see in her eyes Viola wanted her as much as she wanted Viola.

"Would you like that? For me to be bossy?" Gillian questioned.

"Only if you're comfortable. To be honest, I'd consider this year to be a success already if I could lie beside you."

As nice as that sounded, it wouldn't be enough for her; every part of her was pulsing for Viola's touch. She could be commanding. Her first thought fell to needing her clipboard; she shook it away. This was not a clipboard moment.

"I don't want to just lie beside you. I want to feel you, all of y — "

Before Gillian could finish her sentence, she was flat on her back on the bed, Viola straddling her. Heat radiated from between Viola's legs as she pressed and rubbed against her belly. Looking up, Viola met her with a playful and intense stare. Her eyes were dark with desire, lips parted as if she were on the edge of speech or simply overwhelmed by the moment. Gillian's breath caught as she took her in.

Her hands slid up Viola's thighs until they could go no further. Slipping her fingers under the elastic of Viola's knickers, she was met with a wetness that made her burn between her legs. Her fingertips slid against Viola's softness, teasing and rubbing, tracing every inch of her, all the while hoping she was doing the right thing. Viola writhed and moaned at her touch, arching herself back to allow more access. It wasn't enough. Gillian needed to see her, not blindly touch her.

She tugged at the fabric, her voice breathless. "I want these off. Now!"

Viola jumped off her, curls bouncing as she hurriedly slipped her underwear off, almost losing her balance in her haste. Once free, she straightened and nodded towards Gillian's lower half with a playful grin. "And those?" she asked, her voice full of anticipation.

Taking a moment to appreciate the naked woman standing in her bedroom before answering, Gillian let her eyes wander. She drank in every exquisite detail — the way Viola's skin glowed, the gentle curve of her hips, and the way her hair fell over her breasts. "You may remove them," she said, her voice deep and smooth, full of authority.

Gillian arched her body as Viola gripped at the lace trim, allowing her to slowly slip them off. A wave of self-consciousness hit her again, and she crossed her legs. As Viola moved to climb back on top of her, she forced herself to uncross them, to show herself to Viola. There was nothing left to hide.

"Oh, Gillian, you're so beautiful," Viola breathed, her voice low and sultry as she leaned over her. "I love you."

Although she was caught off guard for a moment by Viola's sudden declaration, Gillian found the same words coming from her mouth. "I love you too." There was no doubt in her mind whether she was ready to say them.

Pulling Viola to her, her hand grasped the back of her head, forcing their lips together in a passionate kiss. Their naked bodies brushed against each other, love flowing through their skin as their hands explored each other.

Viola's fingers drifted along Gillian's inner thigh, the touch light yet deliberate, moving closer to where she needed them most. The anticipation was unbearable, making her tremble as Viola's fingers slipped through her wetness. They began exploring, tracing every part before working their way inside with a constant rhythm and intensity that was pure ecstasy.

She wouldn't last long if Viola kept it up, but she didn't want her to stop and encouraged her on, moving with her. She'd never been this aroused before; every nerve in her body was lit with desire.

Viola's tongue teased her nipple, sucking and licking, making her breathless. Catching her eye, Viola smiled, her mouth opening wide as it devoured Gillian's breast, making her moan. She could see the unmistakable passion in Viola's eyes, a sheer desire to please. It was overwhelming, driving her toward the brink. She'd never appreciated how intoxicating it would feel to have someone so focused, so intent on her pleasure. The thought only added to the unyielding feelings coursing through her body, and before she knew it, waves of orgasm crashed over her, leaving her trembling in the aftermath.

Viola's arms were soon around her, kissing her cheek and neck, holding her tight as she regained her breath.

"Was that okay?" Viola whispered in her ear before kissing it and sending a pleasurable aftershock through her.

Gillian could only nod and smile. She couldn't stop smiling. She was going to keep demanding Viola take her; nothing and no one was going to stop her. She couldn't be without this feeling ever again — couldn't and wouldn't be without Viola.

Admitting to herself who she was may have been one hurdle — a rather large one that took decades to climb over; admitting it to Viola felt like another. To admit it to the world — or, in her case, Kingsford — was going to be a monumental challenge. It was something she didn't have a plan for, and she'd never been without a plan before.

∽

Holding Gillian in her arms, listening to her ragged breath gradually slow after the intensity of release, felt surreal. The woman was enchanting, even before the dress slipped from her shoulders, revealing delicate black silk and lace.

There were no words for how Gillian made her feel when she peeled away her outer layers. Seeing Gillian laid out naked before her, vulnerable yet powerful, exposed in every way possible, was something Viola hadn't fully anticipated, and it had stirred a primal desire within her.

It wasn't only her body Gillian had exposed; there was

a new level of trust between them. There was also a new level of trust inside Gillian for her own feelings, which was beautiful to witness. Viola was proud that she was the one to remove her walls, brick by brick, lowering them enough that Gillian could finally step out from her foundations and start again.

Feeling Gillian stirring in her arms, Viola instinctively loosened her hold only to find Gillian on top of her, her wetness pressing against her lower belly. The way her breasts sat, full and enticing, was enough to make Viola's breath catch. She couldn't resist the pull. Her hands moved up, cupping the fullness of Gillian's breasts in her palms. Their softness was intoxicating, but it was the quiet, involuntary moan that escaped Gillian's lips that made Viola's heart race faster.

She was perfect. From the shape of her waist to the curve of her hips where they flared gently before descending into the rounded fullness of her thighs. Viola's hands moved from her breasts as if compelled by instinct, tracing the smooth line of Gillian's body, her fingers lingered at the swell of her hips. Gillian arched slightly into Viola's touch, her movements unguarded as if she'd let down all the barriers she fiercely maintained.

Viola squirmed with anticipation as Gillian leaned toward her, hovering above her breasts before kissing them passionately in turn. Her warm, wet, insistent lips traced over them, her tongue teasing her nipples. The sensation was almost too great, charged with an intensity that made her body ache for more. It ached for Gillian and demanded release, so it could feel these sensations all over again.

Gillian's hands, once tentative, explored with growing confidence, her touch firm on Viola's body as if she had mapped out every inch of it and was now claiming it. Viola gasped, her fingers running through Gillian's hair, holding her close as her lips trailed over her belly.

"I need you," Gillian whispered, her voice demanding and low. The desire in those words made Viola's pulse pound so hard she could feel the pressure in her neck.

"You have me… always," Viola replied, breathless.

The desperation in her tone was unmistakable, and it only spurred Gillian on as her lips pressed firmly over Viola's skin, making their way past her belly button and down. She could only lie back and hope they were heading where she needed them.

Gillian's smouldering lips radiated through her core as they pressed into her. Her tongue was slow and deliberate, as though savouring every moment. Viola gasped, her back arching off the bed, her breath catching in her throat as the pleasure built quickly — far too quickly. Gillian didn't hold back, her tongue moving with precision, exploring her in ways that made Viola's head spin. Her eagerness and the intensity of her movements left Viola trembling. How could Gillian not have done this before?

Every sweep of her tongue sent a new wave of arousal through Viola, her body writhing beneath the exquisite torment. The feelings only intensified as Gillian's fingers teased her, stroking, then gently pushing, until they slid inside her. Any attempt to delay the inevitable was fruitless. Her body tensed, the pleasure spiralling until she finally surrendered.

"Gillian…" Viola moaned, her voice barely audible as

she tilted her head back, her hands clutching the sheets as she unravelled completely.

Lying there, eyes shut tight, she could sense Gillian's movements around her. She tried to move, to reach out, but she was too exhausted. She wrenched her eyes open as the sheets were pulled over her, wrapping around her before she was gently turned onto her side and drawn into Gillian's arms. She'd never felt as happy as she did in this moment. As safe.

It was almost impossible to believe this was where they'd ended up after everything — the tension, the icy glares, the biting words exchanged with Gillian when she moved to Kingsford and took her place. Now, the same woman held her like this, with such affection, after claiming her in a way Viola could never imagine. And yet, despite the absurdity of it all, it felt right.

Feeling a soft kiss to the top of her head caused a bubbling sensation, like champagne fizzing, to flow through her veins. Gillian pulled her closer, their bodies minds and souls fitting together like puzzle pieces. Closing her eyes again, she nestled against Gillian's chest as a smile forced its way to her lips.

CHAPTER 24

⚜

Gillian woke with an unexpected warmth radiating beside her. An arm reached out to her under the duvet, bringing to her the sudden realisation that she was not alone. Her mind filled in the blanks as she trailed a finger along Viola's arm.

"Good morning."

"Morning," Gillian replied quietly, nerves beginning to set in again in the cold light of day.

She spotted Agatha by her feet, glaring back at her with disdain. The cat got up, walking up to greet them before settling between them and purring.

"Agatha. How nice to see you, and here of all places." Viola stroked the cat's soft fur as she stretched out.

"She refused to move back into the manor."

"After refusing to leave in the first place?"

"Yes," Gillian confirmed. "Once you left, I saw a lot more of her."

She'd become rather fond of her feline companion since then. The cat having decided she preferred the lodge after all made her feel as if they were of one mind. Even if it that mind was keeping warm.

"Maybe the manor wasn't the reason she stayed; maybe it was me," Viola suggested as Agatha got back up and returned to her spot at the bottom of the bed.

Gillian laughed. "I hadn't thought of it like that."

"I was joking, but they say cats have a sixth sense about things. She might have known we were destined for each other before we did."

"You returned her to me at the lodge enough times. Maybe it was part of some cunning plan on her part to bring us closer together."

"To make you hate me even more for stealing your cat as well as your house?" Viola chuckled.

"I don't think I ever really hated you. Perhaps a tiny bit," Gillian conceded. "You had everything I lost."

"I had everything you sold. Even if it was a reluctant sale, I only bought and paid for things, including priceless art in the attic, which you stubbornly overlooked."

Gillian couldn't help smiling. "Jonathon ultimately saved the day after ruining it in the first place. Although, technically Arte spotted it."

"I like to think my trained eye for good art helped with that," Viola said with an exaggerated air of importance, waving her hand as if she were some kind of art connoisseur. She flashed a quick, self-satisfied smile even as Gillian raised an eyebrow. Viola continued, undeterred. "I mean, it takes years to develop this kind of instinct, you know? Recognising a hidden gem comes naturally to me now. The brushstrokes, the composition... all very subtle clues only someone knowledgeable would pick up on."

With Gillian's eyebrow still raised, Viola conceded. "Yes, okay, I missed it, too, and then I went and put it on display without realising, only for it to end up in a magazine where someone with an expert eye spotted it."

Gillian laughed as Viola nestled closer to her, their bodies entwined under the cosy sheets. They lay there, wrapped in each other's arms, the quiet comfort of their closeness enough to fill the silence.

Viola's voice, soft yet hesitant, broke through the stillness. "Did you mean what you said yesterday… about not wanting there to be a time when you're without me?"

Gillian didn't even need to think. Her answer was immediate. "Yes," she whispered, her lips brushing lightly against Viola's hair. "I meant every word."

"When was the last time you left Kingsford?"

"Only the other day I went to the supermarket in the next town."

Viola sat up, revealing her bare breasts. "I don't mean travelling locally; I mean further afield."

"Why would I want to leave Kingsford?" Gillian asked, perplexed by the notion.

"I don't know, to look at the rest of the planet. It does exist, you know. There is a whole other world outside those gates."

Gillian wasn't sure what answer to give. She knew that; she just held little interest in it. "I've never felt the need to leave or had reason to," she replied, her voice shaky.

"Now you do."

"What do you mean?" Gillian asked, sitting up.

"I mean, that I can't stay here." Viola pulled her knees up to her waist and leaned into them, hugging them. "I have a career, a worldwide career. I'm leaving for America in a few weeks. Then I will be in Europe for some time. I want you to come with me, at least for some of it."

When the cruel light of day kicks in with all its problems and limitations, it gives a good whack, Gillian thought to herself.

"What is this?" Viola pushed when Gillian didn't respond. "A casual fling."

"Of course not," Gillian scoffed, annoyed at the sheer temerity of the question.

"I have a right to ask for clarification about what the future looks like. What you want," Viola continued, her voice softer now, but no less determined.

"I can't just up and leave; I have Kingsford to run. There's so much to do," Gillian said, her hands fidgeting as if trying to grasp onto something solid, something familiar.

"You have Bridget," Viola urged gently.

"But the business is beginning to bloom."

"Bridget is more than capable."

Gillian scoffed.

"She is." Viola leaned back into the pillow, covered herself with the duvet, and crossed her arms. "You just make her nervous. You know she looks up to you and wants to impress you. As I've come to realise, you are quite difficult to impress."

"What am I without it?" Gillian said with a deep breath.

"Your identity isn't Kingsford," Viola answered softly, her previous hardness giving way. "And I'm not asking you to forget it, Gillian. I'm asking you to stop letting it define you. You've not moved back in; that's huge. You've turned it into a proper business; that's also huge. Maybe it's time to step away, give each other some space to grow."

"Stepping away is very different from stepping back. The former being more permanent than the latter," Gillian said quietly, her voice holding a subtle sadness as the idea of letting go tightened her chest.

"Then step back for a time. You've made great strides this past year."

She had been through a lot — more than she could have ever anticipated. It marked the departure of Jonathon from this world and the unexpected arrival of Viola bringing turmoil into her life. The loss of Kingsford, a place that once anchored her, was devastating. It was a blow that nearly broke her. And then, thanks to the woman who took everything from her, she had regained it. It was returned to her through no effort on her part when she wasn't entitled to it in the first place. She'd felt entitled to it, seeing it as payment for thirty-five years — her thoughts paused - - of what?

How should she describe the last thirty-five years? Her mind was reaching for the word 'suffering', but she stopped it. Things with Jonathon hadn't been that bad; they could have been worse. He wasn't violent; he left her to her own devices, letting her run things like their social life. All her time and energy given to the village she gave willingly; she'd enjoyed her role and embraced it. It gave her something in return, a sense of belonging when she'd never belonged anywhere before. The manor became her refuge, somewhere she could hide away and pretend to be someone else, but she had done that to herself. She allowed it to lock her in time, in a vacuum.

Did she want to escape it? Forging a new relationship with it was one thing, leaving it, walking away from it, for an extended period — how would that look? How would it feel? She'd dipped a toe into a different realm, and now she could feel the door closing behind her. There was no way back, not that she wanted to return; she loved Viola and wanted to be with her. She just didn't know how to navigate this new world.

"How do I go out there now? Who am I when I open the lodge door? Being here with you, naked," she said, smiling at the thought, "is very different than being naked in front of everyone else."

Viola shifted closer, resting her head gently on Gillian's chest, her fingers tracing light circles against her skin. "You," she began softly, "are you. However that looks. Always unapologetically you. People will get used to it, and a lot quicker than you think. I'm sure the village gossips will do most of the work for you."

Gillian let out a soft laugh, but it faded quickly. Her hand absentmindedly stroked Viola's hair as her thoughts turned inward. "The message I took from my experience with Hen was one of shame. It didn't change how I felt, but it added something heavy. A weight. A sense of wrongness."

Viola's head lifted slightly, her eyes meeting Gillian's. "You need to understand," she said firmly, "what we did last night — it was beautiful. There's nothing shameful about it. Two people enjoying each other, sharing something so intimate, what does it matter what those bodies look like? It's a meeting of minds."

Gillian looked away as the words sank in. "I know," she whispered, her voice tinged with a mix of acceptance and hesitation. "I do know."

"It takes time to reprogram yourself from bigoted views forced onto you. You have as much right to be who you are and live how you want as any other person on this planet and, more particularly, in Kingsford."

"In my case, it's taken over thirty-five years. I've just kept telling myself things to keep the feelings down," Gillian murmured, her voice heavy. "It's easier to convince yourself of a lie than face the truth."

"You've already faced the truth," Viola said, her tone filled with quiet reassurance. "I'm here, and as you say… naked." A playful glint flashed in her eyes before she continued. "It's the final navigation into port you need to tackle, and I will be your tugboat."

Gillian pulled Viola into her, stroking her skin and watching as goosebumps appeared on her arms. After savouring her comforting presence for a few minutes, Gillian gently pulled back, brushing a soft kiss against the top of Viola's head. "Shall I make us some tea? Or coffee?"

"Coffee, please. Have you got a spare toothbrush?"

"There should be a new one under the sink," Gillian answered, knowing there would be.

She watched as Viola extracted herself from the sheets. The previous night's events still felt like a dream; however, with Viola standing there, her bare skin bathed in the soft glow of the morning light, the reality of it all was undeniable. Every inch of her body was captivating, and Gillian couldn't tear her eyes away.

Viola glanced over her shoulder as she left the room, her lips curling into a knowing smile. It was a smile that said she knew exactly what was going through Gillian's mind and she knew the effect she had on her.

Gillian pulled on a silk slip hanging on the back of a chair and wrapped her dressing gown around her. She descended the stairs and entered the kitchen, turning the kettle on. The sound of the door knocking echoed through the house. Checking her dressing gown was sufficiently tightened, she headed towards it. Not one for opening her door in a state of undress, she recognised the knock as Bridget's, and knowing she would only knock louder, rather than leave, she opened it.

"Happy birthday!"

"Thank you, Bridget," Gillian said, taking a bunch of sunflowers and a box of champagne truffles from her and placing them on the hall table.

"Do you know where Viola is?" Bridget asked, stepping in and closing the door behind her. "The helicopter is on the lawn, and I checked the manor. She's nowhere to be seen."

Gillian could feel her throat tightening. She hadn't even thought about what to say.

"Err. Yes, she stayed here last night, in the spare bedroom."

"You don't have a spare bedroom."

"No, I don't, do I?" Gillian admitted, feeling foolish for lying. Why hadn't she said the sofa?

Bridget stepped towards her, reaching out and placing

her hand on Gillian's arm. "It's okay, Gillian. I know. I've known for some time. We've been friends for nigh on thirty-five years. You might not speak much about yourself, but I know you. Plus, your eye has a habit of wandering. It wandered quite a bit in Viola's direction."

A sudden wave of panic washed over Gillian. She withdrew her arm and backed away, walking to the sitting room. She felt exposed and vulnerable. Her initial thoughts went into denial.

"I, I… don't — "

"Oh, don't even try to deny it," Bridget interrupted as she followed behind. "There is nothing to be ashamed of; Elouise and Louisa have been together since the Second World War for pity's sake."

"What nonsense! They're just good friends."

"No one is 'just good friends', Gillian. You thought they were or refused to see it. Everyone else knows. It's not like they even hide it, and why should they? You might have had your airs and graces, living in that big house, but you're just another member of this community, and you always have been. Nothing is different about you, Gillian, except you're finally being honest with yourself."

A silence filled the room as Gillian stood speechless. Finding her voice she asked, "Why didn't you say anything?"

"Because you didn't," Bridget replied. "I figured you'd bring it up if you ever wanted to talk about it. Then Viola left, and I knew I needed to step in."

Understanding washed over Gillian. When they spoke about 'living our truth', Bridget knew. She'd always known and was trying to help, more than Gillian had realised at the time.

"Look, no one cares if you're gay, Gillian, or whatever you are," Bridget said, her voice edged with exasperation. "I assume you must have some feelings for men being married to one all those years, even if it wasn't the easiest of marriages. We're not in the eighteen hundreds now, you aren't lady of the manor, and the village does not start and end with the Carmichaels. You are just another villager like the rest of us." She took in a breath and sighed loudly before starting up again. "You've spent so much of your life acting a part in it; it's time to take on the lead role and find some happiness for yourself," she urged.

A noise in the hall caught their attention.

"I will leave you both to it," Bridget said, heading to the door, where Viola stood holding two mugs, dressed in only her knickers and a T-shirt.

"Good morning, Viola," Bridget said as she passed her, placing her hand on her shoulder. "It's good to see you here."

"Morning. It's good to be here."

"I've never seen her like that before," Gillian said, taking a cup of tea from Viola to the echo of the front door shutting behind Bridget.

"Passionate?"

"Vexed?" Gillian corrected her as she examined her tea.

"That was passion, from what I heard of it, anyway. She wants what's best for you, and you can't see that. You were blinded by one bigoted woman with her own agenda and allowed her to define your life."

Gillian nodded. "I have, haven't I?"

Viola offered a soft smile and asked, "Is the tea okay? I thought I should make a start. I found some Earl Grey tea bags, which I assumed were your cheat bags."

"Yes, thank you," Gillian said, sipping at the steaming liquid. "I admit I keep a box for emergency situations when five minutes is too long to wait for a proper brew."

"I feared this was one of those situations."

"Yes. It very much is."

Viola nodded towards the hall table. "Are those from Bridget?"

"Yes, sunflowers and chocolates. My favourite." Gillian sighed. "She gives them to me every year."

"You don't look overjoyed."

"It made me realise something. I have no idea what her favourite flowers and chocolates are. I've known her for thirty-five years. I was her maid of honour. I stood beside her as she buried her husband after only ten years of a happy marriage, and I don't know these things. What's wrong with me?"

"Nothing is wrong," Viola urged, placing a hand on her arm. "You've lived in a different world. A world that wasn't even your world, just a place you hid in, and somewhere where you didn't make a lot of room for others. Now you are changing that."

Gillian nodded. She intended to try. The relief she felt that Bridget knew and was supportive made her feel a little lighter already. "Maybe I have been trapped in Kingsford."

"After what happened with Hen and your mum, you hid here like a butterfly trapped in a box. It's time to set yourself free, Gillian, and see what you can achieve elsewhere in the world. I'll be there to hold your hand, every step of the way."

"I'll see that you are."

"Through your binoculars?" Viola asked through a cheeky grin.

"No. I'm going to need you much closer than that." Gillian stepped towards Viola, careful not to unsettle either of their mugs. "This close."

She placed a kiss on Viola's lips. Finding them dry, she moistened them with her tongue, sending a warmth rushing over her skin.

"Come back to bed," Viola said, pulling away from her with a smile.

That wasn't an invitation Gillian would ever refuse. "I will, but I can't keep Dudley waiting too long for his breakfast."

"Mmm, breakfast. Why don't you bring those chocolates?" Viola added, nodding at them as she passed. "I'm looking forward to seeing Dudley again. I've missed him."

Gillian shook her head, a teasing smile tugging at her lips. "Chocolates for breakfast? Really?" She picked up the box and followed Viola up the stairs.

"Yes. You are doing things differently now, after all."

That was true, but eating chocolates in the morning sounded a step too far, she thought, as she took in how great Viola's backside looked from eye level.

"When is your birthday?" Gillian asked as they climbed back into the bed.

"The twenty-first of April."

"And when does your tour of America finish?"

"The end of March," Viola said, taking a sip of her coffee. "I have a few weeks off, and then I leave for Europe for two months shortly after my birthday."

Viola leaving would be a wrench, but she would put plans in place to allow herself some freedom away from Kingsford. She couldn't be apart from her for too long.

"I shall come with you then, if that's agreeable?" Gillian said, placing her hand between them on the bed. "There's a lot I need to get into place before I can consider leaving."

Viola placed her hand on top of Gillian's. "Very agreeable. I would prefer sooner, but I understand."

"As long as Bridget agrees to take over — if she's still talking to me," Gillian murmured, a hint of uncertainty creeping into her voice.

"She will be," Viola reassured her. "I'm sure of it. She showed you how much she cares about you."

Gillian sighed. It was the only time her friend had ever raised her voice to her, and it had spilled out in a way that had taken her completely by surprise. Bridget was always unwavering in her support, never questioning her decisions or pushing her too hard.

In all their years together, she was the one person Gillian could count on to stand by her, no matter what. Today, she'd challenged her. It had shaken Gillian, even if she knew it came from a place of love. It was exactly what she needed to hear, though, that someone believed in her enough to demand better from her.

"She's never pushed me like that before," Gillian admitted, a small smile tugging at her lips. "But I guess that says everything, doesn't it?"

Viola nodded, her fingers skimming lightly along Gillian's arm. "It does. She'll stand by you, as she always has."

"Will you be okay going alone to America?" Gillian asked, her voice faltering as she looked down.

"Yes, as long as I know you are here waiting for me to return."

"I will be," came the confident reply.

"I'm not sure America is ready for Gillian Carmichael to land on its shores anyway." Viola grinned.

Gillian narrowed her eyes at her and then relaxed them, adding a smile. "I will expect you to return to visit me if your schedule allows, and perhaps we could speak on the phone every day."

"I will ensure my schedule allows for all of that."

"Would you mind if I leave telling people about us until you return? I want time to get used to everything myself first," Gillian admitted, knowing it wouldn't be an easy task to rediscover herself.

"Of course not."

"I will hold a garden party for your birthday and invite the village. I can show you off." Gillian beamed.

"I like the sound of that."

"If you can get through coming out on the world's stage, then I can get through coming out in Kingsford." She took Viola's hand and squeezed it, initially excited at the prospect, only for nervousness to creep in and brush the edge off it. "Did you know Elouise and Louisa are a couple?"

"I had a feeling, yes."

"They've never shown any affection towards each other in public."

"Some people don't. Did you and Jonathon?"

"Not at all, but then we didn't have anything to hi — " Gillian's words faltered, her voice catching as she realised where the sentence was heading.

"I'm glad you didn't finish that sentence," Viola said quietly, though her meaning was clear.

Gillian gave a small nod. "I'll get there."

Viola didn't press further; there was no rush, no expectation, only understanding. Everything had changed between them, and yet, as she sat there next to Viola, the morning light filtering in around them, Gillian found herself grateful for it all. It was strange, the way something that started with tension, animosity, and distance had evolved into this — a space where she could be herself, where she was finally letting someone see who that was.

For the first time in a long while, possibly in forever, she felt truly happy. Fear may still sit at her edges, but with Viola by her side, she knew she could let go of everything that once bound her and embrace the future as a free woman, whatever it might hold for her.

EPILOGUE

FOUR MONTHS LATER

Gillian double-checked the list on her clipboard as she set it down on the kitchen worktop. Satisfied, her pen pressed down to tick the last box. The manor was spotless, and the scent of spring flowers from Elouise and Louisa's garden filled the air, mixing with the aroma of freshly baked scones. Everything was ready for their afternoon tea party.

Under normal circumstances, Gillian would receive everyone herself to make each guest feel personally welcomed. With Bridget noticing her focus was elsewhere — eagerly awaiting the arrival of Viola, the guest of honour — she had volunteered to do it for her.

The effects of a week shared with Viola lingered in her mind, causing its own distractions. It wasn't just the dazzling whirlwind of London — the museums, the art galleries, or the extravagant shopping sprees. Nor was it the evenings spent dining at Michelin-starred restaurants, laughing over exquisite food and wine. It was what had come in the quiet moments: how they searched for each other's hand, gripping the other's when they walked, or the way Viola would rest her head against Gillian's shoulder in the back of the taxi after a long day of sightseeing. Those moments left their mark far deeper than the distractions of the city.

It was liberating to get away and be in a different environment with Viola. On the few occasions she returned from America between concerts, Gillian had met her in the city, keeping her away from Kingsford and the surprise she was planning.

A week had passed since she reluctantly left Viola's penthouse — and, more regrettably, her bedroom — to give her space to prepare for her imminent tour. In the meantime, she returned to Kingsford to finalise arrangements for Viola's party. Although Bridget offered to handle everything, Gillian had immersed herself in the planning and preparation. This was to be her last event for some time, and with it being such a special occasion, she felt compelled to oversee every detail herself.

The familiar vibration she'd grown fond of filled the air around her. A glance out of the window confirmed it as the silhouette of a helicopter gleamed in the afternoon sun — Viola was on her way.

Gillian's heart rate, already elevated from nerves all day, quickened to a nearly panicked pace. Viola's arrival was more than a reunion; it was the moment for everyone to understand exactly what she meant to her

Gillian's stomach tightened at the thought. For years, she had buried parts of herself beneath layers of propriety and grief. The village could be warm and welcoming, yes, but it also thrived on gossip. She could imagine the whispers that would ripple through the room at her declaration.

Despite the fear, a thrill was simmering beneath it, something akin to exhilaration. For the first time in years, Gillian was ready to show the world who she truly was. It was Viola who had made it possible. With her unapologetic confidence and quiet strength, she had swept into her life like a force of nature, peeling back the layers she carefully constructed.

Viola made her question everything she thought she knew about herself, her place in the world, and the limits she'd once accepted. If anyone could make her believe this leap of faith was worth the risk, it was Viola. She felt a pang of shame as she recalled pushing Viola away, letting fear dictate her actions and forcing parts of herself to remain hidden in the shadows.

With another glance out of the window, she could see Viola stepping from the helicopter. Gillian almost ran through to the back hall to greet her, though she quickly stopped by the mirror to check her appearance. Taking a deep breath, Gillian smoothed her floral dress and straightened her shoulders.

She smiled to herself, proud to have found the courage to swallow her pride, voice her true feelings, and ask Viola for the support she needed. That pride swelled even further as Viola entered the hall, setting her bag down and closing the door behind her. She was here — she was hers.

They met halfway, their movements urgent and unspoken. Desperate lips found each other in a passionate embrace; the intensity of Viola's made Gillian's head spin with giddy delight.

"How are you?" Viola murmured.

"Nervous," Gillian admitted.

"Let me stem those nerves for you."

Her warm lips brushed against Gillian's neck, sending a shiver rippling through her body, leaving her knees weak. It soothed the whirlwind of thoughts going through her mind.

"Gillian, Vio — " A voice interrupted them, and both women turned toward the doorway. Bridget's head popped around the edge of the doorframe, her face alight with mischief. "Oh, you found her!" she said, grinning from ear to ear. "Don't mind me. You lovebirds carry on."

"Lovebirds?" Gillian croaked, her cheeks flaming as Bridget retreated into the hall.

"What's wrong with lovebirds?" Viola teased.

"Makes us sound like a couple of teenagers."

Gillian's breath hitched as Viola stepped closer, pushing her against the wall and grasping her breast as she nuzzled at her neck.

"Would teenagers do that?" Viola asked, her voice low and sultry.

Gillian's cheeks flushed. "Yes."

"And this?" Viola asked, sliding her knee between Gillian's legs, sending a jolt of heat searing through her.

"I should hope not, but I expect so, yes."

"And this?" Viola's hand ruffled Gillian's dress, her fingers grazing the skin of her thigh underneath it.

Despite the growing intensity of her desire, Gillian playfully pushed Viola back. "Not here. Can't you wait?"

"No, I can't. I need you now."

"Our guests are arriving."

"Let them. I'm taking what I can get whilst I've got you."

Gillian arched an eyebrow, her tone challenging, even as a smile tugged at her lips betraying her amusement. "Taking? Are you indeed?"

"No, sorry. You're right. You are going to give me everything I want. I won't need to take anything."

Her warm breath against Gillian's wet skin shot a cooling sensation across her neck until Viola's greedy mouth kissed it again.

"Mmm, cotton, not silk?" Viola remarked, her hand having reached as far as Gillian's underwear. "It feels very comfortable."

"Indeed."

"Do you think you'd feel even more comfortable if they were on the floor?"

A soft moan escaped her lips as Viola's fingers tugged at the fabric. The sound of a knock on the door to the great hall made them jump apart. It creaked open, and Bridget's voice floated through.

"Perhaps you could put a lid on it. Everyone has arrived, and the waiters need to come through for more champagne."

Gillian smoothed down her dress. "I never thought I'd say I'm looking forward to some time away from here."

"So am I," Viola laughed, pulling her in for a final kiss

before they checked their appearances in the mirror and joined their guests.

At the heart of the packed-out hall, crisp, white linens and vases of pastel tulips adorned the oak banqueting table. The table was a feast, laden with a delectable spread of triangular sandwiches, mini quiches, vibrant macarons, mouthwatering petits fours, and baskets of scones.

"Let's get this done," Gillian said with a deep exhale as she turned to Viola. A reassuring smile awaited her, spurring her on.

"I'm right with you," Viola replied, taking a spoon from the table and handing it to her. "You've got this."

With a long breath to calm her racing heart, Gillian stepped up onto the staircase and chinked her glass, only realising now how sweaty her palms were as she gripped the crystal.

"Can I have everyone's attention, please? I promise not to keep you from the delicious treats Mrs Johnson has prepared for our tea party, but I can't let this moment pass without saying a few words. It was well over a year ago I stood here at Jonathon's wake to announce that changes would be happening on the Kingsford Estate. It may have taken a little longer than anticipated to begin those changes, and even as they begin to happen now, they aren't quite as I first envisaged. A great deal has changed over the last year."

Gillian's voice wavered until her gaze fell on Viola. The love shining in her eyes dissolved all her nerves and replaced them with a surge of confidence. She still couldn't believe someone so extraordinary was hers. The way

Viola's eyes sparkled at her made Gillian's chest tighten with emotion.

"Everything has changed. I lost my dear manor, only to find it again… but whilst it was lost, I found something dearer to me than I could ever imagine. I found someone special," she began, her voice steady despite the rush of emotion rising within her. "Someone who has shown me life doesn't have to follow a single path, and that there can be beauty in doing things differently. Someone who has made every moment brighter simply by being in it." Gillian paused, her lips curving into a tender smile as she raised her glass. "Viola, happy birthday!"

As the room erupted into applause, Viola stepped up beside Gillian, her cheeks flushing pink. Suddenly blanking on everything she had planned to say, Gillian realised words weren't necessary in that moment. Without hesitation, she closed the distance between them, pulling Viola into a kiss that she eagerly returned.

The clapping faltered, a momentary hush falling over the crowd as gasps rippled through the room. The pause was fleeting, though, as the applause swelled again, louder and more enthusiastic than before.

Gillian tried to focus on the woman in front of her, but she struggled, listening instead for every sound, filtering for words of disapproval. None came. Slipping her hand into Viola's she pulled back, finding a beaming smile to match her own.

She continued her speech, finding her legs were quivering from the adrenaline pumping around her. "I hope she comes to realise that now she is part of Kingsford, she will never be lonely."

"Hear, hear," Louisa and Elouise shouted, clapping enthusiastically at the front of the crowd.

"Viola leaves for a European tour shortly, and I will be going with her."

More gasps echoed around the hall.

"Don't get too excited. I will be back, and nothing at Kingsford will change. I have been repeatedly assured life will go on without me, though I'm yet to be convinced. I will leave you in the competent hands of our dear Bridget. I have every faith in her. My rock and my loyal friend for thirty-five years."

"Over thirty-five years," Bridget shouted from the front of the crowd, much to everyone's amusement.

"Yes, thank you, Bridget," Gillian replied dryly, realising her eyes were beginning to moisten. "To finish, I've added a circular walking route around the outskirts of the estate so even if the manor has an event, anyone who wishes to enjoy its parkland can. I've even added a few benches to offer…" She was about to say 'rest points', and although factual considering the average age of Kingsford's residents, she finished with, "Reflection points. Crafted from the finest teak, these sculptures capture the landscape of the South Downs and its wildlife in intricate detail. We have our local artist, Arte Tremaine, to thank for them," Gillian announced with a gracious nod in Arte's direction, as she spotted her and Charlotte at the front of the group. "She has worked for several local celebrities, including Beatrice Russell." An excited hum of reactions rippled through the crowd. "Now I've kept you long enough, so bon appétit!"

As the hall filled with a lively buzz of conversation,

Gillian's grip on Viola's hand tightened as she led her down the staircase towards Arte and Charlotte, who were mid-discussion.

"I told you they were a couple — " Arte's voice cut off abruptly as Gillian gave a deliberate cough, eyebrows raised. Arte's cheeks flushed. She quickly recovered, flashing a mischievous smile in their direction. "Sorry. We had a small bet on — "

"Well, less so a bet since we both agreed that if you weren't already a couple when we saw you, you very soon would be," Charlotte clarified with a grin.

"It turns out you were both right then," Viola said, kissing Gillian's cheek.

It filled Gillian with warming confidence as her eyes darted around the hall to gauge people's reactions. She scanned the faces of those nearby, bracing herself for murmurings or side glances only to find no one was even looking at them. Charlotte's voice pulled her attention back.

"I can't thank you enough for discovering that gem of a painting, Viola. I can't tell you how it feels to have it in my collection."

"You are more than welcome. If it wasn't for Arte spotting it, I expect it would still be hanging there unnoticed."

"It certainly wouldn't," Gillian remarked stiffly, adding with a playful tone, "It would be back in the attic where it belongs."

Viola shook her head, a playful grin spreading across her face. "Forgive Gillian. She's a bit uncultured when it comes to art."

Gillian's mouth twisted as if to protest until the look Viola gave her softened it into a smile.

"The wait to hear back if it was what I thought it was nearly killed me," Arte interjected. "It was one of the most pleasurable yet nerve-racking moments of my life."

"Even if her instincts are never wrong when it comes to art," Charlotte added, lifting their conjoined hands to her mouth and placing a kiss on her wife's hand.

"Thank you for your generous final bid," Gillian said, nodding to Charlotte. She recalled the moment when Charlotte, clearly frustrated with the meagre bid increments, had added a cool million to silence the competition — and the entire room. Gillian had nearly fallen off her chair again. "I didn't expect it to go for quite so much. They said without the provenance it may have affected the price."

"It's worth every penny, I assure you. I judged it on its own merits, with the dramatic feminist style, subject matter, and strong female character. The CR stamp was the icing on the cake. It was going in my collection at whatever price. I can't believe it was in your attic. Have you any idea where it came from?"

Gillian shook her head. "I remember my late husband returning home with them shortly after he sold off the last piece of Kingsford's arable land. I was furious and wanted them gone. I told him I threw them away and we never spoke about them again."

"Well, it has been a welcome addition to my growing collection, which incidentally will be displayed at the Courtauld Gallery shortly. I'm showcasing a selection of emerging female artists and historical works. At the heart of it all will be the pièce de resistance, *Justitia* by Artemisia Gentileschi. You should come and see it if you can ever tear yourself away from this place, Gillian."

"Oh, she can," Viola said, her eyes shining. "She was in London not long ago, and as she's declared in front of everyone, she's coming with me in a few days for my European tour. So, no backing out now."

"I wouldn't dream of it," Gillian confirmed as Viola's arm threaded through her own. "First Paris, then Monaco. I'm rather looking forward to it."

"Monaco?" Charlotte questioned. "We'll be heading there ourselves soon to enjoy my mother's villa while she's away."

"We find that's the best time to enjoy it," Arte smirked.

The comment hung in the air before they all dissolved into laughter.

"I'm performing at the Opéra de Monte-Carlo," Viola explained, "inside the casino."

Charlotte's eyes brightened. "I know it well; my stepfather, Baptiste, owns the casino."

"I'll have my agent send you some VIP passes then."

"Wonderful, thank you," Charlotte replied.

"Would you like to see around the house?" Viola offered.

Arte's face lit up.

Viola hesitated, biting her lip. "Oh… I forgot it's not my house anymore."

"See how easy it is to forget?" Gillian teased.

Viola nudged her with a playful smile. "I know the owner *intimately*, and she won't mind if I show you around."

"She won't," Gillian confirmed.

As Viola led the two of them away, the nearby sound of the major's voice rose just enough to carry. "The women are getting all the good ones these days. I can't think why."

As Gillian spotted him, she could see him twirling the ends of his moustache.

"Hopefully, Viola will soften her up a bit," Mrs Hawkin's voice came from beside him.

She glanced up to the staircase, where Viola was directing Arte and Charlotte to the first floor, only to find her looking back with an amused glint in her eye. Her smile broadened into a mischievous grin, making it clear she'd heard every word. With a wink, she was gone.

Gillian's lips twitched despite herself. With Viola beside her, the judgement of others mattered a little less. Mingling through the crowd, trying to hold her head high, she spotted the reverend.

"Ah. I was hoping to bump into you."

The reverend turned, startled, and took a step back as though bracing himself for an ambush. She noticed how his expression shifted from wariness to politeness.

"Might I pop over to the rectory tomorrow? I have a small project I'd like your opinion on. It has to do with the church bells. They've been silent far too long, don't you think?"

The reverend blinked.

"With me leaving in a few days," she continued, brushing aside his hesitation, "I may not be at a committee meeting for some time. So I thought it best to leave you with a cheque to cover the costs. You can manage the arrangements, I'm sure. I thought it would be lovely to hear them ringing again for Christmas."

At that, his face lit up, warmth replacing his earlier hesitations. "Oh, yes, of course," he said, his voice brimming with enthusiasm.

"Wonderful. I'll pop by tomorrow, then."

Not wishing to linger, she disappeared back into the crowd, which to her delight appeared to still hold no interest in her or her news. With her stomach more settled, she made her way to the buffet table, where she discovered Bridget scooping some strawberry jam on top of her clotted cream. Biting back the urge to point out that the jam should go first, she approached her.

"I meant what I said," she began. "You are my rock, Bridget. You always have been. I'm sorry if you ever — if I ever made you feel like anything else."

Bridget squirmed and shrugged as her cheeks pinked. "You should be proud of yourself. Your speech was delivered beautifully."

She was proud of herself, and she almost wished she'd made it sooner rather than fretting for months about the villagers' reactions.

"No one seems to care."

"Why would they? What's changed except you have a new partner?" Bridget topped her plate off with two pink macarons and casually added, "Mrs Johnson has put on a marvellous spread. The villagers all agree. I was thinking we could hold a regular social event here, like an afternoon tea, maybe once or twice a month. It would be an opportunity for those who don't go to church to socialise a bit more."

Gillian couldn't help smiling at the woman. Bridget had been right all along, but rather than gloating about it, she casually changed the subject instead.

"That's a lovely idea. I'll leave the particulars to you. I know you can take care of everything. I'm not saddling you with too much, am I? What with Agatha to keep an eye on and Dudley to deal with every day?"

"I have the vet's number in my favourites, not that I'll need it. I've pinned your instructions for Dudley to the stable wall, and I'm sure Agatha will instruct me as to her exact requirements. Everything is under control," Bridget assured her.

"I know. I believe in you. You learnt from the best after all."

Bridget grinned. "Ah, there's the Gillian we know and love."

"I've still got it, don't worry. I don't want to lose her completely. Hannah, my hairdresser, recently lost her horse, so she's agreed to ride Dudley whilst I'm away."

"Good, that bit I can't do. Everything will be easier to manage from the lodge, and by the time my cottage has finished being renovated, you'll be back."

"She will be," Viola said, suddenly appearing beside her. "You can't take Kingsford out of Gillian, but you can take Gillian out of Kingsford — if only briefly."

"And strapped into a helicopter." Bridget chuckled.

Gillian placed her arm around Viola's waist, pulling her into her side as she looked adoringly into her eyes. "There was nothing worth leaving for, until now."

Viola washed her hands in the kitchen sink. Taking a hand towel, she dried them as she wandered over to the window and admired the familiar view. It felt good to be back in the manor, and by Gillian's side — in the open. She'd missed the manor and Kingsford more than she realised she would.

Gillian appeared quietly by her side; she hadn't heard her enter. "The last of the guests have left. Bridget and Mrs Johnson have insisted on clearing up. Shall we go for a quick walk before we lose the light? I need to clear my head, and I have a surprise for you. Well, more of a birthday present."

"A present? Then lead on." Viola smiled, excited to see what Gillian had in store for her as she followed her into the back hall. Her eye caught her bag by the door, reminding her of a task she needed to carry out. Taking a deep breath and knowing there wouldn't be a perfect time to ask this of Gillian, she said, "I wanted to... would it be okay with you if I were to scatter Mum's ashes here? I wanted to do it when I owned the place, but I wasn't ready, and then, as you know, events took a turn. Now it feels right, and I don't want to leave her suffocating in a box any longer."

Gillian gave a small smile, her fingers deftly pulling on her boots as she met Viola's gaze. "Of course it would be okay."

Viola exhaled in relief. "Thank you. It means a lot to me to finally put her to rest. I brought her with me from

London." Viola bent down and rummaged in her bag, extracting a box.

"Could I suggest a suitable place?" Gillian offered. "I've been doing a bit of rearranging outside."

"Of course." Viola followed Gillian outside and along the path to Hen's bench. She noticed the shape was different; in fact, it was an entirely different one and made of metal.

"I commissioned Arte to create this for your birthday. I remember you mentioning how much your mother loved the South Downs and the skylarks."

The new bench featured a backrest with two skylarks in flight, their wings gracefully arched as if captured mid-dance, set against the rolling hills of the South Downs.

"It's beautiful, thank you. Mum would love that Arte made this for her."

"She left a space for you to add a plaque or an engraving if you prefer."

Viola wiped away a tear, her mind already turning over the words she might choose to honour her mother.

"How about spreading her ashes here?" Gillian asked softly. She gestured towards the parkland before them, where the manicured lawn gave way to the sprawling wild meadow blanketing the hill down to the stream.

"It's perfect," Viola whispered in reply.

With a nod of encouragement from Gillian, Viola stepped off the path onto the soft lawn and walked a short way down the slope. The meadow was alive with spring blooms, their vibrant colours popped amongst the long, green grass as it swayed and rustled softly in the wind.

She lifted the lid of the box, her fingers trembling as

she opened the bag inside. With her arms stretched out, she tilted it, letting the ashes fall. The wind caught them at once, carrying them out over the meadow and weaving them through the grasses and flowers. Some fell onto the lawn; others flew high into the sky until nothing was left.

Viola sniffed back her tears, her heart aching as she murmured, "Goodbye, Mum." The words dissolved into the wind, carried away to join the ashes.

Her thoughts drifted back to the day she first collected the ashes. She couldn't imagine then a time when she'd willingly let go of this tangible connection to her mum. Clinging to the last remnants of her had been the only way she believed she could still feel her presence. Closing the lid on the empty box, she paused, uncertainty washing over her at the unexpected sense of peace she now felt.

She made her way back up to the bench where Gillian waited, arms open. Viola stepped into the embrace, and her trembling body relaxed as tears streaked her face.

"Are you okay?" Gillian asked, holding her tight.

Viola pulled back to meet her gaze, nodding as she wiped her eyes with the edge of her sleeve. "Yes," she answered softly.

Gillian reached into her pocket and handed her a handkerchief.

Viola took it with a grateful smile, dabbing at her tear-streaked cheeks. "I'll miss her every day," she admitted, her voice thick with emotion, "but I have you, and I want to focus on what I have, not what I don't — as much as I can."

"You do have me," Gillian reassured her.

Viola felt another comforting embrace envelop her, love overflowing from every part of her being.

"And, as I always said," Gillian continued, "I'm not going anywhere. Now, come and sit."

"Where's Hen's bench?" Viola asked, taking Gillian's hand as she sat beside her. It was comfortable, if a little colder than its predecessor.

"The gardeners are giving it some much-needed attention, and then I will retire it into the lodge garden. It's a little more secluded there; it will make for a peaceful place to sit when the manor is rented out. I want our guests to have as much privacy as possible."

"Privacy you wouldn't afford me," Viola sniffed with amusement.

"Do you wish I hadn't sat here?"

"Of course not," Viola admitted with a smirk, which deepened into a smile as she caught the self-satisfied look on Gillian's face.

"Well then."

"Is this why you insisted on visiting me in London instead of me coming here?" Viola said, tracing her hand along the smooth arm of the bench.

"Yes, I didn't want the surprise ruined before your birthday."

"Everything about today was perfect. Thank you."

"You are very welcome. It was a good day for me too."

They leaned back against the bench, sitting in silence, fingers entwined as the sun gradually disappeared behind the church.

Viola took comfort in knowing that, although her mum had never lived at Kingsford, her spirit was here — home again in the South Downs she had loved so dearly. This was where her journey had begun, where her roots lay, and where she would remain. Giving her mum this final gift brought her a sense of peace.

"We should go before we're surrounded by darkness," Gillian said. "I still need to bed Dudley down."

"I've missed him," Viola replied, rising to her feet, eager to see the gentle giant again.

Gillian smiled. "We'll have to resume your riding lessons."

"I'd like that. And I'd love for us to ride together again. I particularly enjoyed that."

"Oh, I wonder why," Gillian teased.

Their eyes met, smirks curving their lips at their shared memory.

As they reached the back door to the manor, Viola pulled away from Gillian. "I'll grab my bag."

Once inside, she left the small box on the hall table, quietly hopeful Mrs Johnson would clear it away. It was only a box, yet she felt silly for feeling attached to it for what it once held. The idea of throwing it away herself was too much, though, even if she knew it was irrational.

Stepping outside with her bag in hand, she found Gillian was waiting for her, her silhouette framed by the warm glow of the setting sun.

"How do you think your speech went?" Viola asked with curiosity. "Was it as scary as you expected it to be?"

"A bit of a non-event, wasn't it?"

"Mmm," Viola agreed. "Everyone appeared initially shocked, but then no one seemed to care."

"Maybe they were more surprised I could capture a

beauty like Viola Berkley than by the fact we are both women."

Viola linked arms as they walked. "Elouise and Louisa were certainly cheering us on. And Bridget, our biggest champion."

"Seems so. She is moving into the lodge whilst I'm away. I've prioritised upgrading her cottage; the last owner was a little remiss in its upkeep."

"Hey, I upgraded your precious manor," Viola snarked, nudging Gillian as they entered the stables.

"And what a good job you did, too, especially with the size of the bath in the master suite."

"There's definitely room for two, not that I've tried," Viola said before quickly adding, "I'm willing to find out."

"Perhaps we should check before we leave. I'm sure I have a tape measure somewhere?"

"Very funny," Viola said, giving her a nudge. "We'll be testing it out naked and filled with bubbles."

"Not too many bubbles, I hope. We wouldn't want them ruining the view."

Viola's lips curved into a sly smile; she'd never felt so eager to take a bath before.

Dudley was stretching his head out of his stall, eager to greet them as they approached.

"Hey, Dudley, I've missed you." Viola rubbed his nose as he blew through his nostrils at her. "I'll be sad to leave again in a few days."

"We'll be back soon enough," Gillian reassured her. "I was hoping that once your tour is over you would make this your base… your home. I know the lodge is rather cosy for two, but I hope we can make something work. There are plenty of rooms in the manor if you need space to work. The last owner had the gall to leave a grand piano behind, which I suppose you could use."

"Did she?" Viola recoiled in faux horror. "How rude. If only she had left a priceless painting instead."

Gillian smiled. "What I'm trying to say is Kingsford is as much yours as it is mine. I hope you know that — even if you did abandon it."

"You abandoned the manor first."

"I was forcibly removed against my will. It's different to jumping into a helicopter and flying off."

Viola grinned; she'd missed their playful teasing. "I was forced to leave, too, by my feelings for this hot, sexy woman I fell in love with, but now that she's all mine, I guess I could find a way to live with her." Viola stroked Dudley's soft neck as Agatha appeared from nowhere and brushed against her leg. "You and I could brand ourselves as the 'Ladies of the Lodge'."

"I think I'm happy being just Gillian."

"'Just Gillian' has a ring to it, I suppose." Viola grinned and pulled a frowning Gillian toward her, placing a kiss on her lips before she could protest.

THE END
Keep turning for a free book!

REVIEWS

If you enjoyed this book, please consider leaving me a review on Amazon, Goodreads, or BookBub. Just a rating or a line is fine. Reviews are life-blood to authors, boosting visibility and connecting new readers with our books.

AMAZON REVIEW LINK

JOIN MY READERS CLUB

If you'd like to hear about my new releases, sign up to my newsletter and receive a FREE sapphic romance, *The Third Act.* Download here…**www.emilybanting.co.uk/freebook**

At the suggestion of her daughter, Amy, widowed Fiona attends an art course at the local college where she meets the confident, inspirational teacher, Raye.
Raye awakens feelings long suppressed, but as Fiona rediscovers her sexuality, fear grows over how Amy will react.
Can Fiona find the courage to follow her heart, or will she be destined to spend her third act alone?

REVIEWS

5* Absolutely loved this book! Great story line, well developed characters and beautifully crafted. It is really refreshing to see the older lesbian represented for a change!

5* A beautiful story of love knowing no age.

5* A very well written, heartwarming novella that challenges the absurd belief that people over a certain age are "too old" to crave intimacy, to start fresh and fall in love. I thoroughly enjoyed this story and I wish it was longer.

ALSO BY

BROKEN BEYOND REPAIR

A South Downs Romance Book 1

GOLDIE WINNER 2024: AUDIOBOOK NARRATOR (ANGELA DAWE)

GOLDIE WINNER 2023: THE ANN BANNON POPULAR CHOICE BRONZE AWARD

GOLDIE FINALIST 2023: CONTEMPORARY ROMANCE LONG NOVEL

WINNER OF THE LESFIC BARD AWARD 2022: ROMANCE

WINNER OF THE LESFIC BARD AWARD 2022: COVER DESIGN

WINNER OF THE QUEER INDIE AWARDS 2022: CONTEMPORARY ROMANCE

An age gap, celebrity ice queen romance that will pull at the heart strings — even the icy ones!

Sydney MacKenzie, personal assistant to the rich and famous, is looking forward to a well-earned break to go travelling in her beloved VW camper van, Gertie — that is, until Gertie cries off sick. When her boss calls in a favour, one that will pay Sydney handsomely and put Gertie back on the road, she can't refuse.

Internationally renowned actress Beatrice Russell — adored by her fans and despised by those that know her — is splashed across the tabloids, all thanks to her broken leg. She limps back to her palatial English country estate to convalesce for the summer, where she finds herself in need of yet another new assistant.

Enter Sydney, who doesn't take kindly to the star's demands, attitude, or clicking fingers — much less her body's own attraction to the gorgeous diva. If not for that, and Gertie's worn-out engine, she would leave tomorrow. Or so she tells herself.

As the summer heats up, the ice queen begins to thaw, and Sydney glimpses the tormented woman beneath the celebrity bravado, drawing her ever closer to the enigmatic actress — sometimes too close.

Can Sydney reach the real Beatrice and help heal her wounds before the summer ends and she returns to filming in the States, or is the celebrity broken beyond repair?

ALSO BY

THE NUNSWICK ABBEY SERIES

4.6* Rated Series

BOOK ONE: LOST IN LOVE

A heart-warming, quintessentially English village novel, centred on the ruins of Nunswick Abbey...

Historical tour guide Anna Walker is determined to make a good impression on her new bosses, but juggling a full-time job with caring for her ailing father is putting her own health – and potentially his – at risk.

When she meets Dr Katherine Atkinson, a charming yet intimidating new arrival to the village, Anna is infuriated by the doctor's attempts to convince her that her father needs professional, full-time care. She's even more frustrated by her growing attraction to the classy, wealthy doctor.

Anna's determination to prove she can cope forces Katherine to divulge a painful event from her past that still haunts her, hopeful it will make Anna see sense before it's too late.

With Katherine's heart lost to the past and Anna's overwhelmed in the present, can the two women help each other overcome their struggles and move forward? Will a curtain-twitching busy body curtail any blossoming attraction before it even has a chance to bloom?

Anna and Katherine's story continues in book two, Trust in Truth, and book three, Forgive not Forget.

PRAISE FOR THE SERIES

This is one of the best books I've read in a very long time. I laughed out loud, cried, and even became indignant at one point. I love a good age-gap slow burn and this checked all the boxes!! Well done!!

A splendid read. It had the perfect amount of laughs, tears, and feels! Can't wait to read the others in the series

LOVED this quintessential English romance novel!! Beautifully written, the plot is tight and the main characters - and those around them - precisely drawn. It gripped me from the very first page and I finished it less than 24 hours!

I do not think there is a heart string left that this author didn't strum. I am a mess of happy and sad and just all out of sorts hahaha. Superb writing. Everything the characters feel, you are going to feel so maybe a few tissues, a pint of ice cream and a hug from a friend should be added to your list of things you'll need after enjoying this book.

I rated this book 5 stars because it's absolutely breathtaking, the atmosphere of the quaint little village with the ruins of an abbey is such a beautiful picture and reminds me of a town near to where I grew up.

It's so hard to find sapphic books in general and it's even harder to find one as good as this! I'm in love with Katherine and Anna's relationship and I'm so excited to continue the series. Also this was such a fun book to read that I read it in 1 day and I'm usually a slow reader.

Printed in Great Britain
by Amazon